DAYS TO REMEMBER

Ever since they were children, playing Mary and Joseph in the school nativity play, Breda Hanney and Warren Pascoe knew they were destined to become man and wife. Now, in 1943, with only days to go to the wedding, the dreaded telegram arrives – Warren's ship has sunk and he has been killed in action. The wedding ceremony must be changed to a memorial service. Distraught by grief, Breda vows she will never fall in love again, but life has a strange way of turning things around. The arrival of Warren's cousin Max gives Breda a second chance – if she is willing to take it.

DAYS TO REMEMBER

DAYS TO REMEMBER

by

Rachel Moore

Magna Large Print Books
Long Preston, North Yorkshire,
BD23 4ND, England.

British Library Cataloguing in Publication Data.

Moore, Rachel
    Days to remember.

    A catalogue record of this book is
    available from the British Library

    ISBN   978-0-7505-3112-2

First published in Great Britain in 2008 by Allison & Busby Ltd.

Copyright © 2008 by Rachel Moore

Cover illustration © Rod Ashford

The moral right of the author has been asserted

Published in Large Print 2009 by arrangement with
Allison & Busby Ltd.

Magna Large Print is an imprint of Library Magna Books Ltd.

Printed and bound in Great Britain by
T.J. (International) Ltd., Cornwall, PL28 8RW

For my husband,
with love.

Chapter One

March 1943

Breda Hanney helped her mother clear away the plates from the meagre supper table, ignoring the way her young sisters squabbled over helping with washing-up, and unable to get her mind fully off the infants in her class. They were learning the rudiments of adding and subtracting as a kind of ritual, chanting in their shrill young voices that could almost send a person to sleep, but was still the best way for them to remember it all. One and one are two; two and two are four; three and three are six; four and four are eight; five and five are ten...

Ten was the significant number in Breda's mind right now, and it was also the moment when her thoughts swiftly moved away from her small charges. In ten days from now, she would be repeating a different kind of ritual – the words of the marriage service that would make her Warren Pascoe's wife.

Her heart skipped a beat as always whenever she thought of her sweetheart. Before he'd joined the Navy he'd been one of the local fishermen of the small Cornish community west of Padstow. The sea was in his blood. All Cornish fishermen had to be strong in body as well as nerve, fighting the elements off the wild, unpredictable coast,

11

and bringing in the catch that would be sold fresh on the quay and in the local shops, or sent in lorries to faraway markets. Many a larger ship had gone down in these waters, thrashed to a pulp as they crashed into the cliffs by mountainous seas as if by a giant's hand. Breda's mother always said seamen, and fishermen in particular, were heroes, every one.

Breda didn't really care to think of Warren as a hero, not in that sense, not even in wartime. Heroes were always battling against some kind of foe, and she wanted him to be safe, not in terrible danger. But she knew that was a futile hope in these perilous times. Warren was a seaman through and through, as his menfolk had been before him. His father had had to give up the sea after a crippling gash on his back some years earlier, while his late grandfather had ventured as far as the North Sea on the whaling ships, and had told them horrific tales of struggling to conquer the great creatures in all kinds of weathers.

That was heroic, if you like, and Warren had been brought up on such tales, whether or not they were strictly true. In any case, to a young boy they were made even more glamorous by time and distance, and when the time had come for able-bodied men to enlist for king and country, Breda had known there was as much chance of asking Warren not to go to sea when the Navy asked for volunteers as asking for the moon not to rise every evening.

'If you're not writing to Warren tonight, we'd better get down to your final fitting, Breda,' her mother said, breaking into her thoughts. 'Time's getting on now, and I've plenty of other things to see to before your big day. The girls' dresses still need finishing as well as yours.'

Breda nodded. Her mum was skilled with her needle, which was why many local brides came to her to have their special dress made, and it had taken the family's combined clothing coupons to get all the material that was needed for Breda's own. But this dress was extra-special, because it was for her own daughter. It had been virtually ready for ages, but Cornish brides always observed the old superstition about not putting in the final stitches until nearer the day, just in case anything went wrong. But nothing could go wrong, Breda thought, with a surge of happiness, when she was marrying the man she adored, and had done so since they were children.

The image of Warren was very vivid in her mind at that moment. Tall and muscular, his dark hair salt-roughened by wind and sea spray long before he joined up, his skin weathered by daily exposure to the elements, even at twenty-two years old. It gave his handsome face character. It made a man of him, and not a boy. Breda felt her face grow hot. There was none of the boy about Warren when he caught her in his arms and kissed her with all the passion of a man who lived with danger. She knew how much she was loved.

'Did you hear me, Breda?' her mother said impatiently.

'Sorry, Mum. I was day-dreaming,' she said without thinking.

Her mother didn't hold with such things. Agnes Hanney was often heard to say that day-dreaming wasn't for the likes of folk who had a living to earn, but there had to be some excuse for a girl on the brink of marriage – even if she didn't wholly agree with the idea of them marrying until the war was over. But she knew the impatience of young sweethearts and couldn't blame them either.

Seeing the look in her daughter's eyes now, Agnes felt more tolerant. The girl loved her job, and she worked hard. Controlling a boisterous pack of infants couldn't be easy, especially when some of them couldn't even be trusted to go to the lav on their own yet and sometimes left a trail of widdle behind them when they left it too late. Breda could be allowed a bit of day-dreaming when she had so much to deal with in her job – and so much to look forward to. It had been a toss-up for her too, whether to keep on with the necessary job of infant teaching, or doing some more worthwhile job for the war effort. But as she had been told repeatedly, what could be more necessary than preparing little folk to be adults?

'Let's finish up here then, and we'll bring the dress down while your father's out at the pub. We don't want the stink of his pipe tobacco in it.'

Breda agreed, although since the cottage usually smelt of her dad's pipe, she couldn't see that his presence would make much difference.

'We don't want the girls' messy fingers on it either,' Agnes went on, 'so they're going to your gran's for an hour or two. She'll be glad of the company.'

'How was she today?' Breda said, diverted for a moment.

'Not so good,' Agnes replied, and Breda knew that the shortness in her voice hid her anxiety for her elderly mother. 'She has that many pains in her feet and her hands and everywhere else, she don't know which is worse. But once the screws get you, there's not much you can do about it, and at her age, it's to be expected, I suppose. Old age don't come alone, Breda. Never did, never will.'

'I'll call in and see her tomorrow evening,' Breda promised, never wanting to think of her gran as anything but immortal, even though she knew she was being blinkered to think so.

'She'll like that.' Agnes went on. 'Sometimes I swear it's only the thought of seeing you and Warren spliced that keeps her going. She's very fond of that young man.'

Breda laughed. 'I think she always had a secret fancy for him. She once said that if she was fifty years younger she'd marry Warren herself.'

Not much chance of that, nor of anyone else getting their hooks into her boy, Breda thought with a proprietary glow. From the age of six, when she had gazed at Warren Pascoe in wide-eyed wonder when he'd announced that he was going to be a fisherman like his dad, he'd always been the one for her. She had taken him one of her mum's toffee apples to school, and his cousin Max had teased them mercilessly. That year they had been given the parts of Mary and Joseph in the school nativity play, and Max, always the joker, had said they'd be tottering up the aisle of the church next.

Well, all these years later, that's just what they

15

would be doing, and the pity was that Max wouldn't be here to see it. They had tried to get in touch with him in good time, but Max was one of Monty's Desert Rats now, and even though the successful battle against Rommel for El Alamein had been fought and won six months earlier, the Lord knew where in the world Max was now. Letters from him were so infrequent and out of date by the time they reached Warren's parents who had brought him up, that he could be in Timbuctoo. Breda often wondered what the rough desert sands were doing to Max's sensitive musician's fingers, and just as quickly forgot him, with more important things to think about.

A cottage had become vacant in the village when the old couple there had decided to move inland, away from the rough seas that so often battered the coast. On his last leave Warren had wasted no time in renting it for them, and they would have the best start to married life in the world, even if Breda would spend much of her time there alone until the war ended and Warren came home for good. As always she prayed that wouldn't be too long now.

Breda's sisters came clattering in from the scullery, still squabbling. If it wasn't against her principles as an infant teacher, she would have banged their heads together. Not that these two were infants any more. Esme was twelve and Jenna a year younger, and they were constantly in rivalry with one another over the slightest thing. But their mother was more than a match for them.

'Now then, you two contrary little maids, get

on round to your gran's and keep her company for a while. Take this pot of soup to warm up for her supper, and read to her if she feels up to it. And no arguing to make her poor head ache.'

They immediately began fussing over who was carrying the pot of soup. Breda couldn't remember ever being so argumentative at their age, but then she had been the only child in the family until she was eight years old, when Esme was born. Breda had peered with awe at the tiny scrap of humanity cradled in her mother's arms in the bed upstairs. From the moment she set eyes on the wrinkled little-old-man's face, touched the tiny, perfect fingers that had curled involuntarily around hers, and counted the tiny toes, she had simply adored the new arrival. Esme had been her little plaything, her baby doll to be petted and serenaded, and when Jenna arrived a year later, Breda was in heaven. She had rocked the pair of them in the big old pram that was as big as herself and pretended they were her babies. It was inevitable that when she grew up, the job that appealed to her most was that of infant teacher. Her gran had heartily approved, telling her it was good practise for when her own babbies came along.

'Was I ever like them?' Breda said in exasperation once the girls had finally left to make their way down the steep alleyways to their gran's cottage.

'You were a placid enough babby until you got your dander up, and then we had some fair old tantrums,' Agnes said dryly. 'You won't remember the worst of them when you weren't averse to throwing things about and tearing up books and toys, but thankfully, those two seemed to calm you down a lot when they were born. You always liked having somebody to fuss over. The children at school will be getting the benefit of that.'

Breda couldn't remember being as destructive as her mother made out. It was like hearing about somebody else, but her mother never lied, so she knew there must be some truth in it. These days she could show endless patience with little hands that were trying to draw around their fingers, or to fashion their clay into recognisable shapes, or arrange the shells they picked up from the beach from their nature walks on to their nature tables, but she also knew there were times when the antics of some of her charges could drive her almost to screaming point. There were also the dark days when one or another of them would be missing from their classes, after the news flashed around the village that a brother or a father was missing in action – or worse.

Breda shuddered at the thought. But frustrating and sometimes agonising though life could be nowadays, she was never in a black mood for long. The forgotten temper tantrums of childhood were long subdued, and such times quickly passed. Besides, even if Warren was away at sea so much now, she wrote to him every night, sharing her life with him in that way.

When he was home, she could talk to him about anything, and it was one of the things she loved about him, because he was always prepared to listen. Intuitively, she thought she knew why he took so much interest in reading of her

18

everyday domestic happenings with the infants. She sensed that it helped to offset the memories of some of the sea battles he was engaged in now. The newspapers were always full of it, but invariably guarded in how much information they were allowed to leak out, and Breda was sure that Warren too never told her everything. He cushioned her just as she cushioned him in hers.

She could hear her mum coming down the stairs now, the wedding dress over her arm. As always, Breda felt a thrill at just seeing the lovely silky material, and knowing the sensuous feel of it against her skin, as soft as her sweetheart's touch.

She pushed those particular images out of her mind, knowing these were practical moments, when the hem of the dress was to be pinned up to the correct height so that the pointed toes of her white shoes would just show beneath it. A small band of twisted silk would form a coronet to sit on top of the heavy lace veil that was her mother's, and she was anticipating the day she would wear it.

She followed her mother into the front room that they hardly used except for very special occasions. They were well away from the clutter of the parlour where there was more room to attend to finishing the dress.

'Now then,' Agnes said, 'you'd best stand on a chair, Breda. I think my joints are going the same way as your gran's, and I can't kneel for too long. I think we may have to take the waist in again too.'

They both knew the reason for that without saying as much. Food rationing had made them all tighten their belts, and it showed no sign of easing up. It was something else that could only get worse. Breda pulled the curtains across the window to prevent being seen by any passing onlookers before slipping out of her dress and standing in her petticoat. It was the middle of March now and it would be daylight for a little while longer yet, but modesty had been instilled in her from an early age. They might not be rich, but they had standards.

She put on the white shoes she was going to wear for her wedding, and climbed onto one of the wooden chairs, bending down so that Agnes could slip the silky folds of the wedding dress over her head. To her relief it still fitted perfectly, and she relished again the sensual feel of it against her skin. It had been stitched with love as well as all Agnes's expertise. The hem wasn't finished though, and it still needed pinning all round before it could finally be stitched to the correct length.

'Hold the pin cushion for me, and hand the pins to me as I need them,' Agnes said, her brusque manner not betraying how beautiful she thought her girl looked now. You didn't tell daughters how pretty they were, in case it made them swollen-headed, but Breda truly looked like an angel, thought Agnes, with her brown hair that she usually wore neatly tied up for school, falling about her shoulders now.

Breda took the pin cushion and did as she was told, moving gradually round and round on the chair and trying not to wobble as her mother began the pinning. It would be disastrous if she went crashing to the floor, and stubbed her toes or broke her leg or something equally awful. She was so busy imagining the worst things that could happen that she wasn't noticing what she was doing, until she felt a sudden prick in her finger, and realised she had stabbed herself with a pin.

She gave a small yelp, but if that was the worst that could happen, she could put up with it. Then she drew in her breath with a gasp of horror. Right on the bodice of the dress were two small spots of blood, stark red against the purity of the silk. Agnes straightened up at once on hearing her daughter's cry, and she tut-tutted as she saw what had happened.

'Stay right where you are, Breda, and don't move until I get something to put around your finger, and a damp cloth to remove those spots. As long as it's done straight away, it won't stain, and you'd better let me have the pin cushion for the rest of the job. This is what daydreaming gets you, my girl.'

She went out of the room for a few moments and Breda felt her head swim, gripping the back of the chair for support until her knuckles went white. She felt oddly breathless, and she was totally unprepared for the feeling. She wasn't squeamish about blood, and had mopped up enough of it from scratched legs in the play-ground whenever one of her infants went sprawling. But this was different. This was her blood, staining her wedding-dress, and if that

21

wasn't an omen, a sign of bad luck, she didn't know what was. *And it was the second sign.*

'Now then,' Agnes said, bustling back with a bandage and a damp cloth. 'Wrap this around your finger for a minute while I see to those marks.'

Breda spoke quickly. 'I'd rather take it off, Mum, and I think I'll leave the pinning until another day.'

'You can't take it off yet, or you'll risk spreading it farther. Stand still and let me get on with it, for goodness' sake. It won't take a minute.'

Breda did as she was told, biting her lips to stop them from trembling. Agnes's cold hand slid down the front of the dress to hold it away from Breda's body, while her other hand rubbed gently at the bloodstains.

'There now,' she said with satisfaction. 'You'd never know anything was amiss, so let's carry on and get the job done.'

'I'd much rather leave it for tonight, Mum. To be honest, I'm starting to feel a bit faint, standing on this chair.'

Agnes looked at her sharply now. 'You do look a bit white, though why a few spots of blood should upset you I don't know. It'll be as good as new when I've done with it, but you'd better have your way, I suppose.'

Breda suffered the next few moments until her mother lifted the dress carefully over her head, trying not to admit to the feeling of being suffocated as she was enveloped and blinded for a moment by its silky folds. It was no more than a foolish fancy to think there was anything

22

sinister in what had happened, even though she knew her gran would probably think otherwise. Her mother was a practical woman, but like many Cornish women of an older generation, her gran believed in all things mystical, and that everything happened for a purpose.

Breda was thankful when Agnes took the wedding-dress away to hang up in its protective covering, and she quickly put on her own clothes again. She hadn't written to Warren yet that evening, but she was suddenly consumed by an urge to be with him, even if it was only through the medium of writing to him, to sense that he was close, to be reassured that her sweetheart was still strong and alive. The word rushed into her head, making her gasp. She hadn't meant to think it, and she shook herself angrily, feeling a brief return of the childhood rage that had once plagued her, and knew that if anything happened to Warren it would turn her world upside down. It would turn her into a madwoman...

With mild panic, she wondered if she was already on the road to madness to be even thinking such stupid thoughts. And all because of a simple accident that her mother had taken in her stride and put right in minutes. Her head cleared. That was all it was. A simple accident that had been put right.

Right then, her father Gilb was striding down to his local on the waterfront. The old pub with its grimy green bottle glass windows had been there for ever as far as folk knew. It thrived on the reputed history about an ancient law that said a

23

man couldn't be convicted of a crime if it was witnessed through glass that distorted the image. The thick bottle glass frequently used in pub windows upheld the legend. No one actually knew when the name of this particular pub had changed to the Bottle and Jug, nor if such a criminal had ever been saved by the ancient law in these parts, but such legends lived on for locals and strangers alike. Of course, nowadays there were thick blackouts at the pub windows, like every other window in the village.

Gilb enjoyed his pint of ale and a yarn with the old codgers and the fishermen who congregated there, and these days there was always someone ready to stand him a jar and give him some raucous advice, now that his daughter was a nearly married woman. They had to temper it a bit when it got too fruity, though, because it wouldn't do for Gilb Hanney to think of his daughter's good name being bandied about by a crowd of lusty fishermen.

He was almost at the pub, drawing on his pipe in the early evening with the stars just appearing in the sky, when he heard his name being called. He turned with a surprised smile to see his eldest daughter running towards him over the rough ground leading down to the waterfront.

'What are you doing out and about this evening?' he greeted her. 'I thought you and your mother were busy doing women's work of a kind I'm not supposed to see just yet,' he added with a grin.

'We were,' Breda said breathlessly. 'But I decided I'd much rather be out of doors. I was feeling too hot inside the house.'

Her father smiled at her, and all thoughts of joining the men at the Bottle and Jug disappeared from his mind.

'There's nothing I'd rather be doing than spending a couple of hours with my girl, but it's a mite cold for sitting around at the beach yet.'

'I don't mind where we go. Let's take a walk along the cliffs. I feel the need to blow the cobwebs away.'

Her father tucked her arm in his. 'Have the little sprogs been giving you a hard time today?' he said with a sympathetic smile, as they strode out towards the cliffs. 'I knew there must be something. I could tell it from your voice.'

Breda gave a shaky laugh. 'No, it's not the infants. They were no more troublesome than usual.'

'What then? You're not giving Warren the old heave-ho, are you?' he said, grinning at his nautical joke.

Breda kept her head bent as they walked up the steep slope from the beach to the cliffs, and once they were there, they both paused to catch their breath. From here, they could look down on the picturesque, straggling village. From here the cottages, buildings and church spire were darkened because of the blackout regulations, yet they still had an eerie beauty, steeped as they were in moonlight now, all the way to Padstow. In the small bay the fishing boats were crazily lopsided and impotent at low tide, belying the power of the craft and the men who manned them, and even though Warren didn't skipper one of those boats these days, Breda wished momentarily that the tide would never rush in again, and that the boats would stay beached for ever. She had never told anyone of the nightmarish dreams she had occasionally, when the waves started creeping in like greedy, hungry fingers, to capture Warren and take him away from her.

'What is it, my dear?' her father said gently. 'You know you can tell me anything, don't you?'

She leant against him, feeling the steady beat of his heart against her body, and she knew at once that she could never tell him of the premonition that had swept through her at the sight of the two spots of blood on her wedding-dress. He would have been badly troubled to know how she felt. If her gran would have said it was a bad omen, how much more bad luck was it to put into words that she feared Warren's life was in danger? It was something that was tacitly forbidden by all those whose livelihood depended on the sea. She thought quickly of some other explanation for her agitation, knowing now that however much she had needed to get out of the house, it might have been foolish to make her father look so anxious for her. She thought quickly and forced a small laugh.

'Oh, it's only Esme and Jenna as usual. They were squabbling so much tonight, and I've had visions that they'll still be arguing at the wedding and spoil everything on my special day. And now you'll think I'm just being silly,' she said.

He laughed gently. As he gave her a squeeze, the scent of his old pipe was oddly reassuring.

'You're not silly, but I'm starting to think

Warren's marrying a crazy woman. Those two can argue till the cows come home, and it's not going to spoil anything, I promise you.'

He sounded so confident, so protective, the father who could always smooth over all her ills, that Breda told herself she had been getting worked up over nothing. Then they both groaned as the sound of a distant air-raid siren reminded them that somewhere else was getting a visit from Adolf's bombers tonight, and that the best place for any sensible folk to be was indoors.

Chapter Two

Springtime was a time of renewal in the countryside, and for coastal communities like Penbole
the annual Spring tides also heralded the fact
that the seasons were changing. Lush and full,
the tides roared up the north Cornish coast, and
on good days, with the sun glinting on the blue-
green waves, the curling surf and white horses,
there was nothing more beautiful.

The locals took it all in their stride, but
strangers to the area, like the grockles from upcountry, would stand for hours on the cliffs,
admiring what nature provided so effortlessly. It
was said that much farther upcountry, where the
Atlantic narrowed into the Bristol Channel as it
narrowed still more into the Severn river, the
water gathered even more strength, and with
nowhere else to go there was a huge bore like a
tidal wave that surged up the funnel. Such talk
was only fascinating hearsay to the insular, stay-
at-home folk of Cornwall, who could see nothing
but the vast waters of the Atlantic Ocean off their
narrowing coastline.

Springtime came early here, bringing with it the
first annual network of greenery on trees and
shrubs. Wild bluebells, cowslips, furze and forget-
me-nots flourished among the moorland bracken,
and hazel catkins appeared, dancing in the breeze
to delight the schoolchildren, who gathered them

for their school nature tables. Breda's infant class had had the joys of nature instilled in them from birth, and enjoyed their regular walks away from the stuffiness of the classroom.

Right now, it was debatable whether they were more excited about their teacher's forthcoming wedding, or the trip to Padstow for the annual 'Obby 'Oss festivities on May 1st, which fell on a Saturday this year. But since their teacher's wedding came first, they were busy at work drawing pictures of the scene at the church on Breda's big day, which would be proudly hung about the classroom. Breda smiled at the various offerings, encouraging her small charges in their artistic attempts, her silly fears about the spots on her wedding-dress diminishing now.

'You'll look lovely, Miss,' piped up one and another, 'and we're all coming to see you in your white dress.'

Mrs Larraby, the head teacher, smiled at Breda over their heads.

'By the sound of it, you may need to get wed in a far larger church than our little local one, Miss Hanney.'

'Oh, I don't think that would go down very well,' Breda said, hearing the chorus of dismay from her pupils. 'It's the church where Warren and I were christened, and the vicar would have something to say about it if we deserted him for our big day, to say nothing of our parents!'

Mrs Larraby laughed. 'Quite right, and I was only teasing, of course. I'm sure the children are all looking forward to it nearly as much as you are.'

Breda doubted that, but she kept the fixed smile on her face, knowing the older woman didn't hold with arch remarks or double meanings. Nobody could be looking forward to the wedding as much as herself and Warren. It was the culmination of all their dreams, and if only his cousin Max could have been there to stand beside him as his Best Man, it would have been even more perfect. But it wasn't to be, unless a miracle happened and Max suddenly turned up from wherever he was in the world. But it was too late now, and one of Warren's old schoolfriends had said he'd be proud to do the honours. You couldn't start changing arrangements to suit Monty's military manoeuvres. However little the war had touched them in the far west of Cornwall, you couldn't ignore it.

Her attention was quickly brought back to the present at the sound of wailing from the back of the class, signalling that the notoriously damp child had had another accident in her excitement and needed tidying up. This was the real world, Breda thought with a smothered sigh, not fighting battles in far-off corners of the Egyptian desert, which was the last place anyone had had any news of Max Pascoe. She gave a comforting word to the snivelling little girl as she took her outside to the lavs to change her knickers.

That night, as she did so many times now, she dreamt again about Warren's last leave, and in particular, their last evening together.

'It won't be long now,' Warren said, as they walked down the lane to the empty cottage that

30

was to be their home. 'And once this damn war is over, we can spend the rest of our lives together.'

Breda hugged his arm, feeling a thrill run through her. Tonight would be a rare chance for them to be really alone together, other than outdoors. This would be far more intimate, and she knew Warren was as aware of it as she was. Probably more, since she knew what a passionate man he was, and how he had been anticipating their wedding night with all the fervour of a young and virile man.

'We'd better not stay too long,' she told him. 'We don't want the neighbours to think we're doing anything we shouldn't.'

Warren chuckled, his arm clinging even closer to hers.

'There's not much chance of that, my prissy maid, but once I get that ring on your finger things will be different, I promise you.'

Breda laughed back. 'I hope you're not marrying me just for you-know-what!' she said teasingly.

'I'm marrying you because I love you, as you very well know, you witch,' he said simply, the words so honest she could never have doubted them. Not that she ever would, she thought, with a rush of love, and it was as hard for her to resist his passion as it was for him. But long ago, she had made a vow to herself and to him, that their first night together would be perfect in the sight of God, and she had never wavered in that resolve. Warren had always honoured that vow, despite the many times he had told her jokingly that she was probably shortening a man's life by

31

refusing him. She didn't refuse him in so many words, anyway. She just somehow managed to turn the moments when the tension between them became too much to bear into laughter.

Tonight may be different, she had admitted as they walked through the fragrant, flower-filled small garden of the cottage that would be their home. They had already been to see it with the couple who had lived here, and agreed that the furniture would suit them admirably until they wanted to change it. The only thing that was new was the double mattress that had been delivered a few days ago, and tonight they would add the sheets and blankets and pillows their parents had given them, in readiness for the day when they would walk here from the church as newlyweds and close the door on the rest of the world.

That was the difference, Breda had thought, with a small shiver that was more excitement than fear. The pristine double bed would be a confirmation of all that they would be to one another, their future lives together, and the children they might have. With her love of children, Breda couldn't wait, and Warren, being an only child apart from his cousin who had lived with him, was in full agreement that a house only really became a home when there were children in it.

Warren flourished the house-key and opened the front door. The previous tenants had left a vase filled with sweet-scented moorland flowers, and they filled the house with their perfume. It was homely and welcoming at the same time. Breda almost danced from room to room, trying

32

to visualise how it would be when she and Warren actually lived here, using their own pots and pans, cooking breakfast for them both, sharing everything, sharing their lives.

'Let's take this stuff upstairs,' Warren said eventually, and they went up the twisting staircase together, into the front bedroom that overlooked the harbour. It was appropriate that it did so, Breda thought happily, since they would be able to see every changing mood of the sea from the window, and snuggle down indoors when the fierce winds rattled the panes.

Just thinking about it made her face grow warm, and to blot out such thoughts, she turned quickly, right into Warren's arms. She couldn't miss the passion she felt in him now, and she told him that they had better get their business done and go home before it got dark. He laughed and let her go, and between them they put the sheets and blankets on the bed and smoothed down the pillows.

Soon, Breda thought, almost breathless, those pillows would be indented with the shape of their two heads...

'What are you thinking?' she heard him say softly.

'Oh, I couldn't tell you! Private thoughts!' she said, trying to tease.

She felt his arm slip around her waist. 'Then I'll tell you what I'm thinking instead. I'm thinking that this is the room where you and I will prove our love for each other, and where we'll make our babies.'

Breda laughed shakily. It was rare that he said

anything so poetic, but she couldn't miss the meaning in his voice.

'I never thought we had to prove it,' was all she could think of saying.

'Of course we don't. I've loved you since I first set eyes on you, and you know that. And I've waited for all these years, and not always patiently, to make you truly mine. To feel that we belong, body and soul.'

'We've always belonged,' Breda whispered.

'And this is where God will bless our union. Isn't that what the vicar called it when he told us marriage was for the procreation of children, and for the mutual comfort of a man and a woman? I never fully realised just how much I need that comfort, my darling girl.'

She looked up into his face, her cheeks fiery, knowing what he was saying, what he was asking. Her heart was beating very fast, and her limbs felt as if they had turned to water, but she knew how much he wanted her ... and, oh Lord, how she wanted him too. Physical love wasn't solely for the comfort of a man, and their wedding was so very near ... so very near...

'I need you too,' she whispered, her voice no more than a thread of sound. 'So much, Warren.'

And who knew how long this war was going to continue? The unspoken words were that you had to snatch the moment, to make the most of whatever precious time you had together these days. Everybody said it. Everybody knew it.

In her dreams those memories always came flooding back, remembering how she had been cocooned in Warren's arms. But alone in her own bed now, in the wee small hours, she was wide awake, remembering more.

She must have made a small involuntary sound, and he had stirred at once, enclosing her even tighter.

'Now we truly belong,' he murmured against her cheek.

She remembered how her eyes had filled with weak tears, and she couldn't be sure whether it was with joy and a feeling of total completeness, or shock at what had happened. They had waited so long ... and in the end their own natures had betrayed them. As if he was aware of her feelings, he kissed her on the mouth, long and hard and deep.

'I'll remember this night for the rest of my life, my darling, and I'll keep the memory of it with me wherever I am. It will be my talisman.'

He kissed her again, and how could she deny the sweetness of this moment, or the deep and abiding love she had always felt for him? But she had also been steeped in the teachings of the church, and the determination to keep herself pure until Warren placed the wedding ring on her finger, and she couldn't quite rid herself of the guilt, either.

'Then you don't think we did anything wrong?' she said huskily.

'Do you?' he said, holding her slightly away from him for a moment. 'How could it be wrong? We vowed to love one another many years ago, and to be together in the sight of God and the congregation, and we hardly wanted any of them around in the last hour, did we?'

When she didn't answer, he spoke more anxiously.

'Wasn't it what you expected, my love? I didn't hurt you, did I?'

She hugged him fiercely, aware of her own passion rising again at the feel of his flesh against hers. Everywhere they touched, it was as though they were in perfect harmony, and would always be.

'It was everything I expected, and more,' she said, her voice a soft sigh. 'But we've stayed too long, Warren. We must go before we're missed.'

It sounded so prosaic after the wondrous emotions that they had so recently shared, but the consolation was that they would have the rest of their lives to renew this sharing of mind and body. Breda's spirits soared at the thought. They left the warmth of the bed and dressed quickly. He went downstairs ahead of her, and when she pulled the bedcovers back on the bed, her heart leapt as she saw the few small spots of blood on the bottom sheet.

Her breath caught between her teeth. Now, *now*, there was something even more significant to remember about that one night. Now she knew why the blood spots on her wedding dress had made her even more agitated than it was reasonable to be. It reminded her of her premonition ... a double premonition now. On that other night, before she went downstairs she had spat on her hanky and rubbed at the marks quickly until the worst of them had gone. It was a natural happening, she reminded herself. It proved to Warren, if proof were needed, that she

36

had never lain with a man until this night. If anything, it would have been far more disastrous if there had been no sign of her purity, and she had persuaded herself at the time that there were no bad portents in what she had seen.

They had walked back to the village in the gathering dusk, arm in arm, saying little. There was a difference in them now, Breda thought. They had known one another for all these years, but never before in the biblical sense. It was an awesome feeling, and she was sure Warren felt it too. He left her at her home, holding her close for a moment before he let her go.

'Sweet dreams, darling,' he said softly. 'Mine will be all the sweeter now.'

She was too busy at school the next day to dwell on her stupid fears. She had promised to call on her gran that evening, and she called out as she opened the door of the cottage, knowing the door was never locked. Gran Hanney always said she had nothing to steal, and nobody would want an old woman like her, so why should she bother to lock her door? The old lady, who seemed as wizened and wrinkled as she had done ever since Breda had known her, looked up from her chair by the fireside, the inevitable knitting in her hand, her knitting bag at her feet. Her old tortoiseshell cat, as thin and scrawny as a scarecrow, wound itself around Breda's legs as it recognised a familiar face, and purred like an express train.

'How are you tonight, Gran?' Breda greeted her cheerfully.

'Fair to middling and twice as ugly,' she replied,

the way she always did. 'The damn fool doctor says I should keep myself indoors until your big day or I'll never make it to the church, but I shall see him out, and most other folks in the village too. It takes more than a wheezy chest to stop me seeing my best girl safely wed. My herbal tonics will sort me out.'

It was quite a speech. It left her breathless, and made Breda smile. She never changed, and even though it was logical that she wouldn't go on for ever, Breda, too, was quite sure it would take more than a wheezy chest to make her push up the daisies. She hoped it would be a very long while before that happened.

'So come and sit down and tell me about the antics of your infants today,' Gran Hanney went on, 'and then we'll have a cup of cocoa.'

'I'll put the kettle on,' Breda said quickly, and then allowed herself a few minutes more to decide how much she was going to ask her gran. She heard her call out tetchily.

'What are you doing, girl? If you're not going to come and talk to me you might as well have stayed home.'

'Sorry, Gran,' Breda said. 'I was day-dreaming.'

She hurriedly made the two cups of cocoa and took them back into the parlour, curling up on the big old armchair that had been her grandad's. When she was a small child she'd chuckled with delight as he'd swung her around in his arms, saying he was going to cuddle her for ever in that arm-chair ... but for ever had a habit of ending far too abruptly.

She became aware that her gran was looking at

her strangely, and she took a large gulp of her cocoa.

'So you're nearly ready for the big day then?' Gran Hanney asked. 'Has your mother finished your dress yet? I hope she's left a few stitches to do.'

'Of course. She wouldn't dare go against superstition,' Breda said with a grin.

'You may scoff, my girl, but there's no point in inviting bad luck.'

'Do you really believe in such things, Gran? I know you always say you do, but I sometimes think it's a lot of old wives' tales...'

'If it is, then I'm the oldest old wife in the village,' her gran said dryly. 'I know you modern young things don't hold with such beliefs, but they never did me any harm, and I'm still alive to tell the tale.'

'I don't say I don't believe in them, just that I'd rather not, that's all.'

Gran Hanney looked sharper now. 'What's happened, then?'

'It's nothing.'

'Whenever anybody tells me it's nothing, I know very well it's something. And you're not leaving here until I know what it is. Come on now, my dear, tell your old gran. You're not having second thoughts about the wedding, are you?'

'Of course not. We're wildly happy. It's not that. But you do believe in omens, don't you, Gran? You can't deny it. You've told me often enough, scaring me and the girls with some of your old tales!'

'Oh well, I admit some of them were just tales,'

the old woman said with a soft chuckle. 'But there's often a spark of truth in even the wildest story.'

Breda wished she'd never started on this tack, but she knew Gran Hanney wouldn't let it go now. She was like a fish caught on a line, wriggling and fighting like mad, but never able to let go in the end. She gave a small sigh. Cornish fishermen were the bravest of souls, and she wished that was what Warren was doing now, instead of somewhere at sea in a warship, and for some reason she found herself thinking with a moment's rare resentment that his cousin should have been here too, taking Warren off to the pub for a game of darts and having a good old yarn or two. Max *should* have been here. He'd learnt about the wedding from Warren's mother, or at least, the letter had been sent to him in good time. Whether he'd ever received it, nobody knew. Letters were notoriously slow in reaching the troops, sometimes arriving in great batches, weeks or months old, and who knew what arrangements were made in the desert for such mundane things?

'Where have you gone to, my lamb?' she heard Gran Hanney say softly. 'You're off in dreamland, and thinking of that handsome young man of yours, I'll be bound.'

Breda laughed self-consciously. 'Something like that, Gran!' she admitted.

The old woman crossed her hands in her lap. Breda knew that sign. It was as good as digging her heels in, and Breda knew she wasn't going to be able to get home until she'd said what was troubling her.

'So out with it, then. I need to get my beauty sleep sometime tonight, girl, though there's some that would say it's far too late for my wrinkled old face!' she said briskly.

'You always look beautiful to me.'

'And don't think that soft-soaping me is going to stop me from knowing something's on your mind. If you can't tell your old gran, who can you tell?'

'It's daft.'

'No, it's not, or you wouldn't still be fretting over it. For pity's sake, girl, if you dithered this long when Warren asked you to marry him, I wonder he took the trouble to wait for an answer!'

Breda spoke abruptly. 'When Mum was pinning up my dress, I was holding the pins for her, and I pricked my finger and two spots of blood went on my dress. Now you know. It's a bad omen, isn't it?'

When Gran Hanney said nothing for a moment, Breda felt her heart pound.

She could feel the beat of it in her head and her ears. She was a modern young woman, and she should have no truck with omens and superstitions and old wives' tales, but she prayed with all her heart that the incident was going to be pooh-poohed. She saw her gran rub at the hairs on her chin, the way she often did when she was thinking hard. As a child, Breda had been so fascinated by those chin hairs, which seemed to have always been there, and always tickled her whenever her gran kissed her. Now, they seemed to represent a moment of acute anxiety.

41

'I'm sure your mother got the spots out quickly enough,' Gran said calmly. 'You shouldn't let it upset you, Breda. Accidents happen, and I'll bet the dress looks as good as new again now.'

'It *is* new,' Breda said, wanting to weep, even while she knew how foolish she was being. 'I don't want it to *look* as good as new. I want it to *be* new!'

Gran chuckled. 'You're as soppy as when you were six years old and you dropped your favourite dolly in the mud. No matter how hard I scrubbed it clean, you fussed over it, saying it wasn't new any more. Do you think anybody's going to notice anything wrong with the dress once your mother's got the tiny stain out?'

'Probably not, but I'll know,' Breda muttered.

Gran got up and put a bony arm around the girl's shoulders. 'You're a lovely girl, Breda, and you'll have a lovely wedding day and a lovely life with your man, so go on home and have a good night's sleep and think no more about such a trifle. Things always look better in the morning, and by then you'll wonder what on earth you were worrying about.'

She looked at Breda more quizzically. 'There's nothing else you want to tell me, is there?'

Such as what? That I've already lain with Warren, and anticipated our wedding vows? And that there had been several more spots of blood on the virginal sheets?

'No, Gran, and I'm sorry if I sounded such an idiot.'

Gran Hanney kissed her, and the chin hairs tickled Breda's cheek. 'You're not an idiot, dear girl, and being in love makes fools of all of us at one time or another. I'm not so old that I can't remember what it was like,' she added, her old eyes twinkling with memory.

The aged tortoiseshell cat rubbed against Grandad's old chair now, purring ever louder, its amber eyes fixed unblinkingly on Breda, almost mesmerising her. She uncurled herself from the chair and put her feet to the ground, knowing it was time she left. The cat immediately wound itself around her legs again, soft and warm and intrusive, and she felt a wild urge to kick it away.

'I'm sure that scrawny old thing has got fleas, and I wonder why you don't get rid of it,' she said unthinkingly.

'I'd as soon get rid of my right arm,' her gran replied, unruffled, and having heard these re-marks many times before. 'If you're ever old and alone, my dear, you'll know the comfort of a pet to keep you company, so you get on home now and leave me to give him his victuals.'

Breda left her to it and walked the short distance home in the blackout, thinking that she was probably making a mountain out of a molehill. She tried to recapture the feelings she and Warren had shared on that one magical night. They had merely meant to look over the cottage and make up the double bed for future use. Instead of which... Breda felt a rush of emotion so strong it almost took her breath way. Instead of which, they had discovered the wonder and ecstasy of exploring each others' bodies for the first time. It had made her feel different in so many ways. It still did. It made her

43

feel a woman and alive, and it made her feel a part of Warren in a way that nothing else ever could. It made them belong to one another, irretrievably and for ever, and no one could ever take that away from them.

Chapter Three

Max Pascoe's skin was bronzed to a mahogany hue from the blistering sun and desert winds that could so quickly turn a harmless and tranquilly beautiful scene into a raging sandstorm that blinded the eyes and sliced into the flesh with its ferocity. He could have loved Egypt with a passion, but he had to admit that it was mostly because, as a boy, his artistic soul had been charmed by the romanticism of the wonderful discovery of Tutankhamun's tomb by Howard Carter.

Had that been a factor that had made him welcome so eagerly the chance to be posted to this bleak and desolate landscape that could change in a moment from such beauty to a living hell? Maybe so. In any case, the charm of it all had vanished like the taunting mirages that were frequently seen until the reality of the brutal and endless landscape set in. He had been disillusioned even more by the relentless fighting that had gone on in the previous year when even Monty's famed eighth army had faced such desperate times before the final victory against Rommel.

There was no glory in war. And what had he expected? he asked himself bitterly. Allowing the excitement of seeing this place at first hand to blind him to the fact that he was not here as a tourist, but as a soldier, doing what soldiers do. Sometimes he still wondered what the hell he was doing here, when his real vocation, his real love, was to be playing his saxophone in the local dance band back home in Cornwall.

Those days were long ago now, and so were the halcyon days when Howard Carter's discovery of that ancient tomb had gleamed like the gold artefacts he had found, and when every man and his brother had seemed to think he was an amateur archeologist. The desert then had swarmed with ingenues who tore up the sand with impunity and with no regard for the painstaking work of piecing those treasures together. That same desert was now red with blood, and whatever lay beneath the surface had been broken and swallowed up by the armoured tanks that grated over it, as bitter enemies fought to kill one another.

Sometimes, of course, there had been brief respites. No soldier could continue fighting for ever without becoming completely exhausted and war-weary. With his mates, Max had occasionally managed the tedious journey to Cairo to visit the fleshpots for a few days' leave. His handsome mouth twisted into an ironic smile. Such fleshpots as there were didn't appeal to him all that much. He'd seen enough belly dancers and snake charmers to last a lifetime, and knew all the tricks.

Fat chance for any of that now, he thought, in one of his rare lucid moments, while the military medics were deciding what to do with him. The most recent letter from his aunt had told him about his Warren's wedding to Breda, together with a hasty note from Warren saying he hoped Max could make it home in time to be his Best Man. Enclosed inside his blisteringly hot tent while the wind howled outside, he didn't need to read Warren's note again, despite his raging fever, since the words were imprinted in his mind.

Come home, Cuz, and be my Best Man, as we always planned. It won't be the same without you. Breda sends her love too. Your old pal, Warren.

Breda sends her love. The words had given Max's heart a painful lurch. He knew he could have got leave if he'd tried hard enough. God knew he was entitled to it, until the savage wound in his leg had turned septic with the dangerous risk of gangrene, and given him the continuing fever that turned his brain to mush. Was it fate that made it impossible for him to return home to watch his cousin marry his sweetheart, when he himself would have given the earth to be the man by her side, and not the one fading into the background? Fading and crumbling into the desert sand if the hopelessness he felt now had anything to do with it.

In Max's tortured opinion, Best Man was the most ironic title any man could be given. For all these years, he had kept the secret in his heart, but he was also honest and loyal enough to know that if there had been a way for him to be Warren's Best Man, he would have done it, no matter what his own feelings might have been. He owed his support to his cousin, who had always been more like a brother to him, and Breda was Warren's girl, always had been, and always would be – and was very soon to be his wife.

47

The flap of the tent opened and a surge of stinging sand flooded in with a hot stream of air. The medic who entered shook the sand out of his hair and rubbed at his sore eyes. He never stood on ceremony and was blunt with his words.

'Christ Almighty, it's bloody murder out there today, man, and dry enough to parch a camel's arse. But we've decided what to do with you, Private Pascoe. You're to be sent to a military hospital in Cairo, to see if they can save that leg.'

The shock of his last words almost made Max faint. He'd felt so bloody ill and so delirious during these last days or weeks or however long it had been, that it hadn't crossed his mind that his wound could have been that serious. But looking at the medic's grim face now, he knew the truth of it, and the thought flashed through his mind that whatever they did to him, he really didn't give a tinker's cuss whether he lived or died without the love of his life.

But doggedly, just as quickly he knew he wanted to live. He hadn't come this far, and lived through the nightmare of these last months, to die in some Godforsaken hospital in Cairo. It was the first positive thought he'd had in months.

Breda looked at the leaden sky and prayed that the weather was going to brighten up for her wedding. It was the most important day on her horizon, but March winds and April showers were always a threat. They were also a hazard that every fisherman had to contend with, and they frequently encountered far worse than today, but when did a true fisherman ever let such trifles bother him? Certainly not Warren Pascoe. But he wasn't out there now, at least not in Cornish waters. According to the guarded information he'd told her in his last letter, he would be somewhere in the Atlantic, or the Baltic, or in some other ocean that was merely a name on a map that everybody who followed the war progress knew by now. If nothing else, the war had improved everyone's knowledge of geography.

Breda determinedly shook any fears for Warren out of her mind. It didn't help. Instead, she made herself smile, just thinking of his name that was soon to be hers. She would no longer be Breda Hanney, but Breda Pascoe. Like some love-sick schoolgirl, she had practised it several times on an old exercise book, and had then been too superstitious to tear up the page and throw it away. But superstition was in her blood, and perhaps she was more like her old gran in that respect after all.

In her small class of infants now, she heard the children asking if they were going to go out on their nature walk, and she forced herself back to reality.

'We're going to miss it today,' she told them firmly, ignoring their bleating. 'It's far too windy and some of you have already got colds, so we're staying in the classroom and painting pictures instead. There'll be a gold star for the child who does the best painting of a stormy day at sea.'

It was enough to get them scrabbling for their painting overalls and materials. It took so little to interest them in something new at that age,

Breda thought thankfully. It was one reason why she loved teaching the infants so much, when their minds were so receptive to all that she had to offer them. While she was the one person in the class who found it hard to keep her mind on anything but her forthcoming wedding – that, and the uncertainty of the Cornish weather.

As if to remind her, there was a sudden crash as one of the classroom windows rattled in a fierce gust of wind, blowing out one of the small panes in a small shower of glass. It was too far away from the children to hurt anyone, and was soon cleared up, with a piece of cardboard pressed tightly into place until it could be repaired properly. Breda hoped it would hold. Then, in the general melee and excited screams from the children, one of the little ones screeched and crossed her legs tightly. Breda knew only too well what that meant, and she told the rest of the class to get on with their painting as she took the child out to the lavs to change her knickers. She gasped as they went outside, almost knocked off her feet by the strong wind, and the little girl clung to her skirt in terror.

'It's all right, Sara,' she said soothingly. 'It's only the noisy old wind, and it won't hurt you.'

She wasn't sure she believed it herself as the force of the gale began blowing leaves and small branches about the lanes, and the crashing sound of roof slates soon followed. Breda knew she needed to hurry with her task, before the rest of her charges got frightened by the noise, other-wise they would return to find the whole class in uproar. She didn't fancy finding the contents of

50

the paint-pots sploshing about everywhere, either.

'Be quick, Sara, and then we'll have a sing-song to drown out the noise.'

'All right, Miss,' the child sniffed, as Breda almost pushed her inside the small outhouse and reached for the pack of spare dry knickers that always hung on a peg for such emergencies.

Ten minutes later, they battled their way back to the classroom, to find that Mrs Larraby was trying to calm down the children. She had already instructed them to put their paint-pots away, and she looked at Breda uneasily.

'I think we may have to get the children home early today if the weather gets any worse,' she murmured. 'I've never known a storm start so quickly.'

Breda was thinking the same, and she knew, too, that Mrs Larraby's brother was a fisherman and she would be worried on his account. From the first rattling of the classroom window, Breda knew that the whole community would be anxious on a day like this. The north Cornwall coast was notorious for wrecks. Seas that were benign and beautiful could change into raging torrents that could send the biggest ship listing towards the rocks, and they could overturn small fishing boats and dash them to matchwood in an instant.

The thought of that one lovely evening they had spent together in the cottage surged through Breda's mind at that moment. Being more intimate than they had ever been in their lives until then, Warren had told her it was his talisman, keeping him safe, and she had to believe

51

that. Even if he wasn't in their local Cornish waters, he was *somewhere at sea* – that phrase the navy used that she had always thought to be ominous, both disturbing and unreal.

She saw twenty pairs of frightened young eyes watching her nervously, and she shook herself out of her momentary dread, telling herself swiftly not to be so weak-willed. She had these children to look after, and they looked to her for safety and strength. There had been a time when she had desperately wanted to join up, to be a WAAF or a nurse, and to wear a uniform like some of the other girls her age in the village, but her job here was important, and she had been persuaded to stay.

She walked unsteadily to the small upright piano in the corner of the classroom and clapped her hands for the children to be quiet. From long habit, they stopped chattering and looked at her obediently.

'Instead of any more lessons, we're going to have a sing-song to shut out this horrible old noise,' she told the children as firmly as she could, aware that her voice had gone several notches higher than usual. 'Who wants to choose the first song?'

She heard the expected babble of voices at being given a choice, but she began playing what she chose, knowing they would all join in. *Old Macdonald Had a Farm* was a favourite, and they all got the giggles making the animal noises to accompany it. For the next hour they went through the whole repertoire of favourite nursery songs and rhymes, until Breda's throat was hoarse.

Although it was barely past midday, the sky had become as dark as night. Some of the children had begun snivelling and several parents had already come to take their children home, preferring to have them safely indoors with them in their own homes, and unsettling those who were still in the classroom.

Breda didn't blame them. Her head ached with the noise of the storm and the heaviness of the sky, and even from here they could hear the sea churning greedily against the harbour. Eventually Mrs Larraby came to the classroom again and told Breda they should close the school for the day and let the children be with their parents. The older ones could make their own way, but for the little ones there would be a crocodile line, with Breda at the front and Mrs Larraby at the back, to deliver them all safely home.

It was a lengthy task, and when it was accomplished, they were all battered by the wind and lashing rain. By the time Breda reached her own home, she was totally exhausted. Her sisters were also home from school now, drying their hair and chattering like magpies at the chance of an unexpected day's holiday.

Her mother began fussing at once. 'Go upstairs and change out of those wet clothes and take off your boots. They look fair sodden. I hope your gran's all right. Your dad was going to call in on her on his way to the quay to see what's afoot, although you know how she revels in the sight and sound of a storm.'

Oh yes, they all knew what an eccentric old lady Gran Hanney was. Agnes shook her head slightly, as if wondering how anybody could enjoy a storm, and then noticed how much her daughter was shivering.

'For goodness' sake, do as I say, Breda. You don't want to risk catching a cold before your wedding. It wouldn't be a pretty sight to have the bride sneezing all the way to the altar.'

'All right, and then I'll go and stay with Gran as well.'

She couldn't explain the anxiety she felt, nor the reason why she felt in her bones, her intuitive Cornish bones, that there was some parallel between the state of the churning sea here, and the things that might be happening somewhere out there in the vast unknown ocean. *Somewhere at sea.*

She knew all the people in this village. She knew the fishermen, the friends of Warren's and the older men, who still had their strength and skill tested every single day. If the boats had gone out earlier today, it was the last anybody would hear of them until they returned, and like everyone else in a small seafaring community, she shared in the entire village's anxiety for those at sea.

She refused to admit to the real fear in her heart. The parallels with Warren's situation gave no sensible reason for her fear and she tried to subdue it. Upstairs in her room she changed her wet clothes and dried herself quickly, not bothering about the rats'-tails of her hair. It was the least important thing on her mind as she pulled on warm socks and boots and raced down to her gran's cottage. Her dad had left now, and without warning, her throat caught on a sob, and her gran spoke firmly.

'Sit you down, girl, and do as you're told for once. You'll drink some tea if I have to force it down you. I don't know what dark thoughts you're harbouring, but you look as if you've had a shock, and hot, strong tea for shock is what the doctor ordered. How do you think Warren will feel when he gets home, if he sees a maggot for a bride?'

But she wasn't his bride yet. The talisman might not be enough. It might be his downfall. Breda had never thought herself the type of person to panic unnecessarily, and even though she knew their actions at the cottage weren't responsible for the storm or her irrational feelings that went with it, common sense was deserting her today, and she couldn't seem to stop it.

She felt the hot cup of tea being thrust into her hands, and she dutifully sipped it, hardly noticing how it scalded her, but starting to feel angry with herself for her weakness. If she could go to pieces like this when nothing bad had happened, then how much worse would she be for all the years ahead when the war was far behind them, and Warren renewed his life as a fisherman?

'Now then, are you going to tell me what's got into you today?' she heard her gran say calmly, as her wretched cat purred contentedly by the fire-place, oblivious to the racket still going on outside.

'I don't know. A bad feeling. I can't explain it.'

'Well, you're being a proper Job's Comforter for a girl on the eve of her wedding, aren't you, girl?'

55

'I know I am, and I can't help it!' She wandered about the small cottage as jittery as if she had St. Vitus' Dance, until she couldn't stand it any longer.

'I think I'll go down to the quay and find Dad,' she said abruptly.

'It's pouring with rain, my dear, and you'll hardly be able to see a hand in front of your face for the wind and the spray. Warren's not there, you know,' she added, as if wondering if the girl had become confused.

'I *know!*'

'Then at least wrap yourself up in some of your grandad's old oilskins to keep the worst of it off yourself. Remember your wedding's not very far away and you don't want to catch pneumonia.'

Her mother had only mentioned a cold. Now it was pneumonia. Breda wouldn't care what it was, she thought hysterically. How could two women make so much fuss about such things when so many lives could be in danger? But as she saw the guarded look on her gran's face, she knew how well she was hiding her own feelings. Gran Hanney had seen it all before, and knew of more than one family who had lost their menfolk to the sea. All the same, she still couldn't stay here. The cottage had started to feel claustrophobic, as if she were suffocating. As if she were drowning...

She felt the cold, clammy oilskins go around her as her gran insisted she wore them, and she rammed the sou'wester on her head, uncaring whether or not she resembled a circus clown. What did it matter? What did any of it matter, as

56

long as all those at sea came safely back home where they belonged?

Outside again, she was almost knocked over by the ferocity of the wind and lashing rain. She was blinded by it. The noise was terrific now. The waves were mountainous in the small harbour, the sea boiling, and she struggled to join the crowds of waiting watchers.

'Is there any news?' she shouted to anyone near enough to hear, but the wind whipped the sound of her voice away. She couldn't see her father or Mrs Larraby anywhere, though it was hard to recognise anybody, done up as they were. She tugged at the arm of a gnarled old seaman, who must have seen plenty of days like this in his long lifetime, and he turned, recognising her with a nod.

'Nothing yet, Breda love, but the boats will have found a safe harbour by now, don't you fret.'

They still waited, though. It was as though no one was prepared to give up the hope that somehow those flimsy boats would ride out the storm and come back to where they belonged. There were plenty of small coves. There were also high, jagged rocks all along the coast. Where could there be any safe harbour in this notorious graveyard for wrecks? There had been many rich pickings in the past whenever a larger ship crashed against the rocks, carrying spirits and timber, and all manner of precious cargo that could be spirited away by keen-eyed Cornish folk right under the noses of the Revenue Men. They were the spoils of the sea. It was recompense for the way the sea could sometimes rob them of their loved ones and their livelihoods.

Breda felt as though she had been standing rigidly for hours, willing her vivid imagination away from the worst possible outcome of this day, when there was a ripple of excitement farther along the quay. Word passed like wildfire among the waiting crowd. From the clifftop farther along the coast one of the fishing boats had been sighted, listing badly, but seemingly making for a narrow inlet for shelter.

'There's no way of telling which boat it is,' somebody was yelling. 'But if one of them's safe, then you can be sure there's hope for the rest of them. They won't be fish bait just yet.'

Fish bait. That was what they called them ... and the next moment she felt her arm gripped by her father, appearing like a grey ghost out of the mist.

'What the devil are you doing here, Breda?' he bellowed in her ear.

'Just seeing if I can do anything to help,' she stuttered impotently, her voice lost on the wind, and knowing there was nothing anyone could do but wait.

Day had seemingly turned into night, and still there was no news of the small flotilla of fishing boats that had gone out that morning. There were no lights in the cottages, and where once there would have been beacons along the cliffs to show the boats the way home, wartime restrictions had forbidden their use. She was frozen to the bone by now, and she couldn't blame some of those who had been here for hours, for going home. She knew, as they all knew, that when there was anything to tell, the news would spread like a flame among the cottages.

'Go home, Breda,' she heard her dad say gently, close to her ear. 'Whatever's ahead, it'll need the men to sort it out, and the women to offer comfort when it's needed.'

She bit her lips, finding them almost too numb with the cold to tremble any more. She knew his words made sense, but it also seemed as if she was abandoning him. But there was nothing she could do here. Nothing that any of them could do until the storm abated. Finally she nodded.

And then, as she turned away, there were shouts behind her, and looming out of the mist and rain the shapes they had all longed to see were lurching drunkenly towards the quay. Half a dozen boats had gone out, and half a dozen boats were returning. They were all safe, and there was complete jubilation among the small crowds still waiting for their heroes to come home.

It was a sign, Breda thought, just as jubilant. If the fishing boats had come home safely, then so would Warren. She had been a fool all this terrible, miserable day, to think there had been anything portentous about it. She could hear the cheering still going on behind her, but she was too exhausted to turn around and rejoin them. She was soaked through for the second time that day, despite the oilskins, but she went straight to Gran Hanney's house to return them and to tell her the good news. By then, the rain had started to ease, and the sky was clearing, the dark clouds scudding across the sky as if chased by a giant hand.

'Didn't I tell you not to fret so much?' the old lady said complacently. 'You can't take the world's ills on your shoulders, Breda.'

'I know. It was just – oh well, it doesn't matter now. And the storm has broken at last, Gran. That's another little miracle, isn't it?'

Her spirits had risen considerably by the time she went home and heard her dad's report that evening. Not one fisherman had been lost. Not one boat had been damaged. So not all omens and intuitions had to be bad, Breda thought thankfully, and if she chose to think of this day as something that had turned out well in the end, then she chose to think of it as a good omen for all the other days.

She walked to school the next morning with a lighter heart. She nodded and passed the time of day with folk that she knew, some of whom were clearing up the mess the storm had made, from fallen branches and the occasional roof slate. She sympathised with those who had suffered some damage, and waved out to Warren's mother, gossiping outside her cottage with the postwoman. No matter what the time of day, Warren's mother always looked the same, in her flowered overall, her hair pinned back severely as if to counteract her pleasant face, Breda thought affectionately.

Her smile faded a little as she saw a young lad wobbling about on a bicycle as he negotiated some of the debris in the road. His antics might have been funny, had not everyone known the significance of those distinctive red post office bicycles and the telegrams they delivered. Some telegrams were the best sort, of course, but others were not...

As the bicycle slewed to a stop beside Warren's mother, she stopped talking to the postwoman, and after a moment when her heart seemed to stop altogether, it was suddenly thudding painfully fast as Breda began running along the road towards her. She reached the cottage just as the telegram boy was handing out the yellow envelope, and she was just in time to catch Warren's mother, who looked in imminent danger of collapse.

Chapter Four

Almost without thinking, Breda bundled Warren's mother inside the house. In happier times a telegram boy would wait to see if there would be any reply, but these days people preferred to see the contents without prying eyes watching them. Already, there were too many locals who had seen the arrival of the telegram boy, and hearts that were probably praying that it wasn't bad news for the Pascoe family. But of course it would be bad news. What other kind would it be? If Breda had been feeling almost crazily optimistic when all the fishing boats had come safely home, she was thrown completely the other way now, as Warren's mother tried to open the yellow envelope with trembling hands.

'Let me do it,' she said, her own lips shaking. It wasn't addressed to her and it wasn't her place to do it, but in so short a time from now, she would have been the one to be the next of kin, not Warren's mother. *Next of kin* ... was ever a phrase so bitter with all that it implied?

The first five words on the telegram dazzled in front of Breda's eyes.

We regret to inform you...

Mrs Pascoe was clinging to her, her fingers digging deep into Breda's flesh. The woman was wailing now, and so was she. Her whole life was disintegrating in front of her eyes by those few stark words on a piece of flimsy paper, telling her that Warren's ship had been sunk by enemy action with all hands lost, and that her beloved Warren was missing, presumed drowned.

'It can't be true!' she finally managed, the breath seeming to explode from her lungs in an agonised gasp, and she was the one clinging to Mrs Pascoe now as the telegram fluttered to the floor between them. 'I won't let it be true. It must be a mistake. It says, "missing, believed drowned". That's what they always say, don't they? It doesn't mean it's definite. It's a stop-gap until they confirm the truth of it – a heartless stop-gap.'

They were both aware of a loud hammering on the door. The next minute it opened, and Breda's gran was there, holding her chest and swaying alarmingly after hurrying too fast from her cottage.

'I saw the postwoman,' she ground out between breaths. 'She said there was a telegram. Somebody's gone to fetch Jed Pascoe.'

Breda motioned to the floor, unable to speak, and Gran Hanney picked up the piece of paper. She read it silently while she caught her breath and stilled the pain around her heart. 'Sit you both down and I'll make some tea, unless there's some brandy in the house. You both look as if you could do with a drop.'

'I don't want tea!' Breda heard herself sobbing now. 'I don't want to sit down. I just want somebody to tell me this is all a mistake, and for Warren to come walking in the door.'

As if by a cruel irony the door opened again. Warren's father, grim-faced at being called home from the dock with the dire news that had gone round the village like a flame now, went straight to his wife. Even if the locals had no real idea what was in the telegram, they hardly needed telling. Telegrams were always bad news in wartime. Mrs Pascoe wrenched herself out of Breda's embrace and wept in her husband's arms.

'It's our Warren, Jed, and it's the news we always dreaded.'

In those awful moments when his parents hugged and consoled one another as best they could, Breda felt very alone. They had each other and they didn't need her. The only person she needed was Warren, and it was drumming into her brain that she was never going to see him again. She'd had the omens. The bloodstains on her wedding dress. The spots of blood on the bed sheets where they had anticipated their wedding day. The storm, and the fishing boats ... and perhaps *their* safe return was the payment for losing one precious life somewhere on a deeper ocean at the hands of an unseen enemy...

The sharp slap across her face brought her gasping to her senses. She hadn't even realised she was screaming as the incoherent thoughts spun through her mind. She wouldn't have believed Gran Hanney's scrawny arm could have such a forceful swing, either. And then her gran was pushing her down on a chair and forcing her head between her knees.

After a few minutes she sat up slowly, facing the two people who were holding one another closely and quietly, and being far more dignified than she was. But they had each other, while she had no one. As the hysteria threatened to rise again, she took the glass of brandy her gran thrust into her hand and gulped it down quickly. She wasn't used to spirits and it made her head whirl, but now Warren's mother was coming to sit beside her, holding her hands tightly.

'Breda my love, this is a tragedy for all of us, and especially for you, so soon before your wedding. I'm afraid.' Her voice broke for a second. 'I'm afraid we will have other things to arrange now – or rather, to un-arrange.'

Breda looked at her stupidly, and Jed Pascoe cleared his throat noisily.

'If you would rather I went to see the vicar, dear, you just leave it all to me.'

Before Breda could gather her thoughts to say that it was her place to do any arranging and un-arranging, thank you, the door opened again, and her own mother came inside, her face distraught.

'Is it true what I've been hearing?' Agnes Hanney asked in a shaky voice. 'It's all around the village that there was a telegram.'

She hardly needed to ask what it was about. The four faces inside the Pascoe cottage told their own story. And then Breda rushed into her arms and was sobbing uncontrollably.

'Warren's ship has been sunk. All hands lost. Missing, presumed drowned,' she grated out jerkily, seemingly unable to put a coherent sentence together.

'Oh, my dear Lord,' Agnes whispered, holding on tightly to Breda, who still seemed near to fainting.

Gran's voice rang out, the only steady one

among them.

'Would everybody sit down before you all fall down, and I'll pour you all a tot of brandy, if Mr and Mrs Pascoe don't object to me emptying their brandy bottle in the process. I won't give any more to our Breda. If she has any more she'll be roaring drunk.'

It was such an unlikely happening that even Breda managed the smallest hint of a smile. But Gran would have seen all this before, of course. This wasn't the first war where sailors had been lost at sea, never to return, and it was far from being the first loss in the village. The names carved on the granite war memorial in the centre of it bore testament to that. And at the end of this war, Warren Pascoe's would be added to it. The sobering thought was enough to make even Gran Hanney's old hands shake a little as she handed round the small tots of brandy, taking charge, because somebody had to, and these folk didn't look as if they had a sensible thought between them right now.

'I'll see the vicar myself,' Breda heard herself say in a voice that sounded completely unlike her own. Where it had been shrill before, now it was dull and flat, as if all the life had gone out of it. As if all the life had gone out of *her*.

'You don't have to do it,' her mother said swiftly. 'One of us will take care of everything, Breda.'

'Will you take care of bringing Warren back to me so that we can be married in a week's time?' she said, suddenly brittle. Her moods, her voice, her senses, all seemed to swing in an instant. She

66

hardly knew who she was any more. She couldn't cope with this. Nor did she want to hear how other women had learnt to cope when tragedy happened. She wasn't one of those other women. She was Breda Hanney, who had loved her sweetheart from childhood, and now she had to face the fact that he was gone for ever.

Someone else was knocking on the door. Dear God, weren't they ever going to leave them alone? she thought hysterically. Was this how it was going to be from now on, with everybody wanting to add their piece to her grief, asking her how she was feeling, when there were no feelings left inside her? When all she wanted to do now was to go home, to curl up into a ball and hide herself away in the dark the way wounded animals did. Waiting to die. *Wanting* to die.

Mrs Pascoe answered the door and ushered in the vicar, telling him in a few brief words what had happened. It seemed it was no surprise.

'Dear people, I got here as soon as I heard about the telegram. I'm afraid there are lots of neighbours relaying the news, all asking if it is true. I couldn't tell them for sure, but one has to assume the worst these days, and I had to see what comfort I can give to you all. And to you, of course, Breda my dear.'

Was she just an afterthought now, then? Coming a poor second after Warren's parents, who must bear the most of the condolences, naturally? She'd always believed herself to be the most important person in Warren's life, but there were others who would grieve for him as well, and she mustn't be selfish. If it was no more than

67

a sarcastic thought, it simply helped to overcome the dreadful feeling of numbness filling her now. She began to speak feverishly, as if she needed to say it all quickly while she still had a brain to deal with things.

'I have to cancel the wedding,' she said, the high, shrill voice returning. 'You can't have a wedding without a bridegroom, and I'll have to see the landlord about the lease of the cottage sometime too. We won't be needing it now.'

'My dear young lady, I'm so very sorry,' the vicar intoned, 'but I'm sure your family will be only too ready to do all of these things for you. May I suggest that we all say a prayer for Warren and all the brave souls who have died with him?'

Breda looked at him dumbly. And then fury took over, and without knowing what she was doing she raged against him, banging her hands against his chest while her family and Warren's looked on in horror at this affront to a member of the church. The words seemed to pour out of her in a torrent.

'You don't know that he's dead yet, and already you're asking us to say these meaningless words about him. If God had loved him, the way He's supposed to love everybody, how could He have let this happen to Warren? If this is what your caring God is all about, then I *hate* God.'

The vicar caught hold of her hands, trying to calm her, while Agnes tried to pull her away from him.

'Breda, I know you don't mean that, and I'm sure the vicar will forgive you in the circumstances. We're all shocked, and you don't know

68

what you're saying.'

'I know exactly what I'm saying,' Breda shouted. 'Warren and I were meant to be standing up in church and swearing before God to love one another for the rest of our lives, but your precious God has taken all that away from us, and He's the one I'll never forgive.'

'It wasn't God, my dear,' the vicar said evenly. 'It was man's inhumanity to mankind that took your young man away from you. We should never forget that, and even if you think now that you will never forgive God, I assure you that God will forgive you, and welcome you back into his loving care.'

At his pious words, Breda just about managed to resist stamping her foot like a thwarted infant. Couldn't any of them see that this was the last thing she could bear now? She wanted no mention of a higher, all-seeing power. Other people might cling to their faith at times like these, but she wasn't them, and she had an almost greedy need to cling to her pain. It was still too new, too raw, for her to want to abandon it, for when she did, then in some irrational way she feared she would start to lose the last contact with Warren she could ever have.

Through her jumbled thoughts, she heard the vicar saying his prayers now, and she could see the older people in the room standing with their heads bowed, their hands touching. Puppets, all of them. She felt like the only sane one here. And yet she was the outsider, the alien force in the room, but still the one who had lost the most. She had lost her entire future. The terrible truth made her feel totally light-headed, as if she was floating somewhere above all these fine God-fearing folk muttering meaningless mumbo-jumbo along with the vicar.

Someone was pushing an evil-smelling bottle beneath her nose, and she spluttered violently, her eyes watering, as the acrid smell of the sal volatile hit her senses. Her mother was holding it, cradling her in her arms. The last thing she remembered was hitting the floor in the Pascoe cottage. There weren't so many people surrounding her now, and she tried desperately to remember those last few moments, and the moments that had preceded them.

The shock of it hit her like a thunderbolt. Warren was missing, presumed drowned. They all knew what that meant. It was giving them false hope, when it was a certainty. The Admiralty didn't make those mistakes. She stirred in her mother's arms, looking around her as she realised she was no longer in the Pascoe cottage. She was home and lying on her own bed, with no idea how she had got here, and her mother was hovering over her with tear-filled eyes.

'Stay still, my love. The doctor's going to give you something to make you sleep for a while.'

So the doctor was here. The only man she remembered seeing apart from Warren's father, was the vicar. Oh, dear Lord, what had she screamed to the vicar? She must be the most ungodly person he had ever encountered. But none of it mattered. Nothing mattered. She felt the sharp sting of a needle in her arm now. Was the whole world trying to fill her with unspeakable things? First the awful smell of the sal volatile to keep her alert, and now something filling her bloodstream to make her sleep. Maybe if she asked him, he could give her something to let her sleep for ever so that she need never wake up to the reality of what had happened. But she vaguely remembered wanting to keep alert, wanting to keep the pain intact...

For the next couple of days, Breda was kept sedated, but she seemed to be in a state of half-consciousness, knowing she was fighting its effect. She wasn't a weakling to be kept unaware of what was happening. She had always considered herself to be a strong person, although hearing snippets of conversations that drifted in and out of her head, she wasn't sure how strong. As she caught the sound of her mother's voice, it seemed that Agnes wasn't sure of it either.

'She looks more peaceful now, thank goodness,' her mother murmured. 'She took it so badly, as you would expect, that I feared for her state of mind when she first heard the news, Gilb. The doctor says there's no question of her returning to work yet, either. The Pascoes are still trying to get word to Max, though how the poor boy will take it is anybody's guess. He and Warren were always so close.'

'That's if they can contact him,' Breda's father replied in the same low voice. 'Communication's so bad these days, and God only knows where he is now.'

'He'll get compassionate leave, won't he?'

'Probably, but what can he do if he does? By

71

the time he gets here, it will be too late to comfort his aunt and uncle.'

The voices began drifting away again, as Breda's father persuaded his wife to leave their poor girl in peace.

Breda remained with her eyes closed, still in the half-waking, half-sleeping and completely unreal state because of the sedatives she had been given. She knew they were deeply concerned for her, but it was odd to hear them talking to each other in her bedroom, and yet talking as if she wasn't there. She wondered if they were trying to make her aware of what was happening outside these four walls, even if she couldn't cope with it herself.

But once those first days had passed, she knew she had begun to feel a little stronger. She wasn't one to lie in bed when she wasn't ill. She had suffered a bereavement. It was similar to one that happened to thousands of other young women and families in wartime, and she wasn't unique, even if she felt that she was, and that no one else could ever feel the way she did.

On the third day, she was aware of several pairs of eyes gazing down at her, and she opened them a fraction to see her two young sisters at the end of her bed. They looked young and scared and shifty, not knowing what to say, and probably wishing she had stayed asleep, Breda thought, with a touch of compassion for them.

'I won't bite,' she said. 'You can come a bit closer if you like. You're not going to catch anything.'

They laughed nervously, and then Esme spoke up.

'We know what's happened, and it's awful. We really liked Warren.' She swallowed hard and went on determinedly. 'Mum said we weren't to worry you, but we wanted to see that you're all right. We're staying at Gran's, by the way.'

Breda struggled to sit up. 'Are you? What for? I bet you don't like that.'

Jenna added her piece. 'Dad said we had to give you some peace and quiet for a few days, but we'd really like to come home now. Gran's cottage smells, and her cat hates me. He's horrible and messy.'

Oh God, if this wasn't being back to normal, as much as anything was ever going to be normal again, then Breda couldn't imagine what was. And seeing the desperation in her sisters' eyes, she knew it was up to her.

'Well, of course you can come home, and you can tell Mum and Dad I said so. I don't expect the world to grind to a halt just because – well, just *because*,' she finished lamely.

'The children in your class have made a card for you,' Esme said, visibly cheering up. 'Do you want to see it?'

She produced the large card that had all the children's signatures on it in their scrawling handwriting. The words 'Get Well Soon, Miss' were written at the top on their behalf by Mrs Larraby. It brought a huge lump to Breda's throat. In their innocent way, she knew her infants would be missing her, and bewildered by what had happened.

'It's lovely,' she said huskily. 'You can put it on the dressing table, and then you can go downstairs and tell Mum I'm getting up.'

They both looked relieved. It made them less than comfortable to see their older sister languishing in bed. A minute later Breda realised Jenna was still not old enough to know the meaning of tact.

'Mrs Stacey at the butcher's said it's very sad that you won't be getting married to Warren after all,' she said. 'But she said you're young enough to find somebody else, so your wedding-dress won't be wasted, nor our bridesmaid dresses, providing we don't grow out of them.'

'Shut up, you idiot,' hissed Esme. 'You're not to repeat that kind of gossip.'

They both left the bedroom hastily, and for a long while afterwards Breda made no attempt to get out of bed, despite what she had said to them. She sat up against the pillows with her thoughts and her stomach churning, and eventually her mother came upstairs to find out if she really was coming downstairs. She found Breda with her face ashen and her eyes large and full of unshed tears.

'Are people in the village gossiping about me, Mum?' she said.

'They're concerned for you, my lamb, the same as we all are,' Agnes said carefully. 'It's not just idle gossip when neighbours talk about what's happened, and whatever they say, it's always with sympathy and not malice.'

'So they have been talking,' Breda persisted.

Stupid question. Of course they had. She wasn't the pretty Hanney girl now, on the brink of a beautiful wedding to her sweetheart. She was

74

the poor Hanney girl, not going to be a bride, and not even a widow. She was nothing.

'You can't stop folk feeling sad for you, Breda. It was the same when the Tremayne boy was killed in France a couple of years ago. You were ready to offer his mother sympathy then, I remember.'

Breda remembered too. But that was the Tremayne boy, and this was Warren, and she couldn't bear the thought of people stopping her in the street to say how sorry they were, and to ask how she was feeling. It was what everybody did, of course. Saying the usual platitudes and getting the usual responses, which eased their consciences and did nothing to ease the heartache inside.

'I'm getting up,' she said, swinging her legs over the bed and feeling her head spin as she did so.

'Go steady, my love. You've been in bed for a few days and you'll be feeling a bit woozy,' Agnes said, alarmed at this sudden change of mood.

'I've been in bed too long. The sooner I meet people and get over their messages of sympathy, the better. I need to go back to school too.'

Her voice choked, knowing she would have to answer so many difficult questions from her pupils. She had never been one to baulk at them before, but they had never been about anything so personal, nor the inevitable anxiety from those five-year-olds as to where Warren was now. They had been looking forward so excitedly to her wedding, and now she had to explain why there wasn't going to be one. They almost certainly already knew, but she knew they would understand it better coming from her. They trusted her. In a strange way, the thought of their innocent little faces gave her a sliver of courage.

'You shouldn't think of going back to school yet,' Agnes said.

'What else am I to do?' Breda said. 'I can't stay in bed for ever, Mum, and I need to see Warren's parents too. There won't be a wedding, and I suppose there won't even be a – a.' She couldn't say the word.

But you couldn't have a funeral without a body, and presumably there wasn't one. Warren had just disappeared beneath the waves and was lost for ever. The lump rose alarmingly in her throat again and then her mother spoke calmly.

'Your father and I have been talking to Warren's parents, love, and of course you were going to be involved when you felt well enough. But the general feeling was that in time, we could arrange with the vicar to have a special service at the church for Warren.'

Breda nodded, her head bowed as she pulled on her stockings, her unkempt hair falling over her face, knowing she was unable to think about such details yet.

'Whatever you think. How are they?' she asked, to take her mind off anything so macabre as a special service for that vibrant young man.

'They're a stoical couple,' Agnes replied cautiously. 'I know they'll feel better when they've heard back from Max, but so far they've had no word from him, despite sending a telegram to his unit. I'm sure he'll get home as soon as he can.'

For one horrible instant, the thought flashed

76

through Breda's mind that it should have been Max who had been killed instead of Warren. Max, the devil-may-care wanderer with no ties, who had always thought more about his precious saxophone playing than going to war. It was only the thought of travelling abroad to exotic places that had lured him into it. But just as instantly, Breda felt ashamed of the unworthy thought. They had always been as close as brothers, and Max would be devastated as soon as he learnt what had happened.

Her mother left her to finish dressing, and a short while later, she walked gingerly downstairs. It was strange to see that everything here was the same as it had always been. She felt as though she had gone through a lifetime of emotions in the last few days, and yet the cottage was still the same. There was a litter of newspapers on the sofa. The scent of her father's pipe lingered on the air. In the kitchen the kettle was gently whistling on the stove. The laundry basket was full of the ironing her mother was about to do. Life went on.

'Sit down, Breda, and I'll make us a cup of tea,' Agnes said, trying not to reveal how glad she was to see her daughter up and about, despite looking so maggoty and frail.

Neither Agnes nor Gran Hanney had too much truck with the need for the sedation the doctor had prescribed. They were both of the old school that said you had to face up to your problems and get over them, not be sent into unconsciousness while the body sorted itself out, which seemed to be the new way of thinking.

'Mum, you know I've told the girls they can

77

come back home, don't you?' Breda said next. 'It's not fair to inflict them on Gran any longer.'

'So they said, but we thought it best while you were in bed.'

'Well, I'm not in bed any longer, so I'll walk down to Gran's this afternoon and let them all know, and then I'll see Warren's parents. If you feel it necessary, I wouldn't mind if you came with me, though,' she added, not quite ready after all, to face it alone.

But she realised that it felt marginally better to be making decisions at all. She had hated the sense of being in limbo and letting the world revolve around her while having no part in it. It wasn't in her character to be so lily-livered. So today the family, tomorrow the infants, she thought, a mite more resolutely. Although, as today was Saturday, she realised, glancing at the calendar on the wall, that would have to wait until Monday. She ignored the crosses on each day of the calendar leading up to the following Saturday with the large red circle around it. The circle marking the special day that would have been her wedding day.

Chapter Five

Breda couldn't rid herself of the strange feeling that she had been asleep for a very long time, instead of only a few days. The village was still the same as it had always been, if you disregarded the shop windows that were criss-crossed with tape, supposedly to stop too much flying glass if they were bombed. But since no bombs had been heard anywhere near the vicinity, it was all taken fairly complacently now. The reality regularly came home to them with ration books and food coupons and the meagre amounts of food allowed to each person every week. How Agnes had managed to bake a modest wedding cake with so few ingredients had amazed the family.

It was a thought that sharply sobered Breda's resolve as she and her mother started out on the road down to Gran Hanney's cottage. There would be cake for tea for a few days once it was brought out of the tin in which Agnes was keeping it. She pushed the thought away, knowing that another lump in her throat was threatening. She tried to keep her head held high, but it was increasingly difficult to do so.

If she had thought they would get to Gran Hanney's house without hindrance she was mistaken. They were stopped every few steps by neighbours and friends wanting to offer their sympathy, and it was the ordeal Breda had expected.

79

'They all mean to be kind, and just remember that with every one who stops you today, it will be one less who stops you tomorrow,' Agnes advised her.

'I know, but it twists a knife in my heart every time.'

'Would you rather they ignored mentioning a young man they all knew? How would that feel?'

'Terrible,' Breda admitted. But she was never more thankful to reach her gran's cottage and to slide down gratefully into an armchair. She pushed the scraggy, noisily purring cat out of the way by instinct rather than annoyance. She knew her mother was right. You had to face people. You had to accept whatever they said and move on. If it was bad for her, it would be just as bad for Warren's parents, even though she had hardly been lucid enough to give them much thought since that dreadful day when the telegram came. She felt guilty about that. If she was suffering, then so were they, and she was glad she had planned to see them as soon as she left here.

Gran Hanney bustled about with a tray of biscuits and cups of tea. Breda thought she must have drunk so much tea that she would soon be drowning in the stuff ... and as the hateful word entered her mind, she choked over her cup.

'Now then, Agnes,' Gran said, ignoring the spluttering over the hot brew, 'I've got the girls' things packed up so you can take them back with you. Gilb called to tell me they were allowed home again. I made them go to their usual Saturday morning club today, but when they get back I'll tell them they can go straight on home. It won't be too much for you, will it?'

Agnes answered shortly that when would it be too much for a mother to be caring for all her family?

'I was thinking of their squabbling on account of Breda,' Gran said dryly.

'It won't be too much for me to have them around,' Breda broke in, not wanting to be talked about as if she wasn't there – either that, or a delicate flower to be nurtured at all costs. 'It will just be normal. But if you don't mind, Gran, this tea's too hot to drink, so you and Mum have a good chat while I go and see Warren's parents.'

She could see they were both about to protest, so she got up at once and made for the door. It occurred to her that she hadn't been alone ever since the telegram came – not alone and in control of her senses, anyway – and suddenly she needed that. She needed to walk through the village alone, just being herself and not relying on her mother or anyone else. It wasn't far up the hill to the Pascoe house from here, and she only met a few folk on the way who murmured words that she didn't really hear.

The first shock of facing Warren's house again since that fateful day came when she saw the curtained windows, signifying that this was a house of mourning. She swallowed hard, knocked at the door, and went inside.

There was no sign of anyone in the darkened front room. Warren's father would be back at work by now, of course, and through the open back door she could see Mrs Pascoe in the back garden, feeding the chickens. Those chickens had provided the fresh eggs they needed for the wedding cake, since Warren's mother had said there was no need for them to use powdered eggs for such a grand occasion ... and Breda forced herself to stop thinking of every poignant little thing that had such a new significance now.

She walked through the kitchen and out into the garden. Patches of flowers were blooming in the spring sunshine, but they were taking second place to the rows of vegetables that the government urged everyone with a bit of ground to grow nowadays. Digging for Victory, they called it. Breda determinedly kept her mind on such mundane things before she called out to Warren's mother.

Laura Pascoe turned around to face her. Her eyes were still swollen with grief, but she looked fairly calm, considering. It seemed odd to Breda, that during those few days when she had been kept mostly insensible, other folk had been coping in a different way. Even if it hadn't been her choice, they were the brave ones, she thought. They had faced their tragedy there and then, while she now had to do it all over again.

'Breda, love, it's good to see you out and about,' Laura said. 'Come and see if there are any eggs among this straw, then you can take one home for your tea.'

It was such a homely remark, the same remark that she had heard a hundred times before, and it was enough to fill Breda's eyes with tears. She scrabbled about in the straw and produced two brown eggs that were worth more than gold in these belt-tightening days.

'Have you heard from Max yet?' she blurted out.

She really didn't know why she'd said it, except that she couldn't think of another single thing to say. She knew they couldn't possibly have heard anything so soon. She knew it would be what they wanted, though, to have Max back safe. To have at least one of them back safe.

Laura shook her head. 'We sent the telegram, of course, and followed it with a letter. Telegrams are so stark, aren't they?' she said unnecessarily. 'I suppose it will just follow him around, and then hopefully he'll get some leave. But let's go indoors, dear. We have things to talk about.'

'Just don't offer me a cup of tea,' Breda said, attempting a small joke. 'What with Mum and Gran filling me up with the stuff, I shall turn brown soon.'

They went indoors, and as soon as Breda sat down in the front room where she had been so many times, she began to feel stifled. There were photographs of Warren everywhere, some when he was a child with Max, and some with Breda as well. It was as though Mrs Pascoe was surrounding herself with memories – as if she would ever forget them, thought Breda, with a flash of annoyance. The woman caught her looking at the photographs with tortured eyes, and she gave a deep sigh.

'You're probably thinking the same as Jed, that there's no need for all these reminders of Warren. And it's true that we older folk are not like you young ones, Breda. I can't weep and beat my breast for ever. It doesn't mean I don't feel, or

83

that I don't miss him because God knows I do, but I have to get on with things. And seeing him all around me like this,' she gestured to the photographs, 'means he's still here, still close to me. I don't find it easy to show my emotions, but it doesn't mean I don't have any.'

'I know that you do,' Breda said quietly, more touched than she had ever been. She had always thought, as her own mother did, that Laura Pascoe was the most stoical of women, but there was definitely a heart beating beneath that starched overall, and it was a heart that ached as much as Breda's own.

'I'm also practical.' Laura's eyes were more steely now. 'There are things to be done, and we need to discuss them, my dear. When you feel ready, I think it would be a good idea if you and I went to see the vicar together.'

'I think he knows there won't be a wedding,' Breda said swiftly. She didn't want to talk about that, she really didn't.

'Has your mother mentioned anything about a special service for Warren? You may think it's far too soon to even think about it, and of course we couldn't consider it for a while, but his father and I think it would be a lovely gesture, that's all. We thought that when Max comes home would be the appropriate time.'

Despite her resentment that this idea was making the certainty of it all too real, Breda could see how important this was to Laura. It was something to look forward to, especially pinning her hopes on having Max there, her nephew, her make-believe son, her substitute boy.

She caught her breath between her teeth, wishing she hadn't thought of any such thing. Max was her friend, and it wasn't fair to resent the fact that he was still alive, while Warren was not. Nor to blame Laura Pascoe for wanting him home. Through the determination in the older woman's eyes to get on with things, there was still a lost look that Breda recognised so well.

'I can't think of that just yet,' she murmured. 'Please let's leave it a while – and I'd rather see the vicar on my own if you don't mind. I rather think I need to make my peace with him for the things I said.'

'Just as you wish, dear.'

There didn't seem much else to say. They were two women, both grieving for the same man, but in very different ways. Laura had lost a son, but she still had a husband to comfort her, and a loving nephew who would come home someday. Breda had lost the love of her life, and she had already vowed she would never fall in love again. How could she, when her heart still belonged to Warren?

She finally left Laura, clutching a brown paper bag with her teatime egg inside it. She could hardly eat it in front of the family when they were probably having dripping toast, as they usually did on Saturdays, but her mother would probably insist on it, still treating her like the invalid she wasn't.

She hadn't considered that to reach the church she had to pass the cottage that was still rented to her and Warren. She felt a jolt in her heart as she turned into the lane and saw it, as picturesque as

85

ever in the April sunshine, the windows shining as if to welcome the new occupants who were going to live here happily ever after. She meant to hurry by, keeping her eyes averted, but as she did so, the gate creaked in a small gust of wind, inviting her in, as if to reproach her if she turned her back on it. And somehow she couldn't.

The key to the front door was in her bag, and her feet seemed to move of their own accord as she took the few short steps towards it, and inserted the key with shaking hands. The last time she had been here it had been with Warren, a special day that had been so momentous for them both. Her heart was pounding as she looked around the small rooms downstairs, so perfect for a newly-wed couple just starting out on the greatest adventure of their lives.

Her breath caught on a sob, and then, almost unwillingly, she climbed the staircase to the bedroom. She stood motionless for a long time, staring at the pristine sheets and pillows that she and Warren would have shared. *Had* shared, the memory whirled through her mind, and thank God for it, she thought almost feverishly. She thanked God they had at least had that one glorious time together ... and if there had ever been a vestige of shame about it, it was gone from her mind for ever now, knowing that it could never happen again.

The anguished sound that left her lips then was almost an animal cry, and without thinking she rushed across to the bed. She flung herself face down on it, breathing in the crisp cotton of the pillows, her arms outstretched, as if to recapture in that one act of supplication, everything they had been to one another.

How long she lay there, embracing the past and mourning a future that could never be, she had no idea. It could have been minutes or hours by the time she realised the room had grown colder. She slowly rose from the bed, smoothing down the covers almost lovingly, then turned to go back down the stairs without a backward glance.

By the time Breda started to walk home later that day, she felt calmer. She had seen the vicar and made her peace with him. She had also made a special plea. On the day that would have been her wedding day, she asked to be allowed some time in the church alone. She wanted no family, no witnesses, just to be by herself with her thoughts of how differently the day had turned out.

'God will also be with you, Breda,' the vicar assured her.

She didn't answer. Even though it seemed the right thing to do to be in God's house on the day when she and Warren would have exchanged their vows, she wasn't ready to forgive the God who had allowed this to happen. She finally mumbled something in reply and felt the vicar's hand pressed lightly on her head while he said a prayer over her. If she had dared she would have snatched his hand away, but she was too steeped in the church's teachings to dare to do such a thing.

At last he let her go and she almost fled out of the cool interior of the church, glad to feel the welcoming warmth of the sunlight outside. The daylight wouldn't be fading for hours yet, but the sky seemed to glow with a pearly reddish sheen that promised fine days to come. Wonderful, fruitful days, full of colour and lushness, such as Cornwall was blessed with so often. Days that Warren would never share with her.

'Miss. Miss!'

She heard the young voice and gave a groan. She was half-planning to go back to school on Monday, at least for a little while, to let her pupils see that she was still their teacher, still here. She turned around and saw one of the small girls in her class, tugging at her mother's hand as she started to run towards her. Breda had known the child's mother all her life, and she forced a smile to her face.

'Hello Josie,' she said to the child. She couldn't think of another thing to say and the mother looked apologetic.

'I'm sorry, Breda. Josie was so excited to see you I couldn't stop her. She tells me the children are all missing you.'

'It's all right, truly,' Breda said, and then she addressed the child. 'I'm coming back to school soon, Josie, and it was a lovely card you all made for me.'

'Aren't you getting married, Miss?' Josie Dean blurted out, her eyes large.

'Hush now,' the mother said quickly. 'She doesn't really understand what's happened,' she mouthed to Breda.

As Breda bent down to the child's level, she summoned up all her teaching skills and pushed everything else out of her mind.

'Josie, even if I'm not getting married, we've got something else to look forward to next month. I promised I'd take the class to Padstow on May Day, didn't I? I'll be telling you all about it when I come back to school, so if you see any of your friends you can tell them that from me.'

As Josie began to smile again, Breda could see the flash of admiration in the mother's eyes as she straightened up. No doubt the word would soon get around that Breda Hanney was being amazingly brave, considering what had happened to her. She didn't feel brave. She had just done what needed to be done at the time. Perhaps that was the answer. One step at a time, however small a step it was. And she had already decided to take an even bigger step that she would tell her family about when she got home.

Agnes had been there for a long while before her. Her younger daughters were upstairs, arguing about something as usual, and Breda's father was quietly smoking his pipe in the back garden. It was all back to normal – at least, normal in the new order of things, thought Breda.

'Warren's mother gave me an egg for my tea,' she said, marvelling that it had remained intact all this time when she had been to the cottage and then the church and then reassuring the child. 'I don't think I should have it if you're only having dripping toast. Put it in the pantry, Mum.'

'Don't be silly. It's your treat, and of course you should have it. I was getting anxious, Breda. You've been gone a very long time.'

Breda took a deep breath. 'I've been to see the vicar and then I ran into one of my pupils and

89

told her I would be telling the class all about the Padstow 'Obby 'Oss on Monday. You know I'd planned to take them.' She rushed on without stopping. 'I have to do this, Mum. They're so little, and they don't need to be worried by thoughts of people dying. I know they'll be disappointed that they can't come to my wedding, and they need something to cheer them up.'

She tried not to let her voice tremble or her face crumple as she said the words. But perhaps the more she said them the more real they would become.

'Are you sure all this is wise, dear?'

'I know it is, and there's something else I want to talk to you about. How would you feel if I decided not to let the lease of the cottage go to someone else and I moved in there on my own? Would it upset you too much?'

Agnes's face was a picture now. She looked flushed and dismayed. 'I think it's the worst idea I've ever heard of. You need to be with your family now, and it's almost unhealthy to think of such a thing.'

'No, it's not,' Breda said, becoming as agitated as her mother now. 'It's where we planned to live, and where I was looking forward to making a home for us, so why shouldn't I live there? I'm a woman now, Mum, not a child. Besides, it's only a stone's throw from you, and from Gran too.'

'Stop right now, Breda!'

Breda jumped as she heard the anger in her mother's voice.

'What do you mean? Stop what?'

'Stop all this frantic activity. You're rushing into

things too fast. You're not giving yourself time to think and to grieve. You want to go back to work, even before it's decent to do so, and now you want to move into the rented cottage just as if nothing's happened. It's all happening too soon, Breda, and if you don't slow down there will come a point when it hits you hard.'

'It's already hit me as hard as anything in my life.'

By now Breda was almost distraught at this unexpected reaction. It had all seemed so simple to decide to move into their cottage, such a beautiful way of still sharing something she and Warren had wanted so much. And now her mother was throwing cold water on the idea.

Agnes caught hold of her hands and gripped them tight, forcing her daughter to sit down beside her on the sofa.

'Just listen to me, Breda. It's not often your father and I act in a heavy-handed way towards you, and your father was delighted to give Warren permission to marry you, but you're not of age for six months yet. It wouldn't be right for you to live alone, and you do realise that we could stop you doing this.'

Breda looked at her in horror now. 'You wouldn't do that! You couldn't be so cruel, Mum!'

'I'm not being cruel, my love, but you need your family around you now. I'm thinking of your well-being, and I have to say that I'm afraid for you.'

Breda snatched her hands away. 'Well, I'm afraid for me too. I'm afraid of having to live the rest of my life without Warren, but if wanting to

91

be independent and live alone is so alien to you, I happen to think it's a very grown-up decision.'

She jumped up from the sofa and ran up the stairs, banging the door of her bedroom behind her and throwing herself on the bed to sob uncontrollably. Just when she was finding a semblance of control in her life, her mother had taken it away. It was harsh and insensitive and it reduced her resolve to nothing again. If Agnes had some confused idea that she wanted to live in the cottage out of some fanciful notion that Warren was going to come walking through the door at any time, she was mistaken. It wasn't that. If anything, Breda was more and more certain that the telegram had told the truth. She had seen the newspaper that her father had tried to hide, reporting the facts of the ship that had been torpedoed and sunk. It was all true. Warren had drowned. He was never coming home again, and she had to live the rest of her life without him. The rest of her life without love.

Many miles away in a Cairo military hospital, Max Pascoe thrashed about in the throes of delirium, while the doctors consulted one another about whether or not his family should be informed of the seriousness of his condition. Since there was nothing any of them could do, it was decided to leave things well alone and let nature take its course. It would be time enough to inform them then. The blunt truth was that either the man's natural resistance would overcome the dangerous condition he was in, or it would be the inevitable outcome. Added to the serious condition of his leg wound, none of them gave much for his chances now that the ravaging fever had taken such a hold of his body.

'A lesser man would have been a goner by now,' one of the medics observed with grudging admiration. 'He must have something to go home to, and it's a certainty that, if he does recover, he'll be given an honourable discharge and sent home. His fighting days are over, poor sod.'

In Max's tormented dreams he was already home, back in Cornwall and breathing in the sweet fragrant grass of summer, instead of the dry, choking dust of the desert. He was a carefree child again, running wild across the moors with his cousin and the girl who followed them both so faithfully, the three of them closer than Siamese triplets as they explored all that Cornwall had to offer. They had climbed the old mine chimneys and imagined they were on top of the world, and crept precariously down and down into the bowels of the earth in the disused mine-shafts, pretending they were true explorers about to discover a lost empire.

In his hospital ward, Max could frequently be heard moaning and shouting when the dreams turned to nightmares. Then there was only himself, left alone on a high and crumbling mine chimney while Warren and Breda danced around it in some macabre dance of death. She wore a bridal veil, but for some reason it was black instead of the virginal white it should be. By the time the nightmare reached this stage Max was always in danger of falling, falling... And always, just before he awoke he would feel the sharpness of the needle piercing his arm, followed by some faceless person rubbing the stinging stuff into his vein to make it work quickly and telling him to hold on there, mate, and the pain would soon be gone.

He wished to God it would be gone for ever. That he could be gone for ever. Something in the back of his muddled brain told him there was nothing left to live for, anyway, that all his dreams had turned to dust, as dry and arid as that of the desert that had burnt his eyes and drained all his energy. The only thing that gave him any kind of peace was when he heard a fellow patient with his head heavily bandaged over one eye, who was still game enough to play his mouth organ. It was a tinny, tuneless instrument, but it was the sound of the music that calmed Max more than anything. There was music in his head and in his soul. He didn't know why, he just knew it was there, and it was the one thing that gave him any solace in his waking moments.

It was several weeks later that the medics had another consultation, after the arrival of a tattered telegram from England that had been following Max's unit around from place to place.

'Best not to mention it to him until he's stronger,' one of them said. 'It beats me how he's hanging on at all, but I reckon the fever might be passing at last. There's still the leg to be dealt with, but the last thing he'll want to know is if some relative has bought it. In his state it will set him back to where he was before.'

The other man agreed and the telegram was placed in the safe in the doctor's quarters while they turned to other patients needing their immediate attention. There was a new intake of casualties every day and every night. It never ended. There were always more ... and there would be many more before this war was ended. It was these poor devils with torn off limbs and blinded eyes and wounds that would never heal, who needed all their concentration, and one crumpled telegram in the midst of dealing with so much carnage was the least of their problems.

Chapter Six

Breda found a surprising ally in her plan. Gran Hanney always came for tea with the family on Sundays, and she found Breda in the garden with her father, while Esme and Jenna were detailed to help their mother lay the table. Gilb had sided with his wife on the matter of the cottage, although how much of that was his own decision, Breda wasn't sure. Her mother could be a forceful woman when she chose, and Gilb often agreed with her to keep the peace. But not so his own mother.

'What's this I hear?' she greeted Breda. 'You're wanting to fly the nest to live on your own, I understand?'

Breda felt herself tense. She might have known Agnes would mention it as soon as her gran arrived.

'I don't really want to talk about it, Gran. I've already had enough of a lecture from Mum.'

'Well, you won't get a lecture from me. I think it's a very sensible decision.'

While Breda was still digesting this unexpected remark, her father tapped out his pipe on the fence and glowered at his mother.

'Now, Mother,' Gilb began warningly. 'You know Agnes is only thinking of Breda's welfare.'

'Don't "Now Mother" me,' his mother answered crisply. 'The girl needs to come to terms with what's happened, and she won't do it with all of you fussing around her, nor with those young girls badgering the life out of her as usual. I've had to live alone for years, and nothing bad's come of it, has it?'

'It's a bit different, Mother!'

'It's not different at all. After your father died I learnt to live on my own, and that's what Breda has to do. She knows it, and so do you, if you've got any sense in your noddle. We Hanney women aren't made of straw.'

'Would you both stop talking about me as if I'm not here?' Breda said in a cracked voice. 'I'm glad you agree with me, Gran, but you'll have a hard job persuading Mum.'

The old woman's face broke into a gap-toothed smile, creasing her parchment cheeks still more as Gilb gave up on the two of them and stumped indoors. For a man who had been out in all weathers all of his life and was as strong as an ox, Gran always said he knew when he was beaten by the petticoat brigade.

'You just leave your mother to me,' she went on determinedly. 'Have you spoken to Warren's folks about it? I'm sure they'll have a few thoughts on it.'

'No, I haven't,' Breda said, suddenly weary. 'I only thought of it yesterday, for heaven's sake. It seemed such a simple idea, until everybody took a hand in it. I was about to become a married woman, and now I'm being treated like a child who doesn't know her own mind.'

'I'd say you were anything but that,' Gran Hanney told her. 'Walk me home after tea, Breda,

97

and take my advise to call on the Pascoes afterwards. They need to know you're thinking of
them, and I'm sure they'd like to know they're still
involved in whatever you decide to do. Don't shut
them out, my love.'

Impulsively, Breda hugged her gran's small,
wiry frame.

'I'd never thought of any such thing. You're a
wise old bird, Gran.'

Gran Hanney gave a wheezing laugh. 'I daresay
I am. I haven't lived all these years without learning a thing or two about human nature.'

They went indoors to find Agnes tight-lipped
and the girls chattering excitedly about which
one of them was to have Breda's bedroom when
she moved out. The decision had already been
made beforehand, but since the telegram, which
was the yardstick by which everything revolved
now, they had become resigned to knowing that
things had changed. Now, it seemed, the bedroom arrangements hadn't. Little pigs, thought
Breda without malice. But how lovely to have
nothing more on your mind than changing
bedrooms...

'When are you moving out, Breda? We'll help
you, won't we, Esme?' Jenna said eagerly over the
fish paste sandwiches.

Agnes choked slightly and shushed her at once.
'Nothing's been decided yet, young lady, and
you're not to upset Breda by asking such questions.'

'I think it really has been decided, Mum,' Breda
told her gently. 'It won't be until after – well, after
next weekend, anyway, and I still have to see the

landlord to tell him the lease is being honoured, but then I'm sure I'll be glad of all the help you can give me.'

Agnes looked at her husband for support, but he merely raised his shoulders a little and said nothing.

'Well then, of course we'll give you all the help we can,' she said stiffly.

Nobody had yet mentioned what was to be done with the wedding dress and the bridesmaid dresses, and before either of her tactless sisters could bring it up, Breda knew she had to talk about it herself. And far better now, with all the family here, while it was still on her mind. Get it over in one fell swoop, in other words. Agnes had already removed the dress from Breda's bedroom, where it had hung outside her wardrobe door in its muslin dust cover, but she could still see it in her mind's eye whenever she looked in that direction. She spoke quickly, while she could still bear to say the words.

'Mum, about my dress. Material is in such short supply nowadays and it takes so many coupons to buy the stuff, so after all the work you put into it, I think we should offer it for sale. Not here, though. Perhaps we could put an advert in a newspaper in Penzance or somewhere.'

As her voice choked, she didn't need to say any more. Her meaning was clear. She couldn't bear to keep the dress as a permanent reminder, but nor could she bear to see another local bride wearing the dress that she would have worn so proudly next Saturday.

'I think you've made the right decision, and I'll

see to the advert, my love,' her father said, taking over.

It wasn't so much sensible as saving her sanity, Breda thought.

Esme and Jenna glanced at one another, and after a moment Jenna said what she was obviously bursting to say.

'What about us? Will we have to sell our dresses as well?'

'We'll think about that later. Meanwhile, let's all get on with our tea,' Agnes said swiftly, seeing that all this was getting too much for Breda now.

Her face had paled, and Agnes began to regret having been so harsh on the girl over the rented cottage. Perhaps she was doing the right thing after all – and if she decided in the end that she didn't feel comfortable there, she could always come home again. She knew their door would always be open to her.

'If you're going to see the Pascoes this evening, you can tell them you have your family's approval about the cottage, Breda,' she said, before she changed her mind. 'Sometime later we'll put our heads together and make a list of the things you'll need for it.'

'Thank you, Mum.' Her heart was too full to say anything more, but out of the corner of her eye she was sure she saw Gran Hanney give a sly wink.

Contrary to the last time Breda had seen her, Laura Pascoe was in a state of agitation when she called on her after walking Gran Hanney back to her cottage.

'We haven't heard anything from Max yet. I know it's less than a week since we sent the telegram to him, but if it had reached him easily, I'm sure he would have replied by now. I'm so anxious that he hears the news as soon as possible.'

'Don't upset yourself about it, Mother,' Jed Pascoe said uneasily. 'Our Max was always a bit of a wild boy, but we both know that once he hears about Warren, he'll be moving heaven and earth to get back home. He'll probably turn up on the doorstep before you know it.'

'I hope you're right. He's not the world's best letter-writer; he always thinks more about playing his blessed saxophone than writing letters.'

'I doubt if he'll be doing much saxophone playing wherever he is now,' Breda put in, needing to be part of this conversation, even though Max was the last person she wanted to talk about.

Jed gave a short laugh. 'That he won't. It's still packed away in its case, ready for when he comes home.'

Breda realised that they were continually talking about Max coming home. It was like a talisman to them. Warren would never come home again, but they had to cling to the fact that Max would. They had lost their precious son, but they hadn't lost everything. She cleared her throat.

'I just wanted to let you know that I'm not giving up the cottage in Barnes Lane,' she said huskily. 'I shan't move into it yet, but I didn't want to give it up.'

For a moment they both looked at her as if they didn't know what she was talking about. As if their minds were still too full of Max.

'Are you sure, Breda?' Laura said at last. 'It will be a lot for you all on your own, what with your job at the school and everything.'

'I would have been there on my own all the time Warren was away at sea, wouldn't I?' she said before she could stop herself.

She bit her lip, wishing she hadn't been so sharp. She didn't want to fall out with Warren's mother, nor with anybody else, but she wished people wouldn't keep on obstructing her when she had made up her mind. And why did she get the feeling they thought there was something not quite *nice* in an unmarried woman wanting to live in a house on her own? She knew they only meant to be kind, but she was starting to realise she couldn't be doing with kindness any more. She just had to cope in her own way.

'Well, girl,' she heard Jed Pascoe say. 'It's a good solid cottage, but if there's anything that needs doing to the place that I can help you with, you let me know.'

She gave him a grateful smile. 'Thank you. I won't forget your offer.'

She didn't stay any longer than was polite. There didn't seem much to say that wasn't difficult or painful, and she left as the daylight was fading. It was twilight now, that lovely, almost ethereal state between day and night, but already she guessed the lights in the cottages were already being lit. In normal times there would be a fairy-like quality about the village, with its winding narrow streets leading down to the sea. Nobody could see those lighted rooms now, because of the obligatory black-out curtains that covered every window. Wartime regulations had taken the spirit out of towns and villages alike, although Mr Churchill had decreed that since there was no longer any risk of invasion, church bells could be rung on Sundays and special occasions. They would have rung here on Saturday too, Breda thought with a stab of pain in her heart, to celebrate her wedding.

She didn't feel like going home yet, and although she knew her mother would be watching out for her return with the new eagle-eyed worry on her face, she felt perversely like staying out as long as she wanted. She repeated the words to herself that seemed to keep entering her head. She wasn't a child.

Breda reached the small bay and the quay almost before she knew where she was heading. The sandy beach was littered with nets and fishing pots, and the fishing boats lay impotent and lopsided on the beach well away from the water now. Out in the bay, beneath the shadow of the cliffs, the swell of the tide rippled gently and benignly to and fro, belying its great power. The power that could sink the greatest of ships and take a hundred men's lives.

It was impossible for Breda not to think of it, when it was the thought that was so uppermost in her mind. She shouldn't have come here, and yet it had become almost a compulsion to watch the moonlight come slowly into view, turning every undulating wave on the darkening sea into a magical sheet of glittering pin-points of light.

Somewhere behind her she heard the sound of laughing and chattering. She almost shrank into herself, recognising the voices, as young as her own. She would have preferred to become invisible, rather than have to face people she had known since schooldays, people who had known her and Warren well. Almost at once, she was aware that the voices had changed to whispers, and she knew she had been recognised. It was ironic, she thought fleetingly, how older folk thought it necessary to ask constantly how she was and to offer their sympathies, while the friends she and Warren had known hadn't come near her, until now. She could sense them approaching, pushing one another forward, deciding who was going to be the spokesman, seeming to see it all as if it was a scene in a play.

'Hey, Breda,' one of the young men said. 'We were sorry to hear Warren's bought it. It's bloody rotten luck, just before you were getting spliced too.'

Now was the time for the heroine to be brave, to say something heroic and wonderful ... and all she could think of saying was the stupidest thing of all.

'You'll catch it if your mother hears you swearing, Hobbsy.'

The group laughed nervously. Then another of them spoke up.

'How's Max taking it? He'll be as cut up as hell.'

'Nobody's heard from him yet, and Max is the least of my worries.'

She shouldn't be resentful that they were asking about Max. They all played in a band for local dances, and Max had been their saxophone player in better times. It was natural that they should ask after him, but it wasn't Max who was lying drowned beneath the waves.

'What are you doing here, anyway?' she asked in a clipped voice. 'And why aren't you in uniform yet, Hobbsy?'

She knew the other two were farmhands and in reserved occupations, but Hobbsy looked strong and healthy enough to fight.

'They say I've got fallen arches and I'm slightly deaf in one ear. I can still play in the band, but it's enough to keep me out of the army – and don't think I didn't try,' he added, just in case she thought he was being a welsher.

'We're going to the church hall tomorrow night to play a few patriotic tunes for the Ladies' Group,' George put in. 'Do you want to come along?'

She glared at him. 'Do I look as though I want to do any such thing when I've got more important things on my mind?'

'Christ, I'm sorry, kid. I wasn't thinking. It won't be much of a concert without Max, anyway. The old ladies always preferred the sound of the saxophone.'

They said goodbye and moved away from her as hastily as they could. She didn't blame them. She was hardly the best company, and she was annoyed by the way they kept bringing Max into the conversation, just as the Pascoes did. She knew how desperately they wanted him home to share in their grief, but Breda wasn't sure how much she wanted it, not yet. Max was his cousin, but he was uncannily like Warren: in looks, in mannerisms, even his voice. She wasn't sure how she could bear to see him, whole and strong, with his life still in front of him.

She turned away from the beach, her head bowed, knowing it was still too soon to even think of coming to terms with what had happened. She tried to accept it, because there was no other choice, but there were still more dark moments than she could bear. Maybe tomorrow would be better, she thought desperately, when she went back to the classroom and filled the infants with excitement over the coming May Day celebrations in Padstow.

It was only three weeks away now, and before then, it would be the Saturday when she would have been walking up the aisle in her wedding dress; then the Easter weekend when the church bells would all ring out; and then the first of May. She tried to project her thoughts ahead, rather than the ordeal of getting through all the days in between.

In the light from the moon she saw her father walking towards her, and guessed he had been sent to look for her. She sighed, knowing her parents were doing all they could for her, but they were also in danger of smothering her.

'I'm all right,' she said at once, as soon as he reached her. 'Mum didn't need to send out a search party for me, Dad.'

He grimaced. 'How about being sent out on fire-watching duty, then? We all have to do our bit when there's a war on, girl, and I'm off to do the rounds of the village to keep an eye on things.'

'Honestly, do people really think the Germans

are going to drop bombs down here?' Breda said, goaded into responding to something that was of the least interest to her right now. 'They'll be dropping them on London or places like that, not all the way out here.'

'Well, let's hope they don't drop them any-where, but I doubt old Adolf would agree with that. Get off home, Breda, and try to get a good night's sleep.'

She could tell he wasn't pleased with her for what she had said. But for goodness' sake, she hadn't meant to imply that people like her dad doing a part-time job of fire-watching were playing at war – or that Cornwall was in the back of beyond, even though it probably was by city folks' standards.

She wanted to put things right with him, but he was already on his way, the scent of his pipe tobacco wafting after him, so she stuck her hands in her pockets and hurried on home before it got too dark to see where she was going. Even though she knew every inch of the village where she had been born, the cobbled streets had become an added hazard now that the street lights were off for the duration.

Monday morning was bright and sunny. As always Breda's first thoughts were of Warren, the sickening reality of her loss rushing into her mind with her first waking moments. But today had a purpose, and even though her heart was pound-ing, she washed and dressed and tied her hair up tidily as befitted a schoolteacher. Her hands trembled as she saw her face in her dressing table mirror. She looked completely washed out, as if she hadn't slept properly for days, which was true. She hadn't slept properly ever since the news about Warren had come, her sleep disrupted by disjointed, nightmarish dreams, where he was sinking helplessly beneath the waves, interspersed with other dreams, hauntingly lovely dreams of times past when they were together, days to remember all her life.

She rubbed some rouge into her cheeks to disguise some of her pallor and put a touch of lipstick to her mouth. It occurred to her that she had done none of those things recently. No wonder her gran had called her maggoty, but why would anybody bother when there was nobody to bother for? She swallowed, talking to herself sternly. If she was going to school, she owed it to the children to look as much like her old self as possible, not like some pathetic waif.

Her sisters had already set off on the bus-ride to their secondary school by the time she went downstairs, where Agnes put a dish of porridge in front of her. She was sure she wouldn't be able to eat it, but with Agnes's disapproving eyes on her, Breda knew she had better try. It was a sin to waste food nowadays, and she forced some of the wholesome breakfast down her throat.

'You know I don't think you're ready to go back to work yet, don't you, Breda?' Agnes couldn't resist saying. 'The children will ask so many questions, and it will be an ordeal for you.'

'I know, but the questions will still be there next week and the week after, so the sooner I answer them the better.' She knew the words were true, and she hoped she sounded braver than she felt. 'Please don't worry about me, Mum.'

She finished as much breakfast as she could and then, as she fetched her coat from her bedroom, she added some more lipstick almost defiantly. It was like a banner, a badge of office, telling the world that Breda Hanney was still breathing, still alive.

Her bravery almost deserted her as she approached the infant school. The cottage in Barnes Lane was very near to it, but from her home she couldn't avoid meeting so many other people on their way to work, and mothers taking their children to school ahead of her. In such a small, close-knit village, everyone knew everyone else, and there was no escape. But all the while, she tried to keep uppermost in her mind the words she used almost as a mantra now. For everyone who offered their sympathies, it was one less she would have to listen to.

The one thing she hadn't bargained for was how many times she would be asked about Max. It was as if the whole world was trying to make her feel that Max coming home would act as a buffer to all the pain she was feeling. And it wouldn't happen. It *couldn't* happen.

She entered the school with a feeling of relief. The high-pitched chatter of the infants reached her ears, together with the smells of chalk and plimsolls drifting into her nostrils, familiar and safe. Her world.

Mrs Larraby greeted her with a welcoming smile and a sympathetic squeeze of her hands, and then she was surrounded by squealing infants leaping up and down and badgering her to tell them about May Day. Young Josie Dean had spread the word quickly, Breda thought with a faint smile. Gossiping obviously began in the classroom. But as the day began it became a blessed relief to be repeating the story of the origins and traditions of the 'Obby 'Oss celebrations that took place in Padstow every year, with folk dressing up in strange garb and prancing through the houses and streets with music blaring and streamers flying everywhere.

The 'Obby 'Oss was the strangest fellow of all, seemingly half man, half beast, leading the procession in his ragged clothes as the town choir sang traditional songs. The children had heard it all before, but young heads soon forgot the information, and enjoyed having it repeated again and again. The musicians would play the hypnotic tunes that were little more than a medley of accordions, drums and triangles, beating and banging all day, and Billy Green would be done up in his own finery as he added his accordion noise to the rest in the ancient ceremony to welcome the beginning of summer.

'On the day before, we'll make some garlands for you all to wear,' Breda told her pupils, to further whoops of excitement.

They would still be on their Easter holiday then, but they would go into the school on the day before the event to make their final preparations. On the day itself, a bus would take them to Padstow, where they would form a crocodile procession to walk the short distance into the harbour. Mrs Larraby and most of the infants' mothers would be with them, to help keep them all under control.

Despite herself, Breda couldn't help but be caught up in the excitement of so many little faces, even when it meant taking one or two outside to the lavs, when it all became too much for them, with the inevitable consequences. She only hoped that all the mothers would bring spare knickers for their offsprings on the day.

By the time they had their mid-morning milk, the children had calmed down a little and were ready for a proper lesson. And then came the question Breda had dreaded as one little girl put up her hand.

'Miss, my mum says your young man was drowned and that's why you're not getting married now. Is that right, Miss?'

There was a sudden silence, and a room full of anxious eyes looked towards Breda, wanting answers, demanding answers. The words stuck in her throat for a moment, but she knew she couldn't let them down.

'Yes, I'm afraid it's true, Sophie, and I'm very, very sad about it, and I know you were all looking forward to coming to the church next Saturday.'

'Won't you be wearing your white dress then, Miss?' she said plaintively.

'I'm afraid not, dear.'

'My mum's got some confetti for me to throw over you,' said another child.

The voice was almost indignant now, and it was certain that few of them had grasped it all properly yet. Breda guessed that most of their mothers would have shielded them from too graphic an explanation of what had happened to their teacher, and it almost overwhelmed Breda to have to explain that no, she wouldn't be wearing her white dress, or want confetti thrown over her, and that there definitely wouldn't be a wedding next Saturday because there was no bridegroom.

The mood of the class changed in an instant as several little girls at the back of the room began snivelling, and Breda wondered desperately how she could make these moments any better, when she herself felt so bereft.

'I've just remembered that I haven't thanked you yet for the lovely card you sent me last week,' she went on as brightly as she could. 'I was really proud of the way your handwriting has improved. I could read every name perfectly, and I think we should practise some more writing today, so now I'm going to write some new words on the blackboard and you can all copy them in your exercise books.'

She quickly turned away from those enquiring eyes, knowing that her own were brimming with tears. But she couldn't shed them now. It wasn't the right place or the right time, so she blinked them back and swallowed hard as she picked up the chalk and forced her hand to stop shaking.

One step at a time, she reminded herself...

Chapter Seven

'How did things go today?' Agnes asked, when Breda got home that afternoon. 'You look exhausted, just as I expected. I told you it was too much for you, lamb, but you wouldn't listen to me, would you?'

Breda flopped down on the sofa, still catching her breath after what had been an emotional day, yet in a strange way it had been a more worthwhile one than she could ever have imagined.

'No, I wouldn't listen, and I'm glad I didn't, because my children needed to hear everything from me. I'm no saint, but they trust me, Mum, and I managed to tell them in simple terms what had happened. Most of all, I was able to cheer them up and get them excited about May Day, rather than worrying about what happens to a person when he's drowning.'

'Good Lord, Breda, that's a gruesome thing to say.'

'Maybe, but it's probably what a lot of them have been wondering about, and they're too young to have such dark thoughts without some kind of simple explanation. So there was also a lot of talk about God and heaven and angels, which will probably please you,' she added.

She was unable to keep the cynicism out of her voice, because she was still angry with God for taking her life away as much as He had taken

Warren's. But her conscience wouldn't let her reveal to the children any inkling of how she felt, and so she had somehow bluffed her way through it. And it had helped.

'I'm sure God will forgive you for talking that way,' Agnes said in annoyance. 'And I hope you'll soon come to your senses and realise that everything happens for a purpose, however little we understand it.'

This was too much. Breda leapt up from the sofa, her eyes blazing. 'Oh, really! Then perhaps you can tell me what purpose God had in sending Warren to the bottom of the sea to be fish-bait, and how the dickens I'm ever meant to understand it. That's right, Mum. I said *fish-bait!* That's what they call it, isn't it? And I'm not going to listen to any more of your pious remarks, because they don't mean anything to me any more.'

She tore out of the room and up the stairs, slamming her bedroom door behind her. Childish? Of course she was being childish. Rude to her mother? Of course she bloody-well was, because she just felt like blasting against everything and everyone right now, even God. Especially God.

She was still curled up on her bed a while later when there was a tap on her door, and then her mother tentatively opened it and asked if she could come in. She was carrying a cup of tea and a biscuit.

'Is it safe to come in?' she said.

She put the cup and saucer down on the bedside table, and with a little cry Breda got up at once and put her arms around her mother.

'I'm sorry, Mum,' she said, her voice shaking. 'I know I shouldn't have said any of those things, but I miss him so much, and sometimes it just overwhelms me. Today was a strange mixture of the wonderful and the terrible, but I had to do it. And I'm going back again tomorrow and every other day, so don't try to stop me.'

Agnes gave a small smile. 'I doubt that I could if I tried, my love. You must do whatever you feel best. And if those little ones are giving you any kind of comfort, then who am I to argue?'

'I'm not sure that comfort is the right word to use, but the one thing I can't do is to destroy their innocence. If they ask questions, I have to answer them, however painful it might be. I wouldn't be much of a teacher otherwise, would I?'

There was a tattered calendar on the wall of the military hospital ward. Max had no idea who had put it there or how long it had been there. He didn't give a monkey's cuss what day it was, or where he was. Days and nights had all merged into one for so long now, that he might have been at the other end of the world, or even in outer space. He couldn't even find much interest in the fact that he was lucid for longer and longer periods, or that the medics had begun giving him more optimistic reports of late.

The words all flowed over him, especially on that morning when the date on the calendar seemed to burn into his brain with a significance he couldn't remember. He knew it was important, but the way the memories kept slipping in

115

and out of his head was an added torment to all the others. He frequently thought he was losing his mind, and sometimes he didn't even care. At least in oblivion there would be peace from the pain in his leg and the fever that had drained him of energy.

'Soon be Easter, Max, old son,' one of the other patients in the ward piped up, seeing that he was awake. 'I keep wondering what my old woman's doing at home now. Baking Easter biscuits, I shouldn't wonder, if the bloody government's allowed her enough butter and sugar to make them. Me and the kids were always partial to an Easter biscuit, and the poor little buggers will be doing without a lot of their little treats now, especially seeing their old dad on Easter morning.'

Used to his sentimental rants, Max kept his gaze fixed on the ceiling above his bed, and didn't answer. But it gradually dawned on him that the man's words were acting as a trigger, and clarifying his thoughts for the first time in weeks – or maybe it was months – he couldn't tell which. But he quickly wished his thoughts hadn't cleared at all, because the reality of it was almost too much.

If it was nearly Easter already, then the day he had dreaded would have come and gone. His cousin would have married his girl, and Max wouldn't have been there to be their Best Man, as Warren had always wanted. The Best Man duties he would have performed loyally, even if it broke his heart to do so.

'Are you all right, mate?' he heard the other man say as he gave a low moan. 'Do you want me to call the medic to give you another knock-out shot?'

'No,' Max grunted. 'I've just seen the date, that's all.'

'Somebody's birthday, is it?' the man said sympathetically. 'It'll be my youngest's in a couple of weeks. Thirteen, she'll be, and a right little cracker and all, and I won't be there to see it unless they sort out this bloody chest infection. I just hope my missus has got enough gumption to keep the boys from sniffing around her, randy little buggers that they are at that age.'

'Can't you ever shut up?' Max found himself shouting. 'I'm fed up with hearing about your bloody family.'

'Calm down, mate! Christ Almighty, I was only making conversation, but even a good old shouting match goes down better than your usual raving. It's good to see you showing a spark of guts, old son, so I don't take no offence.'

His cough was noisy and disgusting as he reached for the spittoon at the side of his bed, and Max was briefly ashamed of his outburst as the chap lay back in exhaustion. He knew the silence wouldn't last long because the man was a never-ending jaw-me-dead, but at least he was finding enough spirit inside himself to fight back, however briefly it lasted. At least he felt alive enough for that.

'I'm sorry, Higgins,' he said at last. 'It's just that my cousin was getting married and I was meant to be Best Man and I've missed all of it.'

'That explains it then. I suppose it's to this Breda you're always blathering on about when you're half in and out of your senses. From the way you went on about her, I thought she was your girl.'

The older man shrugged and lay back on his bed at the shocked look on Max's face. 'Oh, don't worry, mate, we all share our secrets when we're in the same boat. You'd remember a few juicy stories about me and my old woman if your brain was ticking over properly and not so addled. Gawd knows what I've been telling you,' he added with a cheery grin, 'and I know all about the love of your life!'

'I wish you'd forget it then, like I'm trying to,' Max muttered. 'There's no point in wishing for something you can never have.'

'No, there ain't, but it don't stop you doing it, all the same. Anyway, I reckon once they've sorted you out, you'll be going back to Blighty, and then you'll have to face them both, so you just remember that she's his wife now.'

Max knew he meant well enough, but he'd had enough of his home-spun philosophy, and he thanked God when he saw the doctor coming on his rounds, which put an end to their talking. It didn't stop him thinking about Breda being Warren's wife now though, and everything that that entailed. And that night he had the kind of erotic dreams it wasn't proper or decent for a man to have about another man's wife.

The next day, the doc had some news for Max. The fever was lessening, so they were hoping to operate on his leg as soon as possible. They had every hope of giving him a good chance of walking again, even if he'd never be quite as good as before. It was a vast improvement on the darkest days when it was thought there was little hope of saving the leg at all. Max knew he should be grateful, but it was hard to raise his spirits when there were still so many gaps in his memory.

'Cheer up, man,' the medic said, seeing his downcast face. 'There's plenty worse off than you, and you'll still have your handsome looks to charm the girls. With any luck, you'll be going home soon.'

Once he had left the ward, Smithy, the patient with the mouth organ, began playing a tune. Some hated the tinny noise but not Max. Music was like the breath of life to him, even if he couldn't really remember why. This bastard memory loss was as frustrating as anything that had happened to him, if only because he always felt he was so nearly on the brink of remembering things. Music ... and dancing. He'd probably never be dancing again, but that wasn't it. If he wasn't a hit on the dance floor, he knew he was involved somehow. The tune the chap was playing was vaguely familiar, and if only the shadowy images in his head would clear...

'Bloody hell!' he croaked, sitting up in bed so fast it made his head spin. 'I can play the saxophone!'

'Good for you, mate,' Higgins chuckled, clearly thinking he'd gone doolally again. 'I'll get the doc to bring one in and you and Smithy can give us a duet. But keep it down for now, Smithy, you noisy sod, and let's all get a bit of shut-eye.'

True to her word, Breda determinedly went back to school every day. She didn't try to pretend that nothing had happened. There were times when the reality of it was so overpowering that she spent hours weeping in the solitude of her bedroom. Times when she knew her mother was telling her sisters not to make their usual rumpus because Breda wasn't feeling well. Times when her father would ignore any idea of leaving her alone, and simply come to her room and take her in his arms and let her cry her heart out.

There were other times, too, when she forced herself to face up to it all. Warren was never coming home, and she had to spend the rest of her life without him. Those were the stark facts, and Breda had never been afraid to face facts. One of the worst things was facing the sympathetic faces of people she knew well, and walking through the village, being well aware that there were whispers going on behind her. But she wasn't the only one to have lost someone in this war. There were so many others ... but right here in this close-knit community, she was the youngest to have lost her fiancé on virtually the eve of her wedding. That made her special – in a way she had never wanted to be.

Gran Hanney had her own words of wisdom to give her whenever Breda called in to see her. Gran Hanney was never one to mince her words, and always said she was far too old to waste time on sentimentality. And she told Breda bluntly that she was far too young to think there would only ever be one love in her life.

'How can you say such a thing, Gran? You know

how close I was to Warren, from the time we were children. Do you expect me to forget that?'

'Of course I don't, girl. I wasn't suggesting that you forget him, and I'm sure you never will. But take the advice of an old woman who's seen too many years, and too many lonely widows. It's not disloyal to think of loving again, and if the chance should come along, you should grasp it with both hands.'

'Well, it won't,' Breda retorted. 'I don't even want to think about it.'

'Not now, but in time, mebbe,' Gran Hanney persisted. 'You just remember my words, missy, and right now you can make me some beef tea if you've a mind to make yourself useful. The doctor's recommended it, so I might as well try it to keep the peace.'

'You're not ill, are you?' Breda said at once. 'You know you should be taking things easy at your age, Gran.'

Her gran gave a throaty chuckle. 'No, I'm not ill, and I don't intend to take things easy, neither. There'll be time enough for all that when they put me in my box, so take that worried look off your face. I'm not turning up my toes just yet.'

Breda fervently hoped not, although common sense told her that Gran Hanney couldn't go on for ever. Impulsively she gave her gran's thin frame a hug.

'Get on with you, and make me that beef tea before I get too parched to drink it,' the old woman said. 'But if it'll take your mind off your troubles for a few minutes, I'll tell you about all my other aches and pains. Old age don't come alone Breda, as you'll find out one day.'

'All right, I'll make you that tea,' Breda said hastily, knowing she could be in for a long session of hearing about rheumatics and aching backs and other vague symptoms the doctor had no real answer for, but which Gran Hanney was quite capable of dealing with herself. She always said she had no real truck with doctors, and only took his quack remedies to make him feel better – as if the doctor was the patient instead of herself.

But it was quite true that hearing about someone else's problems took her out of her own, if only for a few minuscule moments. It was why going back to school had turned out to be such a blessing in disguise, because the children needed her, and she had to be strong for them. The worst day of all would be the day she and Warren would have been married, and she wanted to be alone on that day. The one concession she would make would be to go to the church and sit in silence, remembering all the days they had shared together. After that, she was going to be resolute and face the future.

They were brave words, but Breda knew she would have to be determined if she was to survive at all. She had never been one for wallowing in self-pity, and she had wiped too many infants' tears and bandaged too many wounded knees and always tried to cheer up her small patients, to let herself down now.

'What are you doing, Breda?' came her gran's plaintive voice. 'A body could waste away waiting for that beef tea.'

'Sorry, Gran, I wasn't thinking,' she said hastily. *Or thinking too much...*

Her gran looked at her keenly, when she took in the steaming mugs. 'So are you still set on moving into the cottage in Barnes Lane on your own? Are you quite sure it's what you want to do?'

Breda swallowed a mouthful of tea too fast and winced at the heat of it.

'What do you think I should do then? Live at home with mum and dad and the girls for ever more? I expected to be a married woman soon and have a life and home of my own. I think Warren would be proud of me for not giving everything up when the cottage meant so much to us. Sometimes I think I can hear him whispering in my ear that he approves, and not to be afraid.'

She hadn't meant to say any such a thing, and she choked over the words a little, and it was nothing to do with the hot tea. She didn't want it, anyway.

'I'm proud of you too, girl,' Gran Hanney said. 'You're facing up to things like a true Cornish woman.'

'Am I?' Breda said. 'Look, it's time I left, Gran. I have to call on Warren's parents to see how they are. I'm not the only one in mourning, am I?'

She felt as if she was, of course. She felt as if nobody else in the world could ever feel the way she did, nor ever had done. But common sense told her it wasn't so. Warren's parents were grieving too, and even though the last thing she wanted to do was to have to give comfort to them

123

when she had so little to spare, she knew it was what Warren would have wanted. But as soon as she entered their house and saw Laura Pascoe's tearful face she felt the sense of gloom descending on her again.

'How are you today, dear?' Laura welcomed her with a sad and mournful voice. Although it wasn't actually so different from her usual voice, Breda realised. She was habitually a rather sad and mournful woman, and for some reason Breda felt irritated beyond measure at having to cope with all this misery as well as her own. It made her sound brighter than she felt.

'I'm coping, because it's what we all have to do, isn't it?'

'Oh well, some of us find it easier to switch off our feelings, I daresay, and that's no criticism of you, Breda, but you're young, and the young get over things more quickly than us older folk.'

'I'm not *getting over* anything, Mrs Pascoe,' Breda was stung into replying. 'I doubt that I'll ever get over hearing that my fiancé was drowned so close to our wedding, but I have to think about my class at school and they're frightened enough with all the bad things going on in the world right now.'

Laura looked at her silently for a moment. 'You were always a strong person, Breda, but I never thought you could be so hard.'

She turned away, her eyes full of tears, and Breda felt instant remorse.

'I'm not hard,' she almost whispered. 'I'm just trying to get on with life in the best way I know, the same as you are, and I truly didn't mean to

124

upset you.'

Laura gave a heavy sigh. 'I know you didn't, and I'm sorry too.'

'Have you heard anything from Max yet?' Breda went on, hardly caring one way or the other, but needing to cover the awkwardness between them.

'Not a word. I know he'd get compassionate leave if he could, and that's another worry. What if something's happened to him? I couldn't bear it if I was going to lose both my boys.'

Breda forced a weak smile. 'You won't lose Max. He's indestructible. After his eagerness to go out to the desert he'll be as tough as old boots by now. One of these days he'll just come walking in the door, you'll see.'

She could hear herself doing it again ... just the way she did with the infants. Doing the cheering up, keeping positive, patching up the wounds, healing the scars. It was ironic, when she was so in need of somebody to cheer her up, to keep her positive, to patch up her wounded heart and heal the scars...

'You're a good girl, Breda,' Laura was saying now. 'It's good that you've got your work to keep you busy. I know you can't appear downhearted for long when you've got a class of infants hanging on your every word, and they're very lucky to have you.'

'I'm lucky to have them too,' Breda said.

She began to feel stifled by the house with its still-curtained windows and the inevitable staleness that closed-in houses imparted. She had insisted that her mother didn't close their curtains all day long, for which she knew her sisters were thankful. They were young too, and wanted to talk of other things, about school and friends and the approaching Easter holidays. She couldn't blame them, and Mrs Pascoe was right. The young did get over things more quickly than older folk.

On the day that would have been her wedding, her parents respected her need for solitude. She walked to the church alone, and sat inside the protection of its cool stone walls for a long while. It was a strange day. Part of her wanted to abandon herself to weeping. Another part of her couldn't stop imagining what this day should have been like.

The church would have been filled with family and friends. The infants in her class would have been almost overcome with excitement, and there would have been more than one little accident in a pair of knickers at witnessing their teacher in her lovely bridal gown and veil. Esme and Jenna would have behaved themselves in their bridesmaid dresses, and Gran would have shed more than a tear or two as she clutched her mum's arm.

Her dad would have walked her down the aisle as she held her bouquet of roses, and waiting for her at the far end of the church would be her handsome boy. *Two* handsome boys, she amended, if things had gone the way they had planned. Warren and Max, smartened up in their finery, so alike as cousins that were like two peas in a pod. But there was only one handsome boy for her. Only one who would take her hand and repeat the vows that would make them man and wife.

She stayed exactly where she was for more than an hour, her head bowed, allowing the haunting images to flit through her mind and not denying them. Finally she gave a soft, shuddering sigh that seemed to echo all around the ancient granite walls of the small church. The culmination of all their dreams was never to be, yet somehow, being here alone in this quiet place was giving her a kind of peace she had never expected.

By the time she left, her eyes were dry and her footsteps stronger as she walked to the cottage in Barnes Lane. It was hers now, hers alone, and she felt a stirring of independence as she opened the gate and walked up to the front door. She remembered how the cottage had welcomed her and Warren the moment they stepped inside it, and it was welcoming her now. It felt like home. No, it was more than that. It *was* home.

'I'm moving into the cottage the weekend after May Day,' she told her parents at supper that evening. 'There's too much to do before then and I'm still involved in getting everything ready with the infants, but once it's over, I want to be on my own. I know Esme and Jenna will be pleased to get the bedrooms sorted out the way they want as well.'

Her mother looked less than happy at the announcement. 'Don't let them push you out, Breda,' Agnes said sharply. 'You have to be very sure that this is what you want to do.'

'I am sure, Mum, so stop worrying about me. Stop *fussing* over me – please.'

Treat me as the woman that I am, and not as a child. There was a limit to how much sympathy she could take, or want. There was a limit to how many times she was aware that her sisters were being told to shush for fear of upsetting her, and a limit to the surreptitious glances in her direction, just to check that she was all right. Oh yes, it was time she moved out, just as she would have done if Warren hadn't drowned. She forced herself to say the words inside her head, knowing that the more she said it, the sooner she might be able to accept it.

'How was Warren's mother today?' Agnes said, going off on a different tack. 'As miserable as ever, poor soul? She never has a happy face at the best of times.'

'Well, she was just about as miserable as she has a right to be, I suppose. She can't help it, Mum. It's her way of dealing with things.'

She knew she was being a dog in the manger, because she was just as impatient with Mrs Pascoe when they were together. Away from her, she felt nothing but sympathy, but it must be hard on a woman to grieve alone when her man was at work all day.

'It will be easier on the Pascoes when Max gets some leave,' Agnes went on. 'I'm sure they would have heard from him by now if the news had reached him about Warren, and it will be an awful shock for him.'

'I can't spare any thoughts for Max right now,' Breda muttered.

'I don't know why not. The three of you were always so close, and you mustn't start resenting

128

him for being alive while Warren's not, my love.'

'Of course I don't! Why would you think such a thing?'

Breda didn't want to think it either, but she couldn't deny that the hateful and guilty thought had crept into her mind more than once. If it had to be one of the Pascoe boys who didn't come home, why not the one who had no ties, no girl waiting to marry him, no love of his own? She had always been fond of Max, and it was true that when they were children the three of them had constantly run wild over the moors together. As inseparable as the three musketeers, some had said, but Max wasn't the man she loved, and she wasn't even sure she wanted to see him come striding through the village, well and whole. Not yet.

Chapter Eight

May Day dawned with all things bright and beautiful, just as the hymn said. Breda's sisters were cycling to Padstow with their own friends, and set off early in the morning. At a more sensible hour, the infant schoolchildren assembled at the top end of the village. They waited impatiently for the arrival of the bus taking them to Padstow for the celebrations, along with the parents and teachers who were accompanying them. However difficult it was for her, Breda was trying to look on this day as a turning point. There was huge excitement in the air, and she knew she mustn't be the one to put a damper on it. This was an important day in Cornwall's annual calendar, and neither the efforts of Adolf Hitler, nor the loss of one man in the community, however beloved, should deny the infants their special outing.

'All right?' Mrs Larraby mouthed at her. Breda nodded, her head held high as they ushered the children onto the bus amid so much noise that it was impossible not to feel uplifted by their innocent chatter and laughter.

She put out of her mind the many other May Days when she, Warren and Max had cycled along the cliff path on this same route. This day was for the children, not for looking back – although, how could she do otherwise? She felt one of her charges put her small hand into hers, and then heard the child's shy voice.

'My mum said you might be feeling sad today, so I made this for you, Miss,' Sara said, pushing the small bunch of wild flowers into Breda's hand.

'How lovely,' Breda said, her heart tugging at the thoughtfulness, 'and we're all going to have a wonderful day today, so nobody has to feel sad.'

Above the child's head she caught the gaze of Sara's mother, and gave a tremulous smile. But then she made a firm resolve. If anybody thought Breda Hanney was going to break down and spoil things for the rest of them, they didn't know her very well. She turned away from any curious eyes and concentrated on telling the children more of what was going to happen today. Some of the youngest ones had never been to see the 'Obby 'Oss before, and it could be a bit frightening with all the noise of the drums and accordions and triangles playing their hypnotic tunes, plus the weird costumes and the wild dancing, all to celebrate the coming of Spring – or Summer, whichever season you considered it to be.

Max used to say it was a bit late to call the first of May the coming of spring, and it should definitely be the beginning of summer. Max always had strong opinions about anything. And Breda and Warren would always argue that spring or summer depended on the weather, but in their hay days it always seemed to be summer in Cornwall, and the arguments always fizzled out in laughter and teasing.

Her throat tightened, remembering. But as the

131

bus covered the short distance to the town she wouldn't allow any other memories to creep in. Ahead of them they could see the harbour, the sea glittering like diamonds in the sunshine, and thousands of onlookers gathering to watch the festivities. There were decorations everywhere, greenery of every description; cowslips and bluebells, catkins and sycamore twigs, entwined around doors and gates and hedges.

As the bus prepared to unload its passengers with cautions for all the children to keep together, Breda knew such a thing was going to be difficult to implement. The best they could do was to advise the parents to be sure to bring their charges back to the bus in two hours' time. It would be long enough for little feet to stand still or to walk about and it would be tricky to keep them all under control for any longer. To stave off any disappointment at having to leave Padstow while all the festivities were still going on, it had been decided to have a picnic on the moors overlooking the harbour during the afternoon, and for this, the parents had brought a bagged lunch for each child. It was as organised as it was possible to be.

And after all, once the long and exciting day was over, with no mishaps, and praise from the children's parents for arranging it all so well, Breda had to admit that she had enjoyed herself. She had actually enjoyed herself, and with it came the realisation that she could still find pleasure in her days, in just being alive. Her darling Warren would never be here to share such times with her again, but she had to accept that she was too young to shut herself away from the world. It was just as Gran Hanney had said. You just had to go on living – with the one proviso that she vowed never to fall in love again.

She and Warren had been undecided whether to change the original name of the cottage they had intended to rent, but Breda had finally decided what it was to be called. It would be Forget-me-not Cottage, Barnes Lane. The following weekend she enlisted the help of her parents and sisters to move all her belongings into her new home. And not wanting to leave Warren's parents out of her plans, she asked Jed Pascoe if he would make a new sign to go over the door, since he was a dab hand with a bit of carpentry. Warren's mother brought her a large bunch of flowers and a vase to put them in as a small housewarming gift. Breda kept her hands and mind busy, surrounded by people, and it was only much later, when they had all gone and she was alone, that she let her guard down.

It should have been such a joyous occasion when the bride and groom entered this cottage. Warren would have carried her over the thres-hold, interspersing every step with a kiss. She had dreamt of the moment when they would finally shut the door behind them and start their married life. Their happy-ever-after. Alone now, she fought to keep the tears down, wandering restlessly through the cottage that was now her home, disorientated and not knowing what to do with her hands. Everybody had been so kind, wanting to help, wanting to do what they could for her, when all she really wanted so desperately was the one thing she couldn't have.

The tears flowed then. How could they not? Instead of laughter and teasing, and the emotional after-effects of her longed-for wedding-day, there was only silence. With trembling hands Breda put the kettle on the stove. It was an automatic movement. She didn't really want tea, but tea was the usual panacea for shock, and the shock of it all still surged into her mind at unexpected moments. A knock on the door broke the silence and as her heart jolted she almost dropped the kettle, and then the door opened and Gran Hanney was silhouetted against the sunlight.

'I waited till the rest of 'em had gone,' she said, wheezing slightly from the walk. 'I seen 'em going back through the village, and I thought you'd have had enough to cope with if they were all fussing over you. Now let me sit down a minute to catch my breath, and if you're making tea, I'll have a cup.'

'Oh Gran,' was all Breda could choke out.

'Now then, I'm sure you've held up all right so far today, and it looks as though you've done your bit of crying. I'm betting the young uns had a whale of a time over in Padstow, so you can tell me all about it and remind me of my younger days. I've got nothing else to do with my time, so let's have that tea, girl.'

For somebody who needed to catch her breath, she did a fair amount of talking, thought Breda. But she did as she was told, glad to have somebody giving her some direction in those muddled moments when the world seemed to be crashing down on her again. And after all, there were plenty of tales to tell about the day, things to make her gran laugh, and to make her laugh too, remembering some of the antics of the 'Obby 'Oss and his attendants.

'So you had a good day then,' Gran Hanney remarked, dunking her biscuit in her tea and then sucking it through her teeth.

'Yes, I had a good day,' Breda said mechanically.

Why did even putting it into words make her feel the tiniest bit guilty? As if she shouldn't feel that way, knowing that Warren would never be able to feel anything ever again. There was no sense in it, no sense at all, but when did sense come into it, anyway? She felt her head droop, recognising that her moods could change in an instant, and that they would be swinging like this for a good time to come yet. It couldn't be otherwise, unless she forgot Warren altogether, and she would never do that. She knew how fiercely she never wanted his image to fade, and she told herself that it never would.

'You've made a nice job of the cottage,' Gran went on matter-of-factly. 'It looks like home already and your mother would be proud of you. I doubt that you'll be spending much time cooking if you've got your job to go to, though, so if you want to come and have your tea with me now and then, I'll be glad of the company.'

'I know what you're doing, Gran, and there's no need, honestly.'

There was another great slurp of soggy biscuit,

135

and then Gran snorted.

'What, no need to invite my granddaughter to have tea with me? Don't be daft, girl. And before you think I'm speaking out of turn, I wouldn't be able to do it if you had Warren to rush home to cook for, would I? We're a match now, Breda, both without a man to care for, but that don't mean we can't care for each other, does it?'

'Stop it, or you'll have me crying again.'

'Well, you go ahead and cry if you want to. One thing the good Lord won't condemn you for is how many tears a body can cry. The government might try and restrict us on many things these days, and what they don't, the Jerries will, but they've got no monopoly on grief, thank God.'

It was a weird kind of logic, but that was Gran, always putting her own point of view on things, no matter how bizarre it seemed to other people. To Breda, it was what made her special.

'No wonder Warren loved you like I do,' she said without thinking.

'You see? You can already say his name without your face all crumpling up. He'd be glad of that. In fact, I know he's glad of it.'

Now she was getting creepy, and Breda was in no mood to hear of any supernatural meanderings, which Gran was always wont to do if she could get a ready listener. Breda spoke more briskly.

'Why don't you stay and have tea with me today then? Warren's dad brought me a couple of eggs so we could have fried egg on toast if you fancy it.'

'Make it fried bread, eh love? It's easier on my gums.'

Breda fled to the kitchen. The last thing she wanted was for Gran to take out her teeth and resort to champing her way through the food on her gums. So fried bread it would be...

Breda admitted that it was Gran who got her through those first difficult weeks at the cottage. It was surprising how many times she turned up – and then reported back to her parents, as Breda gradually began to realise.

'Are you and Gran in league?' she finally asked her mother in some exasperation when Agnes popped in one evening with some runner beans from her dad's garden. 'I was only saying to Gran yesterday that I really fancied some runner beans, and here they are. So you're either clairvoyant or Gran's been telling tales.'

Agnes's face coloured a little. 'You can't blame us for being anxious about you, Breda. You've had a terrible shock and it takes time to get over something like that.'

'I know that, but it won't help by mollycoddling me, Mum. I have to get on with my life as best I can, and I'm doing all right, really I am.'

She didn't mean to sound sharp and she knew they were only trying to help. But didn't they see that nobody could really help? This was something she had to do on her own, and she had taken the first step by moving into the cottage, even if Agnes still thought it was a bit morbid to do so.

'Well, your dad wanted to come here on Saturday to help tackle the garden, but perhaps you'd rather he didn't,' Agnes said, sounding miffed. 'And of course we expect you for Sunday dinner, unless you'd rather be here on your own.'

Breda's eyes filled with tears. 'I'm always on my own now, Mum. Even at school, where the noise of the children's chatter is a godsend, keeping me busy and stopping me from thinking about anything but looking after them, I'm still alone. And I'm not trying to shut you out, truly I'm not.'

Agnes responded by folding her arms around her daughter, feeling how much she trembled and how fragile she seemed now. She spoke more briskly.

'I know that, love, so how do you feel about helping the girls with their homework now and then? It's beyond anything your dad and I can do, but you've got the brains for it. It would get them out from under our feet for a while too.'

Breda smiled weakly. It was all such a ploy. Keep Breda busy, then she wouldn't have too much time to grieve over the fact that Warren was never coming home again. Keep the cottage filled with noise to cover the emptiness.

'Of course I will, Mum,' she said before she could think twice about it. Though she doubted that her sisters coming here would do much to help her peace of mind. But if it kept her mother happy and let her think she was doing her bit, then so be it, and she dutifully let her family help in whatever way they chose. At least it helped to allay the numbness...

Inevitably, as the weeks passed, and May turned into June and then July, and the countryside burgeoned into a glorious summer, things imperceptibly changed. As Gran Hanney always said, nothing ever stayed the same, even if she still missed Warren horribly. He had been part of her life for so long, it was impossible not to do so. But he wasn't always the first thing on her mind every morning when she awoke, with that rush of pain that had become so familiar. Sometimes she awoke with plans of what she and the children were going to do that day before Warren's image came into her mind. And then she was guilty, because she wanted to keep him uppermost in her thoughts always, even though she knew it could never be so.

Half a world away Max was finally recovering from his rampant fever, the operation to save his leg and the complications that followed. He had been kept informed of the progress of the war by his voluble fellow patients, but he could only raise minimal interest in the successful bombing of the Ruhr and Eder dams in Germany, and the other campaigns that were constantly being reported. He hardly cared about Higgins' cursing at his wife's letters telling of clothes rationing and the ever worsening food situation at home. For a long time he had remained in a weird state of not caring much about what happened anywhere except in the small confines of the hospital ward. It wasn't healthy, and somewhere inside himself he knew that it wasn't, but rousing himself from his constant stupor seemed an impossible mountain to climb until the day he awoke more clear-headed than in many months.

A sense of guilt flooded in then, knowing he hadn't even been able or willing to contact his family to tell them what had happened to him. Ever since the realisation that his cousin's wedding day had come and gone, he had felt bad at being unable to send them any goodwill message, let alone get home to fulfil his Best Man duties. And he felt even more guilty knowing he was also glad that fate had prevented him from being there at all.

But now he was nearly well enough to travel, and unknown to him his doctors had decided against giving him the tattered telegram that had arrived several months ago, and an equally tattered letter that had followed it a couple of weeks later. The senior medic had made the decision that whatever was in it, it was old news now. It could do nothing to aid his recovery, and would more than likely set him back. Whatever news they conveyed was best faced when the boy returned home to his family. Instead, they tied the two items in a piece of oilcloth and tucked it in the bottom of Max's belongings as they made preparations to send him to Alexandria. From there he would board a military ship bound for England.

His fellow patient, Higgins, was still in the ward and they both knew he wouldn't be going anywhere for a long time, if ever. Smithy had been discharged a while back and Max missed the cheery sound of his mouth organ, but there was a new kind of energy inside him now every time he thought of the music. The day he remembered he could play the saxophone had been like a burst of sunshine entering his soul, and he wasn't about to apologise to anybody for sounding so bloody poetic, either. It was enough that he was glad to be alive instead of wanting to go to that other, hellishly dark place, more times than he cared to admit.

He felt expansive enough to even think about sending a letter to Warren and Breda to congratulate them on the wedding, and to try to explain why he hadn't been able to be there. But that was as far as it got – just thinking about it. When the time came to ask an orderly for paper and pencil, his spirit failed him. All the same, he knew he had a duty to let his aunt and uncle know he was still alive, so he wrote to them instead.

But he found it was difficult to know what to say without seeming sorry for himself, or being so brutally blunt about his injuries that it would upset his Aunt Laura. He wrote the letter a dozen times before he was satisfied with it, and once he had begun properly, the words flowed. He finally read it over, trying to see it through their eyes.

You'll be wondering what's been happening to me all this time, Aunt Laura and Uncle Jed, and the truth is, I hardly know how to tell you myself. It seems ages since I've been properly aware of what's been going on. I know I've been at a hospital in Cairo these past months, and they tell me I've had a fever that kept me delirious for weeks at a time, and even when I was lucid I was thrashing about and threatening to do myself an injury – and others around me. Added to that I had a deep wound in my leg that wouldn't heal and got badly infected. It was touch and go whether or not I would lose my leg, but eventually they managed to patch me up. I'll never walk quite the

141

way I once did, nor go racing over the moors with Warren, but at least I've still got two legs.

I feel rotten for missing Warren and Breda's wedding, and they must be an old married couple by now. If I could have got a message to you to let you know my reasons, I would have done, but at the time I'd lost my senses and was living in a kind of twilight world. I don't mean to upset you both, but I want you to know that nothing short of this would have prevented me from being home for the wedding.

I often thought I would never see Cornwall again, let alone ever walk. There were times when I wished myself dead, but that's heathen talk, and I know you wouldn't approve, Aunt Laura. But now they say I can come home as soon as they can get me on a troop ship to England. My war's over now, so I'll be picking up my saxophone again and become one of those pathetic old war crocks. You won't see me standing on street corners begging for scraps though. I've still got my pride, don't you worry about that.

As the letter progressed, Max realised how cynical he was becoming. If he had any sense he should scrub out the last paragraph, but some devil inside him wouldn't let him do it. It was the way he felt. Why shouldn't they know how he had suffered? If it helped to explain why he couldn't have come home for the most important day in their lives, when Warren married his sweetheart, then so be it. Without another thought, he scribbled his name at the end of the letter, signing it with fondest regards, and slid it into an envelope, giving it to an orderly for him to post. With luck and a fair wind, it would arrive in Cornwall before he did, saving the need for lengthy explanations.

He lay back on his bed now, arms behind his head, and felt himself start to unwind for the first time in a long while. He had done all that he could to prepare his family for his homecoming. It was still going to be a couple of weeks before he began his journey, and the next ordeal – apart from the trauma of the travel – would be to face Warren and Breda, knowing that for the three of them, their roles in life had been changed for ever. But that was for another day.

Several weeks later, Laura Pascoe took the letter from the postwoman with trembling hands, recognising the scrawling handwriting on the envelope at once. At last, a letter from Max. Some folk around here had always thought him rather a feckless young man, a musician who thought more of playing the saxophone in a small local dance band than getting what some called a man's job, like his cousin and his uncle. But to Laura he had always been the adventurous, flamboyant one. She adored both her boys equally, and she pressed the letter to her bosom with a feeling of real joy in her heart, knowing it was the first time she had felt anything resembling that for months.

She decided to make herself a cup of tea before she read it, savouring the moment when she would hear of Max's exploits, and knowing, too, that she must expect to read of his shock after learning of Warren's death. It would have been a bitter blow to him to lose his close boyhood companion. Whatever had been the cause of so long a silence from Max, it was forgotten and forgiven

143

in an instant.

Ten minutes later, her cry of despair was akin to grief. It was obvious that Max had no knowledge of Warren's death, and whatever had happened to the telegram and subsequent letter she had sent, they couldn't have reached him.

'Oh, my poor boy,' Laura whispered aloud, her breath catching. 'To come home wounded, and to come home to this!'

Before she had time to think, she found herself ramming on her hat and coat and rushing down the street to the infant school. Breda was the one who should be told first, before Jed or anyone else. Breda would want to know that Max was coming home. She couldn't think of anything else.

She was breathless by the time she reached the little school, and she had to stand with her hand pressed to her chest for a few minutes to let the tightness settle down. She caught sight of Breda with a chattering group of small children in the playground poring over some nature tables on which there were clumps of seaweed and shells and bits of rock. The children were laughing so eagerly and happily at all their teacher was telling them, and Breda was so lovely with them. For a second Laura felt a stab in her heart, because if things had been different, then one day Warren and Breda would have had babies of their own, and this girl would have made such a wonderful mother...

As if aware that someone was watching her, Breda glanced up from the nature tables and gave a smile and a small wave as she saw Warren's mother. And then the smile changed to something else as she saw how white the other woman's face was, and she knew instinctively that this wasn't going to be good news.

She felt as if she was running towards Laura, but in fact her feet were so leaden she could only move slowly. Or was that a different kind of instinct to stave off the inevitable, since everyone knew there was no good news these days? Her heart stopped and then raced crazily on. There had already been the worst possible news there could be for the Pascoe family, and there was only one other thing it could mean. She felt physically sick at the thought.

Unless ... unless ... had there been a mistake after all? Was Warren unbelievably safe, picked up out of the ocean by some unknown person and rescued, and was being cared for somewhere? You heard about these things. You heard about them all the time, Breda thought, with desperate hope clouding her thoughts.

'What is it?' she gasped, her fingers digging into Laura's arms so tightly the woman winced.

Laura was unable to speak for a moment, and then the words rushed out.

'I've had a letter. Max is coming home, Breda. He's wounded, but he's coming home. And he doesn't even know – he still believes...'

To Breda's horror, Laura lost her grip on her arm as she fell to the ground in a dead faint. The terrible, terrible dashing of that brief hope was so great that Breda was unable to register anything else, and she could easily have followed suit. And then she became aware of the children crowding all around them with small screams and frightened eyes, and she swallowed down the nausea that threatened to overwhelm her.

'Children, please go inside and tell Mrs Larraby I'm taking Mrs Pascoe home as she's not well. Go *now*.'

Breda spoke as steadily as she could, considering how her heart was churning and her mouth was as dry as dust. As the other woman began to regain consciousness, Breda helped her to her feet.

'What happened?' Laura whispered.

'You fainted. I'm taking you home and then we can talk. Don't say anything until I get you indoors.'

She was in too much turmoil to want to listen to anything yet. She could hardly take in the few words Laura had said. She should be elated – and so she was – but she was also dismayed at the hideously selfish thought that had entered her mind. The shameful thought that should be safely buried, but had thundered into her head.

Why couldn't it have been Warren who was coming home? Why couldn't he be the one instead of Max...?

Chapter Nine

The cottage was nearer than the Pascoe house. Breda held on tightly to Laura's arm, ignoring the curious eyes of the village folk as they walked the short distance from the school. These days there were often red and weeping faces to avoid as folk got news of their loved ones, and it was more polite to look away discreetly than to intrude with murmurs of sympathy. It was simply understood.

Today's news wasn't anything that deserved sympathy, of course. Today's news was the happiest they could receive in the circumstances. As the thoughts whirled around in her head, Breda knew it, even though it had revived all the grief she had been trying so hard to overcome in the last few months. Now, in what should be the best of news, that grief had all come rushing back, but she daren't let Laura see how deep the pain went. Laura would be overjoyed that one of her boys was coming home, and rightly so. It was only Breda who would harbour this deep and unreasoning resentment that it wasn't Warren.

'You need to prune those roses,' Laura said mechanically, as they opened the gate of Forget-me-not Cottage and walked to the front door.

Breda felt a hysterical urge to laugh at the absurd remark. But perhaps it was the only way Laura could cope with the shock of this day. Any

147

news was a shock, good or bad, and this seemed to have knocked her sideways. Maybe she too, had wondered for a second about the contents of the letter that arrived that morning. Maybe she too, had thought for one wonderful, miraculous moment that it had all been a mistake, and Warren was coming home.

A short while later, sitting down with steaming cups of tea, laced with more than a drop of the brandy Gilb Hanney had insisted his daughter kept handy for medicinal purposes, Breda knew it wouldn't have been the case. As Laura handed her the letter, she recognised Max's handwriting just as easily as his aunt had done. She had seen it so many times over the years, from his first childish scribble at infant school, to the bold, scrawling manner in which he wrote now. This was a man's hand, a man who had seen the world, not the child of her memory.

She opened the letter with trembling fingers, almost afraid of what she would see, and as she read it, the resentment gave way to a deep pity for the strong young man she had known, and who seemed so defeated now, despite his brash words about being a war crock. Then she gave a loud gasp, her hand going to her mouth.

'Dear Lord, he doesn't know about Warren,' she finally stammered, her throat full. 'But how could he not know, Mrs Pascoe? I know you sent him a telegram and a letter.'

Laura shook her head in bewilderment. 'Heaven only knows, Breda. Things do go astray in wartime, and for some reason it seems that Max never received the news. It's a cruel twist of fate, and I fear it will only make it worse for him when he comes home and learns what happened. I dread having to tell him.'

'No more than I do,' Breda almost whispered.

It was obvious, too, that he didn't know the wedding had never happened. Nor that Breda wasn't a bride, nor even a widow. She was nothing. If her life had seemed empty these last months, so had Max's been, when it seemed he had lost so much of it due to fever and delirium. Because she knew him so well, she could only guess at how much of his suffering he had left out of the letter he wrote to his aunt.

'We will have to be strong for him,' she said, sounding far more resolute than she felt. 'He'll need our support when he comes home, Mrs Pascoe, and to know that we love him, no matter what state he's in,' she finished lamely.

'You're a good girl, Breda, and we're all lucky to have you,' his aunt said, with a tinge of colour coming into her cheeks now. That could have been due to the brandy, of course, but whatever it was, Breda was glad to see she was no longer looking so pasty as when she had first seen her. 'You would have been a good sister to Max, and there's no reason why you can't be the same now.'

She would never have been his sister, and they both knew that. Max wasn't Warren's brother, and there had been times as the years passed, when Breda had wondered if Max was seeing her as more than his cousin's sweetheart. As if there had been a certain secret longing in his eyes that she couldn't quite fathom. But before she could really think about it too deeply, it would be gone. She dismissed the uneasy thought. It wasn't the time to start speculating over anything so unlikely or so unwelcome. The three of them had been closer than clams at one time, and she had to be as close as that for Max when he came home.

'I'll leave you now, dear,' Laura was saying. 'I'm going to see if Jed is back at the quay yet, and if not I'm going home to make him a meat and potato pie for his tea with what little meat I can get from the butcher. We need to have a bit of a celebration, and you're welcome to come and share it with us after your school day, Breda. Please say yes. It would mean a lot to us on this day of all days.'

She wanted to say no. She wasn't sure she would feel like celebrating in quite the same way as Laura and Jed Pascoe would at the return of the prodigal nephew, but at the pleading look in Laura's eyes she knew she couldn't disappoint them. She leant forward and kissed Laura's bony cheek.

'That would be lovely, and thank you. And before you go, take a few of Dad's runner beans for us to have with it.'

By the time she got back to school she felt as if she had run a marathon. Nervous tension really took it out of a person, she told Mrs Larraby, and she had had more than enough of it for one day.

'It's wonderful news for the family, Breda, and I can imagine the relief for Max's aunt and uncle,' Mrs Larraby said cautiously.

'Of course, and I'm pleased and relieved too.'

150

'But you wish it could have been Warren,' the older woman stated. 'Oh, don't look so shocked, my dear, you wouldn't be human if you didn't have these thoughts.'

'You don't think it's so very awful then?'

'I think it's perfectly normal, though it's not something I would mention to anyone else, if I were you,' the teacher added dryly. 'Look, you'll have your own family to tell, so why don't you go home? The term's almost over, and none of the children are concentrating very hard now.'

'I know,' Breda said with a tremulous smile. 'Thank you for being so understanding. I'll go and tell Gran and my parents right away. They'll all be glad to hear about Max. He's as much a family member as Warren was.'

She almost wished she didn't have to tell anybody. But of course they had to be told, and they all expressed their joy at hearing the news. Her gran was spending the day with Agnes, so at least she didn't have to say it all twice.

'Stay and eat with us, Breda,' her mother said at once. 'You're looking very thin these days.'

'It's the fault of Mr Churchill's starvation rations,' she retorted lightly. 'But I'm going to take advantage of my day off to do some house-work, and I've been invited for supper with Mr and Mrs Pascoe. I couldn't say no, Mum, not tonight.'

'Of course you couldn't,' Gran Hanney said. 'You're a good girl, Breda.'

It was the second time that day she had been called a good girl. She didn't feel like a good girl. She didn't feel like a girl at all, and she never had done so since the day she and Warren had anticipated their wedding night at the cottage, when she had become a woman in both their eyes. A woman and a lover...

Max was finally on a hospital ship bound for England, after a lot of red tape and forms to be signed. He had been given a letter for his own doctor, informing him of the treatment he had received by the army medics, and he was officially discharged from both the Cairo hospital and the army. As he surveyed the cramped conditions of the cabin in the section of the ship that he'd been allocated, he thought how different his life had become since that first day when he had enlisted so eagerly, wanting to fulfil his dream of going to Egypt, his second most cherished ambition. The first, that of playing the saxophone and making music, he had already accomplished, and knew that he would always be able to return to it.

He just hadn't expected to return so ignominiously, he thought savagely, as a sudden stinging stab in his wounded leg reminded him that he was going home to Cornwall in a far less manly state than he had left it. The bloody operations that had saved his leg had also left it somewhat shortened, and he knew he would always walk with a limp now.

'Think yourself lucky you can walk at all, you ungrateful bastard,' Higgins had told him on his last day. 'At least you ain't going home in a box, nor blown to bits in some godforsaken desert.'

'And at least you can always turn a tune – or

so you tell us,' another patient retorted. 'You
don't need your bleedin' legs for that, mate.'

The echo of those words made him turn restlessly on his narrow bunk. On his worst days, he
sometimes wondered if it would have been better
for all concerned if one of those things had actually happened. Dying under the surgeon's knife,
or being blown to bits in the desert and not knowing a damn thing about it. At least he wouldn't be
going home to face the prospect of seeing the girl
he had always loved married to his cousin. Maybe
Warren would even have struck gold right away
and Breda would already be expecting a child ...
the very thought tore at his gut.

He reached for the kitbag that held all his
belongings, knowing that since this space was to
be his home for however long it took the ship to
reach England, he might as well unpack it. He'd
had no heart for it until now, and he had been so
weary by the time the truck had taken him to
Alexandria to board the ship, he'd thought he
was turning into some kind of namby-pamby.

At the bottom of his kitbag he found a small
piece of oilcloth wrapped around something that
he hadn't seen before. He untied it without much
enthusiasm, and then his stomach churned as he
saw the tattered yellow envelope that he knew
instantly meant a telegram. There was an equally
tattered envelope with his aunt's handwriting on
it. He tore open the telegram quickly, and then
his heart stopped with a sickening thud as he
read the stark words.

*Warren feared drowned. Please come if possible.
Aunt Laura.*

He was almost choking now as the saliva dried in his mouth. He ripped open his aunt's letter, the tear-stained words confirming all that the telegram had put so bluntly. He looked at the date on both the items. Three months ago. *Three months!* Was that just before the wedding, or after it? Max felt completely disorientated, as bad as on the first day he had been carried almost sense-less into the military hospital in Cairo. He read on quickly, the words dancing in front of his eyes as he tried to make sense of them.

So it was all true. His cousin's ship had been sunk and he was not one of the survivors. All that time ago, and Max had known nothing of it. He felt sick with grief. While he had been delirious and thrashing at anything in sight, and alter-nately being away with the fairies on the drugs that had been pumped into him, his cousin had been dying. The wedding had never happened. Warren and Breda had never been married, and his services as Best Man would never have been needed...

The fact that he could even think of such a thing when the horror of it all was still sweeping through him, made his stomach curdle, and with-out warning the contents of it erupted and he vomited over everything. Then he passed out.

A ship's orderly found him a while later and had the unenviable task of cleaning him up and that of everything around him.

'You've been having quite a time in here, matey,' the man said cheerfully, when Max finally recovered his senses. 'Ain't got your sea legs yet, I take it. Don't worry, you'll soon get used to it.

Get yourself up on deck for a bit and get some sea air into your lungs. Folk pay good money to go on sea cruises, donchaknow?'

'For Christ's sake, shut up, man,' Max growled. 'I just had some bad news, and I don't need a lecture.'

'Sorry, mate,' the orderly said more sympathetically. 'I still think you'd do better up on deck for now though, so I can swab this floor down. It niffs worse than an Arab's jockstrap.'

Max looked at him silently, thinking what a rotten job he had, and felt ashamed of his outburst.

'Sorry. All right, I'll do as you say.'

'Attaboy. Do you good to talk to some of the other poor buggers, anyway.'

In other words, he wasn't the only one being sent home in a hospital ship. There were plenty of others worse off than Max Pascoe. At least he had all his limbs and his eyes and his brain were intact – as far as he knew. It was time he stopped feeling sorry for himself and thought instead of how bloody terrible his aunt and uncle would have been feeling to hear of Warren's death. And what must they be thinking of their nephew, having had no word from him all this time? Not until now. Not until the letter he had sent just before he left Cairo, saying all the things he had said about the wedding. He groaned, trying to remember his own words, and failing. But for them to get that letter from him, out of the blue, after all this time...

'Here, are you all right, mate?' he heard a voice say.

155

He hardly realised he had reached the deck, and how a young chap with his arm in a sling and a bandage around his head was looking at him in some concern.

'I thought you were going to puke over the side then. Take a few deep breaths and the feeling will pass.'

'Thanks,' Max muttered.

'Don't mention it. I'm used to it, but it can be hellish at first. I'm Graham, by the way, late of His Majesty's Navy.'

'Max,' he said. 'Desert Rat.'

The other young man whistled admiringly. 'I've heard of you lot. Bought it in the desert, did you?'

He didn't really want to talk about it. He didn't want to talk at all. Being on a ship with the sea churning all around him was the worst possible place to have learnt of his cousin's death, reminding him as it did of all that could happen on an angry sea with enemy U-boats beneath the waves, and the ever-present danger of mines. But Graham seemed determined to keep him talking, to keep up his spirits, and, without meaning to at all, Max found himself spilling out the whole ghastly story to him.

'Blimey, mate, you've had a pill, haven't you?' the sailor said sympathetically. 'All that, and your girl going through it too.'

'She's not my girl. I told you, she was going to marry my cousin.'

'Yeah, I heard you. Nothing to stop you muscling in now though, is there? You can't deny you're sweet on her. It shows in every word, and

I don't mean to be callous, but with your cousin out of the way, well.'

Max didn't mean to hit him. You didn't hit a chap with a bandage around his head and his arm in a sling. He hardly knew he had done so. He just felt a blistering rage, his vision blinded by a red mist, the kind you only read about in books. They happened though, he found himself registering almost hysterically.

'Bloody hell, what did you do that for?' Graham hollered, holding his one good hand to his bloodied nose. 'I was only making conversation, for God's sake. If a bloke can't take a joke these days, he might as well be dead.'

The hospital ship was filled to capacity, and there were others around them now, crowding around to find out what was going on. There were shuffling patients returning home in crumpled and bedraggled uniforms, and orderlies rushing to see what all the commotion was about. The one who had dealt with Max earlier was one of them, and he spoke swiftly to one of the ship's medics. He slapped a hand on Max's arm.

'Come on, old son, I think you've had enough sea air for one day. Let's get you back to your bunk and give you a shot to calm you down.'

If Max intended to protest he got no chance. He just managed to blurt out the one word 'Sorry' before he was hustled away from the glowering crowd around the sailor.

He didn't want to be given a shot of anything. He didn't want to sink back into that state of oblivion where he seemed to have been for so long in recent months. But he had no choice.

157

And perhaps, after all, it was better to be out of things than to register the constant undulating motion of the ship, which was doing his innards no good at all. He succumbed to the sting of the needle, and even though he didn't want to think about them, the last things on his mind were the words the sailor had said to him...

'Nothing to stop you muscling in now though, is there? You can't deny you're sweet on her.'

Of course he was sweet on Breda. But it was far more than that. Love didn't always come like a thunderbolt, and in his case it had grown gradually over the years when he, Warren and Breda had roamed the moors like tumbledown kids, and now he couldn't imagine a day when he hadn't loved her.

He moved restlessly as the drug began to take effect, and he tried to push the memories out of his mind. He willed the even more horrific thoughts away – the knowledge that his dearest pal, his cousin who had been more than a brother to him, was dead. How the hell could any decent bloke ever think of muscling in on a girl's grief when he knew, more than anybody else, how much Breda and Warren had meant to one another? Contrary to what that bloody stupid sailor had said, it was the ultimate barrier to him ever being able to think of Breda in that way again.

In Cornwall, it took a few days for the people concerned to finally get used to the fact that Max was coming home, and that there must be a certain amount of celebrating. There was also

158

great anxiety, because it seemed that he couldn't possibly have known what had happened to Warren, and it was going to be a terrible shock for him when he was told. The celebrating would be marred before it even began, unless there was some way of getting the news to him first.

'Do you think that's being cowardly, Breda?' Laura Pascoe asked during one of their now frequent meetings. 'I'm not sure if I can bear to see his face if I have to be the one to tell him.'

'Of course it's not being cowardly. Just don't ask me to be the one to do it, that's all,' Breda said, more crisply than she intended. But truly, these past days had been difficult enough, with people who knew the families well being cheerful enough whenever they mentioned Max's safe return, but also careful not to underline the fact that his cousin had not come home.

'You know I wouldn't do that, dear,' Laura said hastily. 'But we've learnt that once he reaches England he'll be sent to a hospital in Southampton for a few days before an army vehicle brings him home, to assess whether the sea voyage has done him any further damage. I'm thinking it might be wise to send a letter there, so that he knows what's happened before he gets here. What do you think?'

'I'm sure that's a good idea,' Breda said.

She didn't want to be involved in the way Max was told. The more Laura fretted about it, the more it sharpened the knowledge that it was Max coming home and not Warren. Couldn't the woman see that? Or was she so obsessed by the fact that one of her boys had survived that she

159

had almost forgotten the other one?

One glance around the homely room in the Pascoe house, with its many photos and mementoes of Warren that Laura couldn't bear to put away, even down to the skewed ashtray he had once made in a junior pottery class, and Breda knew it wasn't so. But she was finding it increasingly difficult to be a part of it all, and it seemed that the only person who really understood how she was feeling was her gran.

'It was the same when Mrs Tremayne's boy was killed by a freak wave at sea,' she observed, referring to one of her cronies. 'I mind the day the news came, all those years ago, and the poor old dab couldn't bear to wash any of his clothes for months, for fear she'd lose the smell of him. Eventually she had to do it, of course, before the cottage reeked. It was better than garlic for keeping bad spirits away, mind,' she added.

'Oh, Gran, I'm sure it wasn't like that,' Breda said, forced to smile.

'Well, mebbe not quite, but I can understand why Laura Pascoe keeps talking about young Max and why you find it so hard to take, my lamb. Things will sort themselves out once he's home and life gets back to a bit of normal.'

'Oh yes? And what do you call a bit of normal nowadays? Warren's not the only boy in the village who's lost his life now, and how many more will there be before it ends?'

'At least he died in the service of his king and country,' Gran retorted. 'You can take pride in that, Breda.'

'I'd rather take pride in having him home and

160

being my husband, and that's something I can never say now, isn't it?'

She heard herself descending into misery again, when she had begun to think she was finally coming out of the deep trough of despair. Her gran spoke sternly.

'Now you listen to me, Breda. Did you think young Max would never be coming home? Wasn't this something that was always going to happen, barring another tragic happening? You're not begrudging him the fact that he's alive, just because your dear Warren is dead, are you? Because that's what it sounds like to me, and if that's the case, then I'm ashamed of you, girl.'

'Of course I don't think that. I would never think that, Gran.'

But she did, and she knew she did. In the darkest hours of the night, she still had the shameful thoughts in her head that she wished desperately that it was Warren coming home, not Max. But that was a secret she would never tell.

Max's mates in the village had heard the news that he was coming home and wouldn't be returning to war service. The small group that had formed the local dance band was eager for Max to join them again. They played now to raise money for the war effort, and they told Breda they had begun moving further afield with this in mind, and were gaining a reputation in nearby towns and villages. But they still missed their star performer on the saxophone.

'It's nice to know you think so much of him, but I shouldn't think he'd feel like travelling

161

about the country for a while,' she told them uneasily. 'Give him time to adjust back to civvy life, won't you, Hobbsy?'

''Course we will,' the one called Hobbsy said easily. 'But if I know old Max, he won't want to sit on his backside for long. It's not his style, as you should know. Have you heard when he'll be back?'

'No. You'll have to check with his auntie for that.' She spoke shortly, because she didn't want to be his messenger or his go-between, either. Though she couldn't help but be glad that his old mates were so eager to welcome him back in the fold. The sooner he could pick up the pieces of his life, the better.

Hobbsy put his arm around her shoulders and gave her a quick squeeze.

'It was a hell of a thing that happened to Warren, but at least one of the Pascoe boys made it, didn't he? Have you seen this week's newspaper? A couple more chaps from our school year have bought it. God knows how many names will be on the war memorial by the time it's all over. Anyway, that's enough cheering up for one day. We'll be seeing you, Breda. You be sure to come to the first of our dances when Max is playing, by the way. You can be our mascot.'

They had a funny idea of cheering somebody up, she thought, as they swaggered away. And if they thought she'd be going to any dances in the foreseeable future, whether or not Max was playing, they could think again!

It was a weird thing, though. She *did* feel oddly cheered up by the time she got back to Forget-me-not Cottage. It was sad news that two more chaps in their school year had died, and she didn't yet know who they were. But life went on. People still went to dances and to the pictures and enjoyed themselves, as she very well knew. People like Hobbsy and his mates raised money for the war effort and did their bit, even if they couldn't actively fight the Germans. There were still good people in the world. You had to remember that, or you would go under.

Chapter Ten

The school summer holidays were upon them now, and where once Breda would have welcomed the long lazy days, as the weeks went on she found time hanging heavily on her hands. She welcomed the thought of Max coming home, of course she did, but she was dreading it too. The news of Warren's death had hit her so hard, but the terrible shock of it had inevitably faded as the weeks passed.

She still missed him and thought of him every day. She still wept for him at night ... but in Max's mind those feelings of loss would still be new, still raw, and she didn't need to know how deeply he would have felt his cousin's death. He would have his own guilt that he had known nothing about it at the time, and hadn't been there to comfort his aunt and uncle – and Breda. Because there had been such a close childhood friendship between them, it was natural that he would want to turn to her, to share in their mutual grief, and that was something she didn't think she could bear.

Gran had been right, you had to go on or you would go under, and she was trying so hard to look forward and not back. Max would simply undermine everything she had tried to do so far. It was hard not to feel a sliver of resentment because of it.

So far there had been no word of when he was finally coming home. Several letters had been exchanged between Max and his aunt now, and according to Laura they were keeping him in the convalescent home in Southampton for a week or two until they were satisfied with both his physical and mental state. She had snorted when telling Breda as much.

'Blooming cheek, I call it. Do they think he's mad? He needs to come home to his family and get some good Cornish air into his lungs. That would soon put him right, better than sitting around with other poor folk in the same state as himself.'

'I'm sure the doctors know what they're talking about, Mrs Pascoe,' Breda murmured. 'Don't forget, he's been through a lot, far more than we know, I daresay, and it takes times for such scars to heal.'

'It will be good for the two of you to talk about Warren, dear. You both loved him, and it's easier for you young ones to talk easily. We old 'uns can't put it all into words the way you can.'

She seemed to be doing pretty well, thought Breda as she left her a while later. Besides, she didn't want to talk to Max about Warren yet. What was there to say? It wasn't as if she knew any more about his death than what the official telegram and subsequent information had told her. Even then, it had all gone to his parents, since she hadn't been a wife. The sharpness of that thought seared through her as always, and she was still smarting inwardly as she went to call on her mother. She found her way barred, and

165

her mother looking harassed.

'You can't come in, Breda. The girls have gone down with German measles, and the doctor says you can't risk taking the infection back to your young charges when school starts again. They're both squabbling like mad over who's got the biggest rash now, of course, and in a right stew that this has happened in the school holidays instead of in term time.'

She paused for breath, holding her hand to her side as if she had a stitch, and Breda told her to slow down. Agnes glared at her.

'They're also making a big fuss because they've got *German* measles instead of *English* measles. You'd think the blooming Germans invented the disease just to annoy them. It's all right for you to stand there grinning, you don't know what I've got to put up with with those two little madams!'

'I didn't know I was grinning,' Breda said hastily, trying not to laugh out loud at the thought of her two sisters complaining about which type of measles they had. For heaven's sake, if that was the only thing that would ever worry them in their lives, they had little to complain about. But she could see that her mother had had enough for one day.

'I'm sorry I can't do anything to help,' she said more sympathetically. 'But the doctor's quite right, of course, and I daren't risk carrying it back to school when term begins again.'

'I've told your gran to stay away too. She only annoys the girls even more with her tales, and I wouldn't want her catching it. It would probably finish her off. Anyway, I can't stand here gossiping, Breda. Give it a week and then we'll see what the doctor says about visiting.'

'All right. Give them my love, Mum, and I'll send up a couple of my old jigsaws for them to do to while away the time. I won't want them back,' she added.

She could just imagine how impossible Esme and Jenna were being. They were bad enough at the best of times, without the miserable German measles to contend with. But now she was at a loose end again, and, without thinking, her steps took her down to the quay, where the scents of sea and fish and seaweed were pungently strong in the air. High above, seabirds wheeled and screeched, hoping for morsels of food, or alternatively diving for fish. It was a glorious August afternoon and some of the children from her class were poking around the rock pools, looking for limpets or shells. Her nature lessons were obviously taking good effect.

'Miss, Miss, come and see what I've found,' she heard young Sara Hayes shout out excitedly as she caught sight of her.

Breda walked across the soft sand with a smile, thinking how little it took to excite a small child's imagination. At the same moment, she thought how lucky they all were that here on this north Cornish coast in the far west of England there was no need for the barbed wire that had been erected at many areas along the more vulnerable south coasts, to ward off enemy invaders. She shivered as the thought entered her head, and then knelt down beside Sara and her friends.

The shell had been washed clean by the tides

and shimmered like mother-of-pearl in delicate shades of luminescent blues and pinks.

'How pretty,' Breda exclaimed. 'Look after it until next term, Sara, and perhaps we could think up a story about where it came from, and how many people had seen shells like this one before you found it. What do you think?'

'Perhaps it came from a long way away across the sea,' the child said eagerly. 'I'll keep it on my dressing table and look after it, Miss.'

Her imagination was already engaged, Breda thought, and she had all the makings of a bright child. Breda wandered on around the quay, her thoughts lost in the brightness of the day and the way the sea gradually ebbed and flowed, creating a beauty of its own, with no hint of how it could change in a moment. How it could rage and storm and take a man's life...

'Breda, it's good to see you, girl.' She turned to see Jed Pascoe striding towards her, smelling of fish and sea water in his oilskins and thankfully resisting giving her a hug. 'It's a good day for walking by the sea.'

Did his eyes challenge hers at that moment? Was he reminding her that he spent every day locked in battle with the elements, whether they were good or bad, and that neither he nor his son had ever been afraid to meet whatever lay ahead? Or was he reminding her, however unwittingly, that she had rarely come here since the day she had heard the news of the sea claiming Warren? But that wasn't the fault of the sea that he loved. That was the enemy.

'I've been to see Mrs Pascoe,' she told him. 'I

wanted to see my mum too, but my sisters have got German measles so I'm banned from the house.'

'I'm sorry to hear that, but you know you're always welcome at ours, don't you, my dear? We'll certainly want to see you there when we welcome Max home. I can imagine him champing at the bit, as they say, and giving those hospital nurses a right old time of it by now,' he added with a throaty chuckle.

It was funny how imagination took people in different ways, she found herself thinking as she made her escape and went back to her cottage in Barnes Lane. The Pascoes would be imagining how wonderful it would be to have Max home, and he'd probably be thinking the same thing. Young Sara was already imagining where her beautiful shell had come from, while Breda ... what was she imagining? How different life could have been, if only... And yet, for those few lovely moments back there on the beach, she had been as totally entranced by Sara Hayes' shell as the child herself had been. It hadn't been a sin to forget, even for those few moments, that she would never be Warren Pascoe's wife now.

Max was never going to settle down in this God-awful place, he raged to anyone who would listen. He knew he sounded like a rat for ranting about it, because he knew they were doing their best for him. But, hell's teeth, he'd thought that once he got off the ship at Southampton he'd have a couple of days' repatriation and conva-lescence, if only to get rid of the motion of the hospital troop ship, and then they'd send him home. Instead, it was ten days now, and he was sick of being prodded and inspected as if he were a piece of meat.

It wasn't as if he had to stay in bed, except for the regular morning attendance by the medics. The grounds were pleasant enough in the daytime, and if you ignored the sound of gunfire and the drone of enemy planes making their nightly visits, and the whine of the spitfires and hurricanes on the way to intercept the Jerry planes, you got on pretty well. The trouble was, Max was too impatient to waste time here when all he wanted was to get home and start his life again – whatever kind of life it was going to be. But he knew damn well he was luckier than a lot of them here.

He still had all his faculties, as far as he knew. He could still play his saxophone – at least, his fingers were flexible enough and it would only take a few sessions with the old crowd to get him back in the swing of things. He'd even had a note from old Hobbsy, after his aunt had presumably given him the address of this place, to say they couldn't wait to have him back in the old routine again. So why the hell couldn't he be patient enough to wait a few more days?

His temper was finally rewarded when he was sitting in the shade of a tree in the grounds of the hospital. The refrain of one of the old songs they used to play was running through his head and he couldn't get it out. 'In the shade of the old apple tree...'

Not that this was an apple tree, but it made him

start to wonder how many soldiers had listened to those words and the words that followed, and wondered if their girls were still waiting for them. Well, there was one sure thing. There was no girl waiting for him.

'Well now, Private Pascoe,' he heard a voice say just as he was starting to descend into melancholy again. He groaned. Another man in a white coat. Hadn't he seen enough of them to last a lifetime?

'Come to tell me I'm having more tests, I suppose?' he greeted the medic.

'On the contrary. I'm here to tell you you're discharged. Come inside and sign a few forms for me, and then you're to be ready with all your kit at eight hundred hours tomorrow morning, and a vehicle will be here to take you home.'

For a moment Max simply couldn't take in the words. As he looked up at the medic from his bench the sun dazzled his eyes so much he thought he was going to cry. Or maybe it wasn't the sun at all. Maybe it was the sheer bloody relief that this day had finally come, and never had the word *home* sounded so bloody marvellous.

'Thanks,' was all he could stammer.

The medic put a hand on his shoulder. 'I know. Good news can take you just as hard as bad, sometimes. Take your time, soldier, and come to the office when you're ready. Any time in the next ten minutes will do,' he added, trying to make a joke out of it. 'You'll be one of a group going southwest in the morning, so be prepared for a lengthy journey.'

He wouldn't have cared if it was to the moon and back as long as Cornwall and home was at the end of it.

The following day he was slightly revising his thoughts as the endless journey continued. The road to Cornwall was a long one, and there were patients to be dropped off at various points first, through Somerset and Devon, and finally they were heading for the north coast of the county he knew so well.

'It feels good to be back in familiar territory, eh, Private?' the driver asked him, when there were only a couple of them left.

'You'll never know how good,' Max said.

All his life he had had the wanderlust, longing to go to Egypt in particular, and fascinated by the ancient ruins of a civilisation that had been so advanced long before their own. All those years, teasing his cousin because Warren's only ambitions had been to be a fisherman like his dad and to grow up and marry his sweetheart. While Max had been the daredevil one, for whom the grass in faraway fields had always seemed greener. Well, now he had seen it all, from France to Germany and beyond, and no grass ever seemed greener or sweeter than that of the Cornish moors they were crossing now.

'You might find it a bit tricky getting the vehicle down the steep roads to Penbole village,' he commented a bit later.

'Don't worry, mate, I've taken it in trickier places than this. We'll get there all right, and I've got orders to deliver you to your door. We're taking no chances with that leg.'

'Thanks for reminding me,' Max muttered.

And then he forgot the words as the army vehicle rounded the top of the hill. Below them, like some fairyland place conjured up by a magic hand, was the village of Penbole, sparkling in the afternoon sunlight. His breath tightened in his throat as he took in the familiar sight of a place he had frequently thought he was never going to see again.

'All right, mate?' the driver said. 'Bit of a back-water, ain't it? Especially if you're used to the bright lights of London like me. Not that there's many bright lights in the smoke now, mind,' he added conversationally. 'Jerry's seen to that.'

'Just get on with it, will you, man? I'll give you directions as we get down the hill nearer to the quay.'

As the vehicle began to descend, Max got the most peculiar feeling about this place he knew as well as the back of his hand. Had it ever seemed quite so small, the streets so cramped, the houses so close together? Had the hurrying people ever seemed quite so shabby and careworn, resembling strangers more than the chatty folk he had known since childhood? Or was it more to do with the fact that he had seen a far wider world than the insular Cornish village where he had grown up, and which had been his entire world until the wanderlust got hold of him? He had crossed the sea and seen a world of vast desert plains and dunes, great rocky outcrops of moun-tains, and heard voices that were nothing like his own, speaking in a language he didn't understand at first, but which had eventually become as familiar to him as his own Cornish accent.

'Bit different from where you've been, I daresay,' the driver said, still trying to make conversation with this chap who seemed to have lost his tongue now.

'Go down this street and turn left. The cottage is the last one on the right,' Max said, his voice jerky.

If the man did but know it, Max's heart was beating like a drum in his chest, and he was nervous – he was actually stupidly bloody well nervous of going inside his own home and being greeted by his aunt and uncle. His aunt Laura's letters had been warm and welcoming enough, but he knew damn well that the minute she saw him she would be remembering her son who hadn't come home. He was the prodigal, while Warren was fish-bait somewhere in the Atlantic Ocean or wherever his ship had been sunk. He didn't even know that for sure, and, in any case, the sharks would have made short work of his cousin by now, so there could hardly be anything of him left after all this time.

He felt the bile rise in his mouth at the thought, and fought to keep it down. And for one horrific, shamefully weak moment, he almost told the driver to turn right around and take him back the way he had come, because he just couldn't face it. He couldn't face the people who loved him, and for whom he would always be second best...

'This the place, mate?' the driver said, and he blinked as he saw the cottage right in front of him. From here he could hear the sound of seabirds and smell the sea. His uncle would be there right now, going about his business, while his Aunt Laura would be inside, doing the housework and waiting for him, even though she didn't know exactly when he was coming home, because he hadn't known himself.

But there was no reprieve now, because the driver was getting out of his cab and opening the door for Max to get out. He moved stiffly after the long drive, holding on to the walking stick he had been given, even though he hated having to use it. For now it was necessary, not only because at this moment his legs felt like jelly, but also because his injured leg was still so weak. All the same, as soon as he could he intended to throw the stick away. He was too proud to want to be seen as an old man just yet.

He hitched his kitbag higher on his shoulder and bade the driver goodbye, nodding speech- lessly in return to the man's words of good luck. And then he walked up the path to the front door, hardly able to think that he was actually home. He had dreamt of this moment for so long, yet he felt the awful dread of anticlimax, because he still didn't know what awaited him. Tears of joy and relief? Regrets that he wasn't Warren? Would he see it in his aunt's eyes, even if she tried to hide it? He was a mass of indecision and nerves, as bad as at any time he had been caught in the throes of delirium.

And then he squared his shoulders. Was he a man or a mouse? For God's sake, he was the soldier returning home, battle-scarred but still alive, and none could deny that. He opened the cottage door, knowing that it wouldn't be locked, and stepped inside. He was instantly assaulted by the familiar, homely smells of a cottage that was well-loved and well-cared-for. Laura's touch was everywhere, in the neat antimacassars on the chairs and the homemade rag rugs on the floor, to the highly polished table and chairs and the many photographs adorning the room. All of his childhood was here, Max thought, his throat filling up.

A sound from upstairs made him jerk his head towards the twisting staircase leading out of the room, and then footsteps followed, clattering down the stairs. The next sound was a little cry that could only be interpreted as one of happiness.

'Max!' Laura gasped, holding one hand to her throat and clinging to the banister with the other. 'Is it really you, my dear boy?'

She reached the foot of the stairs at the same moment that Max crossed the small room, and then they were clasping one another tightly, and it would have been hard to say whose tears were mingling with whose.

'Let me look at you,' Laura said after a moment or two. 'Oh, but you've got so thin! Didn't they feed you in the army? It was all that awful desert food, I daresay. We'll soon put paid to that, despite the food rationing. My meat and potato pies will soon put the flesh back on those bones.'

She was talking too fast, trying to cover the distance of time between them in an instant. Trying to cover the pain of what had to be said between them by mundane remarks about food and rationing, and as he felt her narrow frame start to tremble, it was Max who drew her down to sit beside him on the sofa.

'We've got all the time in the world to put everything right, Aunt Laura,' he said awkwardly. 'The army has had its fill of me and I'm home to stay. You and Uncle Jed can have a bit of looking after now. But we've got to talk about Warren, haven't we? I want to know everything about what happened.'

She nodded. 'We'll talk, but not now. Later, when Jed comes home, when we can all sit round the table and have supper together like a proper family again. You don't know how good that sounds to your uncle and me, Max.'

It was all he needed to make the tears come. The unmanly, bittersweet tears he hadn't been able to cry until now, but in this understanding woman's arms it seemed right and natural to do so. They both wept for someone they had known and loved since the day he was born who they would never see again, and it was a healing process for both of them.

After a while he left his aunt as she began to prepare supper and he went upstairs to his old room to unpack his things. It was still the same as when he had left it, although freshly dusted and polished each week, he guessed, with the posters on his wall of the places he would one day visit, God willing. The boyhood mementoes were still on his dressing table, the photos of himself and Warren in the school football team, the model air-planes, the magazines and comics they had collected and swapped between them. And there, in pride of place hanging on his wall, and just as lovingly dusted, he wouldn't mind betting, was his saxophone.

For the first time since coming home, his heart stirred with a different emotion. His fingers tingled as if they were coming back to life, and the strains of long-forgotten songs began running through his head. He took the instrument down and felt the golden coolness of it in his hands, stroking it as lovingly as if he stroked a woman's skin. He was almost afraid to put it to his lips in case the magic had gone, and for a long while he merely lay on his bed, holding it in his hands, for the simple joy of reviving a long lost love. It was truly a love he had once never thought to see again, and one that he had as good as forgotten in the darkest of days.

Jed Pascoe came upstairs while he was still musing over his good fortune in being alive at all. Max heard the heavy footsteps and he stood up hastily, to be greeted by his uncle's outstretched hands as he neared the bed.

'It's good to have you home at last, my boy. Your auntie has been fretting that much since we knew you were back in the country, until she's fair worn me out with watching out for your return. Now perhaps we can get back to a bit of normality, eh?'

If his auntie had wept with him, it was obvious that his uncle had no intention of weeping women's tears and was dealing with things in his own way. God only knew how they had dealt with Warren's death at the time, but right now, it seemed that Max was exactly what they needed.

He clasped Jed's arms in a burst of mutual affection and smiled, seemingly for the first time in weeks.

'So come on then, let's have a bit of music to make us think you're really here,' Jed went on heartily. 'We've missed the sound of that darned thing for far too long.'

Max laughed now. He actually laughed. 'Are you calling my one true love "that darned thing"? I'll have you know she's my bread and butter.'

'Oh, ah, well, that's all right until you find a true love that's flesh and blood, and will do you more good than playing in a band, boy,' Jed teased him. 'Have you tried her out yet?'

Max put the saxophone to his lips, avoiding his uncle's eyes at that moment. His flesh and blood one true love didn't belong to him and never would, and the only way he could get her image out of his mind at that moment was to try to make a bit of music, to see just how rusty he had become.

The first few notes weren't too satisfactory, and his fingers weren't as flexible as he had thought they would be. But after a few minutes he managed to create a few runs and a half-recognisable tune, and his uncle left him to it, telling him to enjoy himself and to come downstairs for supper in half an hour.

Still with more of her dad's runner beans than one person could use, Breda Hanney decided to take them to the Pascoe house to leave them with Laura. The evening was beautifully clear, the sky blue and the sun still high in the sky, and she had spent the afternoon with her gran, until the endless chatter of times past had exhausted her. Now, all she wanted was to deposit these beans, which her gran hadn't wanted either, go home and have a long bath, and then read for the rest of the evening. She was almost at the house when her heart suddenly stopped.

At first she thought it was a sound coming out of the ether. One of those weird, haunting sounds that was almost other-worldly in its purity, and then she realised it was because it was a sound she hadn't heard for a very long time. It was the sound of Max Pascoe's saxophone. No one ever played it but Max. No one else would dare to touch it.

Her heart had momentarily stopped and then it was racing so fast she thought she would faint. *He was here.* She had known he was coming home, she just hadn't known when. But he was here *now*, just a short distance away.

Later, she could no more explain her next actions than she could explain how she breathed. Her hands were so clammy she could hardly hold the bag of runner beans, and then she had dropped them, and she was running, running, running away from the Pascoe cottage, back to Barnes Lane, back to Forget-me-not Cottage, where she rushed inside and slammed the door behind her, as if it was a sanctuary.

Chapter Eleven

How long she leant against the door she couldn't have said. It may have been a minute or an hour. The next thing that registered above the beating of her heart was somebody hammering on the other side of the door and calling her name.

'Breda, let me in,' Gran Hanney said in agitation. 'What's wrong, girl? That old gasbag Mrs Norman next door to me said she saw you flying down the street as if you were on fire.'

Breda's heartbeat still felt as though it was jumping all over the place, but she moved away from the door and opened it to let her gran inside. One look at her granddaughter's white face and Gran Hanney steered her to the sofa and sat her down, holding her hands tightly.

'You look as if you've had a shock. Take a few deep breaths and then tell me what's happened. Do you need the doctor?' she added sharply.

Breda shook her head wildly. 'No, I don't need the doctor, and I'm being completely stupid,' she gasped. 'I knew this was going to happen, didn't I? I was expecting it sometime, but when I heard that sound so unexpectedly I just wanted to run and hide, and now everybody will think I'm mad!'

Gran Hanney released her hands and sat back with her arms folded across her thin chest. 'Well, I certainly will unless you tell me what you're talking about. But I can see I'm not going to get

181

anything sensible out of you just yet, so you just sit there while I make us a nice cup of tea.'

She went into the small kitchen to fill the kettle, more troubled than she let on. Surely the girl hadn't seen Warren in some kind of vision? You heard about these things all the time, especially in wartime, and even more so when there was no real evidence of death. No body to weep over, no funeral to say a proper goodbye to a loved one. Or had she heard Warren's voice coming out of the ether? She had mentioned a sound. Maybe it was the boy's laughter ... they had laughed so much together over the years... She felt a deep sorrow for the girl, realising that her torment was far from over yet.

'Gran!' She heard a thin voice say, and she went back into the other room hastily. To her relief, Breda was sitting up now, looking more shame-faced than terrified of some supernatural experience.

'What is it, my lamb?'

The words came tumbling out. 'I was going to take some beans to Mrs Pascoe, and as I got near the house I heard this sound, and it shook me so much I didn't know what to do except to turn and run.'

'Go on, love. You're not alone in thinking you can hear a loved one after they've gone, you know,' she said carefully. 'It's quite a well-known thing.'

She realised Breda was looking at her as if she was the stupid one now.

'It wasn't *Warren* I thought I heard, and I wasn't imagining things, either. It was *Max*. Max must be home, because I heard him playing his saxophone in the house, and it just knocked the stuffing out of me, Gran. I should be thrilled that he's home, safe and well – and so I am, of course, but I just turned and ran rather than face him. I don't understand myself,' she finished in bewilderment.

Gran put her arms around her. 'It was a shock to you, love, that's all. You didn't know when he'd be home and you weren't expecting it. Now you know, and you'll be just as pleased as his auntie and uncle, I'm sure.'

'Well, of course I am,' Breda mumbled. 'I just hope he didn't catch sight of me rushing away from their house like an idiot.'

It was all very well knowing that Laura and Jed would be welcoming Max home like the prodigal nephew, his wandering ways forgotten and forgiven, but it would be different for her. Max had always been a dear friend to her, but Warren had been her sweetheart and her lover, and now that he was gone, she knew there would be a barrier between herself and Max. She had been coping moderately well until now, but with Max's return, all the emotions she was trying so hard to keep under control were coming to the fore again.

She became aware that her gran had gone back to the kitchen and was returning with two cups of tea. She didn't want tea. She didn't want anything, but she took it dutifully and sipped the hot brew.

'Answer me one thing, Breda. Are you glad Max is alive?'

'Well, of course I am! What a thing to say!'

183

'So what did you expect him to do when he recovered from his war wounds? Did you think he'd stay away from the place where he grew up, or come home to his family and the people who loved him?'

Breda stared into space for a moment, trying to see beyond the words her gran was saying, and not liking what she saw.

'You think I'm being selfish, don't you?'

'No, love. I think you're just human. I think this is one more moment you have to get over before you can move forward. There were two lovely young men growing up in the Pascoe household, and you were so entwined with the pair of them as children that when one of them is no longer around, it's like losing a limb – and from what I hear, Max nearly did just that.'

'I know he did.'

Gran went on relentlessly. 'And when three young people have been such close friends, and then one of them has gone, it's going to be difficult for the other two to feel comfortable with each other for a while. That's natural as well. I daresay Max will be feeling as awkward about the first time he sees you again as you are about seeing him. Have you ever thought about that?'

'Not really,' Breda said slowly. The truth was, she had never thought about it at all. She had never thought about Max's feelings, other than knowing he would be missing Warren badly, and full of guilt that he had known nothing about his death for so many months.

'Well, drink that tea and think about it now,' Gran instructed more smartly.

Breda thought about it for a long while after her gran went home. She prayed now, that neither Max, or anyone else in the Pascoe house had seen her take fright, dropping the bag of beans and rushing home like a scared cat. There was no getting away from the fact that at some stage she and Max had to meet. They had to meet and talk about Warren, and probably weep together. They should be able to comfort one another, but for the life of her, Breda hoped it wouldn't have to be too soon.

And yet, how much more traumatic was it going to be, if every time she walked out of her cottage, she was glancing over her shoulder to see if Max was around? How much better to go straight back to the Pascoe house and break the ice while his aunt and uncle were there? It would be less embarrassing in company – and she acknowledged sadly that until now, embarrassing was a word she had never thought to use in her relationship with Max. Maybe tomorrow...

At home in his own bedroom at last, and still experimenting with his saxophone after so long, Max was unaware of the turmoil going on in Breda's mind. He longed to see her, but he was sensible enough to know things were going to be different between them now. They were both very different people from the two carefree children they had been in the past. With Warren they had been the three musketeers, all for one and one for all, and now there were only two. But tonight was for his aunt and uncle, and everything else could wait.

He was shown the original telegram and sub-sequent letters confirming what had happened to Warren. Instead of a wedding, it had come to this, tearing two families apart, and again, he felt guilty that he had known none of it at the time.

'But what about you, Max?' Jed said at last. 'You didn't have an easy time of it out there, did you? And what do the doctors say about your leg? It's healed properly, I hope?'

'I don't think I'll be dancing just yet, but it's doing well enough. I'm thankful that they saved it, even though I had no idea at the time how dangerously near I came to losing it. I must say I didn't fancy being a peg-leg standing on a street corner selling trays of matches.'

It wasn't much of a joke and he wished he hadn't said it. It was cruel to even mention those poor sods who had to do just that. Far too many spontaneous and sarcastic things came out of his mouth before he could stop them these days, but these good people didn't need to know how bitter he had become. He forced a smile.

'Listen to me. You don't need two good legs to play the sax, anyway, and the sooner I get back to earning a proper crust, the better.'

'You must give it time, my dear,' Laura said at once. 'There's no need to rush into anything. Just get used to being home again before you think about work.'

'There's some that don't consider playing in a band to be work.'

'Well, it's lovely to hear you playing again,' Laura said, determined to keep the evening as cheery as possible. 'Everyone will be glad to know

186

you're home. Perhaps we could ask Breda to join us for supper tomorrow by way of a small celebration. 1 know she'll want to see you as soon as possible.'

'Are you sure about that?'

'Why on earth shouldn't she want to see you?' Jed said. 'You, Warren and Breda were as close as clams in the old days, the best of friends.'

'And then there were two,' Max murmured beneath his breath.

But looking into the honest eyes of these folk who had known the worst pain possible in the loss of their son, and knowing how pleased they were to see him home, he knew he should keep his bitterness to himself.

'Why don't you go and see her tomorrow, Max?' Laura said encouragingly. 'She's not back at the infant school for another week or two, and she'll be glad of the company and to talk over old times with you.'

'I'll see.' He was non-committal. His heart raced every time he thought of a first meeting with the girl he had adored for as long as he could remember. But that was something else these honest folk wouldn't know about, and he never wanted them to guess how passionately he had longed to be in his cousin's shoes when he walked down the aisle with Breda Hanney. He cleared his throat. 'I think I'd like to get some fresh air in my lungs after supper. I'll take a walk down to the quay and back, just to remind myself that I'm really here.'

'I'm guessing you don't want company,' Jed said. 'Sometimes a man needs to be by himself to sort things out in his head.'

'How well you know me, Uncle,' Max said with a half-smile.

In fact, they didn't know him at all, he thought a while later, when he walked carefully down the steep hill to the quay, thankful now for the walking stick he had so despised. They didn't know what new torment he felt, knowing he was so near to Breda, and yet dreading the moment when they would come face to face and he would see the disappointment in her eyes that he wasn't Warren. He didn't know how he could bear that.

He reached the quay and leant on the wall to watch the seabirds resting on the calm swell of the sea. There was no hint here of the storms that could rage through the channel, nor of the enemy's more lethal dangers that lurked below the waves in other waters for unsuspecting ships. He shuddered at the thought, willing away the images of Warren's ship being ripped apart, and of the terrified sailors floundering for their lives in icy waters.

'Max! Hey, Max!' He turned with relief as he heard a familiar voice calling his name. He saw Hobbsy, George and Roy, his mates in the band, bearing down on him. They pumped his hand and slapped him on the back until he had to protest.

'It's good to see you back,' Hobbsy said enthusiastically. 'We've got a few dates lined up for later in the year, so we're in dire need of you, mate.'

'I'm not so sure about that. I'm pretty rusty at the moment,' he began.

Hobbsy snorted. 'Don't give us that. It's like riding a bike, isn't it, boys? Once you've mastered it, you never forget, and you're one of the best, Maxie. A bit of practise and you'll be as good as new. I bet you couldn't wait to get your hands on the old sax again, could you?'

He grinned. 'You're right there. So I'll think about it.'

'Good lad.' George slapped him on the back again. 'Come on then, we're going to the pub, so you can think about it there. The beer's on us tonight.'

It wasn't what he had intended. The Bottle and Jug would be crowded as usual on a summer evening, and he knew he'd have to face people he knew, answering questions and fending off others. But if this was a baptism by fire, he thought grimly, at least he was doing it in the company of good mates, and it would help to boost up some of the confidence that seemed to be missing from his life.

He hadn't expected to see Gilb Hanney, deep in conversation with some of the older men about the way the war was turning into a battle for air supremacy. He didn't want to talk about war or hear about it, but these folk, who had never seen a battlefield – not in this war, at least – couldn't seem to talk about anything else. But then Gilb caught sight of him and left his friends for a moment to come across to the corner where the band quartet were sitting.

'By all that's holy, it's good to see you back safe and sound, Max,' Gilb said at once. 'We thought we'd lost you for ever when we didn't get any news of you. Your aunt and uncle will be mightily relieved to have you home.'

'Thanks, Mr Hanney.'

He didn't know what else to say. The man spoke as if he was personally involved and interested in whether or not Max Pascoe came home. But of course he was. The Hanney and Pascoe families had been so intertwined it was only natural for him to speak that way, but it unnerved Max to realise that all these different folk had worried for him, while he had been so steeped in the throes of delirium he hadn't been able to think about any of them, or to care whether he lived or died.

'Have you seen Breda yet?' Gilb went on.

'Not yet. I'll see her soon,' he muttered.

'She prayed for you.' Gilb pressed Max's hand and went back to his friends.

Hobbsy chuckled. 'I reckon more than a few folk around here have got religion since this war started. I never thought to hear old man Hanney saying it though.'

'Never mind all that. What are these dates you've been talking about?' Max said, determined not to let his thoughts dwell on Breda praying for him. 'I haven't said I'll be able to join you, mind. Only that I'm thinking about it.'

But by God, by the time he went home that night, he realised how good it had been to talk with friends who didn't go on about the war all the time, except in the work they were doing to raise funds and make people happy. The regular village dances had always been a popular part of life here, and now the band was being asked to go

190

further afield in their fund-raising activities. It gave them an added incentive to do what they could for the war effort, and if it did a lot for the people's morale, it also did a lot for the three of them who hadn't been able to pick up a rifle for their various reasons.

He even found himself smiling as he remembered one of George's casual remarks as they all parted company.

'By the way, Tom Greenwood says he's bringing a rabbit round to your place in the morning, Max, as a kind of welcome home. Tell your auntie to leave a tin outside the back door and she'll find it there at first light.'

Tom Greenwood was the local poacher cum spiv who could get anything anybody wanted, and no questions asked. Even the village bobbies generally turned a blind eye to his activities. It would certainly cheer his Aunt Laura, Max thought, who had always been partial to a bit of rabbit stew.

'We'll have it tomorrow evening, so you be sure to ask Breda to come and join us like I said,' she told Max later, obviously set on the idea now.

His heart leapt. That hadn't been his plan at all. He still had no idea how he was going to approach Breda or what he was going to say to her, but now it was as good as an ultimatum, and he knew his aunt wouldn't take no for an answer. But perhaps it was better this way. He had a genuine excuse to see Breda – and it was a source of sadness in his heart to know that had never been necessary before.

'I'll have to see if I can make it up the hill,' he

191

said, as a last token effort to put aside the moment, and knowing what a blow it would be to his manhood if his gammy leg prevented the walk up to the Hanney house.

'There's no need, boy,' his uncle put in. 'She's living in the cottage at the end of Barnes Lane now. She and Warren had planned to move in there together, and she decided to go ahead anyway.'

Laura cleared her throat noisily as Max digested this news. He had been away so long. He had never been good at keeping in touch, and this only emphasised how far apart he had grown from those he loved the best. Time and distance, and memory, had erased far too much from his mind.

'I'll find it,' he said in a muffled voice. 'I think I'll go to bed now though. It's good to be home, but it's been a very long day.'

It was more than that. He couldn't sit here any longer making small talk when the emotion in the room now was starting to unnerve him. He stumped up the stairs and into his old room, closing the door firmly behind him. He was truly exhausted, but when it came to sleeping, he found it was impossible. The sounds of a seaside village should have been so familiar: the late-night revellers making their way home from The Bottle and Jug; the last of the seabirds wheeling and dipping before they went to their nests; the distant sound of waves slapping against the cliffs; the murmurs of his aunt and uncle as they prepared for bed.

Instead of it all being so relaxing and homely

Max found himself missing the camaraderie of hospital life, the backchat between the servicemen and the orderlies, even the moans and groans and occasional screams of those enduring unmentionable suffering. That had been his life for so many months now that this was the part that seemed like being in an alien country. For one irrational moment he even found himself longing for the anonymous stab of a medic's needle in his arm, dulling his senses so that he didn't have to think of anything at all.

Eventually sleep must have come, because the next thing he heard was the raucous mixture of the early morning sounds of cockerels and seagulls, and his Aunt Laura knocking on his door and bringing him a cup of tea. Such a thing was almost unheard of in this practical household.

'I don't expect this treatment, Auntie,' he said, struggling to sit up.

'Don't worry, you won't get it for long,' she said smartly. 'Just let me pamper you for a few days, Max, so I can really believe I've got you home again.'

He could see how important this was to her, and the flash of annoyance at being treated like an invalid faded.

'You should see the fine rabbit Tom Greenwood's left us,' she went on briskly, as if determined not to show too much emotion that one of her boys was safely home. 'We'll have a stew to last several days, so you get up when you feel ready, and I'll have some breakfast waiting for you. And later on, you make sure you talk Breda into joining us this evening,' she repeated like a mantra.

Now he knew why he was so reluctant to start the day, and it was ridiculous. Breda had been in his thoughts for so long, and in his heart for ever, and it was ludicrous that he was so afraid to face her. He had faced far worse, he thought grimly. If it wasn't too far-fetched to say so, he knew damn well he had looked death in the face on more than one occasion. But that was different. That wasn't the girl of his dreams, who would look at him with regret she couldn't quite hide because he wasn't Warren. She had always worn her heart on her sleeve, he thought savagely, but this was one time he wouldn't want her to. But he knew he had no choice, and the sooner he got it over with the better.

The morning was glorious, as blue and golden as only a day in Cornwall could be. It was a glorious Indian Summer day, with not even the hint of a breeze to ruffle the trees or stop the sun scorching down on the glittering sea. The village children were revelling in these last days of freedom before the start of the new term, and by mid-morning their favourite teacher was taking the opportunity to dead-head the roses in her little front garden. The heady scent was almost overpowering, and she tried not to remember that roses like these would have formed her wedding bouquet a few short months ago.

Breda bent to her task, the weak tears blurring her eyes for a moment until she blinked them angrily away. She thanked the Lord she had

194

remembered to wear a hat, because the heat of the sun was already making her neck start to prickle, and with her fair skin she knew it wouldn't be wise for her to stay outside for much longer. She heard the click of the latch on the gate and swallowed the remaining tears, not really wanting company, but unable to avoid it now.

She glanced up, half-expecting her gran, and then she almost fainted. Warren and Max were so alike that except to those who knew them well, they could almost have been taken for twins. Now, against the glare of the sun, for that one staggering moment she couldn't even be sure...

She let out a cry as the point of the secateurs in her hand stabbed her finger, and she felt the hot spurt of blood as she swayed. Instantly, the man was at her side, throwing down his walking stick, holding her up, holding her tight, urging her to come inside the cottage while he ran her finger under some cold water to cleanse the small wound. She moved numbly, as if in a dream, leaning against the man until they got inside the cottage and into the tiny kitchen. He turned on the tap and the shock of the cold water on her finger made her gasp.

'Sorry,' said Max abruptly.

It had taken him ages to walk through the village, with people stopping him every few minutes to welcome him home and wanting to know how he was, until he had hardly been able to bear their solicitude a minute longer. It had been a relief to see Forget-me-not Cottage ahead. And then to see her in the garden, so natural and so beautiful, had all but taken his breath away.

195

She kept her head bent, her mouth working uncontrollably.

'I shouldn't have startled you like that. I should have let you know I was home,' he went on roughly.

Unbelievably, he felt that they were two strangers now, when they had once been so close. As long as Warren had been part of their youthful trio, they had been close, with every right to be. But not any more. He had never realised it more now that he held her slim body in his arms and felt it tremble. Because of course she didn't want him. She had never wanted him, and she never would.

'I knew you were home,' she said in a muffled voice. 'I heard you playing your sax when I was on my way home from mum's last night.'

'Trying to play it, you mean.'

She turned and looked at him then. Really looked at him, at Max, not the echo of Warren that she still loved so much. And she managed a small smile as the colour began to come back into her cheeks.

'You'll play it again. You can't keep a good sax player down for long. And in case I forget to say it, I'm *so* glad to see you home, Max, I really am.'

He turned off the cold water tap quickly, realising they were standing here like idiots with her finger starting to shrivel.

'You need a sticking plaster over that cut,' he said practically. 'Knowing you, you'll have a first-aid box somewhere.'

'On the shelf,' she murmured.

It was such a homely, loving thing to do, to have

him dry her finger and put a sticking plaster over the cut. It was the sort of thing Warren would have done, kissing the finger before he covered it. She was thankful Max did nothing of the sort. Then she shivered as she saw the spots of blood on his shirt where she had leant against him.

'You'd better let me dab that for you,' she said, whitening again.

'I'll do that. You sit down a minute, and then we'll talk,' he ordered.

She did as she was told. He could have no idea why the sight of that small mark had upset her so much. It recalled the memory of the blood-stained sheet in the room upstairs when she and Warren had made love. Even more it revived the memory of the bloodstains on her wedding dress. Bad omens ... and now this.

She took some deep breaths and told herself not to be so stupid. She was a modern, rational schoolteacher, and she couldn't, and she *wouldn't*, let her life be ruled by omens and superstitions.

Max came back to her and sat on an opposite chair.

'All done,' he said, more cheerfully than he felt.

She looked so pale and wan and so unlike the old Breda he knew. He longed desperately to gather her up in his arms and tell her he would love her for ever and wipe all the sadness away, but he knew he could never do that. She looked up at him, her heart in her eyes, and said the first inane thing that came into her head.

'Your aunt and uncle have been very kind to me, Max, ever since – well, ever since,' she said mechanically.

Her face crumpled, and he couldn't bear it any longer. In an instant he was on the sofa beside her, holding both her hands tightly, and barely noticing her small wince as he squeezed her poor finger.

'I loved him too, Breda. God knows I loved him too. He was so much more than my cousin. He was like my brother. You know that,' he said hoarsely, and the next moment they were sobbing in each other's arms as if they would never let one another go.

Chapter Twelve

The door burst open and it was as though two small whirlwinds had arrived.

'Some old bloke's thrown his walking stick in your garden,' Jenna shrieked.

Then she gasped as the two people on the sofa sprang apart as though they had been stung.

'What are you doing with that man?' her sister shouted in a fright.

Max turned around then and as the two girls saw him properly, they both gasped and clung to one another.

'What are you doing here?' Breda said crossly, trying to recover herself as quickly as she could. 'Aren't you still in quarantine? And you know who this is, you idiots. It's Max.'

'The doctor says we're out of quarantine now, and Mum says we're getting on her nerves so we thought we'd come and visit you,' Esme said, her wide-eyed gaze still on the stranger she hardly recognised.

Breda knew it was understandable. He had been away for two years on his adventures, if that was what you called them. Despite his illnesses he was still deeply tanned from the hot desert sun, but he'd lost a lot of weight. He could hardly expect two little girls, who had still been children when he went away, to remember him as fondly as they did his cousin.

He cleared his throat. 'You've grown,' he said inanely. 'Which one of you is the oldest?'

It was enough to make Esme bristle. 'Me, of course. I'm twelve now and Jenna's eleven.'

Jenna was still playing with the walking stick and looking at the two older people as if still trying to make up her mind about Max. Then he smiled, and as he did so, Breda felt her heart turn over. In that split second, it wasn't Max's smile. It was Warren's ... and she couldn't bear it. She stood up.

'Well, since you're here, you can do something useful and show Max around the cottage and I'll get us all some lemonade. And put that stick down, Jenna. It doesn't belong to some old bloke. It belongs to Max.'

If she kept saying his name, it might reassure her that it was really him, and not some ghostly apparition who looked like Warren but wasn't and never could be Warren. She felt guilty at even thinking that way, but she admitted that the shock of seeing him in the garden so un-expectedly had all but floored her.

'Come on then, girls. Give me the guided tour,' he said cheerfully, as if he hadn't a care in the world. And for some reason that annoyed Breda too.

It was hardly going to take long to show him around the cottage, but it would give her a few minutes to recover herself a bit more. She went into the kitchen as she heard the girls starting to chatter now, asking him about the war and about his wound and if it had hurt a lot, and what it was like to live in a different country. She heard them

200

clatter up the stairs, hearing the girls' light footsteps and Max's heavier ones as he leant on his walking stick now.

She heard the creak of the floorboards in her bedroom, the one she had expected to share with Warren, and where they had anticipated their marriage that one beautiful, glorious time.

It was a room where Max would never have been included, intruding on their privacy. She imagined him looking around the small room now, with its candlewick bedspread on the bed and her dressing gown sprawled across it, her nightdress neatly folded on the pillow, her slippers on the floor. He would be seeing her dressing table with her brushes and combs and jewellery box. Private, personal things, that weren't for a stranger's eyes... She couldn't get the wretched word out of her head, even though Max had never been a stranger and never could be.

She poured four glasses of lemonade with trembling hands and called out to them to hurry up and come downstairs.

By the time they did so she could see that Max had already charmed his way into her sisters' senses. They were totally enthralled by him, hanging on to his every word and excited by his tales of what the desert was like and how the people dressed in Egypt, the food they ate and the jobs they had. For heaven's sake, Breda found herself thinking irritably, there was a war on! It hadn't been any joyride, but from the glow in the girls' eyes now, at any minute they'd be wanting to go off and be wanderlusts themselves!

'Max is going to write about his adventures,'

Esme announced.

'Oh yes,' Breda murmured cynically, having never heard an inclination to do any such thing in the past. But that was the past, of course, and he was a different person now. She was beginning to see that. He had sobered considerably, and at the same instant, she hoped he hadn't sobered too much. It would be cruel if the old loving, devil-may-care young man had been lost for ever because of his experiences.

'Don't you think I could, schoolteacher?' he challenged her.

She forced a short laugh.

'Knowing you, I think you could do anything you set your heart on.'

'Well, that's the first sensible thing you've said to me since I got here. Which reminds me. In case I forget, I'm to invite you to supper tonight, Aunt Laura's got a rabbit and we're having stew. You'll come, won't you?'

She had the feeling he half expected her to refuse. But why on earth should she? It wouldn't be the first time she had sat around the Pascoe table for a meal. Four people enjoying one another's company, except that the fourth person had always been Warren in recent times, not Max. She swallowed and unconsciously lifted her chin, pushing the memories away.

'Of course I'll come.'

'Good girl,' Max said softly.

Oh, he understood her so well. If she wasn't wearing her feelings on her face, he could always read her mind. She wasn't sure that she cared to remember it. But she was starting to remember so many things now, not least the fact that she had always loved him. Not in the way she loved Warren, of course, but as a dear and loving friend, and she was sure he needed all his friends now until he was completely recovered. She put out her hand and squeezed his arm as they sat down to drink their lemonade.

'I'm truly glad to see you home, Max,' she said.

He felt a bit like the Pied Piper when he left the cottage, with two small girls strutting along beside him as they walked through the village. He was already their hero, but at least their endless chatter stopped him thinking too much. It didn't stop his thoughts completely, though. If he had ever thought that to see Breda again would in some way exorcise his feelings about her, he now knew it would never happen. If anything, seeing her so vulnerable, still with that lost look in her eyes because of Warren, had increased his feelings a hundredfold. And it would be something that had to be subdued, he told himself grimly.

'Don't you two have something to do?' he finally asked the girls when their chatter was starting to pall.

Esme frowned. 'We'd rather stay with you. What are you doing today?'

What indeed? What did he have to do today, or any other day? The emptiness of his life suddenly hit him like a stone in the gut.

'Lord knows. I might start on my memoirs,' he said extravagantly, for want of something to say.

Jenna giggled. 'What are they? Is it something wicked?'

'No. It means writing up my memories of what happened, but I'm not sure I'm ready for it yet. I'm going down to the quay to take a look around, so I'll see you two some other time. You can tell your mother you've seen me and that I'm all right.'

He hoped that would be enough to send them off. For a minute he thought they weren't going to get the message, but, thankfully, they skipped off in the opposite direction after a minute or two. They were nice enough kids, but he wasn't in the mood for a day of juvenile company. He wasn't in the mood for anything much. People were kind, but it dawned on him that there were varying types of sympathy being directed at him by people in the village that he had known for years. There were those who welcomed him back, avoiding any mention of Warren and what had happened to his cousin. There were others who felt they had to say something, unconsciously trying to probe his mind over his own feelings, and he'd had enough of that from the professionals who had tried to help him come to terms with all that had happened in the past few months.

Eventually, he walked home, to find his aunt already doing things with the rabbit that he didn't particularly want to know about. He told her Breda would be joining them that evening, and then he went upstairs to his bedroom, to pick up his saxophone, his best and trusted friend. He ran his fingers over the coldness of it, reviving memories of old and familiar tunes, and lost himself in the music.

Breda didn't deny that she was unsettled. She had known Max was home and she knew she would have to meet him sometime, and for the life of her she didn't know why she had been so reluctant about it. Well, of *course* she did, she reminded herself honestly. It was because they were the remaining two of a constant threesome, and the difference would be even more emphasised now. But wouldn't it always have been like that if Warren had come home and they had been married as they had planned? Wouldn't Max always have been shut out from the inner circle of their marriage? Even as the pretentious thought sped through her mind, Breda shook her head impatiently. She was a down-to-earth Cornish girl, not a pretentious person, and she hated people who used such phrases. It just seemed the most apt one she could think of at that moment.

Impulsively, she abandoned anything else she was going to do that day and walked down to Gran Hanney's house. Gran was the only person she felt able to talk to in any way that was bordering on the emotional. But she didn't want to get emotional; she just needed someone to talk to.

Gran Hanney was making potato and onion soup for her midday meal. The tantalising smell permeated her whole cottage, making Breda's mouth water. 'Good. I'm glad you've come,' the old lady said matter-of-factly. 'I always make too much soup, and by tomorrow I've usually changed my mind about eating the rest of it. It's wicked to waste food nowadays, so you can share it with me.'

'I hadn't really come for that,' Breda said weakly.

'It makes no never mind why you've come. You know I'm always glad to see you, my lamb, so sit yourself down while I spoon out the soup and then you can tell me what's bothering you.'

'How do you know something's bothering me?'

'Isn't it?'

Breda sighed. Why did she think she could come here and not have her innermost secrets probed? Not that she had any innermost secrets ... well, not too many. And none that were for sharing.

'I suppose it's about Max,' Gran went on. 'I thought I saw him from my window earlier this morning. He don't look too good, so I hope you were kind to him.'

'What a thing to say. Of course I was kind to him. Why wouldn't I be?'

Gran shrugged. 'No reason, I daresay. So what did he have to say to you?'

'Nothing very much, really. I've been invited to the Pascoes for supper tonight, and I don't really want to go.'

There. She had said it. It had hardly been more than a thought at the back of her mind, but now it was out in the open.

Gran banged the saucepan down on the draining-board, wincing as a small splattering of hot soup caught her hand. Her voice was crosser than she intended because of it.

'You can't shut your eyes for ever, Breda. You always knew this day would come, and you should remember the good times you, Warren and Max always had together, instead of grieving for ever for the things that will never be the same again. We know they won't, and you've had a terrible time of it lately, but be glad for the boy who's come home.'

'I am,' Breda mumbled, ashamed of her own feelings and startled by the way her gran seemed to be censuring her. She had always been Breda's champion, and as she saw the way her gran sucked at her finger, she held up her own finger in a comic gesture.

'We're a matching pair now. Shall I put a plaster on it for you?'

Gran scoffed at such pampering. 'It's not necessary. So are you going to the Pascoes for supper tonight?'

'Of course I am. I never said I wasn't, did I?'

'That's my girl,' Gran said in a softer voice. 'So let's have our soup before it gets cold. Get the dishes down, there's a love.'

It would more likely burn the roofs of their mouths, Breda thought grimly, since Gran always liked to boil the living daylights out of her vegetables. But with a good amount of blowing and wafting, the taste was marvellous, and she felt better by the time she had finished the small repast.

She told herself later what an idiot she was to be apprehensive over having supper with Max and his aunt and uncle that evening. It would be an ice-breaker and a celebration all in one, and, as always, Gran had said the right thing. Of course she was glad for the boy who had come home, and she was just as eager as anyone else to hear about his experiences.

Her mother called to see her that afternoon, bringing her an egg from one of her dad's chickens. Breda didn't need to tell her that Max was home. By now, the whole village would be aware of it.

'The girls are full of their new hero,' Agnes announced. 'He had plenty of things to tell them about Egypt and the way it still resembled biblical times in places. He told them to look at the pictures in their bibles to see the way the people dressed and worked with their ploughs and oxen, and it was just the same now.'

'Did he really say all that? It was more than he said here. I daresay he was glad to be rid of them by the time he managed to shake them off.'

'Perhaps,' Agnes said. 'They seemed quite taken with him, anyway. And how about you, Breda? Was it an ordeal for you to see him?'

She wanted to say no, of course it wasn't. But she had been brought up to speak the truth, and she gave a soft sigh before she replied.

'It was, if you must know. Partly because I wasn't expecting to see him so soon. I was gardening when I suddenly heard someone open the gate, and I looked up and for a minute I thought – well, never mind what I thought. Then I pricked my blessed finger, which didn't help matters, and I went a bit doo-lally for a minute.'

'You poor thing,' Agnes said sympathetically, seeing far more than the jerky words actually told her. 'I hope you washed it thoroughly before you put that sticking plaster on it. You don't want any garden germs to get in it.'

'I did, and it's fine,' Breda said, as the image of Max Pascoe holding her finger beneath the cold water tap entered her mind. 'It was only a little scratch but it hurt at the time.'

'Anyway, thank you for my egg. I'll keep it until tomorrow, as I'm having supper with the Pascoes this evening,' she repeated yet again.

'Good. And you're to come and have your Sunday tea with us, now that the girls are no longer infectious. It won't be long now before the school term begins, and you'll be too busy for anything as usual.'

If anything, Breda was longing for it to begin again. The holiday weeks of inactivity had lingered far too long, and she longed for the rough and tumble of school life that kept her heart and mind occupied. She longed for the innocence of the children in her class, with their artless questions and ready acceptance of whatever she told them.

But before any of that happened, there was this evening to get through. And as she walked through the village later, with the day still mellow and warm in the lowering rays of the sun, she lifted her chin high and was determined not to let anyone guess how her heart was beginning to pound. For pity's sake, she had been to this house so many times before ... but never quite like this.

Just as it had been at Gran Hanney's earlier, the aromatic smells of cooking assaulted her nostrils as soon as she entered the house. She followed the smell to the kitchen where Laura Pascoe was enveloped in a large overall as she stirred the

209

rabbit stew. Almost at once, Breda heard the sound of Max's saxophone from upstairs, and his auntie gave Breda a welcoming smile.

'That's when I really know Max is home,' she said. 'He's a bit rusty, but it's all coming back, and it's a real treat to hear him playing again. Will you help lay the table, dear? Jed's still out in the backyard having a last smoke before supper. So we'll call him inside once it's ready.'

It was all so homely, and Breda was relieved that they didn't have to stand on ceremony. She was being treated like one of the family, the way she had always been, being asked to help, and expected to do so.

Max came downstairs, and any awkwardness between them was overcome by Jed coming back indoors at the same time and with Laura tut-tutting at the smell of his cigarette smoke in the kitchen. Nothing much changed, thought Breda – only the most important thing of all. But since this was Max's homecoming, she was determined not to be the one to put a damper on the evening.

Sitting around the table and eating a meal to-gether was always a good thing, anyway. And Max made them laugh by retelling them how Jenna and Esme had hung on his every word about Egypt.

'I'm sure they think it's a glamorous place,' he remarked dryly. 'But I soon put them right about that.'

'Yes, but you always thought so in the past, Max,' Jed said. 'There was a time when you were sure you were going to discover some ancient tomb and make your fortune, I seem to remember.'

'That was before there was a war on, and

besides, Howard Carter got there before me, didn't he? But the girls were more interested in the biblical aspect of the landscape – the bits the Germans hadn't got at, that is.'

As she saw the frown on his forehead at his last words, Breda spoke quickly.

'I'm surprised Jenna and Esme were so interested, but I think the children in my class would be even more so. We have regular Bible classes at school, so how would you feel about coming along one day and telling the children about it, the way you told my sisters? It would make it all seem more real to them if they knew you'd been to some of the places mentioned in the Bible.'

He didn't look impressed by the idea. 'I'd hardly call it that. I just said the clothing and the occupational methods of the people living in the desert seemed to have changed very little in all these years. Besides, I'm no schoolteacher.'

'You don't have to be. You just have to tell them what you've seen, that's all. You're not scared of a group of five-year-olds, are you, Max?'

She challenged him with her voice and her eyes, and she heard Jed chuckle.

'She's got you there, boy. You're not going to admit to it, are you? If you are, you're no nephew of mine!'

'Of course I'm not scared of a group of kids. I just wonder how boring it would be for them, that's all.'

'Well, I think they'd love to have a real live hero coming to talk to them. But it's up to you. Just think about it.'

'I think we should get on with eating our stew before it gets cold,' Laura put in, since the conversation was getting a little too tense for her liking.

Breda could have bitten out her tongue at calling Max a real live hero. Of course that was what he was to all of them, but it drew too much attention to the fact that their other hero was missing from the table.

'I'm planning to get back into some band practice very soon,' Max went on a little later. 'At Gough's Farm where George works, they've got a large empty barn where they do their practice now, with only the cows to worry about. Oh, and the Land Girls. George says they've got three of them working there, which is an added reason for practising there rather than the village hall,' he finished with a grin.

At Jed Pascoe's teasing, and Laura's slightly sniffy look at the mention of the Land Girls, Breda couldn't have said why his words made her feel slightly discomfited. Had she expected Max to come home and be a permanent invalid? Or stay around the house all day being waited on by his aunt? He was far too proud a man for that. It would never have been Max's style, and she was very sure that as soon as he was able, he would throw away the walking stick.

'They'll be glad to have you back in the band,' Laura was saying. 'But don't try to do too much too soon, Max. Give yourself time to get used to being home.'

'I've got plenty of time for that now, haven't I?' he said tightly. 'The army doesn't want me any

212

more, and I'm not much use for anything else.'

'What about this writing you mentioned to the girls?' Breda found herself saying in the small silence that followed. 'Your memoirs, I think they said you called it.'

'What's this?' his uncle said. 'It sounds a bit of a namby-pamby job for a chap, if I may say so.'

Max snorted, glaring at Breda as he did so. 'It was only a passing thought. Don't worry, I'm not going to turn into Oscar Wilde. A better idea would be for me to send in a couple of pieces for the local paper, just to let folk know what it was really like over there. But I'm no writer, as you know from my lack of letter-writing, and of course I'd need some help.'

He was the one challenging Breda now, and she felt her face flush.

'What do you say, schoolteacher?' he went on relentlessly. 'If I do what you want and sit in with a bunch of five-year-olds to tell them about Egypt, will you do what I want, and give me some after-school help with a bit of writing?'

She could hardly say no, not with his aunt and uncle looking at her and silently encouraging her to agree to this. To be the good friend she had always been to Max. Well, she had always intended to be that. She just hadn't expected to be entangled in his life almost as soon as he returned home.

'All right,' she said at last. 'Providing this isn't a five-minute wonder, and also that you can tear yourself away from the lure of the Land Girls on Gough's Farm long enough to take it seriously.'

He laughed, his eyes momentarily sparkling in

the way she remembered, and which she realised had been sadly lacking in his expression so far. There had been a deadness in them, which was almost certainly due to his own terrible experiences, and then the shock of learning about Warren.

'I shan't be going up there for the Land Girls, Breda, just for band practice.'

'If you believe that you'll believe anything,' they all heard Laura say under her breath as she took the dirty plates out to the kitchen and prepared to bring in the apple pie and jug of condensed milk.

When the meal was over and the women attended to the washing up, the men sat and talked more soberly about the war. It wasn't looking good, and it would be a fool who thought that it was. The northwest coast of Cornwall was more isolated than many other cities and towns, and escaped the worst of the bombardments that hit the vulnerable docks of Bristol and Portsmouth, and the capital itself. Rumours had it that London was a shell, with so many casualties it made you wonder if the nation could ever recover.

'Just listen to them,' Laura said to Breda, as the murmur of voices rose and fell. 'Putting the world to rights between them, the way men always do when they get together.'

Then she spoke more softly, her hands stilled for moment over the soap suds in the washing-up bowl.

'It's so good to have him home, Breda. It's good for me to have him to fuss over, whether he wants it or not, and it's good for Jed to have one of his

214

boys safely home and to know he's going to stay. He'll never take Warren's place, but he always had his own place here with us, so I hope you understand what I mean.'

'Of course I do,' Breda mumbled, not wanting to hear any of this, and wishing at that moment that she could simply disappear.

'I'll walk you home,' Max said a couple of hours later.

'Oh, there's no need. You stay here and carry on jawing with your uncle.'

Breda spoke almost in a panic. By now she just wanted to get out of there. During the meal and immediately afterwards while they had all been occupied, it had been fine. But the intimacy of the four of them sitting and chatting, and inevitably sharing memories about Warren, was becoming too much to bear. She had had all these months to get used to the fact that he was never coming home, and that she was never going to be his wife, and tonight had brought all the raw and painful emotions rushing back to the surface. She desperately needed to be alone.

'What kind of a friend do you take me for, if I can't escort a pretty girl home? It's getting dark, and you don't want to fall down and break a leg in the blackout. Besides, I need to get in some walking practise, so don't deny me that small pleasure. Or are you ashamed to be seen walking with a chap with a gammy leg?'

'Of course not,' Breda said crossly. 'Who's going to see us in the blackout anyway? You just mind you don't trip up and damage the other one.'

She got ready to leave and she thanked the Pascoes for a nice evening, and was urged to come again whenever she liked. And then they were stepping out together, the girl and the man, and it was common sense for him to tuck her hand in the crook of his arm as they made their way towards Forget-me-not Cottage.

'I'm not sure who's holding up who now,' Breda said, trying to make a joke of it as she stumbled slightly on the cobbles in the lane and was pressed even closer to Max's side.

'Well, you know you can always rely on me, Breda, the way you always could. I'd like to think nothing's changed between us.'

She nodded, even though they both knew there was a change that could never be reversed. They were two instead of three – and it was the wrong two.

'Here we are,' she said with relief. 'Be careful going home, Max, and I'll see you again soon.'

'You're not going to ask me in then?'

'No, I'm not.' She forced a laugh. 'You've seen enough of me for one night, and you must be as tired as I am.'

He waited until she opened her front door and waved to him. As he left, she was just beginning to realise what a strain the evening had been, but she was suddenly too weary to think about anything any more, and she went straight upstairs to bed.

Chapter Thirteen

Breda told herself a hundred times that there was no reason why she should feel awkward with Max. In the past they had been as close as brother and sister, and it was logical to think that their closeness could be even more special now, in comforting each other after Warren's death. They shared a mutual grief as well as a past. There was no reason why she should feel uneasy at the thought of him coming to the cottage for her to help him with his proposed writing for the local newspaper – or the feeling that he could do it very well on his own without any help from her. She had seen the challenge in his eyes when he offered her a tit-for-tat arrangement for talking to her schoolchildren, though. It was so typically Max.

She called on Gran Hanney a couple of days later to check on her, as she often did, and as usual, Gran had her own opinion on it all.

'Don't you think he needs to be with the people who mean the most to him? He'll be feeling lost without Warren, and apart from his family you're the next best thing. Like most young men, I daresay he thought that when this war was over everything would go back to the way it was before. You can't blame him for wanting to make things feel as near to normal as he can for himself. He'll feel safe with you, Breda.'

'I suppose you're right,' Breda said slowly. 'I never thought of Max as wanting to cling on to something safe. He was always the adventurous one. He went travelling on his own even before the war, though I imagine his reckless days are over for now.'

She wasn't too sure she liked to think of herself as something safe for Max to cling on to. It sounded dull and stuffy, and she was anything but that. At least, she hoped she was.

'Well, you've just said it, haven't you?' Gran Hanney went on. 'I shouldn't worry too much about Max. He'll be busy thinking about the band soon, from what I've been hearing from young George's mother, and he won't have so much time to bother you then.'

'I didn't say he bothered me.'

She didn't really know why she wasn't keen on the idea of helping Max with his project. It was wonderful that he had something definite in mind to do, instead of wallowing in his own misfortune, and feeling less of a man than he used to. Perhaps it was the thought of the two of them in her cottage together, poring over his words and trying to get them in the best order they could. Or perhaps it was because it would open her eyes to all that he had been through during those terrible times in the desert and make her feel sorry for him all over again. Perhaps it was going to be all too intimate for comfort.

She got up from her gran's armchair. She had only come for a chat and to see that Gran was all right, and it had turned into more of a soul-searching exercise than she had intended.

'I'd better go, Gran. I'm going to give the cottage a special clean-through before term starts next week.'

'You're a good girl, Breda, and I know that young man will appreciate all that you're doing for him. Be gentle with him.'

Breda laughed out loud at that. It was an odd thing to say, but just what she might expect from her gran, and as she walked home she thought she knew what she meant. Max was still vulnerable, no matter how much he tried to put on his old act of bravado. He had come through the kind of hell she couldn't imagine, and, on top of that, he had had to face the shock of knowing his cousin had drowned at sea. It must have been dreadful, expecting to come home and find Warren and Breda married, and then finding out the truth.

She tried to put it all out of her mind for the moment as she neared Forget-me-not Cottage. It looked really lovely in late summer, with the full-blooming roses still at their best and the honeysuckle winding around the door frame, filling the air with fragrance. Warren would have loved it here, and he would have loved what she had done to it in turning it into a home. Despite the poignancy of her decision to come here on her own she knew she had done the right thing in continuing their dream, and not remaining at home with her parents. She swallowed the thickness in her throat and went indoors, trying not to let the tears start at the thought of the memories they would have made as they grew old here together.

She couldn't change things, and the only thing to do was to move forward and get on with her life as best she could. She wasn't the only girl in the village to have lost a sweetheart because of the war. There were so many others, not just here in Penbole, but all over Cornwall and the entire country. Wives and mothers lost husbands and sons. Every day there were notices in newspapers, giving lists of names of the dead and wounded and those missing in action, and they were far more than just names to the people who knew and loved them.

'Come on,' she said out loud through gritted teeth. 'Is this how Warren would want you to behave? He'd have told you to get on with it, girl.'

She smiled faintly, knowing it was true. He had never believed in wasting time and energy over things that couldn't be changed. She took a few deep breaths, put on her overall and went to the cupboard to get out dusters and brushes and a tin of lavender furniture polish, then went upstairs to tackle the bedrooms in order to make them spick and span before the new school term started.

Max had begun making plans. He had never been a man to sit on his backside and let the world pass him by. He was fully aware that his auntie would mollycoddle him for a few weeks yet, and probably even longer, but it wasn't his way to be idle and never had been. There had been enough of that in his enforced and endless weeks in hospital. He had already discovered he could ride his old bike again without too much

220

trouble. It had made his leg ache badly at first, using muscles that had been wasted for too long, but he knew the exercise was what he needed, so he had persevered grimly.

The school term had resumed by the time he turned up at one of the fields at Gough's Farm, and the village was returning to normal activities after the summer holidays. He was met at the field by cheers from his pal George and Farmer Gough, and by the stares of three girls he didn't know, clad in the green jumpers and brown slacks of the Land Girls. They also wore the regulation slouch brown hats to keep off the sun, and were leaning on their pitchforks as they helped to get in the hay.

For a moment the green and sweetly smelling pastoral scene took his breath away. It was in such stark contrast to the scorched Egyptian desert that to foreign eyes was either being farmed in pseudo-biblical ways, as he'd told Breda's sisters, or obscenely running red with the blood of the soldiers of many nations.

'Hey, Max! I knew you couldn't stay away for long!' George called out, and Farmer Gough strode forward to shake his hand enthusiastically.

'It's good to see you back, boy. It's about time we all took a break, so come into the farmhouse and my old woman will make us a drink. Tools down, girls,' he instructed, and the Land Girls complied at once, whispering together at the sight of the good-looking young man who had turned up out of nowhere.

He didn't miss their glances, nor the way their long hair bounced on their shoulders beneath the unflattering slouch hats. He'd seen enough nurses recently, with their hair bundled up inside their caps, for him to appreciate the comparative freedom and freshness these girls displayed.

Riding his bike had meant he'd had to dispense with the walking stick, but he felt stiff and awkward after the ride, and he tried not to limp too noticeably as he followed them all into the cool farmhouse. Mrs Gough exclaimed with pleasure the moment she saw him, and then embarrassed him by flinging her arms around him and pressing him against her ample bosom.

'Well, if you're not a sight for sore eyes, Max Pascoe, my love, and looking as roguish as ever, despite the need for a bit more flesh on those bones. Sit you down and let's take a good look at you.'

Her flattery made the Land Girls giggle, and he was fully aware that they were sizing him up as well. It was good for his morale, even though he wasn't interested; there was only one girl in his heart. But he wasn't a monk either. He grinned back at them, and George chuckled.

'So when are you coming back to us for band practice? We might have a go on Saturday night if you're interested. The girls here can be our audience, and I daresay Mrs Gough might have a look in if we get too loud for comfort.'

The farmer's wife laughed. 'You know I enjoy hearing you boys play.'

'I might, but I'm still practising in private,' Max said dubiously. 'I'm a bit too rusty for facing an audience.'

'Rubbish. The day Max Pascoe don't want to

show off his skills is the day we throw in the towel,' his pal scoffed. 'Why don't you see if Breda wants to come up here too? She and Warren used to enjoy our practices.'

In the small silence that followed, the three Land Girls continued to whisper among themselves and George's face went even ruddier than usual.

'I'm sorry, Max, I wasn't thinking.'

'Don't be daft. It would be a poor show if we couldn't mention his name any more. If we did that, it would be as though he never existed.' His voice was jerky all the same. 'I don't think Breda would want to come though.'

'You'll never know if you don't ask her,' Mrs Gough said soothingly. 'Besides, she might like to meet our three city girls here. She wouldn't be sitting there on her own like a spare part.'

'I'll see,' Max said, knowing he would do no such thing.

'Where have you been to get that tan?' one of the girls asked him. He didn't recognise her accent. It was quick and pert, like her, he registered.

'Egypt.' He didn't want to get into conversation. He didn't want questions about why he'd been there and what had happened to him, especially from strangers. He drank his glass of cider quickly and looked directly at George.

'I don't want to stop you from working, so why don't you show me where this barn is where you practise nowadays?'

He stood up, trying not to sway as his bad leg threatened to betray its weakness. But too much small talk was beyond him today – and this from someone who had always had more than his fair share of the gift of the gab, according to his cousin Warren.

'Come on then, mate,' George said, seeing more than Max let on. 'We'll only be practising up here a few more times, anyway. Once the nights get dark it's not worth coming all this way and back again in the blackout, even though Roy borrows his old man's van to bring us and the equipment up here. So it'll be back to the village hall again soon.'

Max couldn't say that the thought alarmed him. It had been more of an effort than he'd expected to ride all this way, especially on the steep hill up through the village to the moors and farmland. At least they'd be transported in Roy's dad's van on Saturday, hoping his relief didn't show.

George slung an arm around Max's shoulder in a friendly gesture, and then dropped it as the Land Girls giggled again.

'Silly little tarts,' he commented once they were outside and walking towards one of the outer barns. 'They're all right for a bit of a laugh, but you wouldn't want to take one home to Mother, if you know what I mean. And they think we're all hayseeds down here.'

Max grinned. 'And that wouldn't do much for your image, would it?'

'It was easy to see they took a bit of a shine to you. It's the glamour of the wounded hero,' he said without malice. 'They quite enjoy hearing us play though, and they usually get up and do a bit of a dance. If you want to make them really jealous, do what I said and ask Breda. She always used to enjoy our sessions.'

'I don't think so. Forget it, George.'

By the time he cycled away from the farm, his interest in the Saturday evening practice session was quickening. It revived his own need to be doing something he loved as soon as he was able, and even if he couldn't walk the way he used to he knew there was nothing wrong with his ability to make music.

It was too good a day to go back home yet, and after the brief respite at the farm he found himself cycling along the edge of the moors and on to the coastal path overlooking the village. It was incredibly peaceful up here, away from everything, with only the whispering sounds of the bracken and gorse to disturb the air. Far below the cliffs the sea glittered in the sunlight, and soaring seabirds circled and dived. He felt his heart soaring with them as a renewed sense of belonging filled him. The fact that a war was raging throughout so many areas of the world could easily be forgotten in the tranquillity of such a scene, if only for a little while. Exploring the desert sands of far distant places had been his dream for so long, but after all, home was where a man needed to come back to. And this was home.

Ahead of him he saw a small group of people coming his way, and for a moment he felt a small resentment that this beautiful place was no longer exclusive to him. He didn't want to share it, and he especially didn't want to have to pass the time of day with strangers. And then his heart jumped.

Breda Hanney and a small group of a dozen or so infants were picking wild flowers and heading ever nearer to him. Even in his startled realisation that it was her, his mind registered that he had never seen anything so lovely as the sight of her in her pale blue floral dress, surrounded by those eager and chattering children. Her hair had come loose from its pins and was falling about her face, and until she caught sight of him she had looked as young and carefree as her small charges – and nothing like the desolate and ravaged girl she must have been at losing her sweetheart on the eve of their wedding.

'Good-morning, Max,' she greeted him once they came close. 'Children, say good-morning to Mr Pascoe.'

'Good-morning, Mr Pascoe,' they chanted, parrot-fashion.

God, she was so much more controlled than he was, Max thought. She was perfect, not betraying for an instant that she might have been dismayed at the sight of him. But perhaps she wasn't. Perhaps it had meant nothing to her...

'Good-morning to you all,' he said, thinking how daft it all sounded, but knowing she was being the schoolteacher now, and not the woman who had wept in his arms so recently. 'What's all this, a nature walk?'

'That's right. We're going to dry these flowers and mount them once we've found out the names of them all. And I've been telling my class about you coming in to talk to them soon. You

226

haven't forgotten, have you?'

If he had, she obviously wasn't going to let him forget. And from the way the kids were jumping about now, he guessed she'd put the idea into their heads pretty thoroughly. He spoke as coolly as he could.

'I haven't forgotten, and as soon as I can find the time we'll arrange it, but I've been a bit busy myself lately. I've talked to the local paper about my idea of writing about my experiences, and they seem quite interested in a couple of personal experience articles, so I shall need some help with that as soon as it's convenient.'

There was an undeniable clash of wills between them again, as sharp as a flash of lightning, and this time it was Breda who gave a soft laugh.

'You always did know how to get round me, didn't you, Max? So we'll see you at school on Friday morning, all right?'

Before he could answer, one of the small girls was shrieking.

'Miss, Sara Hayes has weed her knickers.'

Breda turned around with a smothered exclamation, not so embarrassed by the child's remark as by the fact that Max was grinning broadly now as he leant on his bike. Sara was standing with her legs tightly crossed, and a look of desperation on her face, but it was obvious it was all too late.

'The rest of you get on with picking flowers while I get Sara changed,' she said firmly.

Why didn't he go on his way, she fumed, *instead of asking some of the kids if they already knew the names of their flowers? Why distract them as if he was*

227

being helpful ... which he was, of course, when she absolutely didn't need his help!

She helped Sara out of the sodden knickers and put them in the waterproof washing-bag she carried in her large canvas bag on these occasions, and helped Sara into a replacement pair of dry knickers.

'I couldn't help it, Miss,' the child said in a small voice.

Breda gave her a hug. 'Never mind. We've been out a long time today, so it's time we all went back to the classroom before we have any more little accidents,' she said with a smile as she straightened up.

'Well done, teacher,' Max said under his breath as she shepherded the children into a crocodile. 'You're obviously cut out to be a school marm.'

He didn't really know why he felt like mocking her at that moment, unless it was because it tugged at his heart to see how gentle she was with a distressed child, and he had a sudden vision of how she might have been with Warren's child.

Or his own.

'I'll expect you at the school on Friday morning to talk to the children,' she told him crisply, ignoring his remark.

'Maybe. And how do you feel about coming to Gough's Farm with me on Saturday evening to hear my first practice with the band? I could do with some support, and you'll help to offset the attentions of the Land Girls, if you know what I mean. It will do them good to see a wholesome Cornish girl.'

'I don't think so,' Breda said, echoing his own

first thoughts.

She marched off to catch up with the straggling children now, unduly ruffled to think Max only thought of her as a foil to some city girls who had taken a fancy to him. The implication was obvious. And why should she be in the least interested in going to a band practice? It had been fun in the past when she and Warren had joined them, when they were barely more than enthusiastic amateurs. The sessions then had caused more laughter than anything else. They took themselves more seriously now, and it may be just what Max needed. But she didn't.

'I think you should go,' her mother said. 'You can't hide yourself away from the normal activities of a young girl for ever, Breda. And Warren wouldn't think any less of you for getting out a bit more, my love.'

'I never thought any such thing!'

'Didn't you? How often have you been anywhere in these past months? You made a great effort in taking the infants to Padstow for May Day and we all admired you for that. But do you ever go to the pictures? Or to a social evening at the village hall raising funds for our soldiers and sailors and airmen?'

'It's not much fun on my own,' Breda muttered.

'You don't have to be on your own,' Agnes went on relentlessly. 'There's me and your gran, and the girls too if it's something that suits them. Don't turn into a recluse, my dear.'

Breda was becoming impatient with all this

badgering, but she knew very well it wasn't going to stop once her mother got a bee in her bonnet about something. And if her mother couldn't talk Breda round, she'd be just as likely to get Gran Hanney involved as well. Breda gave in.

'Oh, all right, Mum, if it will please you I'll tell Max I'll go to this blessed band practice with him. Now can we talk about something else?'

She saw the satisfaction in her mother's eyes and gave a small sigh. She knew the signs. She had no doubt her parents and gran had been getting their heads together and decided it was time Breda took an interest in the world around her, and that Max Pascoe was just the chap to revive her. They would never think of it as any kind of romantic attachment, any more than Breda herself would, but he was an old and familiar friend, and friends were what she needed right now. In fact, in all her growing up years, when she and the Pascoe boys had been such close friends, tomboys all, running wild over the moors – and later, when she and Warren had fallen in love, there had been little need for other friends. She had never really noticed it before, but she was noticing it now.

Max turned up at the school on Friday morning. She wasn't sure he'd actually do it, but she felt a frisson of pleasure that he'd taken the trouble, and that he was dressed casually in a way that wouldn't alarm the children. His tall frame filled the remaining space in the classroom as she clapped her hands for silence and reminded the infants what he was here to do.

'Now then, children, this is Mr Pascoe, who

some of you met the other day on our nature walk. What do we say when a visitor arrives?' she said in her usual schoolteacher voice, fully aware of Max's amused smile.

'Good-morning, Mr Pascoe,' they chanted in unison.

'Good-morning to you, children,' he said gravely.

Breda continued. 'Mr Pascoe is going to tell us what it's like to live in Egypt today. You all know where Egypt is now, from the large map on the wall. There are some bad things going on there these days because of the soldiers fighting, but we're not going to hear about any of that. Mr Pascoe is going to tell us about the ordinary lives of the people who live and work there.'

She looked at him encouragingly and sat down, hoping this wasn't going to turn out to be a gigantic mistake. As he said, he was no schoolteacher...

Max cleared his throat. 'Miss Hanney tells me you've seen some pictures in your bibles about Egypt, and about the people working and ploughing in the fields. What did you think of those people? They didn't look very much like us, did they? Have any of you drawn pictures of what you think Egypt might look like?'

There was a babble of excitement and a number of hands shot up and a flurry of pictures were produced to show him. Breda relaxed. He was handling this in just the right way, bringing the children into the discussion and drawing them out.

'Very good,' he said approvingly. 'Now I'll tell

231

you a bit more about it, shall I? How many of you have been to Egypt?'

There were hoots of laughter at that, and he had them enthralled as he went on to tell them about the desert and the wonderful River Nile that wove its way like a wide blue ribbon through the banks of greenery and fertile land, and then the vast expanses of barren desert beyond. He told them about the exciting discoveries of the archeologists and the wonderful temples that were still standing after thousands of years with their hieroglyphic writings and drawings. But mostly he told them about how he had seen the people at work, looking exactly as they had in those biblical pictures, and using the same tools and methods after so many years. He used simple terms that five-year-olds could understand, and by the end of it Breda was filled with admiration. He may not be a teacher, but he had the gift of communication.

'I think that's enough, don't you?' he said finally to Breda. 'Any more information and they'll have forgotten half of it by teatime.'

'You were wonderful,' she breathed so that only he could hear among the babble of excitement in the class now.

She noticed how tired he looked. It was probably more of a strain than he admitted to revive so many of his own memories of a country he had always wanted to see, and yet to leave out so many of the worst memories of all. This wasn't the time or place to speak of the atrocities that wartime brought, nor of his own injuries. That was for another time and another audience, and

Breda was full of confidence at how he would bring it to life for newspaper readers. In a personal column he could reveal many of the things the government never would.

She called for silence, and the chattering class reluctantly obeyed, clearly still agog at all they had heard.

'We've all had a wonderful morning with Mr Pascoe, haven't we? And I think we should show our thanks to him for coming along today.'

She began to clap and the children followed suit at once. Max waved a hand at them and made for the door, with Breda following to show him out.

'Thank you so much, Max. They'll be talking about it for the rest of the day and much longer. And if your offer of tomorrow night is still on, I'd like to come.'

Her eyes were shining with the pleasure and success of the morning, and impulsively he leant forward and kissed her cheek.

'Of course it is, and that was instead of an apple for the teacher. Be at my house around half past six, and Roy will take us all in his dad's van with the equipment.'

He walked away before either of them could say any more. He hadn't meant to kiss her like that, but he hadn't been able to resist it, and he didn't want to see any sign of recoil in her eyes. He knew he had been standing still for too long. His leg ached intolerably and he was glad of the walking stick as he went back to his aunt's house.

Breda watched him go for a moment before she went back to the classroom. She hadn't been affronted by his kiss. It was far from the first time he had kissed her, and far more enthusiastically than that in times past. Today it had been nothing more than a sweet gesture, and she felt a small glow at being able to help him in some small way towards regaining his self-confidence. It had been so evident in the way he spoke of Egypt and his experiences, and the children were so excited over all he had told them.

She couldn't help a small amount of preening that she had suggested it. In fact, she felt more alive than she had done for some time. The shock of seeing Max so unexpectedly on that first day was finally over. He was here, and he was here to stay. And of course she was glad of it. He was her closest friend, and the nearest thing to Warren in her life. Not that he was in any way a substitute, or ever could be. He was simply her friend. Her good friend.

Before she examined just how much this meant to her, she turned back to the clamouring children with their eager questions. They spent the rest of the morning drawing pictures of the narrow strip of fertile land that bordered the River Nile, and the intriguing images of the dark-skinned men in their long robes working at their ploughs in the fields.

'Just like Jesus in the Bible,' as one awe-struck little boy had whispered.

Chapter Fourteen

By Saturday evening Breda was getting cold feet, and wondering why she had agreed to go to the band practice. In the old days she and Warren would have gone together. Then, the sessions were always held in the village hall, and were always pretty disorganised affairs in between the Mothers' Meetings and whatever else was going on. They were lighthearted evenings, when the band members hadn't had much hope of doing other than playing at village hops. But recently the three members who had carried on without Max had become quite popular locally and had even got the occasional engagement in nearby towns, especially now that there were American servicemen in the vicinity, who were always keen on a dance. With Max adding his saxophone playing, who knew where they could go? It gave Breda a small shiver that was part excitement, part nerves.

She turned up at the Pascoe house still telling herself not to be so feeble and to enjoy the evening. She could see the van that belonged to Roy's grocer father already there, and when she went inside the house, the boys were talking excitedly with Laura and Jed.

'I wondered if you'd come,' Max greeted her after she had said hello to everyone.

'I said I would, didn't I?'

235

'It's great to see you, Breda,' Hobbsy said. 'Now we're all here, let's get going. We can't keep those city girls waiting all night.'

If there was anything guaranteed to put her off, that was it. Breda didn't know any city girls and wasn't sure that she wanted to. She imagined that they probably hated being sent to the back of beyond instead of living among the bright lights. Not that there'd be any bright lights in the cities now, of course. Blackout regulations were every-where, so they were all in the same boat. She began to feel annoyed with herself for being so in-sular and narrow-minded. After all she had been through, it would take more than three strangers to upset her. The idea was to enjoy herself, not to be gloomy.

The instruments were already in the back of the van. Hobbsy's drum kit took up most of the space, along with George's piano accordion and Roy's cello. Max was holding on to his precious saxophone as they all piled inside. The other three were squashed into the bucket front seat, while Max and Breda perched in the back, ignoring the varying smells of food and produce that lingered.

'You do realise I don't know what the heck we're going to play, don't you?' Max said. 'I've been playing a few of the old songs in my bedroom, but I suppose you've got plenty of new ones now.'

He tried not to show his apprehension. The last thing he wanted was to appear a fool beside these three who had been playing together all this time while he'd been serving his country.

'George has got a list of the songs we're doing, and some sheet music for you, Max,' Hobbsy said. 'Don't worry, mate, we'll all be getting to grips with being a quartet again. Anyway, we've got a bit of news for you. You know Roy's dad's on the local parish council. Well, they've asked if we're interested in doing a Harvest Festival dance at the village hall at the end of September. What do you think about that for our first performance back together?'

'I think it's too bloody soon,' Max said without thinking.

'I'm teaching the schoolchildren how to make corn dollies next week to help decorate the church for the special Harvest Festival service,' Breda said quickly, to cover the awkward silence. 'I don't suppose we'll get much produce this year to take to the hospitals though, except what people can spare from their own gardens.'

'It won't be too soon to play at a dance if we get enough practise in,' Hobbsy said, ignoring Breda's words completely. 'If this session doesn't work out well tonight, then we'll just have to get more time in. They can't refuse to let us use the village hall if they want us for the Harvest Festival dance. I never thought you'd be welshing on us, Max.'

'And I'll fight any man who says I am,' Max snapped back.

Breda put her hand on his arm as the van lurched up through the village and out towards the farm. 'Calm down, Max. It will all turn out all right, you'll see.'

Aware of his tension, she felt acutely sorry for him. He was no sissy and never had been, but she could sense that however much he wanted his life to get back to normal, all of this was a bit of an ordeal for him. In any case, it wasn't the normality he wanted, or had ever imagined for himself. Max the adventurer had always dreamt of being the hero in far away places. Penbole and home must seem very humdrum to him now – and so much less than he had ever wanted.

She felt his hand cover hers and give it a squeeze. It stayed there for a few minutes and she didn't push it away. She didn't want him to feel bad. Playing his sax was surely his lifeline, and if he felt uneasy about that, it wasn't going to help his general well-being.

'Have you got that list of song titles, George?' she said.

After a minute or two he handed it back to her. It was light enough in the back of the van for her and Max to open the piece of paper and scan down the list.

'There's nothing very new here, is there?' she said in some relief.

'People like the old songs,' Hobbsy said. 'They like waltzes and quicksteps, but there's also a few more fast numbers than the ones we used to play, so the kids can do the jitterbug if they like. But you'll soon get the hang of it, Max, no trouble.'

George glanced back. 'We thought we should have a new name for ourselves now that we're back together again. What do you think, Max? Any ideas?'

He didn't, but Breda was glad they were involving him. He was far more vulnerable than he used to be, and he needed to feel needed. Didn't everyone?

They had almost reached the farm now and there was no need for an answer.

The three Land Girls were already at the barn, not wearing their regulation uniforms now and with their hair down. They looked pretty and smart in their summer dresses, and Breda felt annoyingly countrified beside them, even though there was probably no need for it.

'I suppose they'll be giggling their empty heads off and chattering away like magpies all through the practice,' Max whispered in her ear. 'If there's anything to put a chap off when he's concentrating, it's that.'

His opinion of the girls was hardly damning, but Breda gave him a sudden smile that took his breath away. He didn't know the reason for it, but it made him feel good all the same.

Breda realised that the Land Girls were looking at her a bit enviously, and also a bit nervously. It dawned on her that they had almost certainly heard her story from Mrs Gough, and they'd be feeling a bit awkward with this girl who had had the terrible experience of losing her fiancé just before their wedding. The whole village knew of the circumstances, and Mrs Gough wasn't averse to passing on a bit of local gossip. It gave Breda a weird sort of feeling to know that she was a kind of tragic heroine in the eyes of these girls. But they were out of their normal environment down here in Cornwall, and she tried to revise her earlier opinions.

In any case, the evening wasn't about them. It was about the band recovering their old style and becoming a group of four again instead of three.

Previously, Max had been the acknowledged leader, but it was Roy who seemed to be taking the lead now. He wasn't very good at it, and Breda hid a smile as she heard them arguing now and then over a piece of music, or the way it was arranged. If she knew anything about it, it wouldn't be long before Max regained the leadership.

'They're not bad, are they?' one of the girls commented to Breda.

'With more practice, they'll be great,' she agreed. 'It's been a long time since they've all played together, so they're doing pretty well.'

'Max had a bad time in Egypt, didn't he?' another of the girls said. 'We heard that he nearly went mad.'

'That's a stupid thing to say,' Breda retorted. 'He nearly lost his leg and was delirious for a long while, and it was enough to make anybody wonder if they were ever going to recover. But he's made of strong stuff, and he did recover.'

'Fancy him, do you?'

Breda glared at her. 'He's one of my oldest friends, that's all. Perhaps it's different where you come from, but we value our friends down here.'

'Oh, hoity-toity!'

Breda was relieved when Hobbsy gave a loud drum roll and called out to them before the conversation began to get heated. 'Hey, you girls, stop talking and listen to this new arrangement and tell us what you think of it.'

Max had already skimmed through the list of song titles and was relieved to remember most of them.

'Don't Sit Under The Apple Tree' was one of

240

the newer numbers, but he'd heard the tune being played on the mouth organ in the Egyptian hospital several times. In any case, he had always been able to play by ear and rarely needed to follow the music on the song sheets once he had got the melody in his head. It didn't take long for the quartet to get it all together and to produce a reasonable sound. It was enough for the Land Girls to prance about on the dusty floor of the barn, anyway, while Breda preferred to sit on a straw bale with Mrs Gough and just listen to the music.

After a couple of hours they decided they had had enough. The daylight was fading now and they wanted to get back to the village before dark. They had worked out a presentable programme of songs, mixing fast ones with slower ones to suit all tastes, and Breda was full of admiration for the way Max had slid into the old routine so effortlessly. Once a musician, always a musician, she thought.

'I'm glad you came, my dear,' Mrs Gough told her delicately. 'It's good to see you smiling again after the time you've had.'

Breda knew she was right. She had done a lot of smiling that evening. It was fun listening to the fast-moving 'Chattanooga choo-choo', even when the Land Girls had added their tuneless singing. But she mustn't be uncharitable, she reminded herself, even though they weren't the sort of girls she'd choose as friends. Was she being snobbish? She didn't think so. They were simply from different worlds.

The only time she had had to bite her lips

241

tightly was when the band played 'You Are My Sunshine'. This had been a particular favourite of hers and Warren's during the past year. Max probably wasn't even aware of it, but now it was a poignant reminder of all she had lost. It would have been a favourite of many other couples too, and if the band were keen to include it in their repertoire, then so be it, she told herself.

By the time they all piled into the van again and were on their way back to the village, she was feeling very tired, Max must be feeling that way too, but he never showed it, buoyed up as he was by the success of the evening, and the excitement of the other three.

'We'll do a couple more practice sessions in the barn, and then I'll see my dad about getting time at the village hall,' Roy said, taking charge. 'It'll be easier on all of us, right?'

They were all in agreement, and then the van rattled back up the hill to drop off the other three, leaving Max and Breda outside his aunt's house.

'Come inside for some cocoa and then I'll see you home,' he said. 'Aunt Laura will be dying to know how it all went tonight.'

'I should really get back,' she said hesitantly.

'Why? What will you do? Make your own cocoa and go to bed? You might as well give Aunt Laura the pleasure of hearing what you thought of it all tonight.'

Breda could see at once that he was being his old masterful self. Tonight had given him back a lot of his old self-confidence. He wouldn't see the irony in his words about her going home with

242

nothing more to do than make her own cocoa and going straight to bed. Alone, of course.

'All right then. But you don't need to see me home.'

'Yes I do. It'll be dark, and I don't want you falling about in the blackout, so don't argue.'

Never mind the fact that she had been walking or cycling about in the blackout ever since the restrictions had begun! But he was being very sweet in wanting to take care of her, even though she had been taking care of herself for all these months.

He was right about Laura and Jed wanting to know every detail about how the evening had gone. They were interested in it all, and Breda could see how the fact of Max being home – one of Laura's boys – was restoring a lot of their well-being. They sat around the table and drank their cocoa, and coaxed Max to give them a small rendition of some of the songs they had played.

'You always did have music in your soul, Max,' Laura said with a sigh.

'I don't know about that,' he said with an embarrassed grin. 'I know I can forget a lot of bad things when I'm playing. It might have helped me when I was in hospital all those months instead of listening to one of the old boys squeaking away on his mouth organ. Mind you, I didn't even remember my sax at all until his playing triggered something in my memory, so I should be grateful for that, shouldn't I?'

'You had a rough time of it, Max, but it's behind you now,' Jed said.

Breda cleared her throat. She could see the

signs, and it was starting to get all too emotional for comfort. She couldn't bear it if they began reminiscing about Warren. Not now, not tonight, when the evening had begun so well and finished so happily with Max and the band rediscovering their old skills.

'I really must be going home, so thank you for the cocoa, Mrs Pascoe,' she said quickly.

Max got up at once, and she knew there would be no stopping him. But she admitted that she was glad of his company. There was no moon that night, and it had become very dark. There had been more than one nasty accident in the blackout, and she didn't want to be another one. He tucked her hand into his arm automatically, and they strode out towards Barnes Lane. It wasn't until they were halfway there that she realised he was limping again.

'You forgot your walking stick,' she said accusingly. 'You really shouldn't try to do things too fast, Max.'

He shrugged. 'I suppose I got carried away with the practice and the ending to a good evening. Don't worry; I'll live.'

She caught her breath at his words, wondering how long every innocent remark was going to turn a knife in her heart. He must have realised why her head suddenly drooped, because he went on in a low voice.

'We can't change things, Breda. Warren's gone, but we have to go on. He wouldn't have expected anything else, would he?'

She just nodded, because she wasn't in the mood for any philosophical discussion tonight. It

244

wasn't far to the cottage and she was thankful that they were nearing it now. All she wanted was to go indoors and go straight to bed without the need to think any more at all. But she couldn't ignore the fatigue in Max's voice either, and without the walking stick to ease the strain on his leg...

'Max, please borrow my bike to go home. You can bring it back tomorrow. I'll feel much better if you do.'

Without warning, he leant over and kissed her. She wasn't ready for it and she moved her head slightly, which meant that the kiss ended on her mouth instead of on her cheek. It was no more than a brush of his lips against hers, and no more than a friendly gesture.

'You're a good kid, Breda, but you always were, weren't you? All right, if it'll make you feel better, I'll borrow your bike.'

She fetched it from the lean-to at the side of the cottage, and watched him go on his way. The lights were dimmed as usual, and were hardly likely to be seen from any stray enemy aircraft overhead, she found herself thinking scornfully. But you had to obey the rules these days.

Without bothering to put on any lights in the cottage, she went upstairs to bed. It had been a good evening, and far more enjoyable than she had anticipated. Her mother was right, she should get out more. She had adored Warren and those feelings would never die, but she was too young to grieve for ever for something that couldn't be changed. Even Max had said that, and she knew his feelings for Warren were as

245

deep as her own.

As she undressed in the dark and got into bed, she curled up in a ball and closed her eyes, trying as always to bring Warren's image close. She hugged the pillow, wishing desperately that it was his warmth that she could feel next to her. Holding him close and kissing him goodnight... And she was so tired now that she imagined she could almost feel that kiss on her mouth...

It must have been the heady excitement of the evening that muddled things in her mind, because as she drifted into sleep, just for the briefest moment, it wasn't Warren's kiss at all. It was Max's.

She couldn't have said what woke her in the cool, early hours of the morning. It may have been a dog barking in the lane, or the early sounds of the roosters. Or maybe the birds rising from their nests along the cliffs. Whatever it was, she awoke with a shiver. She was still hugging her pillow as she had been when she had gone to sleep, and as always when she awoke the first thing that came into her head was Warren. In those first delicious moments before realisation came rushing in, she could still see his face in front of her, feel his breath on her cheeks and his arms around her. This day was different. She couldn't see him properly, and she couldn't feel his touch, and it was as though some elusive devil was keeping them apart.

She felt a small sob in her throat. The memories that were seeping into her brain now weren't the same, familiar ones that gave her a brief, bittersweet comfort. There was music in her head now, and she had heard a lot of it last night. And the song that was uppermost in her mind now was the last one the band had rehearsed. 'A Nightingale Sang In Berkeley Square' was another tune that she and Warren had loved. They'd even joked about how they didn't even know where Berkeley Square was, but it sounded very posh, and he used to tease her that they were going to go and find it one day. But in these waking moments it wasn't Warren smiling at her. And it wasn't Warren's voice she could hear. It wasn't anybody's voice. It was just the haunting sound of a saxophone. Max's saxophone. And with it, the memory of that fleeting kiss as he had said goodbye to her last night.

She caught her breath between her teeth. It was Sunday morning and it was barely dawn, but she couldn't stay in bed a moment longer. She threw on her dressing gown and slippers and padded downstairs to make an early morning cup of tea. She wasn't quite sure what was wrong with her. Last night had been good. She had enjoyed listening to the band and she could put up with the Land Girls cavorting about with their flirtatious eyes as they eyed up the boys in the band.

It was none of that. She had always thought that this was the hour of the day when you could be brutally honest with yourself. Most of the village hadn't come to life yet, and there was no one to intrude on her thoughts. But she knew what was troubling her. It was that kiss.

As the kettle started to give its piercing whistle, Breda quickly took it off the stove and poured the water into the teapot mechanically. She made herself a cup of tea and started to drink it, hardly noticing how scalding hot it was. Why in heaven's name was she making such a fuss about a fleeting kiss from a boy she had known all her life? She wasn't some kind of wishy-washy Victorian miss who thought no one had the right to ever kiss her lips again after Warren. Her parents had kissed her often since then, and so had Warren's parents. Gran kissed her. Kisses were an expression of affection between people who cared for each other and wanted to show that affection, especially in times of trouble. Her eyes blurred a little and she leant back in her chair, holding the hot cup in her hands.

So what was it about that kiss that hadn't felt right? Max had kissed her a thousand times in the past, sloppy youthful kisses and enthusiastic adolescent ones. Kisses on birthdays and at Christmas. Kisses to celebrate passing exams. They had all been real, expected, and reciprocated. Yet last night's was somehow wrong.

The dog in the lane barked more loudly, making her jump, spilling her tea on her dressing gown. And she asked herself the question she hadn't been willing to face. Was she actually disappointed that the kiss had been so brief, so platonic, instead of the way a kiss should be when it ended a lovely evening?

Her heart raced erratically, but before she could examine just what her thoughts were trying to tell her, she heard the clop-clop of a horse's hooves and the chuntering sound of the milk cart in the lane, accompanied by the milkman's tuneless whistle, and the rattle of bottles.

She jumped up and threw the remainder of her tea down the sink, furious with herself for letting her imagination go to places she didn't want and certainly didn't need. The very idea of Max kissing her in any kind of romantic way was repellent. He was her dear, good friend, and nothing more. She doubted if he had ever thought of himself as anything more, and she was the wicked one for allowing these thoughts into her mind. She had been alone too long, and she really should do as her mother said and get out more, she thought savagely.

There was no going back to bed now, and she buried herself in a book until the sun was properly up and she could decently get dressed. She busied herself with household chores that didn't need doing, and by midmorning she had told herself she had been acting like a fool to get so het up over nothing. A little later she heard the swish of tyres on the gravel outside, and she saw Max returning her bike and propping it up alongside the house. For a ridiculous moment she wondered if she should pretend not to be there. She should have gone to church, but she had been a bit slacking in that of late, she thought guiltily, finding no comfort in the vicar's words. Then she told herself not to be so stupid and opened the door.

'I brought your bike back,' Max said unnecessarily. 'I did the right thing in borrowing it last night. I was more tired than I realised but I still found it hard to sleep after all the excitement of the evening. How about you?' He looked at her quizzically. 'There's something different about you this morning.'

'No, there isn't. I'm the same old me,' she said quickly.

'You look a bit peaky. Come out for a walk and get some sea air in your lungs. You can borrow my stick if you get too tired. We'll share it.'

She bristled a little. 'I'm hardly likely to do that. I'm the girl who could walk for miles, remember? There were plenty of times when I could beat you and Warren up to the moors and back again!'

'I remember,' he said evenly. 'I wasn't planning on anything like that today. Just down to the quay and back. Are you game?'

'All right. My gran will probably think I've gone halfway to the devil already, anyway, for missing church again.'

'Nobody could think that about you. How is the old girl, by the way? I must drop in and pay my respects sometime.'

'She'd like that. She was always very fond of you, Max, and she had a sneaking admiration for the way you weren't content to do the ordinary things that everyone else did.'

'What, like settling down and getting married before I was wet behind the ears, and ending up with a parcel of kids, you mean?' he said lightly as they left the cottage and set out along the lane.

Breda laughed. 'No, I didn't mean that. I mean going off to foreign shores and having adventures like some comic book hero. Gran always thought you were a bit like one of those devil-may-care characters.'

He kept looking straight ahead. 'Well, she was partly right. I do care though, Breda, about a lot of things. I'm not as shallow as that makes me sound.'

'I know that. But if you're going to get all serious with me, I'm going back home. It's too nice a day for deep discussions, and I just want to enjoy the sunshine.'

'And the company, of course,' he said more casually.

'And the company,' she agreed.

Breda had promised to go home for tea that afternoon, and, as she expected, her mother wanted to know how it had all gone last night, saying she was glad she'd done it, and that she'd gone out with Max this morning too, because it all helped to take her out of herself.

In Breda's opinion, that was a silly thing to say, because how could anything take you out of yourself – and why would you want it to? But she was getting used to well-meaning folk telling her how she should feel and what she should do, and told herself to stop getting so critical and just accept it.

'Are you going to marry Max now then?' Jenna said matter-of-factly.

Breda jumped at the unexpectedness of the question, and Agnes scolded her daughter at once.

'Jenna, what a stupid thing to say. Breda's not thinking of marrying anyone, and certainly not Warren's cousin.'

'Well, I thought they liked each other,' Jenna said, starting to look a little tearful now.

'We do, Jenna,' Breda broke in before her mother could go off on one of her tirades and upset the child even more. 'We're good friends, that's all.'

'Won't you ever marry anyone now then, not ever?' the girl persisted, while her twelve-year-old sister looked on, seemingly quite happy to let Jenna put her foot right in it.

Breda sighed, wishing this conversation had never started.

'I don't know. Perhaps one day, years from now. I couldn't think of anything like that for a long time though, and I don't want to talk about it.'

Esme piped up now. 'One of the girls in my class at school has just got a new stepfather. Her dad died six years ago and her mum's got married again. She likes him, because he buys her things and they live in a new house.'

'Well, good for her,' Breda said, not knowing what else to say and feeling her palms getting damp. 'Shall I call Dad in for tea, Mum?' she said desperately.

He'd been out in his shed for the last hour, away from too much female talk, as he called it. Agnes nodded, seeing from Breda's face that it was high time he came in to deflect the probing and un-settling questions of their younger daughters.

They were worse than the infants sometimes, Breda fumed as she went out to the back yard. She remembered how one of the little ones had once asked her the same innocent question about marrying Max. It was as absurd then as it was now, and she didn't even want to think about it.

Chapter Fifteen

In a village the size of Penbole, Breda knew she couldn't escape seeing Max, even if she had wanted to. In fact, she told herself that the more she saw him, the more they could resume the old easy relationship they had always had. In any case, she had promised to help him with this article for the local paper, and she knew he was going to hold her to it. It was quite odd how some folk had always thought him a bit feckless because of his wanderlust and his love of music, she mused, when anyone who knew him well, knew that when he got an idea in his head, he could be as tenacious as a limpet.

She knew, too, that even though he was no longer in the thick of it, he followed the progress of the war as seriously as any of the men in the village. Evenings spent at The Bottle and Jug were not only to share a few pints of beer. They were to mull over all that was happening around the world.

Long ago, the village had organised its share of volunteer firewatchers, even though it always seemed unlikely that the Jerry planes would come this far west to drop their bombs. All the same, you had to be on your guard these days, and it had happened.

Although there had been plenty of air-raid alerts, people had become accustomed to them, since they were so often false alarms. It was more likely to be a serious threat on the south coast than here. Sometimes planes could be heard in the daytime, and people had learnt to recognise the different sounds of the engines, and to know whether they were enemy planes or British ones. The only time this part of the county had been rocked was in October 1940, when Padstow had been hit by six incendiary bombs. Three people had been killed, all generations of one family, which made it even more tragic for those who were left. A number of houses were damaged, and although it gave a great jolt to the community concerned, the general feeling was that north Cornwall was getting off lightly compared to other parts of the country.

There was plenty of news now about the American forces arriving in the area, and ever more whispers about the important day when the allied forces were going to make a great push on the French coast. It was going to take months of careful planning, but everyone had their say on it, and how it was going to be a turning-point in the war. The Americans were finally in it, and for many it was exciting to see them in the vicinity, with their seemingly endless supplies of chocolate, sweets and nylon stockings, which were unheard of locally. It was no wonder the local girls were eager to go to any dances the Yanks were going to attend, although not everybody was pleased to see them.

'You can't escape the buggers now,' one of the grizzled old fishermen grunted at The Bottle and Jug. 'Flashing their money about like nobody's

254

business, and turning our girls' heads. There's word that they've even got a naval supply base set up on Exeter golf course now. That'll upset the nobs, won't it?'

'Pipe down, Gabriel,' Jed Pascoe told him. 'You'd grumble if the Pope came to visit.'

'You bet your damn belt and braces I would,' the old boy bellowed. 'We don't want none of their lot down here.'

Jed grinned at his nephew, knowing how easy it was to rile the old man. It was no more than a harmless village sport, and it always raised the atmosphere to see how Gabriel Finn spluttered and blustered when something got his dander up.

'You shouldn't taunt him like that,' Max grinned at his uncle. 'He'll have a heart attack one of these days and then you'll be sorry.'

'Don't you believe it. He'd like nothing better than to pop his clogs here in the pub, ranting and raving at the rest of us. There's no better place for old Gabriel to end his days than with his head stuck over a pint pot. Anyway, never mind him. What do you think about the Yanks establishing an amphibious training centre over in Falmouth? They say it's on the cards in a couple of weeks. If that don't mean business for getting ships across to France for an invasion in due course, I don't know what does.'

'It's about time,' Max said evenly.

Jed looked at him sharply. 'You're not fretting over not going with them, are you? If Warren was still with us, I know he'd be champing at the bit and all. But he's not here and you ain't fit, and we've all got to make the best of things, boy.'

'I know. I wasn't thinking about that at all.'

Not even about the fact that it was good that he and his uncle at least, could finally start to talk about Warren more naturally. Unless they were able to do that, it was as if he'd never existed at all.

'What then? I can see you've got something on your mind,' Jed said, under cover of the general mêlée of noise and chatter going on all around them.

Max sighed. He hadn't been going to say anything, but as usual both their tongues were loosened a little in this atmosphere. 'You know I fancied doing a bit of writing for the newspaper and that Breda's agreed to help me put my words into a bit of sense. Well, now I'm wondering if I should do it after all.'

'What's stopping you? I can't say I thought it was such a clever idea myself, but if it keeps you occupied, then why not?'

Max ignored the implication that it was just something for him to do to while away the time, or his surprise at his uncle's comment.

'I think it will upset people,' he said flatly. 'If I'm going to do it at all, then I have to be honest about the things I saw and experienced, and it's not going to make comfortable reading. God knows how much the government keeps things hidden from the public, and we all know the papers don't tell us everything about what's going on, do they? Is it right for me to blab about my side of it?'

Jed sounded cautious. 'I daresay it depends on how much you need to say it all, boy. If it's a case of letting it fester inside you and twisting your brain, then it's probably better out than in.'

'Yes, but who am I doing it for? To educate the public into what's really happening in the middle of a war zone, and to let them know what happens to a chap's brain when he's delirious and half-dead? Or would I really be doing it for me, just to indulge myself and let them see what a hero I was? Which is not what happened at all,' he added with brutal honesty. 'I didn't come home as the conquering hero, more like a total wreck.'

'For God's sake, Max, listen to yourself,' his uncle said angrily. 'You've got a story to tell, but if you don't want to tell it, that's up to you. Plenty of old soldiers from the first world war never said a single word about what happened to them, because it was too bloody painful. They kept the memories locked up in their heads until they died. If they had nightmares over what had happened, it was their private nightmares, and not something to be inflicted on their wives and families. Those old soldiers kept their traps shut, and you don't see them going loopy because of it, do you? They just carried on and made the best of it, and were bloody thankful to be alive. And if you want my honest opinion, I think you should do the same.'

It shocked Max to hear his uncle speaking so forcefully, and at such length, and it told him Jed really meant what he was saying.

'You think it would be a mistake to bring it all into the open, then? You don't think folk would really want to know what conditions were like in the desert?'

Too late, Jed realised how he had let himself be talked into the opposite of what he'd been saying in the first place. But he had to admit he'd been uneasy about Max's whole plan.

'You're a clever chap, Max, but I think some things are best left alone. Soldiers are trained to fight and they know what to expect, but I'm not sure that ordinary folk can really cope with the reality of it all. And that's my last word on it. I'm not making up your mind for you. You're the only one who can do that. Now go and get us some more beer. All that talking's made my throat parched.'

It was still hard for Max to sleep at night. The soft bed that should be so familiar to him was still strangely alien after the rough camp conditions of the desert and the hard, narrow beds of the various hospitals he'd been sent to. He was always restless for several hours, trying to get his leg into the most comfortable position before he finally dropped off to sleep. Tonight was even worse, because he had a lot to think about, and the more he thought about it, the more un-decided he became.

He tried to think of what Warren would say. He thought of his cousin's fresh, enthusiastic face, and how he used to encourage him in whatever he wanted to do. Being two years younger than himself, Warren had always looked up to him, seeing him as a bit of a god... As his thoughts twisted and turned, he grimaced, because he had never felt less god-like himself. He felt more like a rat, knowing he was in love with Warren's girl, and always would be. And if ever a love was destined to remain unfulfilled, it was this one, with the shadow of Warren always between them.

God, this wasn't helping! He wanted Warren's advice on whether or not to write of his experiences. But Warren wasn't here to help him. Breda had to be the one. The clever schoolteacher could tell him what to do if anybody could. He tried to think of her in those terms and not to allow her image into his mind at all. He wouldn't think of her long hair bouncing on her shoulders as she walked, nor her fresh, clear complexion, and the mouth that he had kissed... He wouldn't picture her at all, he thought desperately, and he finally fell into an exhausted sleep.

Breda wasn't expecting visitors the following evening, and she and Max hadn't made any special arrangements for him to discuss his newspaper article with her. She certainly wasn't in the mood for it now. She was tired after a day at school that hadn't gone well, with several of the infants being sick, and praying that none of them was going to go down with German Measles as her sisters had done. It would be ghastly if it ran through the school. So she looked up with no great enthusiasm when she saw Max walking up the path of the cottage.

'You can come in,' she greeted him, 'but I'd better warn you that I'm not the best company this evening.'

'That's all right. Neither am I,' he said.

'What's wrong?'

He sat down heavily on one of her chairs, staring gloomily into space for a moment. What was wrong was that he was turning into a prize idiot, unable to make up his mind about anything. It was a hell of a comedown for somebody who had always been so decisive in planning his own future and his own destiny. Maybe after all, it was like the old biddies of the village said, and there was no changing what fate had in store for you, anyway. He had never had any truck with all that mumbo-jumbo stuff, and he didn't want to give it credence now.

'Max, are you all right?' Breda said sharply when he didn't answer.

His mouth twisted. 'No, I'm not bloody well all right. I've only got half a leg that hurts like hell every now and then. I had to give up the life I wanted, and I might as well give up the rest of it and admit defeat,' he finished half-jokingly.

Breda was startled by his words. She didn't answer immediately, but her brief pity disappeared as she felt a sudden rage boiling up inside her, and she couldn't contain it a moment longer.

'You make me sick,' she finally burst out. 'There's nothing much wrong with you except a great big dose of self-pity right now. You've got a damn sight more than half a leg, and even if you didn't, it's better than no leg at all, isn't it? So you can't go traipsing all over Egypt and anywhere else you please like some damn wandering minstrel. You've got a life, and you've got your music. You should be glad you've got what you have, instead of being so pathetic over things that can't be changed. Other people are dying in this war, Max, and there are plenty more who will never come home. Remember that!'

She was shaking all over by the time she finished speaking. It had been a miserable and worrying day at school with the children, and to come home to this was too much to take. She was red-faced and tearful with him for bleating so much. It wasn't the Max she knew. It wasn't the Max she wanted. Before she had any idea what his reaction was going to be, he had leapt up from his chair and put his arms around her, holding her tight.

'God, I'm such a thoughtless pig,' he said roughly. 'I didn't come here to say anything like that Breda. It just came out, and you know I'd give anything to have Warren back with us. I'd gladly give my bloody leg and anything else, just to know he was still alive.'

'Don't be daft,' she said, her voice trembling and muffled against his shoulder. 'He'd never have wanted that. You'd never be able to chase him and me over the moors with a peg-leg.'

For some reason the bizarre image of the three of them prancing over the moors in that fashion whirled into her head, and even though it should have been horrific, she found that her shoulders were shaking with a different emotion.

'Oh Breda, sweetheart, you know I didn't mean to upset you like that,' she heard him whisper hoarsely, not realising that the tears were turning into silent laughter. 'You know you mean the world to me.'

He clamped his lips tightly together, afraid he was going to say more, things she wouldn't want to hear, especially not now when her head would be filled with bittersweet thoughts of Warren. She moved slowly out of his arms.

'Sometimes these things are better said,' she murmured back, unconsciously opposing every-thing his uncle Jed had told him. 'We both loved Warren and we both miss him dreadfully, and those feelings can't disappear in a day or a year, if ever. We just have to go on as best we can, don't we?'

'And you're so much wiser than me, school-teacher,' he said, trying to lighten the moment, while wondering too, if she was unintentionally telling him that she would never love anyone else. If so, the loss of his old wanderlust days was even more frustrating, knowing that he could never leave here, at least not while the war lasted, when his aunt and uncle were so grateful to have him home.

'I'll make us some tea,' Breda said, moving farther away from him. 'And then you can tell me why you really came here tonight.'

It gave him time to compose himself, and to curse himself for being so feeble. He hadn't meant to say anything so stupid to her, and now she'd think he was in a precarious mental state after all. Perhaps he was, he thought uneasily. Perhaps it took far longer than he had believed to regain every part of yourself when something traumatic happened to you.

'You should go and see my gran,' Breda told him. 'She's got more pills and potions for calming people than anything the doctor can prescribe.'

'Is that so? And do you think I need pills and potions to calm me?'

She came back with a tray of crockery and a pot of tea.

'I don't think you should mock it. These old methods have proved as effective as any new-fangled medicine, and often more so. What harm would it do?'

'That's not what I said. I asked if you think I need pills and potions to calm me. Do you think I'm crazy?'

'Of course I don't,' she said crisply. 'I only know that Gran helped me in many ways after Warren died, and I'm not saying anything more. Just talk to her and make up your own mind, unless you think it's beneath you to take any notice of an old lady who's lived more years than the two of us put together.'

'All right, I give in,' Max said to please her. 'I'll pay her a visit sometime, just to be sociable, but I'm not promising anything.'

'I didn't ask for promises. Now, what did you want to talk about? I'm not in the mood for discussing your writing tonight, so it had better be something else.'

He took the cup of tea she handed him, not missing the way her hands still shook. He hated himself for having upset her so much, and he blurted out the first thing that came into his head.

'Will you come to the pictures with me on Saturday night? There's a Western film on at the fleapit, and I'd rather go with you than go on my own.'

She felt her heart jump. She hadn't expected this.

'I don't go to the pictures any more,' she said abruptly.

'Why not? Are you afraid of seeing make-believe

people enjoying themselves on the screen? We used to enjoy cheering the cowboys and booing the Indians and all that stuff. Or are you turning into a martyr and shutting yourself off from doing normal things? You're not a hundred years old, Breda.'

He didn't know why he was taunting her like this, but it angered him to think of her retreating into herself, and he wondered uneasily if she felt she owed this kind of loyalty to Warren.

'I know all that, and I'm certainly no martyr or a saint! I sometimes have to bite my tongue a hundred times when the schoolkids drive me mad.'

'Oh, come on. I know you're good with them. You take them on nature walks, and I heard you went with them to the May Day celebrations at Padstow, which must have been a bit of an ordeal for you at the time. I know you enjoyed our band practice the other night, so what's wrong with coming to the flicks? It won't make the village label you a scarlet woman, Breda.'

She gave a deep sigh. He didn't physically dig his heels into the hearthrug, but he might as well have done, because she knew he was going to make every argument under the sun until she gave in.

'If I say yes, will you stop badgering me?' she said finally.

He grinned. 'I've stopped already. And if you think I came here to discuss my article for the newspaper, you can stop worrying about that, because I've decided against doing it.'

'What? Why?' She couldn't think of anything

264

else to say. It had seemed such a positive step for him to take. Something to do to occupy his mind until he decided what else to do with his life besides playing in the band.

He shrugged. 'I'm not sure I want to bare my soul, and I'm even less sure the village would want to hear the truth of what conditions were like in the desert, nor how I coped with nearly losing my leg. I can't see the point in stirring up worries in people's minds with no good reason, and my uncle agrees with me.'

'Does he?' Breda said. 'So what are you going to do instead?'

'I haven't thought that far ahead. I'm still getting used to being home.'

There was an awkwardness between them now that they couldn't seem to cross, and Max finished his tea and got up to leave.

'Anyway, I just wanted to let you know, so I'll see you on Saturday night.'

She had to admit she had mixed feelings over his change of heart. It had seemed such a good idea, but she was beginning to see now that it might well upset people in the village who still had sons and brothers serving in the most violent parts of the world. It might well have been some kind of release for Max to get it all out into the open, but it could have proved an added torment for other people. She began to respect what his uncle Jed had apparently told him. He'd have to find some kind of a job, though. It was early days yet, but Max wouldn't want to play the wounded soldier for long. It wasn't in his nature to ever be content to do that.

Max was thinking much the same thing as he strode back through the village. Playing in the band was not a full-time occupation and never had been. For the sake of his own pride, he had to do something worthwhile. He found himself nearing Gran Hanney's cottage, and on an impulse he knocked at her door. She peered out of the window to see her visitor, and then answered the door with a toothless smile.

'Well, this is a nice surprise, Max,' she said, 'It's not often I get handsome young men callers, so come inside and jaw with me for a while.'

'I'm not exactly a handsome young man caller. More like a lopsided one.'

Gran Hanney cackled as she led him into the cluttered parlour with its collections of shells and knickknacks and family photographs on every surface. She shooed her old cat off a chair, ignoring its yelping, and told Max to sit down.

'Now then, young man, would you like a glass of my home-made cordial before you tell me what you've come to see me about?'

'No, I won't have anything to drink, thank you. I've just had a cup of tea with Breda.'

'Ah-hah.'

'Is that comment supposed to mean something?' he asked when she didn't say anything more.

She cocked her head on one side as if to take stock. When she narrowed her eyes to look at him thoughtfully, they almost disappeared into the wrinkles on her face. Her hair was thin and wispy and there was no knowing how old she was; she seemed to have been in the village for ever and never looked any different, and as children he and Warren had always known she had the reputation of being a wise woman. Right now, Max had the uneasy feeling that if anybody could see inside another person's head and know what they were thinking, it was Granny Hanney.

'You're fond of Breda, aren't you, boy?'

'Of course I am. Warren was like a brother to me, and when we were kids Breda was like our sister. Except that things changed between them, of course. But I don't have to tell you that, Gran.'

He had the uneasy feeling he didn't have to tell her a lot of things. He cleared his throat, wishing he'd never had the impulse to come in here at all. Breda had put the idea into his head, and he'd simply followed it.

'I didn't come here to talk about Breda,' he said.

'What's troubling you then? I can see that something is.'

'Well, I suppose it was something Breda said.' He was unconsciously still talking about her. 'She thinks I need something to calm my nerves. I don't think she's right, but I've just changed my mind from doing something I'd planned, and it's left me high and dry in a manner of speaking.'

'What was this then? Is it about writing something for the newspaper?'

He might have known that Breda would have mentioned it. She was very close to her gran, and nothing much escaped the old lady.

It half-opened the door for him to say a little about it. That was all he intended. He certainly

267

didn't intend blurting out any details of those terrible days in the desert when his unit had been under fire from the vicious German assaults, when their desperate advances into enemy lines had seemingly been going nowhere. He hadn't meant to tell her how several of his good mates had been blown to bits, and many more of them had suffered horrific injuries in more ways than should ever be recorded in a family newspaper. He could see now how insensitive that would have been for families still worried for their loved ones. He didn't mean to talk so graphically about how the desert so often turned red with blood until the hot, fierce winds came and covered all trace of it, burying those who couldn't be saved, blinding the eyes and searing the souls of those who were left behind to carry on. He had never intended saying any of that.

He wasn't aware that the old woman had left him for a few moments until she returned with a glass of some strange liquid that he didn't recognise, urging him to drink it. He did so without thinking, feeling the bitter brew seep down his throat, and in a few seconds she slowly came back into focus again, sitting opposite him with the scrawny cat on her lap, its inscrutable yellow eyes watching him. He felt as if he had been a long way away to a place he didn't recognise, and was slowly returning.

'You'll feel better now,' Gran Hanney said complacently.

'What was in that drink?' he said hoarsely.

'Nothing to harm you, my dear. 'Twill merely calm the nerves and give you a sense of well-being, nothing more. The rest of it you've done for yourself.'

He stared at her, not understanding. 'What have I done?'

'You've said what you could never have written down for public viewing, and rightly so. You've scoured your soul and got rid of your demons.'

'I'm sorry. I never meant to have such an outburst,' Max said in agitation.

'It had to come sooner or later. Who better to tell than an old woman whose shoulders might not look very strong, but who's heard it all before, rather than your family who couldn't bear it? You've put your ghosts to rest, Max, and you need to concentrate now on looking forwards, instead of backwards.'

He gave a small smile for the first time since coming here. 'We always called you a wise woman, Gran, but I never realised quite how wise you are until now.'

He also saw how tired she was looking. In absorbing all that he'd been saying, it was almost as if she had lived through it with him. He was tired too. Extraordinarily and desperately tired. It was quite an effort to get up from the chair and reach for his walking stick.

'I'll remember what you've said,' he mumbled. 'In fact, I'm taking the first step on Saturday. I've asked Breda to come to the pictures, and she's said yes.'

'Good. It's what you both need,' Gran Hanney replied.

She got up and kissed him before she showed him out, her lips parchment dry and scratchy on his cheek, but somehow like a blessing.

He walked home slowly, thankful that he didn't meet too many people on his way. The night was already drawing in, and it would soon be dark. His auntie was out for the evening at one of her meetings, and his uncle would doubtless be down the pub by now. With any luck, he could go home and go straight to bed. With a bit more luck, he might even sleep more easily than of late, with none of the nightmares that still plagued him. He could only hope.

Chapter Sixteen

The courting couples in the village always headed straight for the back row of the cinema they called the fleapit. As the usherette shone her torch, Breda deliberately walked ahead to halfway down the darkened room. There was no way she wanted people to think of herself and Max as one of those cosily cuddling couples in the back row, and nor did she want to be anywhere near them. It would have been all too emotional, remembering the evenings that she and Warren had spent here, seeing comparatively little of the film they were supposedly watching.

'Does this seat suit you, ma'am?' Max whispered in an amused voice.

'It's fine,' she told him, guessing that he knew very well why she had walked ahead. Anyway, now that she was here, she was going to give all her attention to the Western film. First, though, there was the Pathé Newsreel, giving as much information as was allowed about the war.

Max was quiet throughout the news items, but he visibly relaxed once the small cartoon began before the main feature. It was a good film, and it was easy to lose themselves in the fictional battles of the cowboys and Indians, and even join in the whoops and hisses of some of the audience. By the time the lights went up at the end of the evening, and they had all stood to attention

271

as 'God Save the King' was played, Breda felt more relaxed than she had in a long time.

'Gran told me you'd been to see her the other night,' she said socially as they went outside into the night. 'I'm glad you did, Max. She talks a lot of sense.'

'I think I did most of the talking, but she's a good listener as well, and that's all I'm going to say about it, so don't think you can pump me. She didn't tell you anything else, did she?'

'No. Gran never gives away any secrets. That's why people tell her things.'

'So what do you want to do now?' he said.

He was glad to move away from the memory of just what he'd told Gran Hanney, even though some of it was decidedly hazy, and he wondered again just what had been in that brew she'd given him. Whatever it was, he hadn't had any nightmares that night, nor any night since, he realised.

'Now? Go home, I suppose!' Breda said.

'Why don't we get some chips?'

It was what they often did after the fleapit. The fish and chip shop in the village was very near the cinema, and most of the young people who spilt out of the fleapit seemed to end up there, and on summer nights they took their newspaper-wrapped chips down to the sea wall to eat under the stars. For a moment Breda's heart baulked at doing what she and Warren had so often done, but the smell of vinegar and hot chips was wafting this way, making her mouth water. The September nights were still balmy, and she was suddenly hungry.

'Why not?' she said recklessly.

It was the kind of night for feeling reckless. There were plenty of young people about now that the cinema had emptied, and it was like being part of a clan. Breda knew she had missed this, and it was just as Max had said. She *had* chosen to shut herself off from joining in so many things, almost revelling in her grief and misery in a way that was unhealthy. She knew her family had been worried about the fact that school and her little cottage had seemed to occupy all her thoughts, when she was still a young girl who should be making the most of life.

But as Max bought the chips and handed her a packet liberally sprinkled with salt and vinegar, just the way she liked them, she felt a small burst of resentment against her well-meaning family, and Max in particular. She knew she was being contrary, but he needn't think she was going to throw herself into every bit of village entertainment there was, just to keep him company.

'I'm not sure I want to sit on the sea wall after all,' she said.

'All right, but they'll be cold by the time we've walked home with them, unless you have no objection to eating in public.'

'Everybody else is doing the same thing, and besides, it's nearly dark.'

It wasn't just sitting on the sea wall and eating chips and the emotive memories it would evoke. It was being within sight and sound of the sea that had taken Warren away. He had always loved the sea... Without a breath of wind and the air so still, that sea would be so benevolent tonight, but

273

it only made her think more bitterly of how cruel it could be to take her sweetheart from her.

'Where have you gone, Breda?' she heard Max say, as they walked away from the village towards Barnes Lane.

'I'm all right,' she said in a muffled voice. 'Just thinking, that's all. And you should go, Max. You don't need to come all the way with me.'

'Warren wouldn't have left you halfway home,' he said roughly, 'and I've no intention of doing so either, especially when I can tell that something's upset you. I thought we had a good time tonight.'

'We did. Oh, take no notice of me, Max. I get these black moods sometimes. I surely don't need to explain why, do I?'

She felt angered that she might need to do so. Of all people, he should understand. Her footsteps had quickened, and she realised that he was limping a little more. He was trying to do without his walking stick as much as possible, but sometimes by the end of the day it was too much.

'Let's slow down,' she said. 'Do you need to rest a minute?'

'There's plenty of time for resting. I'll just walk you to your gate and go back, so don't worry about me.'

They were talking like strangers. She didn't know how the old loving mood had changed between them, or how to bring it back. She was still clutching half a bag of chips. There was a bin at the end of the lane and she flung the bag inside. Max did the same as if all taste for them had gone now.

'Max, I'm sorry,' she said more softly. 'It's just

that sometimes I get an overwhelming feeling of sadness inside, and it's hard to shake myself out of it. I think about Warren all the time, and I miss him so much that it's unbearable.'

He put a friendly arm around her shoulder and squeezed it hard.

'I know, sweetheart. I miss him too. It's like having part of your life snatched away. You've lost half of what's past, and you've been cheated out of the half that should be in front of you. Does that make any sense?'

'You do understand then,' she murmured. They had reached Forget-me-not Cottage now, and were leaning on the gate as if reluctant to break away.

'Of course I do. You don't have a monopoly on grief, Breda, even though mine must be a very different grief from yours. I know that.'

Well, you may think you do. I know that yours is the deeply felt grief of two boys who were as close as brothers. But mine is the grief of a girl who was so nearly a bride, but who knew the sweetness of my lover's body but will now never know it again. And I long to feel him in my arms again ... so much...

She felt something like an electric shock run through her, wondering if she had actually said those words aloud. She knew she couldn't have done, because Max was not looking startled or disgusted at hearing what was really going through her mind at that moment. She was still half held in his embrace, and her thoughts were so mixed up that she needed to be alone.

'Go home now, Max,' she said shakily. 'We had a lovely evening, and it's a shame for it to end

275

sadly. Let's just remember the good times.'

This time, because she felt she had unintentionally upset him, she was the one who reached up and put her lips to his. The tangy taste of vinegar and salt was on both their mouths, and although it was only intended to be a friendly gesture, before she knew what was happening, his arms had tightened around her and the kiss had turned into something more.

She broke away quickly, and said goodnight to him in a strangled voice before rushing indoors.

It was reaction, nothing more, she told herself wildly. It was the mere fact of being close to someone who cared for her, when she needed to feel someone's love so badly. It was nothing more than that. To imagine, for a single moment, that the tingling sensation running through her veins when that kiss had deepened, had any other meaning, was to be disloyal to Warren's memory, and she wouldn't allow it inside her head for a single, furious moment.

'I heard you and Max went to the pictures last night,' her mother said casually when she went home for tea on Sunday, which seemed to be the expected order of things now, with her gran there as well.

'The way news gets around this village, there can't be a more gossipy place in Cornwall,' Breda said. 'They'll be putting banners out soon.'

Agnes looked at her silently for a minute. 'There's no need to be waspish, Breda. Mrs Lumley's daughter next door has just started work as an usherette, and she happened to mention it over the garden fence this morning, that's all.'

'So Mrs Lumley's daughter told Mrs Lumley, and Mrs Lumley told you. Why not Old Uncle Tom Cobley and all!'

She didn't know why she was taking on so. There were plenty of folk who had seen her and Max at the pictures last night, and afterwards at the fish and chip shop, and walking home. The village had hardly been empty. At least Barnes Lane had been quiet when they said goodnight, but that was something she didn't want to think about.

'Are your bowels all right, my dear?' Gran Hanney enquired.

Breda looked at her gran without speaking for a moment, and then her mouth twitched. Trust Gran Hanney to bring matters down to basics. If your bowels weren't in working order, then it could put you out of sorts for days, but when Gran administered a good old dose of syrup of figs, it usually did the trick.

'They're fine, Gran, and I'm sorry for snapping, Mum. But you're right. Max and I did go to the pictures, and it was a good evening.'

'He's a nice young man,' Gran Hanney observed. 'And probably ready to settle down now.'

Well, not with me, Breda thought. *So you can get any little ideas like that right out of your head.*

She was doing it again. She had to stop talking to herself. It was what old ladies did who had no one to talk to, or only a cat who couldn't answer back. Maybe she was turning into her gran...

'I don't think Max is ready to settle down,' she said swiftly. 'He's getting adjusted to being home

277

again, and I daresay we'll be going out together again from time to time. I'll be sure to give Mrs Lumley notice,' she couldn't resist adding.

Her sisters came home from their Sunday School class lesson in time for tea, and had some news of their own.

'We've been invited to a party in Padstow,' Jenna shouted. 'The whole class is going, and it's being arranged by the Yanks. What do you think of that?'

'I think you had better ask your father and me before you go accepting any such thing,' Agnes said sharply.

'You've got to let us go, Mum,' Esme said. 'We'll look stupid if we're the only two left out. It's not just our Sunday School anyway, it's all the Sunday Schools round about who are being invited to say thank you from the Yanks to the local people for being so friendly. We've got a letter about it.'

She thrust a piece of paper into her mother's hands as Jenna began wailing.

'I knew she wouldn't let us go. It's just because they're Yanks, isn't it?'

'I didn't say I wouldn't let you go, providing it's properly supervised,' Agnes went on. 'I said you should ask your father and me first. And stop calling them Yanks. It's not proper.'

She ignored Gran Hanney's mutterings that there were some folks who were being *too* nice to the Yanks, and out for all they could get. Gran didn't get around much, but she heard plenty.

'What harm will it do, Mum?' Breda said. 'There's safety in numbers, and if the whole class is going from Penbole, I suppose they'll be taken there and brought back.'

'Breda's right,' her father spoke up now. 'How would we look if we said no? A party's harmless enough, and we wouldn't want to be seen to be snubbing them. They are our allies, remember.'

Against her better judgement, Agnes gave in. She didn't really know why she was objecting. Only those who worked and moved outside of Penbole had met any Americans yet, since they weren't based in the immediate vicinity. There were some people in Padstow who had had several billeted on them and spoke well of them. The only ones most Penbole folk had seen were in the films that came out of Hollywood, and they were mostly fast-talking gangsters or slow-drawling cowboys. The occasional film depicting wartime events showed them as heroes, every one. Agnes tried to be realistic. It wasn't as though her younger girls were in any danger of having their heads turned by these Americans. They would be far from home and missing their families, and if they were looking for female company it would be young women of Breda's age who would be more likely to attract them. At least she had no worries there. She couldn't imagine that Breda was likely to have her head turned by any of them.

Agnes busied herself preparing tea, and let her thoughts turn to her eldest daughter. Breda was a lovely young woman, and what had happened to her in April was the worst thing any young woman on the brink of marriage could experience. It took time to get over such a thing, and five months was probably nothing, but you couldn't grieve for ever. She was glad when Max Pascoe came home at last and that they had resumed their old friendship. It was what her girl needed. Max wasn't Warren and never could be, but he was the next best thing, in Agnes's opinion.

Her hands paused over scraping the margarine on the bread for the fish paste sandwiches. Max was no substitute for Warren, and she knew Breda would never think such a thing. But a mother always wanted the best for her children, and in all honesty, if she had to choose someone else for Breda to share her life with, she could think of no one better than Max.

'Do you want some help, Mum? You're taking ages,' she heard Breda say behind her, making her jump. 'You're not still fretting over that party, are you? If I know Miss eagle-eyed Strachey, she won't let her Sunday School charges come to any harm!'

'Oh, I know you all thought I was making a fuss over nothing,' Agnes agreed. 'It's what mothers do, my love. When you've got babies of your own, you'll know.'

She spoke rashly, and immediately wished she hadn't made such an emotive remark. She turned to apologise to Breda, and then saw that her daughter was half-smiling.

'I think I've got a pretty good idea already. I know I'm more like a mother hen with my infants sometimes.'

Agnes gave a sigh of relief. The last thing she wanted to do was to stir up thoughts in Breda's mind about something that could never be, not with Warren, anyway. But it was also a relief that she hadn't closed in on herself at the mention of babies. It was a good sign that maybe, just maybe, she was finally coming out of the terrible feeling of loss that had gripped her for so long.

The party that the Americans were hosting was arranged for two weeks' time. It would almost coincide with the Harvest Festival events in Penbole. Breda wondered if Americans celebrated Harvest Festivals too. They probably had different celebrations at different times of the year. She wasn't really sure, but it seemed a good idea to brush up on it a little, and use it as a small lesson for her class. The Americans were over here now, and the children couldn't help but be aware of it. She liked to introduce topical things as well as the regular lessons, but before she could inform them, she had to find out the details for herself.

She thought she might have found out something from the small library in the village but it didn't have that kind of information. So after giving it some thought, Breda went to the family source of all knowledge. She called on her one evening after school.

'Gran, what do you know about American customs and traditions?'

'What a question to ask!' the old matriarch said. 'How should I know about such foreign things?'

'Oh well, I thought you were my best hope, but if you don't know anything, I suppose Dad or Mr Pascoe might be able to tell me something.'

'Now just hold your horses. I might be able to think of something, but why do you want to know? You're not taking a fancy to any of these

281

Yanks, are you?'

Breda laughed. 'Of course not. I don't know any! No, I just thought it would be interesting to tell my class something about them, that's all. It seems as though the Yanks are going to be around for a while, so we shouldn't be ignorant about their way of life.'

'The infants are a bit young for all that, my love!'

'I don't think they are. They may be only five years old, but they're ready to absorb everything at that age, and they loved hearing Max tell them about Egypt.'

'It's a pity he hasn't been to America, then he'd be the one to ask.'

'Well, he hasn't, so do you know anything or not?'

Gran pursed her lips in thought until they almost disappeared. She wrinkled her brows, sending them into even more pronounced corrugated lines.

'The only thing I can recall is something about a Thanksgiving Day at the end of November. It's something to do with when the first settlers from England landed there, but my memory's hazy. What you want is to find out from one of these Yanks first-hand. Get one of them to come and talk to your infant class.'

Breda jumped up excitedly. 'Gran, you're a genius! I'm sure Miss Strachey will tell me how I can get in touch with them.'

'You want to watch these Yanks, mind,' Gran warned her with a toothless grin. 'They'll see a pretty girl like you and want to whisk you off across the ocean.'

'That'll be the day! But thanks for your advice, Gran. Actually, I'd better talk it over with Mrs Larraby first of all and, if she approves then I'll go and see Miss Strachey.'

She kissed her gran quickly, and whirled out of the cottage. With a real purpose in mind now, she felt more animated than before. It would be wonderful if one of the Americans themselves could be persuaded to talk to the children. They were always being told to be friendly towards their American allies, but so far, the people of Penbole village had had little chance of doing so, or even to know what they were like.

She was concentrating so much on the idea as she walked home, that she hardly noticed some-one walking towards her until she almost bumped into him. Then her heart leapt. Just as she had thought the first time she had seen him after so long, for a moment she thought she was seeing Warren. She quickly covered any sense of shock or disappointment that of course it wasn't.

'Oh Max, I'm sorry,' she said. 'I was deep in thought.'

'I can see that,' he said. 'I've just been to your place and discovered you weren't there. What's wrong?'

'Nothing! I've just had the most wonderful idea. Come on back with me and you can tell me what you think. I'll tell you when we get indoors, and I'm sure you'll approve.'

Without thinking, she linked her arm through his, hugging him to her. She was so overcome with the simplicity of the idea that she was longing to tell someone, anyway, and who better than Max, who would surely be as enthusiastic as she was?

'I don't think it's a good idea at all,' he said flatly, when they were sitting indoors with glasses of lemonade in front of them.

'Why on earth not? I thought you of all people would see the sense in it. You told them about Egypt because you'd been there and knew it first-hand, so what's wrong with asking an American to tell them about one of their traditions?'

She was bitterly disappointed by his reaction. It was almost as if he was jealous – and that was ridiculous, because he'd never been to America, and couldn't know any of their customs. Or was it because he didn't want one of the dashing Yanks, in their tailored uniforms and their flash good looks, invading his territory? But that was just as ludicrous.

'I suppose you've met some of them, have you?' she challenged him, expecting him to have to admit that he hadn't.

'I've met more than a few,' he said shortly. 'You've forgotten the times I've spent in various hospitals and rubbing shoulders with patients who weren't English. There were many others from our allies.'

'So what have you got against them?'

'Nothing. Some of them were all right.'

She gave an exasperated sigh. 'Well, what's your objection then? You seemed to think it was a good idea to broaden their education when you told them about Egypt. I was hoping you'd back me on this, Max. You know how much I value your opinions.'

'Oh, well then, and I'm probably just being a dog in the manger.'

Breda took a proper look at him then, and realised that he looked more agitated than usual. 'What were you coming here for tonight, anyway? Did you have something to tell me?'

'I certainly did, but all this has put me off my stroke.'

'You'd better tell me now then. I know you, Max, and something's up, isn't it? What's happened?'

His voice was guarded. 'It's nothing to worry about.'

If it wasn't so childish, she felt like stamping her foot. And then some sixth sense told her that whatever she was going to hear it wasn't going to be good news. She folded her arms and refused to move until he came out with it.

'I'm a big girl now, Max,' she said, trying to lighten the moment. 'I've coped with plenty in the last five months, so whatever it is, I'm sure I can cope with this.'

'All right, and don't go off half-cocked, but Aunt Laura's had a funny turn. Uncle Jed thought it was a heart attack and sent for the doctor, but he says it's nothing of the sort. It's either a simple panic attack or mild asthma. She has to stay in bed for the rest of today and then take things easy tomorrow. She made a great fuss over that, of course, complaining that there was nothing wrong with her and grumbling at Jed for fetching the doctor.'

Breda had jumped up now. 'Why on earth didn't you tell me right away? I'll come back with you and see if there's anything I can do.'

'I don't know that you can do anything. I'm there and so is Uncle Jed, and we can see to everything.'

'Oh, is that so? She'll need proper looking after, and when was the last time you cooked a meal?'

He snapped back. 'It was in the desert, Miss Gourmet Chef, with the most basic of tin cans and the kind of meat your delicate stomach wouldn't want to know about. I can rustle up something for us tomorrow, and we won't starve.'

'Well, you may not need me, but I'm still coming to see her,' Breda said, decidedly ruffled now. She hardly knew why she was arguing with him, when it was obvious he was concerned about his aunt, and really cared about her. Maybe it was the fact that he implied Breda wasn't needed, when all anybody wanted was to be needed by somebody.

As they retraced their steps through the village, she thought how strangely this day was turning out. Her excitement over the possibility of finding one of the Americans to come and talk to the schoolchildren was fading fast. For the moment this was far more important. She was nearly as fond of Warren's parents as she was of her own family, and Mrs Pascoe had never seemed a weak woman.

You just never knew, though. It could even be the delayed shock of Warren's death, followed by the second shock of Max's homecoming, however joyful that had been, that had given her this panic attack. She prayed that was all it was.

'I'm sorry, Max,' she said abruptly as they neared the Pascoe house.

'What for?'

'For mentioning the blessed Yanks at all when you were worried about your aunt. I don't know if Mrs Larraby will agree to it, anyway. It was just an idea.'

'And probably a good one. I just wasn't in the mood to hear about it.'

She was mollified by his words, but she couldn't be bothered to think any more about it now. She just wanted to see for herself that Mrs Pascoe was all right.

She found her sitting up in bed, looking decidedly cross at being ordered to stay upstairs. The aromatic smell of steaming Friar's Balsam wafted through the room, and Laura gave a sigh of exasperation as soon as she saw Breda.

'Don't tell me they've sent for you too. It's a lot of bother about nothing, and I'm getting up tomorrow. This steam will soon get my tubes opened and I'll be as right as rain. Not that I'm not glad to see you, my dear,' she added, 'but men do fuss so, don't they?'

'It's because they care about you, Mrs Pascoe, and I'm really glad to see you looking like your usual self.'

And sounding it too, Breda thought, hiding a smile. Like most hardy women of her age, Laura Pascoe never had much patience with illness in herself. But Breda was relieved to hear her grumbling. This family had had enough to cope with in recent months without anything happening to the mainstay of it, which was what the woman of the family always was. She glanced around to see Max hovering at the bedroom door, still looking troubled. He did care, she thought. He was one of the most caring people she knew, for all his undeserved rakish reputation. The sudden rush of warmth she felt for him took her by surprise.

'Why don't you put your cooking skills to work and make your auntie and me a cup of cocoa, if it's not too much trouble?' she said, her voice a little shaky.

Chapter Seventeen

To Breda's surprise, Mrs Larraby didn't jump at the idea of inviting an American to tell the children about their customs and traditions, and she knew far more about it than Breda had imagined.

'My father became quite an authority on them at one time,' she told Breda. 'He used to tell me about it, and I know one of the important dates in their calendar is Thanksgiving Day, towards the end of November. It goes back to when the Pilgrim Fathers first landed there in 1620 and they had a very bad season with failing crops and so on. The following spring, the local Indians showed them how to grow corn and about the crops that were more suited to that part of the world. They also taught them how to hunt for game, and to fish, and after that they flourished.'

'It's a bit different from the cowboy and Indian films then when they're always fighting one another!' Breda said.

Mrs Larraby laughed. 'Yes, without those first Indians, the pilgrims would probably have starved, and history might have been very different.'

'So why don't you think it's a good idea for one of the Americans to talk to the children?'

'I think the history is a good idea, Breda, but they'll be telling them about a celebration when the tables are loaded down with all kinds of food for a feast, with turkey and pumpkin pie and many rich dishes that they've never heard of. I'm not sure it's the right thing to do, considering our pathetic wartime rations.'

'I think the children are too young to worry about that.'

'But their parents are not. Look, I can see you want to follow this up. If you like, I can borrow one of my father's books for you to read, and instead of asking a stranger to talk to the children, I think it would come better from you.'

'Do you?' Breda said dubiously. She couldn't deny she was disappointed by this response, but as the headmistress, Mrs Larraby would have the last word on it, and she hadn't finished yet.

'Don't forget that the children here haven't seen any Americans, especially those in uniform. They're still foreigners as far as they're concerned. I think that with the help of my father's books and your imagination, you would do very well.'

This hadn't been part of the plan at all. Breda had been rather proud of getting the Americans themselves involved. Now, it seemed it was not to be. But that was being stupid, she told herself, and she was forced to say that she would be glad to see the books. In any case, there was no hurry. If the Americans' Thanksgiving Day was towards the end of November, that would be time enough to make a lesson out of it.

She was going to see Laura that evening and she knew she would have to let Max know what had happened. If she didn't tell him, he would surely ask. He might even crow a little that she wasn't being allowed to invite some smart American to talk to the infants, she thought cynically. But then, remembering how the children had almost hero-worshipped him when he had told them about Egypt, she felt that strange sense of warmth running through her again, recalling his easy smile and his voice, and the gentle way he had connected with the five-year-olds. Perhaps he should swot up on the Yanks' customs and do the talk himself! She squashed that notion right away.

Getting ready to go out that evening, she paused as she eased her long hair out of its ponytail and brushed it into a simpler style. The frisson of warmth she had felt towards Max suddenly changed into a flash of anger. It had been too warm, too tingling, too everything she didn't want to feel towards anyone else except Warren. It was too soon for any of those feelings, and especially not towards someone who looked like Warren and talked like Warren, but could never *be* Warren. Even if the old friendship she and Max had always shared ever turned into something else, how could she be sure it wasn't because he was so like Warren? How could she be sure she wouldn't be thinking of him as a substitute for the love of her life?

If she had felt warm before, she felt a cold chill run through her now. She didn't want those feelings invading her body. She wished she didn't have to see him constantly, but there was no way she could avoid him, and if she couldn't trust her own emotions, there was only one way to deal with it. If it was the only way to keep a certain distance between them, she would have to try to be cool towards him. But how difficult was that going to be with her dearest friend? All the same, she couldn't risk letting these treacherous emotions enter her heart.

She had steeled herself by the time she reached the Pascoe house that evening. Laura was doing what she always did, pottering in the kitchen, while Jed read his paper and smoked his pipe, filling the house with its evil smoke. Breda felt a sense of annoyance. Where was Max, who had implied so sincerely that he was going to take care of his aunt? And why couldn't Jed have helped for once?

'Why aren't you sitting down, Mrs Pascoe?' Breda said at once. 'Let me finish the washing-up for you.'

'Now then, Breda love, the day I can't do my own washing-up is the day I might as well turn up my toes, and I'm not ready for that yet.'

'Is Max upstairs?' she asked casually, aware that her heart was thumping for the ridiculous reason that she was planning to act differently towards the young man she had known all her life. And he wouldn't like it – any more than she would. But the fact that she thought he should be here with his aunt was definitely going to help.

'He's gone out for a band practice. They've got the village hall for two nights a week now, to get ready for the Harvest Festival dance. It's doing him good, Breda, and he's already looking more like his old self again. And before you say anything, I insisted that he went. I don't need a nursemaid, my dear.'

'Are you sure you're feeling quite well?'

Laura sniffed. 'Of course I am. Those two made a fuss over nothing, and a bit of Friar's Balsam over a bowl of steam always puts me as right as ninepence. They caught me at a bad moment, that's all. It's good of you to come and see me, Breda, but you don't want to sit indoors with we two old codgers. Why don't you get down to the village hall and enjoy the band practice?'

'Well, I did want to have a word with Max,' she said reluctantly.

'There you are then. And once I've cleared up here I'm going to sit down with my knitting, so don't go worrying about me any more.'

There seemed nothing more to say, and Jed hardly looked up from his paper as she left the house, merely grunting that he'd look after Laura, never fear. He didn't make much of a show of it, thought Breda. But that was the way they had always been, and he'd sent for the doctor soon enough when he'd thought there might really be something wrong with his wife.

She walked back towards the village hall, and as she neared it she could hear the sound of music. It didn't sound at all bad. The three who had been left behind all this time had evidently kept their hands in, and Max was so adept with his saxophone it was as if he had never been away.

As she heard the sound of giggling behind her, she turned around to see three girls approaching, and she realised they were the Land Girls from Gough's Farm.

'You're that girl we met the other day, aren't

293

you?' one of them said. 'Do you know where this village hall is? We can tell it's around here somewhere, so we're going to give the boys a surprise.'

Breda felt an unreasonable stab of jealousy run through her. They wore makeup and they looked quite smart now. Their accents were quick and fruity, and there was no reason why they should make her feel inferior, but they did, damn it, they did.

'I should think you could follow the sound of the music,' she said. 'But in case you can't, it's over there.'

They giggled again, whispering something that she couldn't hear, and then they said a casual 'thanks', linked arms and waltzed on ahead of her.

For a moment she was undecided about what to do. She needed to see Max, and if she didn't turn up at the village hall his auntie would ask why he hadn't seen her. Then her chin lifted. Why should she stay away from the band practice on account of some simpering girls? She strode ahead and went inside the hall.

The boys were taking a pause now, and George was chatting to the three girls. As soon as Max saw Breda he came across to her.

'Aunt Laura's much better today, in case you were asking.'

'I don't need to ask. I've been to see her, and I was surprised you weren't there,' she replied.

He didn't miss the coolness in her voice, and he replied just as coolly.

'I wasn't there because she didn't want me fussing around her, as you very well know. Besides,

Uncle Jed was staying in all evening in case she felt unwell. You can't put people in cotton-wool, Breda. Are you checking up on me now?'

She couldn't believe the way they were talking to one another. Surely even strangers wouldn't talk to one another in such an aggressive manner. Annoyed, she reminded herself why she had wanted to see him.

'Of course not. I just wanted to tell you that Mrs Larraby doesn't want an American soldier to come and talk to my infants. She wants me to gen up on the information and talk to them myself. Her father's got a lot of information about American traditions, and she thinks the kids would prefer to hear a voice they know rather than a stranger's. What do you think?'

She could hear herself saying it far too clumsily and hastily, and almost as if she resented having to tell him at all. As if she was a failure because she hadn't got her way. As if she would far rather have had a dashing American soldier come to the school and talk to her class. She hadn't meant to sound so petulant, and it wasn't the right time, when the other three band members were already tuning up and calling out for Max to join them. He almost snapped at her.

'I don't think it's anything to do with me, but we'll talk about it later. You're hanging around until we've finished here, I take it?'

Before she could answer, he had gone back to the others, and there was no more time for talking. She was tempted to slip straight out of the hall and go home, but how pointless would that be, when he would almost certainly come knocking on her door when the session had finished? She had asked for his opinion now, and he wouldn't let it go until they had thrashed it out one way or another.

She could see the three Land Girls giggling together as they sat near the back of the hall. Did they ever do anything else? Breda wondered. They were out of their own environment and she should probably try to befriend them, but they didn't need her. They had each other.

For a moment it was a thought to make her feel unutterably lonely, wishing she had a special friend she could talk to. But for all her life, growing up as a tomboy, there had only been two special friends: Warren and Max. Now there was only one, and she had pretty well alienated him tonight, she thought miserably. She determinedly sat tight through the practise session, applauding when the girls did, and listening to them wheedling the boys to walk them back to the farm – or better still, for Roy to get his dad's van and run them back. Did they think there was petrol to spare for joyrides these days? But Roy being Roy, he said he'd see what he could do, and they all went out of the hall together, leaving Breda and the others behind to pack up. The instruments were going to be kept safely locked up in a cupboard until the next practice evening.

'I'll walk you home and we can talk about this idea of yours,' Max said.

'It wasn't my idea. It was Gran's.'

Max gave a heavy sigh. 'I don't remember you being so argumentative, Breda. Anyway, I might as well tell you my news too. I'm tired of hanging around the village every day doing nothing except exercising my blasted leg, and it's not doing so badly now. There's a limit to how long a chap can pretend he's still convalescing without being bored to death.'

'You're not thinking of moving out of Penbole, are you? Max, it will kill your auntie if you have to tell her that.'

She was so alarmed at the thought it didn't occur to her how much it would hurt her too.

'No, of course I'm not moving away. But I've got a job. It's only just been arranged and I haven't even told the boys in the band or my aunt and uncle yet.'

'What kind of a job?'

It wasn't what she had expected to hear. And yet, how long could he have been content with doing nothing? He had never been one for wasting time, and these last weeks and months must have hung very heavily on his hands.

'Well, it's obvious I can't go globe-trotting any more like I used to,' he said, with a slight bitterness in his voice. 'In fact, I don't think I've got the heart for it any more. But I did plenty of driving in the desert in all kinds of vehicles. Rowan's Taxi Service is looking for a new driver, and I went to see them this evening, and I start on Monday.'

'I didn't think there was much call for taxis in Penbole.' She didn't want to put a damper on his enthusiasm, but she had to say it.

'People will always need transport to take them from place to place, and with no railway station or very frequent bus service, well, with a licence to take people to and from the nearest hospital,

297

Rowan's is ideal, and fully covered for the necessary petrol. I've been doing my homework, Breda, and they don't just operate in Penbole, so I shall be fully occupied from now on.'

And she didn't need telling that it was giving his confidence a great boost to be doing a proper job again. She hugged his arm impulsively.

'Well, good for you, and I'm relieved that you aren't moving away. For a minute I thought that was what you were going to tell me.'

'Would it have worried you so much?'

'Of course it would. I couldn't bear to lose you too.'

He didn't say anything for a minute, and then his voice sounded strange.

'I wish you meant that, Breda.'

They had reached her gate now, and she felt a small shiver run through her.

'Why wouldn't I mean it? You know how much you've always meant to me, and I couldn't have been more pleased when I knew you were coming home safe.'

'You'd rather it had been Warren though.'

She felt the heat rush into her face then.

'That's not fair, Max, and you shouldn't say such things.'

'Why? Don't you think I always knew I was second best? It was Warren you were going to marry, so it stands to reason it was him you wanted back.'

She shook herself away from him. 'You're in a very odd mood tonight, and I'm not listening to any more of this. I thought you'd have been pleased enough about your new job, but you seem determined to torture yourself. Go home, Max.'

'Give me a goodnight kiss to cheer me up then, and let's give the neighbours something to gossip about. You can do that for the wounded hero, can't you?' he said mockingly.

Before she could reply he had pulled her into his arms and pressed his mouth to hers. It might have been intended to be a teasing kiss between friends, but it quickly turned into something far more passionate. He held her so tight that she was aware of every inch of his body pressed against hers. She could feel his heartbeats, matching the drumbeat of her own. She could taste his breath, and her own arms were winding around him, holding him close, wanting the feel of someone else's arms holding her and loving her, so much...

'Dear God, if you knew how often I've longed to do that, Breda. How often I've dreamt of holding you in my arms like this.' He mouthed the words softly, as his lips moved a fraction away from hers.

She wrenched away from him then. Her lips were tingling, but no longer with an answering passion. She felt outraged that he had used those words to her. Even more so, she was upset that he had overstepped the mark of the loving friendship they had known for so many years, and made her forget, in those exquisite moments, that her heart still belonged to Warren and always would.

'I think you had better go now,' she said, her voice throbbing, and her eyes brimming with unshed tears. She felt she had betrayed Warren.

And Max had betrayed them both.

'I'll go, but just remember that you can't mourn him for ever, and he wouldn't want you to,' Max said harshly, just as if he could see right inside her head now. 'You have a whole lifetime ahead of you, Breda, and someday you may look back and see how much of it you've wasted. And I hope you'll save a dance for me at the Harvest Festival night. I'll need to take a break from my sax now and then.'

He swung away from her before she could say angrily that she had no intention of dancing with him or anyone, and didn't know if she was even going to go to the dance at all. But she knew that she would. Of course she would. Everyone would want to support their local boys in the band, especially when it was the first time Max Pascoe had been home to join them.

She went indoors and slammed the door behind her, knowing she was being as petulant as any of her infants and not caring. She didn't want him kissing her. She didn't want to dance with him and feel his arms around her. And just as instantly she knew that she did. The shock of it hit her like a blast of cold air. It was far too soon after Warren. It was all wrong. Especially with *him*. It could never be with him.

A treacherous thought crept into her mind. Was she so attracted to Max, her old friend, because he was so similar to Warren in every way? And if that were so, who did she really love? Was she tentatively falling in love with Max against her will? Or was it the ghost of Warren who was still so dear to her heart? How could she be sure?

How could she ever be sure?

The breath tightened in her throat. Just as before, Breda resolved to be as cool as possible towards Max. She didn't want to let him think for a moment that she had soft feelings about him. But what about his feelings for her? Was he really implying that he loved her, and had always loved her? He had never given any indication of this before. But she knew he wouldn't have done so, out of loyalty to Warren. He had too much integrity for that. But now Warren was gone, and there was nothing to stop him declaring that he loved her, if he really did so.

Unless he was just desperately sorry for the girl who was so nearly a bride, and wanted to show her that she was still desirable. Her thoughts were so muddled she was close to tears when she went to bed that night. She longed to bring Warren close to her in her dreams, but the dreams didn't come, and she spent a restless night, hardly sure of anything any more.

Daylight brought sanity, and she told herself she had simply overreacted to a kiss. It wasn't as if she was never going to kiss anyone else in her life-time, for goodness' sake. And Max was right in one respect, she thought reluctantly. She couldn't mourn for ever. Gran Hanney had told her that.

'Do you think we can all love more than one other person in our lifetime, Gran?' She asked casually the next time she saw her, knowing it was a question she could never ask her mother. 'I don't mean the love we have for our parents and friends, but the love between married people.'

Gran cocked her head. 'Do you have a special reason for asking me such a question, my lamb?'

Breda felt her face go hot. 'I'm not speaking personally, but I was thinking the other day about the women left behind when their men are killed in wartime. There were a great many single women after the first world war who never married again, weren't there?'

Whether or not Gran thought Breda *was* speaking personally, she kept her opinions to herself. 'There were that,' she agreed. 'And a great many babbies who were never born because of it.'

'What do you mean?'

'Well, it makes sense, doesn't it? If some of those widow women had married again, they'd probably have had babbies, and had a happy life. Some of those women had a struggle in their lives when their men died, and I think there was a lot of unnecessary hardship because they were too wrapped up in what was past instead of looking to the future.'

'You've got some very modern ideas for a lady of mature years, haven't you?' Breda said, wishing she had never started any of this.

Gran cackled. 'More like an old duck, my dear. But when you get to my age, you start to see things, and what I see is the way some people can forget that they've still got a life to live. Don't you forget it, Breda. Your Warren wouldn't want you to turn into one of those sour old biddies who decided they were going to be martyrs to a memory.'

'You never married again though, did you, Gran?' she said daringly.

302

'I wasn't widowed young, and there's the difference. I had a lifetime of marriage with your grandad until he passed away, God rest his soul, and when you've been Darby and Joan for so long you don't hanker after anything else. And that's enough talking for one day. I need to have a bit of shut-eye, so if there's no other little problem you want ironed out, go and leave me be, there's a love.'

Breda wasn't really sure she had ironed out any of her little problems, but as always her gran had spoken a lot of sense and given her something to think about. Or not, as she chose. Right now, she was going to put the whole troublesome thought of Max Pascoe out of her mind, and concentrate on planning things for her class now that the Harvest Festival was imminent.

She cycled up to Gough's Farm on Saturday morning. Farmer Gough was always agreeable to giving her a bundle of straw for the children to make their corn dollies, and it was a bright sunny morning for being out and about. It seemed abnormally quiet that morning, and she found the farmer and his wife talking in the farmhouse kitchen, both looking far more subdued than usual.

'Hello,' she called out cautiously. 'Can I come in?'

'Oh, Breda love, of course you can. I'll put the kettle on,' Mrs Gough said at once. She looked red-faced and puffy-eyed.

Breda thought frantically. They had no sons away at the Front, so nothing bad could have happened there.

303

But, clearly, something had happened.

'Is everything all right?' she asked tentatively.

Farmer Gough cleared his throat. 'It's Gina, one of our Land Girls,' he said. 'Her mother's written to say her brother's been taken prisoner, along with his best pal, and Gina's fair cut up about it.'

'We've had to let her go,' Mrs Gough put in. 'She wanted to be home with her mum and dad now, of course, and the other two girls are just as upset. We've sent them off into Padstow on the bus for the day, rather than have them hang around here being miserable. I don't know if Gina will be back or not. I daresay it depends on how much her mum needs her.'

Breda felt shocked. Every bad thing she had ever thought about the Land Girls being flighty flew out of her head. She could imagine just how Gina must feel, not knowing what was happening to her brother and his best pal. You heard such terrible tales about conditions for prisoners of war. Some said it was better to be killed outright than taken prisoner... She gave a shudder as the grim thought entered through her mind.

'Here, my dear, have a cup of tea,' she heard Mrs Gough say kindly. 'I can see this has upset you too, what with your own trouble and all.'

She pulled herself together. 'It's all right. I know you were fond of the girls, and this will have been a blow for you too.'

Mrs Gough spoke tearfully. 'They've been like a breath of fresh air to we old bodies, and we looked on them almost like our own. But they weren't our own, of course, and when something like this happens, you realise it all the more. Folk are only ever on loan to you, aren't they? God reminds us all of that in the end.'

'Now then, my love, Breda didn't come up here to be miserable, and you put a smile back on your face before the other two come back for their dinner.'

For a moment Breda had forgotten why she was here at all, and then she remembered. Asking for a bundle of straw seemed such a puny request compared with the fate of two young men being taken prisoners of war. But life went on, and never was there a sharper reminder of it than in the life of the farm, when cows had to be milked and eggs collected from hens day in and day out. She told them quickly why she was here, and was glad to get away as soon as she could.

'Please tell the other two girls how sorry I am to hear of their friend's news,' she said before she left the farm. 'I hope Gina gets positive news of her brother and his friend very soon.'

She cycled back to Penbole, and the salt breeze blowing in her face made her eyes smart a little. But she knew it wasn't merely the breeze that was making her feel sad and somehow humble. She felt an acute sense of loss for all the young men who would never come home again, and at the same time there was a small prayer in her heart for those who would.

Chapter Eighteen

Breda couldn't quite explain why hearing about the Land Girl's brother and his friend should have sobered her so much. Apart from herself, it certainly wasn't the first time people in the locality had heard bad news. There had been other tragedies in the village, and other reports of prisoners of war too, but it was the first time she had been with the people closely involved so soon after the news had broken. It was obvious that Mrs Gough had been fond of Gina and taken her news to heart.

Breda admitted she had more or less dismissed the girl as being a bit flighty, and looking down her nose at the quaint Cornish folk. She had even been slightly scathing of the Land Girls and their easy, flirtatious ways. She regretted those feelings now, knowing that Gina and her family must be feeling as devastated as she had done when she had the news about Warren. Her brother was still alive as far as anybody knew, but who really knew anything these days? She wondered if or when Gina would come back to the farm, but if she did, Breda resolved to be more tolerant towards her in future.

In any case, there were busy weeks ahead. Her sisters had returned happy and excited from their party in Padstow that the Americans had hosted, each child having been given a small bag of gifts, which included a bar of chocolate and a tin of fruit. The Harvest Festival was almost on them now. The schoolchildren had finished making their corn dollies for the church, and the band was making its last preparations for the dance at the village hall. It seemed as though most of the village was planning to attend, according to Laura Pascoe. She and Jed intended to look in for a little while, just to hear the band in action again, but Jed didn't dance on account of his old back injury, and didn't care for these occasions.

'I don't know where they'll all fit in, I'm sure,' Laura went on, 'but to hear Max talking, you'd think they had sold a thousand tickets. He's more excited about it than I've seen him in a long time, and he's looking more like his old self again.'

'Well, I can't comment on that as I haven't seen him for several weeks. I'm sure he's busy now he's working for Rowan's Taxi Service, so they must be doing good business.'

Breda tried not to let a note of resentment creep into her voice, but ever since that night when he had kissed her so passionately and she had pushed him away, she hadn't seen him at all. She was probably being a dog in the manger, but he was her oldest friend, and she wanted to keep it that way.

'It's more like a part-time ambulance service,' Laura said with a small sniff. 'I'm sure some of these old folks could easily catch the bus for their appointments, but they don't bother when they've got a handsome driver like Max on the doorstep, and a concession from Rowan's. Besides, they like his chat and his cheery smile.'

Breda wouldn't mind a bit of that herself, she was thinking as she went home. She really missed his chat and his cheery smile. She missed *him*. And yes, she was definitely being a dog in the manger.

Almost as if she had conjured him up, she saw the black taxi cab trundling down the hill towards her. Her heart skipped a beat. It was ridiculous. She knew him as well as she knew herself. Why should she feel so nervous just because he was pulling to a stop, as she wondered just how he was going to be with her now?

'Are you coming to the dance on Saturday?' he called out through the open window of the car.

'Of course,' she said, forcing a smile. 'It's all for a good cause, isn't it?'

'And don't forget you've promised me a dance. I'm going to hold you to that, mind. Can't stop now, though; I've got to collect one of my old dears to take to her foot clinic.'

He waved his hand and drove off. The smell of the exhaust stung her eyes for a moment, and she blinked it away. It was just as his auntie had said then. *Lucky old dear*, she was thinking, to be having the chat and the cheery smile ... and what the dickens was wrong with her to even think like that?

Gran Hanney had always been the person Breda found it easiest to talk her problems over with, and her gran was full of sympathy for the Land Girl when she heard the news of her brother. But Breda found her gloomier than usual that day, with news of her own.

'She's not the only one. It's happening everywhere nowadays. My old friend Ethel Payne's
grandson's just been reported as missing in
action, and another woman at my Monday meeting has lost her son in a plane crash, and she
hasn't had any word from her nephew for weeks
either. The war's coming to Penbole, Breda, and
there's nothing we can do to stop it, except to
keep them all in our prayers.'

'I'm not sure that prayers are doing any good,'
Breda muttered. 'It doesn't bring them back,
does it?'

'Now, don't go losing your faith, my girl. It's all
that holds us together in times of trouble.'

'It didn't help Warren, did it? I prayed for him
hard enough. I prayed for him night and day to
come back safely, and it didn't stop him being
drowned, and no amount of prayers helped me
after he died. It was you and Mum and Dad who
got me through it, not any meaningless mumbo-
jumbo from the Church.'

She hadn't meant to say any of that. She certainly hadn't meant to burst out with something
almost blasphemous that was sure to upset her
gran. But Gran Hanney didn't seem shocked or
come back at her in the way Breda half expected.
Instead, she looked at her sorrowfully.

'What's got into you, my love? You're not
usually like this. Has somebody upset you? If it's
all this talk of other young men dying and being
taken prisoner, then we'll say no more about it
and talk of happier things.'

'It's not that. I don't know what it is. It's something I don't even want to talk about, or think

309

about. It's not even something I've put into words myself.'

She knew she sounded irrational and almost incoherent, and the next minute she found her gran pushing a small glass into her hand.

'It sounds as if you need a bit of a pick-me-up, my love, so you'll take a drop of my medicinal brandy and no arguments. It will do you good.'

'I don't need brandy.'

'Drink it anyway,' Gran insisted, and because she was used to doing what her elders told her, Breda swallowed the bitter liquid, ignoring the way her head swam as she did so.

'Now tell me what's really bothering you,' Gran said gently.

'I feel too ashamed to put it into words.'

'Well, I'm sure it can't be that bad, Breda. I've never known you do anything in your life that you need to be ashamed of.'

Oh no? You've always put me on a pedestal, darling Gran, but what would you say if you knew about Warren and I making love before we were married? Isn't that a sin in your eyes? Wouldn't you say how wicked I was that we lay together and adored one another in carnal knowledge, which is how your precious and unforgiving Church would put it? How big a sin would it be in the eyes of the village too? Breda Hanney, the scarlet woman, shaming her family.

She gave a small sob in her throat. Because it wasn't that at all. She so fiercely clung on to that one glorious time they had shared. The one time that they hadn't known then was going to have to last them for all eternity. It wasn't that.

310

'I loved Warren so much, Gran,' she whispered.

'I know you did, my dear.'

'And the awful thing is that now I sometimes find it hard to picture his face. He's been gone such a little time, and already he's fading a little in my memory and I can't bear it. I want to keep him with me for ever, and he's already slipping away, and it's far too soon. I would go to sleep thinking about him, and when I awoke he was always the first thing on my mind. But he's not there the minute I awake any more, and it really upsets me. It's as though I'm losing him all over again. I have his photos and I look at them all the time, and I read his letters over and over again, but I still can't picture him the way I used to, and I want him back!'

She was almost gasping by the time she finished speaking. She had truly never put these thoughts into words before, nor allowed herself to believe that it could possibly be true that in a matter of months Warren's image was already fading. She felt fickle and ashamed, as if she was betraying him through no fault of her own.

She didn't want it to happen, and it was cruel that something more powerful than herself was taking him away from her all over again. Of course she could bring his image back by looking at his photos, but she wanted him there when she awoke, still beside her, still loving her from wherever he had gone... She wanted those blissful first moments of the day before the sick shock of remembering that he would never be with her again...

'Now you listen to me, girl,' she heard Gran

311

Hanney say firmly. 'Do you think that what's happening to you is unique? Don't you think this is what happens to everyone who loses a loved one? You can't hold on to a dream for ever, Breda.'

'But what about all the women whose menfolk are away fighting, and are gone from home for months at a time?' she cried out. 'Do they all go through this kind of thing? I can't believe it. I *won't* believe it.'

'Why not? Do you want to be the only martyr in the village? Because that's what you're going to turn into if you don't accept that it's the same for everybody. Yes, for those folk whose men are away for long periods of time too. Think about young Max for a minute. Didn't you forget something of what he looked like all those times he was off wandering? I'm sure his auntie did so at times. But the minute you saw him again you recognised him instantly. He wasn't gone for ever. There's no sin in the way you're feeling, Breda; and we're all human.'

It wasn't the same, and the last person she wanted to think about was Max right then. She wished her gran hadn't mentioned him at all. But she reluctantly admitted it was true. Max's image had never been uppermost in her mind all the time he was away, but she had been able to bring it back, just as she could now bring Warren's back. In that instant Warren was right there in her imagination and in her heart, as real as he had ever been.

The rush of relief she felt then was an almost physical pain, and she knew it was only the morning thing that had upset her so much. It was this yearning for him to be with her the moment she awoke, so that in those first blissful moments before reality rushed in she could believe he was still alive, still coming home, still her sweetheart, her lover.

'Thank you, Gran,' she murmured weakly. 'As usual, you know just the right things to say to put things right.'

'Ah well, my dear, when you've been in this world as many years as I have, there are few things a body doesn't know, so dry your eyes, go home and remember all the good times you and Warren shared. And then believe that it's time to move on and don't waste the rest of your life in mourning things that can't be changed.'

'So you think I should go to the dance on Saturday night?' Breda asked with a watery smile, as if it was the only important thing in her life.

'I'd say that's a very good place to start.'

It felt odd to dress up and brush out her hair until it shone and apply a bit of make-up. It was the first time she had done such a thing for ages. There would be people there who knew her, old school friends, and older matrons. They would be watching to see how she was coping, poor girl, and her pride wasn't going to let her look down-trodden. Her parents had said they might put in an appearance as well as the Pascoes, just to support Max and the band, and they too would be watching their girl carefully, but she was going to hold her head up high. She told herself she was doing this for Warren too. He would want her to be brave and not fall apart at the first real social affair she had attended since April.

The band was already playing when she arrived, since she hadn't wanted to get there too early. Max didn't see her at first, and she couldn't help thinking how handsome he looked now. He had lost much of the gaunt look he'd had when he first came home, but he had certainly lost none of his skill on the saxophone.

Something must have alerted him to her, as in a little pause in the music he turned his head and saw her, and the smile he gave her then made her heart turn over, because, oh God, it was so like Warren's smile. She swallowed hard and gave him a small wave before she wove her way through the crowds to where she could see her parents. Before she reached them she was stopped by two girls in bright summer dresses.

'It was nice that you sent a message to Gina,' one of them said a bit awkwardly. 'I'm Tess, by the way, and this is Ellie.'

Breda was so surprised that she didn't know what to say. Did they want to be friends with her? She'd never thought so for a minute before. She hadn't even asked their names. But that was when there were three of them, as close as clams, and these two looked suddenly unsure of themselves, despite the make-up and the high heels. Remembering how the three of them had been such friends, Breda guessed it was Gina who had been the leader, and without her, they were a bit lost. As if to reinforce her thoughts, Ellie gave an uncertain laugh.

'Gina's not coming back, and we don't know a

soul except you and the boys in the band, and they ain't going to be very chatty tonight, are they?'

'Come and meet my parents, if you like,' Breda said without thinking, and they tagged along behind her almost gratefully.

It was strange, when she had thought them so standoffish and superior before, and now they were the odd ones out, and probably wondering why they had come here tonight at all. But, after all, they were just people, and once they had had a couple of dances with the boys who dared to ask them, they seemed more relaxed.

As well as the modem tunes, the band played some old tyme dances for the older folk, and plenty of excuse-me and progressive dances too, which got everybody in a sociable mood. Half-way through the evening there was an interval when the band could take a breather, and Max came across to where Breda and the Land Girls were sitting.

'I'm glad you came,' he spoke to them all, but his eyes were on Breda. 'How do you think it's going?'

'Everyone's enjoying it, Max,' she answered. 'You must be very pleased.'

'We are, and when we start up again, I'm claiming my dance. I've told the others, so no excuses, mind. Now I'm off to get a drink because I'm parched. I'll bring some over for you three as well.'

The girls giggled as they watched him go, and Tess nudged Breda.

'He really fancies you, doesn't he? I reckon he's

315

a real good catch for some lucky girl, that one.'

'I don't know about being a real good catch,' Breda said with a forced smile. 'He's just someone I've known all my life, that's all.'

'So what's wrong with fancying someone you've known all your life? Sorry if I'm speaking out of turn, by the way. Mrs Gough told us about how you lost your boy earlier, but if you don't snap this one up, I reckon someone else will pretty soon. He won't stay unattached for long.'

'I'd rather change the subject if you don't mind,' Breda said, starting to feel uncomfortable as she saw Max coming back with four glasses of lemonade balanced precariously on a tray. These girls had a far more outspoken way of talking than they did in Penbole, and she wasn't sure she liked it.

'Take no notice of Tess,' the other girl said. 'She's always a bit of a matchmaker and she don't mean no harm,'

'It's all right,' Breda murmured. The annoying thing was, she was sure Tess was right. Max wasn't going to stay unattached for long. And how would she feel then...? She told herself she would be glad for him, and that it would mean nothing to her, except for the pleasure of seeing him happy. But somewhere deep inside herself she knew she was being a total hypocrite, because if and when that happened she would be as jealous as hell.

The music started up again with a drum roll, making her jump.

'My dance, I think,' Max said steadily, holding out his arms to her.

316

'Go on, girl,' she heard Tess say beneath her breath.

And then she was moving forwards with Max, moving into his arms as the band played a dreamy waltz to begin the second half of the evening. The thought fluttered through her mind that she would much rather it had been something wild and lively like the Gay Gordons, instead of a sentimental tune that was all too emotive for comfort.

'Relax, Breda, I won't bite,' Max said in her ear.

'I never thought you would,' she said crossly.

She was very aware that people were watching them. It was probably just her imagination, but right then it seemed to her that everyone in the hall was taking note of the way Max Pascoe and Breda Hanney were dancing. Holding one another close in the crush of dancers, their hands clasped, his arm around her waist, her head so near to his shoulder.

It should have been Warren. How sweet it would have been if he had been home on leave, and it had been the two of them floating around the village hall in time to the music. How much sweeter still if there had been no war, and they had been married the way they had always planned. The music ended, and Max squeezed her hand for a moment before leading her back to the other two girls, and then making his way back to join the rest of the band.

'You certainly looked as if you were enjoying yourself, gel,' Tess said cheekily, and then two eager young men in army uniforms came to ask the girls for the next dance, and Breda was left temporarily alone until her mother came and found her.

'We're not staying until the end, Breda. Your gran's been at home with the girls tonight even though she had the screws real bad earlier. She won't want to be too late, so we'll be going in about half an hour. She might stay for a bite of supper, so do you want to come back with us when we leave as well?'

'Yes, that would be nice, and then I can walk home with Gran.'

It would also give her the perfect excuse not to stay until the end of the dance, and hearing the band playing the goodnight song they had been practising. She didn't want to listen to 'Who's Taking You Home Tonight?' and know that it wouldn't be Warren. Better by far to be long gone before then.

'Are you all right, Breda? You look a bit flushed,' Agnes said keenly. 'I saw you dancing with Max earlier. He's looking much better, especially now he's got his new job with Rowan's Taxis.'

'Yes, it's good that he's getting back to normal, and I think Dad's looking for you, Mum,' Breda said desperately. For pity's sake, she didn't want to spend the evening discussing how well Max looked, or whether or not he fancied her, or what a good catch he was going to be for some lucky girl...

She saw one of the boys she'd been at school with coming towards her, wearing a soldier's uniform now, and she gave him an extra-special smile as he asked her tentatively for a dance. Well, this was why she was here, wasn't it?

All the same, she was glad when her parents decided it was time to go. They walked home with the strains of the music fading into the background behind them. When they got back, Gran was dozing in her chair, and the girls were in bed.

'Now then, Mother, are you having a sandwich and a cup of cocoa with us before Breda walks home with you?' Agnes said brightly.

'I don't think I will,' Gran said. 'My old bones are paining me something terrible tonight, and I'll be better off in my own bed.'

'I don't want anything either, Mum,' Breda said quickly. 'I'm tired as well.'

She listened to herself, sounding like a hundred years old when down at the village hall people would be dancing the night away for a couple more hours yet. But she wanted to be home, inside her own four walls, and to shut out the memory of what might have been and what could never be. The dance had been something of an ordeal, she admitted, because in the old days it would have been Warren who was whisking her around the floor, even though he always said he had two left feet.

'Come on then, girl, let's make a move,' she heard Gran say as she heaved herself up out of the chair. 'Did you have a good evening?'

'It was a great success,' Breda answered, which didn't exactly answer the question, but seemed to satisfy everybody.

They walked back to her gran's cottage slowly, on account of her gran's creaking old bones, as she called them, and Breda went indoors to make sure she was going to be all right before she left her.

'Don't you worry about me, Breda love. I'll probably be as right as rain by tomorrow, but I'm glad you went out tonight. It's what you need, and I'm sure the company did you good too.'

'I get plenty of company every day at school,' she said with a grin.

'So you do, but it's not the same, is it?'

Breda couldn't argue with that. A class of chattering infants couldn't compare with a person of your own to come home to. She kissed her gran quickly, having been assured that she didn't want any cocoa and just wanted to get to her bed.

'I'll see you tomorrow at Mum's for tea, then,' Breda said.

''Course you will, if I'm spared,' Gran said, as she often did.

It was just an expression, no more. Older folk used it all the time, and there was no need to think it was in any way prophetic, just because her gran had looked older and more frail than usual that night. No need to shiver at the thought that one day her gran wasn't going to be there any more, and when that happened, Breda would feel that she had lost her best friend, and was more alone than ever.

She spent a restless night, sometimes sweet-dreaming about the dance, with the music running through her head, and sometimes having nightmares about death and dying, and being alone. She woke up in a cold sweat, sure that something bad had happened. It was barely dawn, but she knew she couldn't sleep any more, and she dressed quickly, and made herself some breakfast simply because it was the usual ritual. She couldn't go to her gran's cottage yet. If she was still sleeping, it would frighten the life out of her to be woken so early. And if she was not...

She hardly knew why she felt so apprehensive. Maybe part of it was because of seeing so many young men in uniform at the dance last night. Young men who were still boys in her eyes, boys she had known all her life from her schooldays, acting like men, ready to die like men. She smothered a sob, telling herself not to be so damn stupid, because they were all living out a dream, anyway. Boys always wanted to be heroes, and so they were, every one. Like Warren.

It was Sunday morning and even though the village was still sleeping, Breda knew she couldn't stay indoors a minute longer. She pulled on a coat, for there was a real autumnal chill in the early morning air now. She walked down to the quay, watching the fishing boats bobbing on the water and the waves rippling towards the beach, and breathing in the familiar tangy smells of salt and seaweed and fish. The sun was rising higher in the sky now, and the sea was pink and gold and almost heartbreakingly beautiful, with no hint of how cruel and treacherous it could be.

She sat on the sea wall until she began to feel numb, and eventually she turned away, knowing she couldn't put off the moment any longer. She had to see if her gran was all right, and to rid herself of this sense of doom.

Her gran had always been an early riser, and

Breda found her in the little back garden putting out bread crumbs for the birds, as sprightly as ever. The overwhelming sense of relief brought tears to her eyes, and she dashed them away.

'You're all right today then,' she said stupidly.

Gran straightened up with only a twinge or two in her back.

'Of course I am. Didn't I tell you I would be? And what are you doing up and about so early on a Sunday? You weren't fretting about me, were you?'

'Just a bit,' Breda muttered.

'Well, come inside and make us both a cup of tea and a piece of toast, and then you can stop worrying. I swear I've never known a girl worry as much as you do, Breda. I'm going to church later, and you can come with me. I may not be able to kneel as easily as I used to, but the good Lord won't mind that.'

There was nothing much wrong with her then, and over tea and toast, Gran Hanney looked at her thoughtfully.

'You know, Breda, facing every occasion when you used to do things with Warren is going to make you sad, but you'll get over that. Last night was the first dance you've been to without him, and of course you remembered other times, but you've done it once, and it'll be easier next time. You'll remember other Christmases and birthdays, and it's only natural to grieve for those times. Every milestone and anniversary is a reminder that everybody goes through, and there are plenty of others in the village who'll be feeling exactly the way you do.'

'I know,' Breda said.

Her gran patted her hand. 'But it's too early for me to be giving advice, and I'll be wearing my old brain out before the day is done at this rate. Put on a happier face and come back when it's time for church.'

In other words, she was dismissed. But Breda walked home with a lighter heart. Her gran wasn't indestructible. Nobody was, but Breda had a certain feeling that it wasn't Gran Hanney's time yet, and that was the biggest comfort of all.

Chapter Nineteen

Breda saw little of Max during the next weeks. Meeting his auntie at the butcher's shop for her weekly ration, she learnt that the band had been engaged for several dates in out of town areas, including a dance at an American army base, which they were very excited about. The taxi service was also keeping him busy. As the year drew to a close, more and more of the old folk in the town needed ferrying about to hospitals and clinics, and chose the taxi rather than wait for an ambulance to come all the way from Newquay, especially as they had such a friendly local driver.

'He's doing all right then,' Breda murmured.

'Better than all right, dear. It's so good to see him smiling again,' Laura said. 'This year has been a sad one for all of us, Breda, and I know it hit Max as hard as any of us when he learnt about Warren's death, but we have to go on as best we can, don't we, my dear?'

Well, you certainly seem to have recovered with the help of your second boy, Breda found herself thinking, and immediately hated herself for being so churlish. She knew, as well as anyone, how devastated Laura and Jed had been when Warren was drowned. She squeezed the older woman's hand.

'Tell him I'm pleased for him,' she said inanely, not knowing what else to say. What else could she say, when he was obviously in no hurry to speak to her himself?

But, as always, she told herself it was pointless fretting over something that couldn't be changed. Gran Hanney told her that often enough. And with the end of the year fast approaching, Breda had plenty to do to keep busy without wondering why an old friend didn't seem to have time for her any more.

Mrs Larraby had decided, after all, that telling the infant class about the American Thanksgiving Day wouldn't be of any benefit to them. It would have been different if there were any Americans based anywhere near Penbole, so that the children knew who they were, and, anyway, they were too young to appreciate exactly where America was. Even with the help of maps and globes, the concept of the distance was beyond them. When Max had spoken to them about Egypt, they had the bible stories to identify with. So the idea was nipped in the bud before it had even got started. In any case, by the end of November thoughts were turning to Christmas. The children were going to make paper chains to decorate their classrooms, and there were already plans for the annual Christmas nativity play, which was always held in the village hall, so that families and friends, and as many people as could be crammed inside, could watch the children perform.

Inevitably, as the children practised their carols and tried to get their lines right for the parts they were to play, there were questions about God and death and heaven. It was the same every year

325

with each new intake of children, but this year Breda found it especially difficult to answer their innocent queries.

'Did your boy go to heaven, Miss?' one little boy asked. 'My dad said he went down to the bottom of the sea, so how did he get up to heaven?'

'Did God send down a special boat for him, Miss?' somebody else asked, which started a small clutch of different questions and opinions.

'If the angels had to swim down to fetch him, they would have got their wings wet, wouldn't they, Miss?'

'Perhaps they all wear special macs.'

'Does God have room in heaven for all the people who die, Miss?'

'What's it like up there, Miss? Will we still have to go to school there, and will you be there with us?' came another anxious question.

On and on it went, until Breda had to call a stop. The questions got wilder and wilder, and some of the youngest ones were starting to look tearful. She tried to answer them as best she could.

'Now, just listen for a few moments. First of all, Neville, God has got plenty of room in heaven for all of us when we die. How he gets us there is one of His secrets. We don't know how He does it, because it's one of His miracles, but it's not something any of us needs to worry about. What God wants most of all is for us to be happy here on earth, so let's do just that by singing some of our favourite carols. Who wants to choose the first one?'

She breathed a sigh of relief as a dozen hands

shot up as they shouted out their favourite carols. These questions occurred every year, and every year it was just as impossible to answer them. She could only hope that she did her best.

All her infants were going to be either angels or shepherds in the nativity play, so there were few words for them to learn. All they had to do was to dress the part and know where they had to stand or sit in the play. Each child was to take home a letter to their parents, advising them of the costumes they would need. A good many old sheets would be turned into angels' robes, and just as many tea towels would adorn the heads of the shepherds. It was the same every year; the same ritual that had continued for generations over the whole country.

There had been one year, long ago, when Breda and Warren had been Mary and Joseph, with Max being one of the three kings. She didn't want to think of that, nor how Max had preened over being a king, when she and Warren had always known they had the most important parts.

Planning the Christmas story at school, plus the children's growing excitement, was making Breda restless. It was as Gran Hanney had said. Every anniversary of times she and Warren had spent together was going to be a poignant reminder, and once each first time was over, it would be a little easier. Nobody actually told her how to get over that first time, though, and the only way she could think of was to keep busy.

She spent that evening at home writing the letters to all the parents for the children's costumes, still praying that they wouldn't get complete stage-fright when they were faced with so many people in the village hall.

By the time her fingers were starting to feel stiff, she began to feel as though the cottage was stifling her, and she had to get out of it for some fresh air, even though it was hardly the right time of year for wandering about. The summer was long gone, and although Cornish weather was generally kind compared to the rest of the country, anywhere at all could be dangerous in the blackout. There was no more than a sliver of moon above, but in any case she knew her way through the village blindfolded, and suddenly she needed to be with people. She needed to be with her family.

Before she had gone halfway she heard the distant drone of aircraft engines, followed by the sound of shouting as one of the ARP men loomed up in front of her.

'You'd best get off the street, love,' he said importantly. 'It sounds as if Jerry's decided to pay us a visit tonight, and the safest place is indoors.'

She wanted to laugh. She felt almost light-headed, and she knew the feeling was probably because she hadn't bothered to eat any supper that evening. But German planes hadn't been this way for ages now. They attacked Plymouth and the coastal towns and the docks, not small villages in the back of beyond that had nothing worth bothering about except to the people who lived there. But as the man moved away to do more of his ARP duty, Breda supposed she had better do as he advised, and she kept her head down as she went on towards her parents' house.

The drone of the planes was still in her head, and the sounds of anti-aircraft fire followed in their wake now, but it was still distant, and it was obvious they weren't coming this way. She glanced up, and felt her heart give a lurch as she saw two ghostly slits of light slowly approaching her. For a few seconds she panicked, not knowing what it could be. She felt disorientated, her head seeming to swim as the ominous lights approached, like some unknown alien monster menacing her out of the darkness.

When they stopped right in front of her, she almost fainted. The sound of engines was very loud now, and then she realised it wasn't only coming from somewhere overhead, but from a very real vehicle on the ground. At the same instant, someone opened the door of the car, and a figure jumped out.

'Breda, what the hell are you doing, wandering about in the dark? I almost ran into you,' she heard Max say furiously.

She felt dizzy and sick at hearing his angry voice, and then all the strength seemed to go from her limbs and she slid down to the ground in front of him.

When she regained her senses she was in the back of the taxi and Max was sitting beside her, rubbing her hands to bring some life back into them.

'What happened?' she said dully.

'You fainted. Are you ill?'

She couldn't understand why he should still

sound so terse and aggressive towards her. What had she done to make him like this?

'No, I'm not ill. And why have you been avoiding me lately?'

The words were out before she could stop them. It was totally the wrong time and place to snap at him, when presumably he was concerned for her. Although if he was, he certainly didn't show it!

He didn't answer for a moment and then he released her hands. 'Look, I'd better take you home. I was just about to put the taxi away for the day, but you're my next case from the look of you. No charge,' he added mockingly.

Before he left her to sit in the front seat, her stomach gave a great grumbling roar, and she clutched it as he gave a short laugh.

'From the sound of that, I'd say you hadn't eaten for hours. Sit tight, and I'll get you home in one piece.'

It was hardly worth driving the short distance back to Forget-me-not Cottage, but from the way she felt, Breda wasn't even sure she could have walked it. She sat in the back of the taxi numbly, knowing she had been foolish to concentrate so hard on the parents' letters without stopping for supper.

Max parked the car and turned off the engine, before coming round to the back door to help her out. For heaven's sake, she wanted to protest, she wasn't one of his old dears who enjoyed the company of this handsome young man when they had to be taken to and from their hospital visits. But she didn't argue. All she wanted was to get indoors, and then he could go. But obviously he had other ideas.

'Sit down and I'll do you an egg and fried bread,' he ordered. 'You do have some food in the house, I suppose?'

Well, now he really was treating her like an idiot.

'Of course I do,' she snapped. 'And there's no need for you to do anything for me, or to stay. I'm sure you've got more important things to do.'

'No, I haven't, and even if I did, I'm staying here until you get some colour back in your cheeks. You look like a maggot.'

He had the most charming way of making her feel attractive! But as she heard him moving about in her tiny kitchen, opening cupboards and finding things, she simply sat back in a chair and closed her smarting eyes and let him get on with it.

In a very short while the tantalising smell of frying eggs and bread teased her nostrils, and then he was bringing in two plates of food, together with some tomato sauce to slosh onto it.

'I thought I'd join you, since you look as though you could do with the company,' he said.

She didn't answer. She truly felt ravenous, and once she started to eat she couldn't stop, and never had anything tasted so good. It wasn't a huge meal, but nobody ate huge meals nowadays.

'Thank you for that,' she muttered. 'I won't keep you any longer.'

Max merely took the plates away and put them in the kitchen before coming back to sit at the table again.

'I'm not going anywhere until you explain what you meant earlier.'

'I'm sure I said a lot of things.'

'No, you didn't, and anyway, there was only one thing that mattered. Why do you think I've been avoiding you?'

'Well, haven't you?'

'Of course I bloody well have. And you know the reason why, don't you?'

She flinched as he swore. She wished she'd never said anything so provocative. She might have known he would seize on it, and she didn't feel like entering into a soul-searching discussion right now. The letter-writing had taken half the evening, and coupled with her hunger, she was now feeling very tired and she just wanted him to leave so she could go to bed.

'Go home, Max,' she said tiredly.

'You never used to be like this,' he replied. 'Whatever happened to healthy and lively discussions between us? Can't we thrash anything out any more?'

'I don't feel like thrashing anything out, and nor do I think there's anything *to* thrash out. I'm tired and I just want to go to bed.'

'That's the first sensible thing you've said all night.'

Her heart leapt uncomfortably. She couldn't believe he'd just said those words in such a seductive way. Or was she imagining it? She stood up, hoping the action would put an end to the evening, but he stood up too and caught hold of her hands, pulling her towards him. For the first time, she recognised that his voice was tortured.

'If you don't know why I've been avoiding you, then I'm starting to think you don't know me at all. Warren wasn't the only man who loved you, Breda, and I've had to keep my feelings hidden for years now. I'd never have said anything at all if he had come back and married you as you always planned. But he didn't come back, and one day you'll learn to love somebody again. When that time comes I desperately hope it will be me, but don't make me wait for ever.'

Was that a threat?

Before she could stop her head spinning at his words he had pressed his mouth to hers in a hard and passionate kiss. She didn't even have the time to struggle to get out of his arms before he let her go again, and then he was twisting around and making for the door.

'Goodnight, sweetheart,' he said in the mocking voice he often used to hide his real feelings. 'I'd better get the taxi away from your door, before the neighbours start to think I'm staying all night, and that would really give them something to think about, wouldn't it?'

Breda stood still for a long while after he had gone, and then she turned with a sob in her throat and made for the stairs and her bed. She couldn't sleep, of course. Her mind was too active now, going over and over the things he had said, and finally professing that he loved her. She had always known he loved her, but she had thought it was the love of a friend who was almost like a brother to her. But he wasn't a brother and never could be. Against her will, she found herself wondering how it might be if she loved him too.

She didn't even want to consider it, but the nagging thoughts wouldn't go away now, and even when she finally fell into an exhausted sleep, he was there in her dreams, unwanted, but unavoidable.

Although she awoke with a splitting headache, a few things were clearer than before. She had to face what he had said, and what her gran had said, and probably what everybody else was thinking. Warren was gone, and no amount of longing would bring him back, and she had a lot of years ahead of her to be lonely. Perhaps, one day, she might even be ready to love again, however impossible it seemed to her now.

She jumped out of bed angrily, ignoring the way her head throbbed as she did so. She might be lonely in her personal life, but she had her family and her work, and the constant company of her infants. And no amount of gentle persuasion for the poor almost-bride to go courting again was going to push her into places she wasn't ready to go.

Christmas was nearly upon them now, and the infants were becoming more and more excited and taking up all Breda's energy. The classrooms were decorated with their paper chains and the fir cones they had gathered and painted silver. There were sprigs of holly that had to be carefully tied and hung so as not to prick any small fingers, and the small school was beginning to look very festive.

'Why aren't you decorating your cottage, Breda?' her sisters asked when they called to see her, with orders to keep out of their mother's way. They were always ready to oblige at this time of year, in the hope that presents were going to be wrapped and hidden away from prying eyes.

'I'll be at home with you all for Christmas Day, so I didn't see the need,' Breda replied, knowing that if things had been different, she and Warren would probably have turned this little cottage into a veritable fairyland of colour and tinsel. No coloured lights would be shining in windows or on the branches of garden trees, of course, since the war wasn't going to come to a halt just because it was Christmas, and extravagances they had once taken for granted were forbidden.

'Well, I think it looks a bit sad, so me and Esme will make some paper chains for you,' Jenna said generously. 'You'll have to give us the money, mind, and we'll go and buy some papers and paste in the village.'

She could hear the enthusiasm in her sister's voice now, and she knew they weren't going to take no for an answer, so she might as well give in. Truth to tell, once she got home from school, she didn't have much incentive to do anything about Christmas, but a couple of hours later, she had to admit that the girls' chatter, and the way they were getting down to their task, was bringing back some of the old excitement she had always felt herself.

'There!' Jenna said in triumph as they hung the last of the paper chains across the room. 'That looks better, doesn't it?'

'Much better,' Breda said with a smile. 'And since you've both been so helpful, you can stay and have some soup with me, and then I'll give you something to spend for your trouble. Don't forget to get Gran something for Christmas. You know she sets a lot of store by those things.'

'Yes, but we don't know what to buy,' Esme complained.

'Well, you don't have to buy her anything. She'd far rather it was something you had made yourselves. Make her a calendar for next year with some pictures of flowers on it. She'd like that.'

'You'll have to show us how. You're so clever at things like that, Breda,' Jenna wheedled.

Breda laughed. 'All right, just as long as I don't end up making it myself. This is your present, remember.'

It occurred to her that her sisters were becoming more sociable companions than the nuisances they had sometimes seemed before. Especially when she and Warren had wanted to spend some time by themselves, and these two little pests had always wanted to hang around. Their mother may have had an ulterior motive in sending them down to Forget-me-not Cottage today, but it was having other benefits as well. It occurred to her, too, that she had thought of herself and Warren at that moment without the pang that the unexpected memory of his name usually evoked.

'Let's have that soup before we do anything else,' she said quickly. 'I can't think when I'm hungry.'

It had certainly stopped her doing anything at all on the day she had almost been startled by Max's taxi into thinking she was being accosted by some weird monster. How foolish that had been – and how careful she had been ever since to remember to eat at the proper times of the day, no matter how busy she was.

'We'll have to come back on Sunday for you to help us make Gran's calendar, because we're going to Gran's when we leave here,' Esme said next. 'We're helping her unravel two old cardigans so she can use the wool again. She's going to pay us sixpence each.'

'You didn't ask her for money, did you?'

'Of course not,' Esme said indignantly. 'She offered, so we didn't say no. She says it'll give her something to do for the winter, and stop her poor old fingers from seizing up. That's what she called them, not us,' she added, before Breda could accuse her of being sarcastic.

Esme was getting far too clever for a twelve-year-old, Breda was thinking. She was growing up and getting taller too, and she wouldn't mind betting that the bridesmaid dress she would have worn last April might even have been a bit short for her now, and a bit tight around the chest, since she was already filling out in that department. Breda felt a softening for her sister, already on the brink of adolescence and all that it entailed. And she really couldn't blame her and Jenna for taking Gran's sixpences, and if it meant they would be keeping the old lady company while they unravelled the old cardigans, it was no bad thing.

'You're not bad kids, are you?' she said lightly, and then Jenna spoilt it all.

'We were wondering if you've got any jobs you

337

want us to do for you too. You don't have to pay us unless you want to, of course,' she said.

Breda laughed at her cheek. 'I'll think about it,' she said. But she had to admit that she was enjoying her sisters' company.

By the time the school nativity play was almost upon them, there was a frenzy of activity at the school, along with tears and tantrums as angels' wings wouldn't stay fastened and shepherds' headdresses kept falling off. In Mrs Larraby's class, Mary now had a sniffling cold, Joseph wasn't sure whether he wanted to be in the play at all, and the original Jesus doll had been dropped on its head, causing uproar from its owner, and was now replaced with a lesser model with fierce red lips, startling blue eyes, and a shock of blonde curls.

'Considering this is supposed to be the season of goodwill to all men, it seems to have missed out on us,' Breda complained to Mrs Larraby.

'It will all come right on the night, just as it always does,' the other woman said soothingly. 'Your angels and shepherds will all look lovely, and I'm sure they'll behave beautifully. And if they don't, they'll still be perfect to their families. A few mishaps on the night are only to be expected and just makes it all the more endearing, so don't worry.'

For a woman who had never had children of her own, Mrs Larraby had a great understanding of children and their parents, which obviously came from a lifetime teaching, Breda thought shrewdly. And she had more problems of her own with two of the Wise Men being away with colds and having to be replaced with two brothers who giggled through their lines. It could only be hoped that Mrs Larrraby's confidence was going to be proved right.

It seemed as though most of the village was planning to attend, and the village hall was filled to capacity on the evening of the play. The Virgin Mary took one look at the sea of faces and took fright, despite the fact that she had no lines to say. She proceeded to hide her face into the shawl covering her head, sniffling her way onto the stage until she was sternly instructed to sit down on the bed of straw with baby Jesus and be quiet.

Breda had no such trouble calming her angels, since most of them were too excited to be scared and, anyway, there was safety in numbers as they clustered together like a glorious white and silver cloud. She thought she was going to be very emotional when it began, but in the end she was just too anxious for everything to go right. And so it did, just as it always did, with thunderous applause from the audience, and proud parents and grandparents having a little weep at their offspring.

At the back of the hall, Breda could see her parents and sisters with Gran Hanney. She had hardly had time to register that they were there until it was all over and the lights went up. Alongside them were Laura and Jed Pascoe, and Max. She had wondered if he would come, but she might have known that he would. Warren would have been here too, since the school nativity play was such a tradition in Penbole, just as it was in schools around the country.

As Max saw her looking his way, he waved and smiled, and gave her a nod of approval and a thumbs-up.

The village hall was quite large, and there was a host of people between them. They were all milling around now, chattering excitedly over how wonderful it had been as usual. The children were dispersing, falling into the arms of doting parents and grandparents. And across it all, Breda could still see that one smile, especially for her, making her heart turn over.

She turned away, filled with sudden confusion, knowing she had needed that smile, that nod of approval, that thumbs-up. It was what Warren had always done. Telling her she had done a good job in getting the infants to perform, and that now she could go home and kick off her shoes, knowing that the school term was finally over, and that Christmas really started from here.

It was *exactly* what Warren would have done ... and Max had slipped into that role so effortlessly, probably without either of them realising it, that it brought a lump to her throat. And there was something more. It made her wonder, if, after all, she was actually having stronger feelings for him than she had ever expected – and just how foolish it would be to acknowledge it.

He was waiting for her outside the hall when she and Mrs Larraby had finally cleared up all the mess left behind. Most people had gone home now, taking their children with them, and only a few stragglers were left gossiping over the success of the evening.

340

'Walk you home, lady?' Max said, and before she had time to say anything, he had tucked her hand in his arm and was starting out for Barnes Lane.

She was still mute from the shock of her own feelings, but she realised that neither of them seemed inclined to be making small talk. In any case, it didn't seem necessary. It was still early evening, and in the enforced blackout the velvet, indigo night sky was studded with a million stars, and it had never seemed so beautiful. On a night that had seen so many innocent children celebrating the age-old story of the birth of a child two thousand years ago, thoughts of a war raging across the English Channel and in so many other parts of the world seemed as remote as those stars.

'Warren would have been proud of your part in tonight's performance, Breda,' Max said softly, as they neared her cottage.

Her eyes prickled, because with those few words, Max had brought Warren near; not leaving him out, not forgetting him.

'And if he was here, he'd have come indoors and had a mince pie without much mincemeat in it, and a cup of something with me to wind up the evening, so why don't you do it instead?' she asked huskily.

Chapter Twenty

As the year drew to a close, Max was doing a lot of soul-searching, and not only about Breda. Even if the war seemed as far away as ever from Cornwall now, it was truly a world war, with desperate fighting going on in occupied Europe and beyond. News of fierce battles in Italy and Russia had become more intensive, and Germany was being bombed by the British night after night. Max still grieved for friends and comrades he had left behind in the Egyptian desert, wondering how they fared – and how many of them were still alive to tell the tale. He still had occasional nightmares, reliving those days and nights, that kept him tossing and turning and unable to sleep. Sometimes he wished desperately that he could still be out there with them, finding the comparatively inactive life he led now more frustrating than rewarding. There were other nights when his wounded leg still throbbed so badly that he felt useless and impotent.

The hell of it was, he had always had such a vivid imagination that he could picture in his mind exactly the kind of hell-hole those places would have become, especially with the winter snows and bad weather on the Continent now. Common sense told him he would have been a liability and done the cause more harm than good. He was better off here, doing what he could with the band to raise funds, and at least raise the spirits of those who came to their dances. He admitted that driving the taxi and cheering the folk who needed him was also boosting his own spirits and he had to be satisfied with that – coupled with the fact that his aunt and uncle were still mightily relieved to have him safely home. He knew damn well it could have been so much worse.

Breda had also been examining her conscience during the last few weeks of the year. Her thoughts were far more personal. She faced the fact that she was still young, with all the needs of a healthy young woman, and she couldn't help questioning whether it would be so very wrong to fall in love again. In the initial sharp grief over Warren's death, the thought had been totally repellent, but the questions were in her head now and she couldn't get rid of them. What would Warren say if he were here? She had no way of knowing that, but he had always been a practical person, far more practical that Max in many ways, and she was darned sure he'd tell her not to waste her life over something that couldn't be changed. In fact, it had been a kind of motto of his: if something couldn't be changed, then you just had to adapt to the new arrangements.

What made it an added anxiety was the fact that the one person she was thinking about more and more was Max, and Max was his cousin. What would the family think? What would the village think? And why did it have to be Max, for heaven's sake? But she already knew the answer to that one. It was because he had always been a dear friend to her, and she knew in her heart that he could be dearer still, if she wanted him to be. But did she? She knew it was far too momentous a thought to be worrying about at this time of year, when her whole family was getting ready for Christmas, and she wouldn't think about Max Pascoe at all. Determinedly, she put him right out of her mind.

On Christmas Eve, she joined her family for the midnight carol service at the church, which was a family tradition, along with most of the village. She had made another resolution by then. It would be the first Christmas without Warren, and she had fully expected to be his wife this year and for it to be an extra magical time. But it wasn't to be, and she wasn't going to spoil her family's Christmas by being morbid.

The fact that Max and the Pascoes were at the midnight carol service too was to be expected. It was one of the rituals they always followed, and they all wished each other a happy Christmas as they parted later. To Breda's relief, Max didn't offer to walk her home. In any case, there were plenty of people going her way, all offering cheerfully to help each other along in the blackout. She had much to be thankful for, she told herself, almost fiercely.

Christmas Day fell on a Saturday that year. The day was cold and bright, with nothing more than a smell of snow in the air, and Breda was spending the whole day with her family. She had already left her bag of presents with her mother to

344

keep hidden from the girls, and she was collecting Gran Hanney on the way. There were few people about on Christmas morning, save for those like her, on their way to join their families, and the diehards going to church for the Christmas morning service.

'The war don't stop for Christmas,' Gran Hanney greeted her. 'I've been listening to the wireless this morning, and there's poor devils having a bad time of it in other places. I'll have to step up my knitting output. They might scorch in the desert all day, but Max told me it can even get cold there of a night-time. I don't suppose they'll mind a few fancy socks from my unravelled cardigans, do you?'

'Oh, Gran, I'm sure they'll be grateful,' Breda said with a laugh, trying to imagine war-toughened soldiers wearing bright green socks.

'You might laugh, miss,' Gran said keenly, 'but when your feet are near to freezing and there's danger of trench foot, you'll be glad of anything.'

'I don't think you get trench foot in the desert,' Breda murmured, 'but I'm sure you're right. Now then, have you got everything you need for the day?'

Gran never travelled light. There was always a bag of essentials which was never opened to anyone but herself and which nobody ever questioned. There was also the small bag of presents for everyone in the family, which they all knew would be mostly knitted scarves and gloves, and for which they all professed the same exclamations of surprise every year.

Inevitably, the time would come when Gran's

presents wouldn't be there any more, and Breda hoped that time would be a long way away. Impulsively, she put her arms around her gran and hugged her.

'I do love you, Gran.'

Gran's old face went pink. 'Good Lord, girl, what's come over you?'

'I just think we should tell the people we love how we feel about them. We don't say it enough, do we?'

'Well, if you start telling your sisters such things, they'll think you've gone soft in the head. I think we all know how we feel, my love. So come on now, let's go or your mother will wonder what's happened to us.'

They had to pass the Pascoe house on the way, and Breda couldn't resist a glance in its direction.

'Do you want to call in to wish them a happy Christmas?' Gran said.

Breda shook her head. 'I don't think so. We did all that last night, didn't we? Mrs Pascoe will want us to stop and chat, and probably have a drink and a mince pie, and that will delay us even more.'

And besides, she couldn't bear to go inside the house, knowing that someone was missing. At that moment the feeling of loss was so over-whelming she had to turn her eyes away from the house before they became too blurred to see where she was going. Her gran was holding on to her arm, and she felt the grip tighten.

'It will get better, my love,' Gran said softly. 'Every milestone you cross will be less painful, you'll see.'

'I know it will. You just have to ride them out, don't you?' Breda answered, more calmly than she actually felt. But it was true. You had to ride these things out, and hope that you came out stronger on the other side of them.

But in the end, Christmas was Christmas, despite the privations that food rationing had put on the country. Like Agnes Hanney, housewives everywhere somehow managed to produce enough tasty Christmas fare to satisfy a family, and the toast in every house was for absent friends, and the hope that this time next year the war would be over. In fact, the atmosphere in the Hanney house developed into something rather more jolly than expected. After the meal Gilb Hanney went out to his shed for a smoke and to fetch a bottle of his homemade beetroot wine, of which he was very proud. The beets had done well that year, and despite having to eke out the sugar ration, he had managed to produce a few bottles.

Breda and her mother were doing the washing-up when there was a sudden explosion. Esme screamed and clung to her grandmother, while Jenna dived under the table, yelling at her sister to do the same.

'It's the Germans!' Jenna screeched. 'They've come to get us!'

'Don't be stupid,' Breda shouted to make her listen. 'We didn't hear any sirens nor any planes, and it wasn't loud enough to be a bomb anyway. Come out from there, Jenna, and don't be such a baby.'

'Well, it was certainly something,' her mother said, not bothering to dry her hands as she rushed out to the back garden with the rest of them following her.

They were met by the sight of Gilb staggering outside the shed, blood-red and dripping from head to foot.

'There's no need to panic,' he yelled. 'It's only beetroot wine. The cork shot out of one of the bloody bottles and the stuff flew all over me. I'm not sure about the rest of it, so I'm going to uncork them all, and once I've changed out of these clothes we'd better drink what's left of it.'

By now, the neighbours on either side had also come outside, hanging over the fences and wanting to know what had happened. Explosions of any kind were enough to make every heart pound these days, but once they were assured that everything was all right the relief was making everyone near-hysterical, especially with the sight of Gilb still dripping with beetroot wine. The neighbours were finally invited in to take a Christmas drink with the Hanneys to get rid of any suspect bottles before any more explosions disrupted the whole street. So what began as a quiet family Christmas Day ended up as a loud and raucous event.

'You know, this reminds me of the old days,' Gran Hanney said with more than a slight slur to her words as she and Breda made their unsteady way homewards in the early evening.

'Does it? And what kind of things did you get up to in the old days?' Breda said with a grin, decidedly light-headed herself.

Gran sniffed. 'I wasn't born old, my love. I must say, your dad can make a fine bottle of beetroot wine, though. Me and your grandad used to like a little tipple on the quiet, never so much as to make us silly, of course, and never in public! Your grandad was a fine-looking man in his younger days, and we did a bit of drinking now and then, and a bit of dancing too.'

'Did you?' This was a side to Gran Hanney the younger ones didn't know!

'Oh yes. We had an old gramophone machine, and when we didn't go out to dances, we liked to dance in the cottage. You couldn't do much, mind, as there's not enough room to swing a cat properly, but it was enough to just be together and sway to the music, and none of this jitterbug stuff I've heard tell of nowadays.'

'It sounds lovely,' Breda murmured, wishing for a bittersweet moment that she could have had the same kind of memories to tell her grandchildren. She couldn't remember more than the odd dance she and Warren had been to together, and the memories were nothing like as sweet as those of her gran's. The dances were more of the village hop variety with two gawky and awkward adolescents trying to look sophisticated and failing miserably.

'It *was* lovely, and one day you'll have those memories too. They may not be with Warren but they'll come, you'll see. Now, see me indoors and right up the stairs to my bedroom, if you don't mind, my love, since I'm not sure my old pins will get me there safely tonight.'

349

It was another half hour before Breda finally walked home to Forget-me-not Cottage, feeling oddly relaxed and calm. By then her gran had insisted on giving her an extra Christmas present, as she called it: a beautiful butterfly comb for her hair, that Gran herself used to wear. It was a lovely and poignant gesture, and Breda was feeling quite emotional by the time she went home. It had been a good day, and she hadn't realised how much she had been dreading it all this time. But the family had all been together, the girls had been on their best behaviour, and the excitement of the beetroot wine exploding had added an extra dimension to the day that none of them had expected. Families, neighbours and friends ... that was what it was all about. They had ended the evening by singing a few carols, after persuading Breda to plonk away on the old piano, as Gilb called it.

It was a cold night and there were stars in the sky, and in a fanciful state of mind, Breda wondered if one of them was Warren, shining down on her, *smiling* down on her, approving of the way she had got through this first milestone day without him, and telling her to get on with her life from now on.

'I definitely had a little too much beetroot wine,' she muttered, fumbling her way into the cottage and feeling as weak-kneed as her gran now. All the same, as she went up the stairs to bed, she told herself again that it had been a good day, a very good day, and one that Warren would have enjoyed so much. She hardly registered that she could think of his name without the usual pain that such a thought might have produced.

Max called to see her on Boxing Day morning with a message from his auntie.

'She'd like you to come for dinner for bubble and squeak and leftovers and pickles, like you always did, and she's sorry she hasn't mentioned it before,' he said abruptly. 'We didn't have too good a day yesterday, and she really wants you to be there, Breda. What do you say?'

She felt almost guilty for knowing that the Hanneys had had such a good Christmas, while the Pascoes apparently had not. They would have been so conscious of the empty place at the table, while the Hanneys had had their house filled to overflowing with neighbours and good cheer...

'Of course I'll come,' she said swiftly. 'And then I'll tell you about our Christmas Day and I promise it will bring a smile to their faces.'

'Good. Then you can bring a smile to mine by saying you'll come to a New Year's Eve dance. It's a special fund-raising dance in Newquay and it's been arranged by the Yanks so there'll be plenty of them for you to dance with while I'm playing with the band. It's quite an honour to have them ask for us, but our reputation has obviously got around. And in case you're wondering how to get there, you'll have your own private taxi service. As it's a charity affair, I've got the use of it for the evening. So say you'll get dressed up in your glad rags and come.'

New Year's Eve would be another milestone to get through. She hadn't intended going any-where. She hadn't even thought about it. But

1943 had been such a terrible year for her, when she had expected it to be so wonderful, that 1944 could only be better. Almost feverishly wanting it to be so, she said yes.

Max's face broke into a smile. Only then did she realise how anxious he had looked until that moment, and she wondered just how bad a day it had been for the Pascoes yesterday. Impulsively, she reached up and kissed him.

'Gran told me that every milestone we cross will be less painful, Max, and I told her I knew it and we just have to ride it out. Think of yesterday as just another milestone, and now it's over.'

'I always said your gran was a wise old bird,' he said irreverently, making her laugh. 'And I'd say it's rubbing off on you, sweetheart.'

'I don't know about that, but she's not a bad act to follow, is she?' And Breda didn't want the conversation to get any more emotive than that.

'I've got something for you,' he said abruptly. 'Call it a belated Christmas present if you like, although it's hardly that.'

Oh God, she didn't want him to give her anything. She hadn't got anything for him. She had wanted to avoid anything remotely personal.

He handed her something in a brown paper bag. Inside was something hard, and when she went to open the bag, he stopped her.

'No, wait until I've gone. I don't want you blubbing over it or I might start. Be careful how you handle it. It's carefully wrapped. It's a piece of shrapnel they dug out of my leg. I can only vaguely remember somebody giving it to me, and it's been stuck in the bottom of my kitbag all this time. I was going to frame it, but then I thought your infants might be interested in seeing it.'

He finished almost curtly, and then he turned away from her and was gone from the cottage before she could say anything. In fact, she was so startled by what he'd said that she couldn't have thought of a suitable reply at all. She opened the paper bag and unwrapped the twisted piece of lethal-looking metal with its jagged edges, as sharp as a dagger. She shuddered, knowing the history of what she held in her hand. This had pierced Max's leg, and it would have gone deep from the look of it. It could have severed an artery, and it must have been excruciatingly painful. It brought home to her more graphically than any amount of reporting just how cruel war could be. And she wasn't at all sure her infants would appreciate the truth of what it was, unless she merely told them it was a piece of metal from a bomb blast. She owed it to Max to do that much at least.

She felt humbled by the sight of the thing. Cornwall had got off lightly compared to many other parts of the country. London had been badly blitzed, almost to annihilation, and so had Bristol and Coventry and the south coast towns. They were lucky here in this southwest corner of the country. But they all read the newspapers. They listened to the wireless reports. They went to the cinema and saw the propaganda and sanitised reports of what was going on, and how our gallant troops and allies were winning every battle. It was only something like this, that Breda held in her hand now, something so personal that had so nearly killed someone she loved, that told the stark reality of it all.

She didn't know what to do with it. Max had said he'd been going to frame it. She wasn't sure if he meant it or not. He'd sounded so odd when he said it. Perhaps he, too, sometimes looked at it, and realised how near to death it had brought him. In the end she placed it almost reverently on the mantelpiece. She knew her family would want to know what it was when they came to visit, and perhaps it would bring home to her sisters how evil war really was.

His visit had sobered her considerably, but as she remembered what he had said about the Pascoes' Christmas Day being less than good, she resolved to be cheerful and to make this day at least, one that was happier for them.

By the time she arrived at the house, she was determinedly cheerful. She had brushed out her hair until it shone and wore a fresh white blouse and a plaid skirt, tightly belted at the waist. She brought a pot of Gran's homemade pickle to add to the festive table and made a point of kissing Laura and Jed, following the same small rituals as on previous Boxing Days, when Warren had been there.

'Did you have a good Christmas Day, dear?' Laura asked out of habit, when they were all sitting at the table, as Laura prepared to dish out the bubble and squeak onto the sparsely covered plates of cold meat.

'We had a hilarious one, and I'm going to tell you all about it while we eat dinner,' she said.

'You could never guess how it turned out, nor how squiffy Gran and I ended up by the middle of the evening!'

'What's this?' Jed said, his normally gloomy face breaking into a more interested expression. 'You and your old gran getting squiffy? What's the world coming to?'

'I always said she was a game old bird,' Max said with a grin.

'I thought you said she was a *wise* old bird,' Breda corrected him.

'That too. So just what did happen at the Hanneys' yesterday?'

'Yes,' Laura said. 'It sounds rather an unusual way to spend Christmas Day this year, if I may say so.'

Breda could see that Laura was none too happy at the thought that they had all been very jolly, when they should have been sparing a thought for Warren. Well, she had done that and more, Breda thought, with a moment's indignation, but it didn't mean she had to sacrifice her whole life to mourning him. She caught a glance from Max, who gave a small nod, just as if he could read her mind.

'You wouldn't have said that if you'd been there, Mrs Pascoe, but of course we did all the usual things. We said a little prayer for absent friends and loved ones, and after we ate our dinner Dad went out to his shed to fetch a bottle of his home-made beetroot wine so we could make a toast to King and country. I would have brought you a bottle today, if there had been any left.'

She couldn't help giggling at the memory, and

as Laura looked askance, wondering what she was talking about, she came out with the whole tale in a tumble of words. By the end of it, to her relief, she had them all laughing, and the mood of the day was lifted. Thank God for her dad's beetroot wine, Breda thought fervently.

'I can just imagine Gilb's annoyance at losing all that wine though,' Jed remarked, seeing the practical side of it.

'Oh well, he didn't lose much of it other than the first bottle. The neighbours helped us to drink the rest,' Breda said, her eyes still alive at the memory of the buxom housewives on either side of their house singing carols in tuneless voices to her piano playing.

Laura cleared her throat. 'Well, I'm glad you had such a good day, dear. We were rather more sober here in every way.'

'Now, Auntie, don't go disapproving,' Max said. 'It gave us all a good laugh, and I'd say everyone needs a bit of laughter these days.'

'Max is right,' Jed said. 'And you'll be making the most of it on New Year's Eve with this dance in Newquay too. It'll be a new year and a new start, and let's hope that by the end of it the world will be at peace again.'

'Hear, hear,' Breda murmured, glad the brief awkwardness had passed. 'I suppose you'll be busy practising all this week then, Max?' she said, turning to him.

'Every night,' he said. 'I won't have time for much else, what with the taxi service and all.'

'It's nice of Mr Rowan to let you use it for the dance.'

Jed chuckled. 'He'll have a full house too, what with you and those two girls from the farm.'

Breda's heart jumped. 'The girls from the farm?'

Max shrugged, watching her steadily. 'They've been home for Christmas, according to George, but they'll be back in a couple of days, and as soon as they knew we'd be playing for the Yanks, of course they wanted to come as well. Roy will be taking the others and the instruments in his dad's van, so I said the girls could come with us. That's all right, isn't it?'

His eyes challenged her, and she said airily that of course it was all right. It was his taxi. And what had she expected? That it would just be a cosy ride for two? But Breda couldn't deny it was exactly what she had thought, and she didn't like the sound of sharing it with those Land Girls one little bit.

'Anyway, it will be company for you, Breda,' Laura went on innocently, unaware of the sudden tension between the two younger people in the room. 'It can't be much fun being in a dance hall on your own, especially when Max will be playing most of the time. It'll be good to have those girls to talk to.'

'I daresay *those girls* will be eyeing up the Yanks most of the time,' she couldn't help saying.

'Plenty of friendships have started on the dance floor,' Max said. 'You never know, you might find a Yank taking a fancy to you.'

'Well, if one does, he won't get any encouragement from me,' she snapped.

'Come on, Breda, I daresay some of them are

357

quite nice,' Jed commented. 'We're supposed to be friendly to these folk far from home.'

'But not too friendly,' Max added.

There was something in his tone that stirred a little devil inside Breda, and made her eyes sparkle. He had obviously thought she was being quite serious when she said no Yank would get any encouragement from her. So she had been, but it wouldn't do any harm to let him think otherwise!

'I'll have to think about that,' she said lightly. 'I won't want to sit like a wallflower all night, and I won't want the GIs to think I'm stand-offish, will I?'

It wasn't the kind of thing she would normally have said in front of Warren's parents, but it was worth it to see the small flash of jealousy in Max's eyes at that moment. He had teased her about the Land Girls, but two could play at that game. True to form, Laura put in her little spoke.

'I'm sure these Americans will respect our decent Cornish girls,' she said firmly, 'so you just have a good time, Breda love. You deserve a nice night out.'

If she was surprised to get such approval from Mrs Pascoe, Breda tried not to show it. The Land Girls weren't decent Cornish girls, although from what she had seen of them she was sure they would be well-behaved too, she thought hastily. For the first time a shiver of excitement ran through her veins. She hadn't met any GIs yet, and it would be an experience, if nothing else.

'I won't stay much longer if you don't mind, Mrs Pascoe,' she said, before she let her imagination run away with her. 'I want to call in on Gran to see that she's all right after yesterday's excitement.'

'All right dear, and thank you for coming. It was what we all needed.'

Before she could start to wallow in times past and bring the mood of the day down again, Breda kissed her swiftly and said her goodbyes. Max walked her to the door, but she had forestalled any thought of him walking with her by mentioning her visit to her gran. He caught hold of her hand and held it tightly.

'Don't get too carried away by the Yanks, will you, sweetheart?' he said softly. 'Remember that home's best.'

'That's rich, coming from you,' she said with a half-laugh. 'You could never wait to get away from home in the past, could you?'

'That was before I realised that what I really wanted was right here.'

She wrenched away from him, feeling her face go hot in the chilly Boxing Day air at all that he was implying. She didn't need this, and she didn't want it.

'I'll see you on New Year's Eve, and thank you for the piece of shrapnel,' she said in a choked voice, and as she hurried away she was well aware that he stood for a long time watching her go.

Chapter Twenty-One

All too soon it was New Year's Eve. The threatened snow didn't come to anything, and the evenings were as crisp as befitted the season, but the days were still mild enough to be pleasant. Breda's family thoroughly approved of her going to this dance. She had almost hoped for some sign from them that it was wrong for her to think of enjoying herself, and in the company of American soldiers too. But the general consensus was that Max would be her guardian angel, and she would have those nice Land Girls to keep her company. It was almost as though the whole world was conspiring to make her accept the inevitable.

Of course, what none of them knew was that Max Pascoe had already declared his love for her, and that she was in a turmoil of indecision as to just what she thought about that. But she had reckoned without her gran's uncanny intuition, which she should have expected.

'You know, Breda, that young man thinks a lot of you, and you could do a lot worse than to give him a chance,' Gran Hanney said calmly when Breda first told her about the dance at Newquay.

Breda's heart jumped. She wanted to deny that Max ever thought of her as anything other than his cousin's sweetheart, but she took one look at those knowing old eyes and gave a small sigh.

'Yes, I know he thinks a lot of me, Gran, but it's

not right for me to think about courting, and certainly not with Max – or anyone,' she added.

'It's absolutely right, my love. Warren's been gone for nearly nine months now, and you know he's never coming back. It's time to look to the future, and who better to do that with than someone who loves you like he does?'

Breda's eyes widened at that, and Gran chuckled.

'Don't look so shocked, and don't turn your back on what's right in front of you, love. But take no notice of me. I'm just a daft old woman.'

'You're anything but that,' Breda said swiftly.

She was still thinking of that conversation as she got ready for the New Year's Eve dance. She was wearing a silky blue dress, with the precious pair of stockings she would have worn to her wedding, and white shoes. Her hair was long and loose, and she had fastened it with the butterfly clip that Gran had given her for Christmas. She remembered how Gran had told her that she, too, had worn it to dances. It was a thought to give Breda a deep sense of continuity. It had been lucky for Gran, and maybe it would be lucky for her too, she thought, without much conviction.

As she heard the taxi arrive, her heart began to beat faster, and she quickly slid her arms into her coat. She resisted wearing a hat, as that would disturb her hair, and she was ready just as Max opened the door.

'You look beautiful,' he said simply.

'So do you!'

'Blokes don't look beautiful,' he said with a grin.

'Well, splendid then. I didn't know you were going to look so smart!' she said with a small gulp.

'We decided we should look the part now that we're playing for more out-of-town engagements, especially in front of these Yanks. We don't want to look like complete country cousins.'

He looked anything but that. He wore a dark jacket and trousers with a red stripe down each side, an immaculate white shirt and a red tie. She couldn't imagine where he, and presumably the others in the band, had got these outfits, but on Max, it looked wonderful, and right now he was the most handsome man she had ever seen. She had never seen Warren dressed like this, and he had always looked far more boyish than sophisticated. For the first time she knew that the likeness between them was only superficial after all. Max was a man in every way, and would always be so.

'Your carriage awaits you, ma'am,' he said in a pseudo American accent that effectively broke the tension between them. 'We have to call at the farm to collect Tess and Ellie, and then we'll be on our way.'

The brief sense that this was in any way a date vanished with those few words. They had to collect the Land Girls, and there would be no chance for private conversations once the taxi was filled with their chirpy laughter. It was probably better so, Breda thought, aware of an odd sense of regret all the same.

In no time, it seemed, they were at Gough's Farm, and the girls were climbing into the back of the taxi, highly excited and chattering nineteen to the dozen all the way to Newquay. With Max responding in kind, it, was hardly necessary for Breda to talk at all. But she was determined to put any reservations aside as they entered the dance hall the Americans had taken over for the evening. As well as the remainder of the Christmas decorations, it was adorned with streamers, and a huge net of balloons hung over the hall, ready to drop at midnight.

'They don't do things by halves, do they?' Tess said excitedly. 'I'm going to nab myself a GI tonight if it kills me.'

'You mind that it doesn't,' Breda said, half joking.

The other girl squeezed her arm, more serious than usual. 'Enjoy tonight, Breda. After all you've been through this year, you deserve it, and dancing never did anyone any harm, did it?'

Her sympathetic tone took Breda by surprise, and she nodded and smiled back. 'I mean to enjoy it, don't worry.'

There wasn't much chance to do otherwise. Almost as soon as the band was in position, a compere in a smart US army officer's uniform announced how honoured the Americans were to have a local band playing for them that evening, and they were applauded loudly before they even began playing. Breda felt a swell of pride for the boys she had known since childhood, who were now being feted.

But there was little time to feel nostalgic because the music began in earnest, and she quickly realised the band had been learning tunes to please the GIs as well as the regular ones the locals were

363

used to. Waltzes and old tyme dances were interspersed with fast tunes for jitterbugging, for those who had the nerve and the stamina, and there were a good few excuse-me dances for those without partners.

The hall was crowded, and almost before she had time to think, there were three American soldiers bearing down on the three girls sitting at the side of the hall. Tess and Ellie were whisked straight onto the dance floor, while she took the hand of the fresh-faced GI smiling down at her.

'May I have the pleasure, ma'am?' he said in a broad accent that was so like the one Max had feigned earlier on that she felt a wild desire to giggle. And an even wilder desire to enjoy herself, just as she had said she would. Tonight was for having fun, not for looking back with regrets over times that would never come again.

He told her his name was Greg and that she reminded him of his girl back home. He said it right away, which might have put some girls off, but which Breda found reassuring. They weren't all outrageous flirts then, and he had nice manners. He told her his home was in Iowa, where they respected the ladies. It could all have been a line, of course, but she knew sincerity when she saw it, and she saw it in Greg's eyes.

He was very easy to talk to, and by the time they had danced a few dances and sat out one or two to get their breath back, she had told him about Warren, despite it being the last thing she had expected to do. They were strangers, ships that passed in the night, and she found that particular simile rather too emotive for comfort.

364

But it had been easier to talk about Warren to a stranger than she had expected, and it undoubtedly released something inside her.

Halfway through the evening the band took a break while records were being played, and Max came over to her side, looking none too pleased.

'I see you're having a good time,' he said.

'Isn't that what you wanted? I thought that was the idea.'

'I thought you might have danced with several partners, not just one.'

'You're not jealous, are you?' she asked, her eyes sparkling with mischief.

'What do you think? Do you want a drink?'

'Greg's fetching me one. Don't look so cross, Max. I can't dance with you when you're playing, can I?'

'Just make sure you save the last dance for me then, and I'll make sure I take a few minutes out for that one.'

He was gone before Greg joined her with two glasses of lemonade.

He spoke thoughtfully. 'That guy looked a bit annoyed. The saxophone player, I mean. He's pretty good. Is he somebody special, honey? I'm not treading on anybody's toes, am I?'

She thought for less than a minute. 'You're not treading on anybody's toes, Greg. And yes, he is somebody special.'

She didn't know why she'd said it. The other girls were coming back, chattering like magpies with the GIs they had in tow, and in any case, Breda didn't want to share any more confidences that evening.

As it neared midnight the mood in the hall became even more frenetic. Everyone counted down the last ten seconds of the old year, and then there were cheers as the net above them released the balloons. People were kissing each other, and wishing each other a happy new year. Before Breda knew what was happening, Greg had kissed her too, to be thrust aside almost immediately, as someone else's arms claimed her. Someone else's mouth was on hers, and her eyes closed as she recognised Max's familiar kiss, and because it was the start of a new year that held the hope of peace and goodwill, she was kissing him back as if her life depended on it. There were records playing again now, and as the strains of 'Auld Lang Syne' rang out, people linked arms and sang their hearts out.

The dance wasn't licensed to go on much after midnight. Cinderella had to put her finery away and go back to her everyday life, though it was not the way Tess and Ellie were thinking.

'The boys are going to try to get over to the farm next weekend to take us out,' they said excitedly. 'How about yours, Breda? Do you want to come with us?'

'I don't think so,' she said.

'Oh well, suit yourself,' Tess said, clearly thinking she was getting on her high horse again.

But it wasn't that. Greg hadn't made any suggestion for them to meet again, and nor had she encouraged it. This was a night to remember, but it ended here, as far as Breda was concerned.

The last dance of the evening was playing now, and she saw Max put down his sax and weave his

366

way through the crowds towards her just as Greg appeared too. Before he had a chance to speak, Max was at her side.

'My dance, I think,' he said, and she moved into his arms without a second thought, knowing that Greg would have no trouble finding another partner.

They didn't even speak. They just moved around the floor in time to the music, reminding Breda all too poignantly of the way her gran and grandad must have danced in their cottage. They broke apart reluctantly when the music ended, and after he escorted her back to her seat, he lifted her hand and kissed it. It was no more than a fleeting touch, a charming, old-fashioned gesture, and in no way could it have been called passionate, yet it was somehow electric.

'Back to work,' he said, 'and in another half hour it will all be over.'

'Boy,' Greg said at her side, materialising from somewhere near. 'That guy's sure romantic, isn't he?'

'I suppose he is,' Breda said with a shaky smile.

She wasn't sorry when the evening finally ended, even though they had to wait until the boys in the band packed up their instruments before she and the Land Girls could get settled in Max's taxi. It had been a wonderful evening, she admitted, and she felt more alive than she had in a long time. More ready to face whatever future that the new year heralded.

They left the girls at the darkened farmhouse, laughingly shushing them for fear they would wake the farmer and his wife. And then Max

367

drove the last couple of miles down to the village and along Barnes Lane to Forget-me-not Cottage.

Should she ask him in? Would he expect it? For one ecstatic moment she found herself picturing how it would have been if Warren had been ending this evening with her. Married now, they would have gone inside their cottage, kicked off their shoes and everything else, fallen into bed and into one another's arms and made glorious, uninhibited love. The memory of that one blissful time was suddenly an exquisite pain in her heart, making her catch her breath between her teeth.

'Are you all right, Breda?' Max said, leaning towards her as he brought the taxi to a stop.

'I'm fine,' she said in a choked voice. 'Thank you for taking me, Max, and for a lovely evening. Good-night.'

She was halfway to her front door before he could get out of the car. For all that the evening had been so good, this was how it had to end. She couldn't bear anything more. She went inside, and a few minutes later she heard the car start up again, and then she was alone, her heart beating rapidly.

Had there been a moment when the thought that it could be Max making love to her had been so enticing? If it was, she didn't want it. Not now. Not until she could really sort out the muddled feelings in her head. For now, she felt very tired, and all she wanted to do was sleep and, hopefully, not to dream. There was a lot to sort out in her mind, not least the fact that she finally knew her feelings for Max had changed. What she didn't know was whether the excitement and emotion of the evening was distorting those feelings, and making them seem more than they actually were. She needed to return to normal again, before she knew for sure. Almost frantically, she welcomed the fact that school would be starting again in a few days' time, and the infants would take up all her attention and her thoughts.

It was several weeks into the new year and already it was feeling remarkably like the beginning of spring in the village of Penbole. The climate was always balmier in the far southwest of the country than upcountry, and dark green shoots of daffodils were beginning to push through the ground in gardens and hedgerows. A few clumps of snowdrops were already blooming here and there, and would be growing wild on the moors, and it was a good time to renew the children's interest in the changing seasons. They were feeling a bit dull and restless after the excitement of Christmas, and they needed something to boost their enthusiasm.

'It's early in the year, but in a few more days we'll go on a nature walk on the moors to see what we can find,' Breda promised them at the end of an exhausting day, when they were at their most tiresome. Their mood was starting to affect her, and although she knew it was up to her to lift them out of it, it wasn't always as easy as it sounded.

Before she could put the idea into practise, she wished she hadn't mentioned it at all when the bright sunny mornings gave way to late afternoon mists that rolled in from the sea and dropped down from the moors, blanketing the village in a ghostly white pall. Even though it was still daylight, each late afternoon the village seemed to take on an eerie silence, and it was a time for huddling indoors around the fire. Gran Hanney always hibernated with her cat and her knitting at such times, and Breda felt very much like doing the same thing every day when school ended and the children had gone home.

About four o'clock one afternoon she was stoking up the fire when someone came knocking rapidly at her door. When she answered it, she saw Sara Hayes' mother standing there, white-faced and distraught.

'Is Sara with you, Miss Hanney? She hasn't come home yet, and nor has Tommy Weeks from next door. Mrs Weeks said Tommy mentioned something about finding wild snowdrops on the moors and that he and Sara knew where they could find them.'

Breda felt a huge jolt at the words. 'They're not here, Mrs Hayes, and they all left school an hour ago as usual. I'm sure they haven't done anything foolish.'

She wasn't sure at all, and her heart was starting to thump painfully hard now.

'That's all very well for you to say, but there are two five-year-old children missing, so what are you going to do about it?' the woman said, her voice rising shrilly.

'I'm sure they're not missing,' Breda began.

'Well, if they're not at home and they're not

370

here, where are they?'

She was becoming angry and tearful now and Breda felt a huge weight of responsibility for the children who had been in her care until an hour ago. The village was so small and safe that the children could easily find their way home on their own, and always did so without incident, until today. Her own voice was tense now, catching the anxiety from Sara's mother.

'I can't think they'd have been foolish enough to walk up to the moors, Mrs Hayes, but if they did, then I think I know where they'd be. We always followed the same nature trail just off the main road. Look, I'll get my coat and come with you to look for them.'

It was a sure bet that Mrs Weeks wouldn't be able to come with them. She had breathing problems that the winter mists always made more troublesome. Her husband was away in the army, as was Sara's dad, and she knew that this situation must be so much worse without a man around to comfort and reassure them.

'Well, make it quick,' Mrs Hayes went on, almost hysterical now. 'If anything's happened to my Sara, I'm blaming you for putting ideas into her head, Miss Hanney.'

That wasn't fair and Breda knew it, but Sara's mother was feeling anything but fair right now. She was hardly rational any more as she turned and ran ahead of Breda through the village. Through the gloom of the mist they both saw a large black car outside the Pascoe house.

'Hold on a minute,' Breda gasped to Mrs Hayes, already with a stitch in her side as she

371

kept up with the woman. 'I'll ask Max if he'll take us. It will be quicker.'

She didn't stop to think how long it must have taken Sara and Tommy's little legs to walk up to the moors, although from where they lived, they were already halfway there. Presumably they had got nearly home, and decided to go further. At least, she hoped that was the answer. It was one answer ... and, pray God, the only feasible one.

Max took in the situation at once. 'Get in the car, both of you,' he ordered, 'and you direct me, Breda, to where you think they might be.'

He drove slowly up the hill through the village, telling them to keep looking for the children all the way. His voice was strong and calming, even though it did nothing to appease Mrs Hayes, nor Breda. She was just so thankful to have him beside her, and for him to keep talking and trying to put a sensible solution to it all.

'If we don't find them quickly, I'll contact Mr Rowan from the taxi and ask him to alert the local police and get out a search party, but I'm sure it won't be necessary. I'd rather give it half an hour before we do anything so drastic. I'm sure that between the three of us we'll soon track the little devils down and they'll be back home in no time, Mrs Hayes, and you'll be giving them a good telling off like my uncle used to do my cousin and me whenever we went missing for an hour or two.'

As he went on talking in that crisp, authoritative way, Breda prayed that he was right. In an hour it would be dark, and who knew what might happen to two small children out on the moors then? If they wandered far from the road they could get disorientated, and there were disused mine shafts farther out on the moors. A child could fall into one of them and be lost for ever. She smothered a panicky sob in her throat, not wanting Mrs Hayes to know how truly terrified she was becoming. She felt Max put his hand over hers for a moment before returning it to the steering-wheel, and she had never been more thankful for his strength.

They reached the road at the top of the village that gave way along the edge of the moors. It was here that Breda often took the class for nature walks, venturing a little way to left or right to collect wild flowers or to examine insects and the like. It was a charming way of educating children into the delights of country life that townies didn't know, and the children adored it. But not today. Today this was an alien place, full of frightening possibilities that she didn't even want to think about.

'We'll leave the car on the side of the road,' Max declared. 'Once we're outside we'll start to call the children's names. Wait a moment after you've called them to hear for any replies, and remember to stay together. We'll continue to the places Breda usually takes them if we hear nothing, but we need to stay together. If we separate we'll only end up having more people to search for, so don't go off on your own, either of you.'

He was strong, taking charge, knowing what to do, when by now Breda's nerves were in shreds, and she couldn't imagine what Mrs Hayes was going through. Sara was her one precious child, but both Sara and Tommy were part of Breda's life too, and she ached to find them, and to find them safe and well.

The air was becoming more chilly, and it was hard to see very far ahead of them now. They began calling the children's names as Max instructed, but they heard nothing in reply. There were no bird sounds, no rustling of leaves or bracken, nothing at all but their own erratic heartbeats.

'This is doing no good,' Mrs Hayes said shrilly. 'You'd better get on to Mr Rowan, Mr Pascoe, and get a proper search party organised as quick as you can. We're never going to find my Sara if we just stand here shouting. I'm going to go and look for her myself.'

Max put a restraining hand on her arm as she made to rush away from them.

'Trust me for a little while longer, please. All that will take time, and we're here now. Besides, neither you nor any search party would know where Breda brings the children, and we really do need to stay together, so lead on, Breda.'

'We don't go very far from here,' she said shakily, feeling close to tears herself now. 'The snowdrops are usually found on the side of the road rather than over the moors, and the children know that. I'm sure they wouldn't have gone off the main road.'

Not intentionally, anyway. Not unless they had completely lost their way. And not until darkness fell and they couldn't find their way back. The sobs inside her were very near to the surface, and she clung on to Max's hand.

The three of them shouted out in unison, first Sara's name, and then Tommy's, waiting in vain for a reply. The mist seemed to muffle any sound there might have been. It seemed as though they had been shouting for a very long time, but it probably wasn't very long at all before they heard a thin sound coming out of the mist.

'It's coming from across the moors,' Mrs Hayes gasped.

'It was Sara, I'm sure of it. It must be Sara.'

They shouted again, and this time there was a weak chorus of sound from the direction of the moors. The three of them stumbled across the damp ground, legs scratched by bracken and gorse, but unnoticed in their haste. They followed the sound, and at last two frightened young faces seemed to loom up at them out of the mist.

'Sara fell down and hurt her ankle and she can't walk,' Tommy Weeks' frightened voice screeched at them. 'She's peed herself too, Miss,' he said, recognising Breda's voice.

Sara's mother almost fell onto the two children in her relief, gathering Sara up in her arms and weeping all over her, regardless of the damp state of the child, and babbling hysterically about what naughty children they were to come up here on their own, where anything could have happened to them.

'He made me come,' Sara shrieked. 'It was all Tommy's idea. We wanted the snowdrops for you, Miss,' she said to Breda.

'Never mind all that now,' Max said roughly. 'Let's get them back to the car and down to the village where they can get warm, but let me have a look at Sara's ankle first, Mrs Hayes. You could be making it worse by squeezing her too tightly.'

It was clear that the woman had gone to pieces now and was only too thankful to hand over her daughter to Max. Breda was touched by the tender way he felt the child's ankle, soothing her all the while. He took out a clean handkerchief from his pocket and wrapped it around the ankle, saying it was only a sprain and it would soon get better, and she could borrow his walking stick if she liked, which brought a trembling smile to her sobbing face.

Nobody cared about the fact that she was wet and dirty, only that she and Tommy were safe, and Max took her in his arms and carried her to the taxi while Breda held on tightly to the excitable young Tommy Weeks' hand. She had been pretty certain that he would have been the ringleader in this little escapade, and she would be very sure to warn the rest of her class tomorrow about the dangers these two could have been in.

Max drove carefully back down through the village, where the night was already closing in. In normal times there would have been welcome lights shining out from cottages, but these were not normal times, and Breda shuddered, imagining the letters that two mothers might have had to write to two serving soldiers about their children. It didn't bear thinking about, and she was mightily relieved when at last they had reached the children's homes, and they could deposit them all.

'I can't thank you enough, Mr Pascoe,' Mrs Hayes said clumsily. 'If it hadn't been for you, we might never have found them.'

'Well, we did, and that's all you have to think about now. That, and getting young Sara clean and dry and into her bed with a hot drink. The same goes for you, Tommy. No bragging to your mum about what a hero you've been, mind, because you haven't.'

'No, mister,' Tommy said glumly.

They drove the rest of the way to Forget-me-not Cottage in silence. Breda knew the reaction to all that had happened was quickly setting in, and she could hardly stop shivering. It wasn't from cold, but from the terrifying realisation that she had started all this by her innocent talks to the children about nature and the early arrival of the wild snowdrops up on the moors. She couldn't possibly have known that Tommy and Sara would go looking for them by themselves, but it didn't do anything to stop her enormous feeling of guilt.

'Thank you, Max,' she said in a choked voice when he finally stopped the car. 'I don't know what we'd have done without you.'

'Well, it's over now, and you did the right thing in calling for me. You know I'll always have a strong shoulder when you need one.'

She began to shake all over. 'Don't, Max, please.'

He caught hold of her hand, feeling how icy cold it was. 'Don't what? Don't pretend that I don't love you and that I was glad that you needed me? You know I can't do that. And I'm not leaving you like this. You're not the only one who needs a hot drink to warm you up. You're freezing, so listen to Doctor Max and do as

377

you're told for once. Come on, get out of the car.'

Numbly, she did as she was told, too limp to argue any more. She felt as if all emotion had gone from her now, and all she wanted to do was to bury her head under a pillow as if she was an animal licking its wounds, and forget that this day ever happened. But she couldn't do that. She knew she couldn't do that. She was a teacher, and she would have to explain to her class how wrong those two children had been, and the dangers they could have been in. But that was for another day, she thought wearily, not for now.

She sank down on the sofa, hardly aware of Max moving about in the cottage. She heard another log being put on the fire, and saw the sparks as it caught light and threw out a welcome heat into the room. She heard the rattle of cups and saucers from the kitchen and then the sound of water boiling in the kettle. She saw and heard it all as if it was all part of a dream. Nothing was real any more, until she felt the coolness of a glass being put to her lips and was ordered to swallow. The bitter taste of brandy slid down her throat, making her wince at its sharpness.

'Why are you being so good to me?' she mumbled without thinking.

He didn't answer, but in any case, she knew why. Of course she knew why. It was because he loved her, and had always loved her. And she loved him. She had always loved him, as a friend, a dear friend, her sweetheart's cousin. And more, she thought, with a little inward gasp.

Slowly his face came into focus, his handsome, concerned face that she knew instinctively wouldn't be making any demands of her on this night when she was so vulnerable, and would probably give him whatever he wanted. But that wasn't Max. He would want a woman to give him her love freely and unreservedly. She touched his face, feeling the warmth of his skin as if she had never done so before. His eyes were so like Warren's, but they weren't Warren's eyes. They belonged to Max, and they were watching her warily now, knowing that her thoughts had been in turmoil for all these months, but unaware that they were becoming crystal clear.

'Stay with me, Max. I don't want to be alone tonight. Will you stay, and risk what the neighbours will say in the morning?' she said huskily, knowing what she was asking, what she was promising, knowing her reputation might be in tatters and not caring. But maybe he would care too much about his own.

His reply was tense. 'I'd stay, but only if I could be sure that this isn't out of sympathy or gratitude over what happened earlier. I have to know that I mean more to you than that, Breda.'

She put her fingers on his lips. 'Will it do if I tell you that you mean everything to me, and that I've been too blind to see it until now? Will it do if I tell you that I love you, Max?'

There was no time to say anything more, and no space between them as he pulled her into his arms, his mouth on hers in the sweetest kiss, and she knew in her heart that whatever else this uncertain new year had in store, this was the man who was making her feel alive again, and that there was a future for them together.

The publishers hope that this book has given you enjoyable reading. Large Print Books are especially designed to be as easy to see and hold as possible. If you wish a complete list of our books please ask at your local library or write directly to:

Magna Large Print Books
Magna House, Long Preston,
Skipton, North Yorkshire.
BD23 4ND

This Large Print Book for the partially sighted, who cannot read normal print, is published under the auspices of

THE ULVERSCROFT FOUNDATION

THE ULVERSCROFT FOUNDATION

... we hope that you have enjoyed this Large Print Book. Please think for a moment about those people who have worse eyesight problems than you ... and are unable to even read or enjoy Large Print, without great difficulty.

You can help them by sending a donation, large or small to:

**The Ulverscroft Foundation,
1, The Green, Bradgate Road,
Anstey, Leicestershire, LE7 7FU,
England.**
or request a copy of our brochure for more details.

The Foundation will use all your help to assist those people who are handicapped by various sight problems and need special attention.

Thank you very much for your help.